In a scandalous age, England's royal family shocked the nation.

His mother, the Dowager Princess was passionately in love with a married man, Lord Bute. Between them they intended, through the innocent young King, to rule England.

His brothers were involved in legal actions because of their amorous attentions to certain charming ladies, famed for their attractions.

On the continent his young sister was imprisoned for adultery and treason.

Worst of all, the King himself was haunted by a secret folly of his early youth, when he had fallen madly in love with a beautiful young Quaker woman, and had secretly married her. Should she still be alive—and he had heard that she was—George's royal liaison with a German princess would be illegal and the arrogant young Princess of Wales would be illegitimate, no longer heir to the throne.

THE THIRD GEORGE

Jean Plaidy

FAWCETT CREST • NEW YORK

A Fawcett Crest Book
Published by Ballantine Books
Copyright © 1969 by Jean Plaidy

Library of Congress Catalog Card Number: 86-22686

ISBN 0-449-21599-7

This edition published by arrangement with G.P. Putnam's Sons, a division
of The Putnam Publishing Group, Inc.

Manufactured in the United States of America

First Ballantine Books Edition: July 1989

CONTENTS

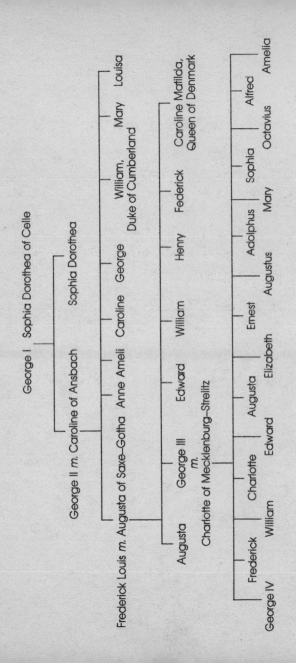

The Fateful Letter

One day in the year 1760, when she was sixteen years old, the Princess Charlotte Sophia of Mecklenburg-Strelitz wrote a letter which many believed set in motion those events which lifted her from a little German principality, where she would doubtless have spent her days in obscurity, to the throne of England.

Charlotte had been out driving in the company of her elder sister, the Princess Christina. Once a week—on Sundays—they took their places in the coach drawn by six horses and drove through the countryside with as much state as they were ever allowed, which merely meant that they were escorted by guards. They were dressed in their best gowns, which they were only permitted to wear on Sundays, and they had been warned constantly by their mother, the Dowager Grand Duchess, as well as their governess, the admirable Madame de Grabow, that they must be careful not to soil them as there was no money available to buy more.

Both Princesses were made aware of their poverty, being obliged to mend their own garments and darn their stockings for as long as there was any possibility of continuing to wear them; and as the Grand Duchess—and Madame de Grabow—believed in discipline and that it was always necessary to have a piece of work in the hands, they must perform these tasks themselves.

Their poverty had increased since the war, which had been going on now for four years, and it was the effects of this war of which she was made deeply aware on that particular Sunday afternoon, which made Charlotte act in such an unprecedented manner.

The coach pulled up suddenly to avoid a woman who had

stepped right in its path and Charlotte saw her quite distinctly as she shook her fist at the coachman.

"You'd run us down," cried the woman. "We're of no account. You take our men for the wars and our money for the taxes . . . so what matter if you run us down!"

Charlotte noticed that her eyes seemed as though they were sunk deep in her head and that her flesh showed through her torn dress.

She had seen the Princesses in their Sunday gowns and she came to the window of the coach and went on: "That was our farm." She pointed vaguely. "Who's going to till the land now, eh? They've taken my man. They've taken my sons. And the Prussians come marching through."

The guards were about to arrest her, but Charlotte cried: "No. Drive on! Drive on." And she and her sister were thrown back against the upholstery of the coach as it jerked into action.

Charlotte was looking out of the window watching the woman.

"It was . . . terrible," she said. "Did you see her face, Christina?"

Christina shook her head.

"It was so . . . tragic," burst out Charlotte. "You heard what she said. This war . . . this *fearful* war! What good is it doing the country? We're all poor because of it. Not that that is important. They'd taken that woman's husband and son. You heard what she said."

"You are too vehement, Charlotte."

"What else can one be . . . when that is happening?"

Charlotte stared gloomily out of the window while Christina quickly dismissed the incident and continued to smile at her own thoughts. It was no use trying to interest Christina in anything since the Duke of Roxburgh had come to Mecklenburg.

So Charlotte gave up the attempt. Perhaps if she had talked to her she would not have felt compelled to give vent to her indignation on paper. She could have expressed it to Christina, could have discussed with her what they could do about it. But Christina was too absorbed in her own delicious thoughts.

The effects of this terrible war are everywhere, thought Charlotte. Yet never had they seemed so obvious as they did on this afternoon. When she had looked into that woman's face she had seen something which she would never forget—a reproach, an appeal. She must do something.

It was not easy when one was sixteen. Her mother would tell her that the war was no affair of hers; and Madame de Grabow would agree with her mother. As for her brother, the ruler of Strelitz, he never had time for her, so she would soon be sent back to the schoolroom if she attempted to talk to him. Her friend and companion Ida von Bülow was too frivolous. She would agree—she always agreed—but she would sigh and say, "Yes, Princess, but what can we do about it?"

"There must be something I can do," she said aloud.

"What?" asked Christina idly.

Charlotte did not answer, and Christina did not notice that she had not.

So Charlotte gave herself up to studying the countryside and was appalled afresh by the effects the war had had on it.

She saw the people inadequately clad, inadequately fed; she saw villages through which the soldiers had passed, and plundered as they went. They had even desecrated the churches and in doing so robbed them of some of the sacred ornaments. And these were the Germans, their own people—the Prussians, the most brilliant makers of war in the world.

When the coach arrived back at the castle Charlotte was in a militant mood.

The castle, like the villages through which they had passed, was in a state of crumbling decay. There was a rampart, but the tower was almost in ruins and the old grenadier who was supposed to guard the drawbridge had laid his musket down beside him so that he could get on with knitting a stocking.

He looked up and nodded a greeting as the coach rattled over the bridge and into the courtyard.

Charlotte, to whom the schloss had been home ever since her brother had inherited the ducal crown eight years ago, noticed for the first time how shabby it was. Only the glass lamps over the gateway and the two cranes set there like guards reminded one that this was the ducal residence.

We are all poor, thought Charlotte, and it is all due to this terrible war.

Never before this afternoon had the war seemed so terrible. She had followed its progress on the maps her governess Madame de Grabow had made—for Madame de Grabow was an expert map-maker and had a passion for geography which she had imparted to Charlotte. She knew that the war was due to the desires of Frederick of Prussia to dominate Europe and of Maria Theresa of Austria to take back from Frederick the province of Silesia. On Maria Theresa's side were France, Russia and Poland, while the English had promised assistance to Frederick. There were strong family ties between the English and the Germans and Madame de Grabow was constantly referring to the island off the coast of Europe which was becoming increasingly powerful and was even at this time at war with the French over their colonies.

And these ambitious rulers, thought Charlotte, were seeking their victories at the expense of the people of such poor little dukedoms as Mecklenburg-Strelitz.

She glanced at Christina. One must not be hard on Christina who after all was twenty-six years old and in love. One could not mix love and war and Charlotte supposed the first was a more inviting subject for thought than the second.

Charlotte had no reason to think of love, so she gave herself up to the contemplation of war and continued to ask herself what she could do about it.

There was one man who could stop this wicked waste, this pillage; who could by the stroke of pen and one word of command prevent his soldiers from laying waste villages, robbing churches and plundering the houses which stood on their routes. This was Frederick of Prussia, whom they called Frederick the Great.

But he would never listen to a sixteen-year-old girl. If she wrote to him her letter would never reach him. He would say she was a silly young creature. What if he complained to her brother? Then there would be trouble.

Yet, thought Charlotte, if I did nothing I should never be able to forget that woman's face. Perhaps she was put in my path today for a purpose.

No, certainly she would never forgive herself if she did not take some action.

But what?

She found her attendant, Ida von Bülow, and her governess, Madame de Grabow, in her apartments. Ida was a frivolous girl, but the governess was a very distinguished lady indeed; she was now a widow and her father had been Mecklenburg's ambassador at the Court of Vienna. She was so learned that she was known throughout Mecklenburg as the German Sappho; an ideal governess for the Princesses, approved of by both their mother, the Grand Duchess, and their brother, the Duke.

Madame de Grabow said: "News has reached us of King Frederick's latest victory. I will show you on the map."

The map was spread out on the schoolroom table, but Charlotte who loved maps almost as much as Madame de Grabow could find no pleasure in it today. She saw those delicately tinted areas as stricken villages, occupied by hopeless old men, women and children because the young ones were away from home fighting on the battlefields; she saw the desecrated churches, the desolate homesteads.

She did not speak of her emotions to Madame de Grabow, for she was sure that lady would heartily disapprove of what she intended to do, but as soon as she was in her bedchamber she called to Ida to bring her pen and ink; and when it was brought she settled down to write:

May it please your Majesty,

I am at a loss whether I should congratulate or condole with you on your late victory, since the same success which has covered you with laurels has overspread the country of Mecklenburg with desolation. I know, Sire, that it seems unbecoming in my sex, in this age of vicious refinement, to feel for one's country, to lament the horrors of war, or wish for the return of peace. I know you may think it more properly my province to study the arts of pleasing, or to inspect subjects of a more domestic nature; but however unbecoming it may be in me, I cannot resist the desire of interceding for this unhappy people.

It was but a few years ago that this country wore the most pleasing aspect. The land was cultivated, the peasants were cheerful and the towns rich and gay. How they have changed! I am not an expert at description, nor can my fancy add any horrors to the picture; but surely even conquerors themselves would weep at the hideous change. The whole country, my dear country, is one frightful wasteland, presenting only objects to excite terror, pity and despair. There is no longer work for farmers and shepherds for they have become soldiers and help to ravage the soil they once cultivated. The towns are inhabited only by old men, women and children; while perhaps here and there a warrior, by wounds or loss of limbs rendered unfit for service, is left at his door, where little children hang round him, to ask the history of every wound, and grow themselves soldiers before they find strength for the field. But this were nothing, did we not feel the alternate insolence of either army as it happens to advance or retreat, in pursuing its campaigns. It is impossible indeed to express the confusion which they who call themselves our friends create, for even those from whom we expect relief only oppress us with new calamities. From your justice it is, therefore, Sire, that we hope redress; to you even children and women may complain, whose humanity stoops to the meanest petition and whose power is capable of redressing the greatest wrong.

Your Majesty's humble servant
Charlotte Sophia Mecklenburg-Strelitz.

Charlotte's usually pale cheeks were tinged with pink. Dare she send such a letter? If her mother knew, if her brother discovered, what would they say? They would be horrified. How dared she, a girl of sixteen, a girl of no account, write such a letter of reproach to King Frederick of Prussia. She was more or less telling him what he should do.

"I will send it," Charlotte told herself fiercely. "For I shall despise myself for ever more if I do not."

She sealed the letter and kept it in her secret pocket; and when the messenger next left with letters for Prussia she gave it into his hands to be put in no others than those of King Frederick.

Then began the misgivings; then the realization of what she had done.

She waited for the inevitable reverberations.

Charlotte folded the petticoat she had been mending and laid it carefully on the table and, grimacing, picked up a gown from the pile of clothing which lay between her and Ida von Bülow.

Ida was aware of the Princess's mood and thought she knew the reason for it. She was after all sixteen and must wonder often whether she would ever escape from the monotony of life here in the schloss. It was certainly dull, Ida conceded, and surely Charlotte must be wondering whether marriage would ever rescue her from it.

But what chance would she ever have? The dukedom of which her brother had become reigning sovereign eight years ago was an insignificant one—about one hundred and twenty miles in length and thirty in breadth—and since the war it had become more impoverished than ever. No, Charlotte's chances were small. She was not even handsome, but rather what kindly people called "homely." Though her expression was pleasant, and a lively intelligence lightened her face, she was so pale as to be colourless; small and thin, she entirely lacked that fleshy rotundity so necessary to Teutonic beauty; her nose was too flat and her mouth so large that had she possessed the most perfect features otherwise, it would have prevented any claim to beauty.

Charlotte held up the gown. "There is not much life left in it," she declared. "I may patch the skirt but I shall be out at the elbows the next time I wear it."

"A waste of time, Princess," agreed Ida.

"But," went on Charlotte, smiling a little wickedly and imitating Madame de Grabow's voice to the life, "at least I am occupied. Idle hands are the outward manifestation of an idle mind."

Ida laughed but Charlotte went on judiciously: "Madame de Grabow is right. I am indeed fortunate that she should be my governess."

"Very fortunate."

"I must always remember it. Oh dear, I don't think I can do any more with this gown. If only . . ."

"You will not get a new one until the war is over."

The war. She daren't think of it. What would he say when he received her letter? Whenever the door opened she started, expecting to see a page there summoning her to her mother . . . or worse still to her brother.

Ida must be regarding her curiously so she threw aside the gown and picked up a piece of embroidery. "That's better. It's a pretty pattern. Don't you agree, Ida? But of course you always agree. Ida, how deeply do you think my sister is in love?"

Ida gave a spurt of merriment. "She couldn't be in deeper."

"Do you think she will be allowed to marry the gentleman?"

Ida thought it likely. Christina was ten years older than Charlotte. If she did not find a husband now she never would; and an English duke would not be an impossible match. The daughter of a minor German duke could not hope for European royalty. Yes, Ida thought, an English duke might do very nicely.

"I do hope so, Ida," said Charlotte fervently. "Although I should miss her. She would go to England."

"And they are our allies in the war . . ."

Charlotte wanted to put her fingers into her ears. Phrases from that most impertinent letter kept wringing in her head. Sometimes she would awake in the night and hear them. Did I really write that? Did I? And did I really send it to the King of Prussia?

"I heard it was very grand at the English Court," she said quickly. "And Christina would of course go to Court. Ida, perhaps it is a good thing that we are a poor little dukedom because that means that no great king would ever ask for our hands . . . and therefore Christina may be allowed to marry her duke. Be careful. Here she comes."

The Princess Christina came into the apartment. There was a resemblance between them, but she was more handsome than Charlotte and being in love had transformed her.

"What news?" cried Charlotte.

"News of what?" demanded Christina. "The war . . ."

"No, no, no! Of you . . . and your duke."

"What news should there be?"

"That Mamma and our brother have given their consent to your marriage."

"Not yet, but . . ."

"They will," said Charlotte. "They must. Christina, when you are an English duchess will you invite me to visit you in England?"

"You may be sure I shall."

"I wonder what it's like there. I wonder if all the stories we hear of it are true."

"Some are." Christina was knowledgeable through conversations with her lover. "The new King is very young—only twenty or so. And the people have long been waiting for the old one to die. They believe everything will be different now he is gone. It will be a change for the better for the King is a very good young man . . . modest and virtuous. Unusual qualities for a king."

Charlotte shuddered, thinking of that other king whom she could not get out of her mind.

"I have heard manners are free and easy at the English Court," said Ida.

"Oh, the English!" laughed Christina. "They are not so . . . disciplined as we are. If they disapprove of the royal family they don't hesitate to say so."

"That is good," said Charlotte with vehemence.

"Charlotte!"

"I . . . I believe that people should speak their minds."

"But to kings!"

"Yes, to kings."

Christina went on: "Oh, yes, there are lampoons and songs always being circulated. The people get together in the coffee and chocolate houses. They are all over the town, these houses . . . and people go there to drink coffee and chocolate and stronger things and talk . . . and talk . . ."

Madame de Grabow came into the room.

She said: "I have just come from the Grand Duchess. I have orders to prepare us to leave for Pyrmont to take the waters."

Christina looked a little downcast, guessing this would mean a temporary separation from her duke.

Charlotte, watching her, thought wistfully: I wonder if I shall ever have a lover. I wonder if I shall ever marry.

"Come," said the efficient Madame de Grabow, "there is much to do. The Grand Duchess is anxious to leave without delay."

It was pleasant at Pyrmont. The Grand Duchess took her daughters to the rooms and it was certain that they benefited by the change. They lived simply, staying at a nearby country house and partaking in the life of the place—like any noble family on holiday.

Christina was a little sad, regretting the parting from her lover who had stayed in Mecklenburg, for he had no excuse for following them there; but she confided to Charlotte that she was very hopeful that soon after their return the betrothal would be announced.

In the rooms where they mingled with other visitors after taking the waters a Colonel Graeme was presented to them. He was a charming Scotsman who was, the Grand Duchess was informed, a great friend of Lord Bute who in his turn was a close friend of the King and the Princess Dowager of England.

Colonel Graeme was very courteous and made a point of speaking to Charlotte. In fact he seemed very interested in Charlotte who was surprised that her mother allowed him to spend so much time with her.

"It can scarcely be that he has fallen in love with you," cried Christina.

That made Charlotte laugh. "You think of nothing but love. No. He is just a nice old gentleman who likes to talk."

And how he talked! It was all about England. He seemed determined to make her *see* St. James's and Kensington, Hampton and Kew; but chiefly he talked of the young King.

"He is not only extremely handsome," he told Charlotte, "but *good*. I can tell you that there was great rejoicing when he came to the throne. We looked forward to a time of prosperity, for the King cares, as few have before him, for the good of his people."

"He sounds a very worthy king," Charlotte agreed. "Is he . . . warlike?"

Colonel Graeme looked at her oddly and she flushed. She said quickly: "I hate war. You will see what it has done to our country. But kings seem to take to it mightily. I was wondering whether the King of England enjoys going to war."

"Indeed he does not," replied Colonel Graeme. "The King of England is opposed to war. He hates suffering of any sort. He wants to see his subjects happily at peace. When his father, the Prince of Wales, died, he was deeply affected. He scarcely touched food for days and we feared for his health. He loved his father; but when two gardeners fell off a ladder in the gardens at Kew he was upset for days."

"He sounds a very virtuous king."

"I believe Your Highness would think him the best king in the world."

"If he loves peace, I should. But His Majesty of England will care little for my opinion."

"I believe His Majesty would be deeply gratified by Your Highness's good opinion."

Colonel Graeme was indeed a courtier, thought Charlotte.

She was not sorry for Christina's sake when they returned to Mecklenburg.

It was pleasant to be back, for the summer was now with them and they could spend a great deal of time in the gardens.

They must not think the sun was an excuse for idleness, said Madame de Grabow; they must not sit about, their hands in their laps, merely because the sun was shining. Such a sybarite existence was to be deplored. They could read in the sunshine, study their Latin verbs, answer Madame de Grabow's questions on history or geography; they could set up a table and make maps of the world; and there was always the needle. When their garments were all repaired they could take up their embroidery or lace; but not before.

Christina was a little anxious.

"I cannot understand why there must be all this delay."

"Does the Duke know why?" asked Charlotte.

"He is as puzzled as I. Why, before we went to Pyrmont it was as good as settled. Now it is: 'Wait . . . You must be patient.' We have been patient long enough."

Poor Christina! She had lost the look which love had put upon her, for the anxiety took the sparkle from her eyes.

It can't go wrong, thought Charlotte. It must not go wrong. And why should it?

Madame de Grabow had ordered them to set up the table and their sewing was laid on it in little bundles. Not much today, Charlotte was thinking. She would soon be working on her embroidery.

It was very pleasant stitching in the sunshine; she had almost forgotten that letter she had written to the King of Prussia, and when she did think of it she assured herself that it had never reached him. Had she not been a little naïve to imagine it would? She pictured the scene; the messenger arriving and the letters being taken from him by one of the King's secretaries. And what was this one? A letter from the Princess Charlotte Sophia of Mecklenburg-Strelitz! Who was she? A girl of sixteen! She pictured the secretary opening the letter, casting his eye over it and, laughing, tearing it up and throwing it in the waste-paper basket or holding it in the flame of a candle.

She had been foolish to worry.

"You're thoughtful," whispered Ida. "I can guess what you're thinking. You're wondering when there will be a suitor for you."

Charlotte did not answer for a moment; she carefully threaded a pale blue strand of silk; she loved working with beautiful colours.

"Oh come, Ida," she said, when her needle was threaded and she was plying it again, "do you really think a husband will ever be found for me?"

"He may find you."

"You are too romantic. I believe you read romances."

"Well, they're more interesting than your Greek and Latin."

"How can you tell since you don't know Greek and Latin. At least they teach me to be realistic, whereas your romances teach you to dream impossible dreams."

"Why impossible? Why shouldn't you have a husband? Many people do . . . particularly princesses."

Charlotte looked across the table where Christina's head was bent over her sewing. She desperately hoped that everything would work out well for Christina.

"Now who," said Charlotte almost testily, "would want to marry a poor little princess like me! Be realistic, Ida, for once. My mouth is too large and my person too small, I have neither attractions nor fortune. No man whom my brother and my mother would consider worthy, would consider me worthy, so there's an end of the matter."

Just as she finished speaking the sound of the postman's horn was heard in the distance.

"Letters from afar," said Christina, lifting her head.

Ida's eyes sparkled. "Perhaps this is a sweetheart come to claim you, Princess," she whispered to Charlotte.

Charlotte laughed at her; and they were all silent. Again the postman's horn was heard—this time nearer.

They listened to it until it was right at the door of the schloss.

A page was coming across the gardens, straight to the table where the girls sat at their sewing.

Christina was watching eagerly. Poor Christina. She was always believing that she would be summoned to her brother's presence and there told that she had his consent to her marriage.

"His Highness commands the presence of the Princess Charlotte without delay."

Charlotte's knees were trembling as she rose. This was how she had imagined it a hundred times. The letters arriving from Prussia. The King's fury; his angry letters to the Duke who allowed his sister to be so disrespectful to the King of whom every little German duke must stand in awe.

Christina and Ida looked alarmed; even Madame de Grabow was ill at ease. The letters had just arrived. It seemed strange that Charlotte should have been summoned so soon. This could not have happened unless it was a matter of the utmost importance.

She followed the page into the castle. It was so hot out of doors, so cool behind those thick walls; but it was not the change of temperature which made her shiver; it was apprehension.

She was saying to herself: I don't care. It was right to do it. I know it was right.

The door was flung open. There they stood; her brother and her mother, side by side. Oh, this was a very important occasion.

"Charlotte!" It was her mother who spoke. She approached, still rehearsing her excuses. "Charlotte, my dear child." Her mother embraced her. "I have wonderful news for you. This is one of the happiest days of my life."

Charlotte looked from her mother to her brother. He, too, was smiling.

The Duke said almost teasingly: "So you thought fit to write a letter to the King of Prussia?"

"Yes," answered Charlotte, trying to be bold but hearing her voice end on a squeak which betrayed her fear.

"Telling His Majesty how to conduct his armies."

"No, that was not so. I merely told him of what the war had done to us here. I begged him to stop his soldiers pillaging the land—which was doing no good to any of us."

"It was an impertinent letter," said the Duke.

"But," added the Dowager Duchess with a smile, "it amused His Majesty."

"It . . . it was not meant to amuse."

"It touched him too. He has given orders that his armies shall not plunder the villages through which they pass."

Charlotte clasped her hands and smiled. She did not care now. She had achieved her purpose. They could punish her if they wished. She would sew a hundred of the coarsest shirts to be distributed among the poor; she would not care; she would rejoice as she pricked her fingers as one always did with that coarse stuff. And she would think all the time of the King of Prussia, reading her letter and deciding that she was right.

"The King thought it a remarkable letter for a sixteen-year-old girl to write. Though you are seventeen now, Charlotte."

"Yes, Mamma."

"That is good too. It is a pleasant age. Now for my news. The King of Prussia had copies of your letter made and

showed them to his friends. He even sent one to the Dowager
Princess of England—the mother of the King.''

"To England! So far!"

"It was the biggest stroke of good fortune that has come to
our House for a long time," said the Duke.

"Your Highness means my letter . . ."

"Your letter," said her mother. She smiled at her son.
"The Princess Dowager thought it a remarkable letter; so did
her son."

"The King! The King of England?"

"He read it, they tell me, and tears filled his eyes. He said:
'What a remarkable girl the Princess Charlotte must be.'
And so he sent Colonel Graeme to see you and to report to
him what he thought of you. It seems that Colonel Graeme
thought very highly of you."

"Mamma . . . what are you telling me?"

"That you are fortunate beyond our wildest hopes and
dreams. The King of England is asking for your hand in
marriage."

"What did I say?" demanded Ida. "Did I not say it was a
sweetheart? I never thought it would be the King of England,
though."

"But Ida . . . he has not seen me!"

"Colonel Graeme has seen you. And he evidently liked
what he saw."

"What a strange way in which to choose a bride!"

"All royal brides are chosen in that way."

"Colonel Graeme must have flattered me. I hope it won't
be a shock for the King when he sees me."

"Perhaps he's not as handsome as he's been made out to
be," comforted Ida.

Christina came in.

She said: "So you'll be the first to be married after all."

There was talk of nothing else but Charlotte's coming
marriage. There was to be no delay. The English were sending Lord Harcourt to Strelitz immediately and as soon as he
arrived the proxy ceremony was to take place, and immediately it was over she was to sail for England.

"It seems there is an undue haste," whispered Charlotte to
Ida. "Do you think they are afraid the King will hear the
truth and not want me after all?"

"What truth? He's heard the truth."

"I think they've told him I'm a beauty."

"Not they. He read your letter and he knows you're a wiseacre. He's more interested in that than a pretty face."

At least Ida was honest. Charlotte studied her face in her mirror and her misgivings were great. Homely is the kindest way to describe me, she thought; plain would be more truthful.

She hoped that the Prince did not like pretty women.

Why should the King of England select her . . . a humble princess of a tiny state without beauty and riches?

Ida had the answer. "Because you're German and Protestant. There are other princesses in Europe, but don't forget they're all Catholics . . . and they're not German. English Kings ever since George the First always marry Germans."

"And I can't speak his language."

"Never mind, he'll speak yours. Remember, he's German too."

"That's a comfort. But I expect I shall have to learn to speak English. Oh, Ida, it's a terrible thought. I shall leave home. I shall live in a strange country for the rest of my life . . ." She looked at Ida. She would doubtless leave her too, for it was hardly likely that she would be allowed to take Ida with her.

"It's better than living here, Princess . . . doing the same thing every day. Why, you've never dined publicly yet. You haven't been living royally at all."

"I know, but now I feel I want to go on as I have been for a little longer at least. I wonder if Christina will come to England with me." Her face lightened. "Of course she will. She will marry and we'll go together . . . perhaps we'll be married together. That will be a comfort. I shan't be alone after all." She was serious suddenly. "I can't help thinking though, Ida, that there is something extraordinary about all this. I am so humble and *he* is the King of England . . . and it is all so sudden."

And although Ida did her best to comfort her, Charlotte could not rid herself of the idea that there was something strange about this good fortune which had been thrust upon her so unexpectedly—and the speedy manner in which affairs were being hurried to their climax.

Christina was heartbroken; there was no comforting her.

She walked up and down Charlotte's bedroom, her eyes wide with misery.

"There's nothing to be done," she said. "No, Charlotte . . . I know you would do anything, but there is nothing to be done."

"Oh, Christina, that it should be due to me!"

"It's not your fault. It has to be. I've had a feeling lately that we were doomed."

"It's so foolish. Because I am to marry the King of England you may not marry an Englishman! Why? Why?"

"It's in the contract. No other member of the family must marry into England. They have their reasons."

"There seems no sense in their reasons."

"Charlotte, you don't realize what this means. You will be the Queen of England."

"Why should my sister not be Duchess of Roxburgh?"

"It is in the contract. Our brother has signed it . . . eagerly. You can guess why. His sister will be Queen of England. Think of that. He would sacrifice a great deal to bring about that state of affairs, and all he has to sacrifice is me."

"Oh, Christina, I wish this had not happened."

"Wished this piece of luck had passed you by? Don't let anyone hear you say that! They will say you are mad. The King of England might hear of it and decide not to marry you after all. Do you want to break our brother's heart . . . and our mother's? Oh, no, Charlotte, be content with mine."

What could she say to Christina? If she could have made the sacrifice she would most willingly. She was afraid when she thought of going to England. The monotonous routine of her days had become precious; she did not want to leave it . . . for the unknown.

But both she and Christina knew that it was not for her to make momentous decisions.

When she offered to give up her marriage that Christina might have hers Christina only laughed with the new bitterness which had crept into her voice.

"Do you want them to marry you by force?" she asked. "Make no mistake, Charlotte. It is not what you want or I want. This is a brilliant marriage—Mecklenburg will be allied with England. We are of no importance. Don't forget it."

No, there was no comforting Christina.

*   *   *

Lord Harcourt had arrived at the schloss.

He was a handsome man in his late forties, extremely courteous, and he behaved towards Charlotte as though she were already the Queen of England.

Before his arrival the activity in the schloss had reached a feverish pitch; the Dowager Duchess had gone through her trunks and produced dresses which she had been saving for very special occasions. There could not be a more worthy occasion than this. The gowns were altered to fit little Charlotte and she stood patiently while velvets such as she had never worn before were fitted.

Every jewel in the schloss must be produced to adorn her for the ceremonies which must take place; but her mother had said that as it was her simplicity which had charmed Colonel Graeme she must be as she was and not pretend she lived less simply than was actually the fact.

Therefore when Lord Harcourt arrived she was seated in the schoolroom darning a stocking and his lordship was conducted to her there.

Lord Harcourt bowed low over her hand and told her that he came on his king's most happy business and that his master was impatient for that business to be concluded and to see his bride in England.

She wanted to ask why his master was so impatient. He was after all only twenty-two years of age. Why the need for such haste? But she did no such thing and modestly lowering her eyes remarked that it gave her great pleasure to welcome Lord Harcourt.

"I have a gift from His Majesty with the instructions that I am to put it into no hands but yours."

She received it with exclamations of pleasure. It was a miniature—a picture of a handsome young man with flaxen hair and candid blue eyes—set with diamonds.

"It is beautiful," she said. "I beg of you convey my thanks to His Majesty."

"It is something Your Serene Highness will be able to do yourself," Lord Harcourt told her; then she understood that her days at Strelitz were indeed almost over. The proxy ceremony would take place and she would leave without delay with Lord Harcourt.

"The . . . the diamonds are so brilliant," she stammered.

"And the picture of His Majesty I see delights you."

"He is very handsome," she said; and her voice trembled

on a note of enquiry, but Lord Harcourt did not understand that she was wondering how such a handsome young king could be so eager to make a homely and insignificant girl his queen.

Christina walked about the schloss like a grey ghost. There was nothing to be done about Christina. The Duke of Roxburgh stayed on in Mecklenburg, hoping, always hoping that something would happen to make his marriage with Christina possible.

But Charlotte's brother was eager for the wedding to take place. He summoned her and told her that the proxy marriage would be performed in a few weeks time and then there would be no reason why her departure should be delayed.

Her departure to a strange land! Charlotte thought about it with mingling dismay and excitement. It would be like being born again. An entirely new life in a strange country—with a husband whom she had never seen.

She would have liked to confide in Christina, but how could she talk of marriage to her poor heartbroken sister.

If only something would happen to allow Christina to marry. But how could that be unless something happened to stop Charlotte's marriage?

Charlotte knew that every day Christina was hoping for the miracle.

And then something did happen.

The Grand Duchess's attendants went to her room to rouse her one morning and found her unwell. Before the day was out she was dead.

This was bewildering.

Events were happening too fast. Christina had been plunged from the heights of delight to the lowest despair; Charlotte was to leave home and go to a strange husband; and this had all taken place in a few weeks after years of monotonous existence. And now change had come from an unexpected quarter. The mother who had governed their lives was dead, and there could be no talk of weddings for a while.

Charlotte, standing by her mother's coffin, looking down into that autocratic face now so white and still and oddly enough younger than Charlotte had ever known her, was suddenly overcome by a fear of the future. Life was ironic, mocking almost. Here you are fussing about weddings, so I will give you a funeral.

How can we know from one moment to another, thought Charlotte, what will become of any of us? One must be strong; one must be prepared.

Throughout the schloss they were saying: "This will delay the wedding. The Princess Charlotte cannot think of marriage so soon after her mother's death."

New hope was springing up in Christina's eyes. Delay meant hope. Often that which was postponed never took place at all.

The Royal Family

The King of England was perplexed. It was less than a year ago when his grandfather, George II, had arisen as usual, taken his dish of chocolate, asked, as he did every morning, which way the wind was blowing, announced his intention of taking a walk in Kensington Gardens, gone into his closet in his dressing room and fallen dead. The old king had been in his seventy-seventh year so his death was not unexpected; all the same George, his grandson, had found the mantle of kingship oppressive.

The shock had not been so great as that he had suffered nine years before at the death of his father. That *had* been unexpected. Frederick Prince of Wales had seemed a normal healthy man until a blow from a tennis ball had triggered off a series of illnesses and at the age of forty-five he had died leaving his widow, the Princess Augusta, pregnant and already the mother of a large family to support her claims to importance in the country and to make her a formidable figure in the eyes of her father-in-law, King George II. She was the mother of this George who had become Prince of Wales on his father's death—her dear George, her meek and malleable George through whom she intended to govern England, although at this time none was aware of the fact. Then there were Edward Duke of York, William Duke of Gloucester, Henry Duke of Cumberland and young Frederick William. She also had daughters—Augusta who was the eldest of the family and a year George's senior, and Elizabeth, poor deformed clever Elizabeth, who had died when George was Prince of Wales; and lastly there was Caroline Matilda, Frederick's posthumous child who was born four months after his death. But it was her eldest, George, who commanded her attention, for he was the King and on him rested her power.

But all the intricacies of state affairs had been overshadowed in George's mind by thoughts of marriage; for he was betrothed to the Princess Charlotte Sophia of Mecklenburg-Strelitz and he was in love with the Lady Sarah Lennox. As he confided to Lord Bute, that man whom he regarded as his closest friend and who was more than a friend to his mother. George "boiled for Sarah Lennox." All day he thought of Sarah; and Sarah was angry with him, which he would be the first to admit was reasonable. Had he not openly shown his feelings for her; he had even proposed—obliquely it was true through innuendoes to her cousin and friend the Lady Susan Fox-Strangeways. And everyone had believed that he intended to put up a fight at least. There might not have been great opposition. He would have had Henry Fox, Sarah's brother-in-law, on his side and, apart from William Pitt, Fox was perhaps the greatest politician of the day.

But that would not be for long, George knew. His friend Lord Bute was already making plans to remove all those who stood in his way including Mr. Pitt—for the reason that Mr. Pitt was no friend to Lord Bute and had made it quite clear that he would not give him a high place in the Government.

George had decided that he must do his duty which his mother and Lord Bute had made clear to him. Kings of the House of Hanover always married German princesses; he could not marry this young English girl, although she had royal blood in her veins (the wrong side of the blanket, the Dowager Princess of Wales pointed out, for the girl's great-grandmother was Louise de Keroualle, Duchess of Portsmouth, and her great-grandfather Charles II). As Sarah was the sister-in-law of Henry Fox this would mean that that very ambitious politician would have far too much influence with the King; moreover, the girl was frivolous and both Lord Bute and the Princess Dowager agreed that if they were going to maintain their hold on the King he must marry a docile German princess—preferably one who spoke no English. This would leave them entirely in control of George as they had been since his father's death.

So together they had managed to persuade George of his duty, which had been made easier by that earlier disastrous affair of Hannah Lightfoot, the beautiful young Quakeress with whom George had fancied himself in love over several years and was so besotted that he had set her up in a house in Islington, had had children by her and even committed the greatest indiscretion of all by going through a form of marriage with her.

It was the memory of Hannah which had made George realize the folly he was capable of when he acted without the advice of his friend Lord Bute and his mother.

And so while he yearned for Sarah Lennox, he agreed to this marriage which they had arranged for him. And now he was desperately trying to put all thought of Sarah from his mind and fall in love with the Princess Charlotte, for he was determined to be a faithful husband and a good king. He was eager that the Court under his direction should be a moral Court. His grandfather and his great-grandfather had openly flaunted their mistresses. That was shocking, George declared, and had determined that a new standard of morals was going to be set in the reign of George III; if he had to make sacrifices, he was ready to do so.

Never in his life, he assured himself, would he be asked to make a bigger one than this. Therefore he set about making plans for his wedding, throwing himself into the arrangements heart and soul, in this way hoping to drive Sarah from his thoughts.

"There shall be no vulgar ceremony in the bedchamber," he announced. "I have long thought it time we dispensed with that ceremony which after all comes to us from the French."

His mother and Lord Bute listened delightedly. "Let him do what he will as long as he agrees to the marriage," said Lord Bute.

"I shall not wish her to bring more than one or two attendants with her," went on George. "These people are apt to meddle."

His mother and Lord Bute agreed sympathetically that this was true.

"Your Majesty does well to take a firm stand," Bute told him.

The Princess Augusta shot a warning look at Lord Bute. Perhaps they should not remind George that he was the King and could do as he pleased. What if he decided to use the royal prerogative and insist on marriage with Sarah Lennox?

But Lord Bute knew what he was doing. The Princess smiled fondly at the man who was her secret lover—though perhaps not so secret, for the whole Court was aware of their liaison and these titbits of gossip never remained inside the Court but always filtered through to the people.

Lord Bute gave her their intimate smile which seemed to say: "You can trust me." And she believed she could.

"How long, I wonder," said George, "before the Princess arrives."

"We shall press forward with all arrangements as soon as possible," Bute assured him. "Harcourt will see that there is no delay. Your Majesty is impatient for your bride."

George hesitated. Perhaps, he thought, when she comes it will be easier. Once I am married to her I shall think only of her. It would be wonderful to put an end to this continual ache for Sarah.

"I am very impatient for that moment to come which will join me to her, I hope for my life."

The Princess and Bute exchanged glances. George was so reliable—except of course when he tried to act without their guidance. They both still shivered now when they contemplated the Lightfoot affair. The Sarah Lennox matter had been far more manageable.

But once George was married all would be well.

The marriage must take place at the earliest possible moment. Therefore it was comforting to hear from George's own lips that he was impatient for it.

When they were alone Lord Bute and the Dowager Princess of Wales began discussing events more candidly than they were able to in the King's presence.

"I cannot wait for Charlotte's arrival," declared the Princess. "I shall not feel safe until they are married."

"This will surely be one of the most hasty royal marriages that ever took place," smiled Bute.

"I keep feeling that something will go wrong."

Bute took her hand and kissed it tenderly; his eyes regarded her affectionately. He had good reason to feel affection for her. His fortunes had been going up ever since that day fourteen years ago when at Egham races a shower of rain had driven the late Prince of Wales into a tent and he, Bute, had been invited to join the royal party for a game of whist. He had immediately become a favourite of the Prince—and an even greater one of the Princess. In those days Frederick had welcomed Bute's devotion to his wife; it had left Frederick to dally with his mistress of the moment while Bute took care of the Princess. They had been a happy foursome and nothing could have been more amicable. But since Frederick's death, Bute's fortunes had risen fast. Not only had he made himself indispensable to the Princess but to her son; and George looked upon him as a father, for he had always played the part to perfection; and now that George was king, Bute's eyes were on the greatest power available. He wanted the position which was now held by William Pitt—the man who was known throughout the country as the Great Commoner, who had dreamed of an Empire for England and had set about obtaining one for her. How he had succeeded was only too apparent. Horace Walpole, that old gossip, had remarked that each morning he must ask what fresh English victory there had been for fear of missing one. Pitt had declared that he could save England and he was the only one who could. He had taken over the ministry in all but name when England was engaged in a war that seemed disastrous, for her only ally was Frederick the Great, and he and England stood together against the combined forces of France, Austria, Russia and Spain. Pitt was fighting out the conflict in America and India and doing what he had said he would do—turn a kingdom into an Empire.

Recognizing the man's genius, Bute would have been contented to work with Pitt. It was Pitt who had shown so clearly that he would not work with Bute. Pitt had stood firm against the folly of nepotism. The right man for the job, was his cry. And he was proving how right he was. Yet if ever a man hoped to climb through favouritism that man was Bute. He had relied for years on the love of the Princess Dowager; now he relied on that of the King. Bute wanted to rule England; and Pitt had already declared that if the unfortunate day arrived when Bute moved in, he, Pitt, would move out.

Ever since that day Bute had made up his mind that Pitt should go and he was waiting for the time to come when he would have an opportunity of disposing of his enemy.

As he smiled at the Princess he was thinking how safe he was with her. She adored him and he was very fond of her. They worked together, saw eye to eye; Augusta was not a promiscuous woman; she had been the perfect wife when Frederick had been alive; she had stood firmly beside him, accepting his policies, hating those whom he hated, favouring those whom he favoured; and she had not been unfaithful, although Bute knew that often she wished to be . . . with him. And as soon as Frederick died there was nothing to prevent their union; neither of them asked for the impossible, which marriage would have been. They were wise enough to do without that mixed blessing. They were as one—in mind and body; and they asked nothing more.

Lady Bute came to Court. Thank God he had been wise enough to choose a sensible wife. She knew of the relationship between her husband and the Princess. He had given her a large family: "Fourteen children," the Princess Augusta had remarked admiringly, "in as little time as it takes to get them." She had special privileges as the wife of one of the most prominent men at Court, and so did her children; Bute himself had become a member of the Privy Council, Groom of the Stole and First Gentleman of the Bedchamber; the King consulted him at every turn and he was fast becoming, to all intents and purposes, the Prime Minister. Lady Bute had been created Baroness Mount Stuart of Wortley; and this, her husband had assured her, on one of the rare occasions when he could absent himself from the side of his mistress to spend a little time with her, was a beginning. Yes, Lady Bute was a sensible woman, determined to put no obstacle in the way of her husband's advancement.

So with his women he was singularly blessed.

"Nothing will go wrong with this, my love," he said firmly. "But I agree with you that the sooner our Princess arrives and is formally married to His Majesty, the happier we shall all feel."

"The girl should be grateful," said the Princess. "After all, what is this place Mecklenburg-Strelitz? Can you imagine their feelings when Colonel Graeme made our intentions clear to them?"

"They must have been overwhelmed with joy."

"I should think so! And Charlotte should be grateful. I hope she will be. We do not want any interference from her."

"You will know how to manage her, my dearest. I am sure of that."

"Oh, yes." The Princess was very confident. "I shall let the child see that she must do as I say. She is very young and will need guidance."

"Let us hope that she will be wise enough to take it."

"My dear, I shall insist on that wisdom."

Bute laughed. "I am sure of it. But His Majesty . . ."

"What of George?"

"If he should become enamoured of her and she plead with him for her own way . . ."

The Princess nodded. "George does become enamoured in the most single minded fashion. That Sarah Lennox . . ."

"It was not insuperably difficult to part him from her. It is not Sarah Lennox who alarms me so much as . . . the other."

"That was when he was young and I believe he was led into that folly. He would never be so foolish again surely. It is merely a matter of managing Charlotte. And I am sure I shall be able to do that. Sarah Lennox is a minx . . . and Hannah Lightfoot must have been a strong-minded woman. German women are brought up much more sensibly. They know their places. So it will be with our little Charlotte. And I shall be hoping that she becomes pregnant as soon as possible."

"Then your mind is at ease?"

"As much as it can be until George is actually married to a safe little German princess."

While they were talking the King burst in upon them. It was clear that something had happened to alarm him. His face was pinker than usual—a sure sign that he was distraught. His mouth with its thick Hanoverian lips was trembling a little.

"George . . . my dearest son, what is wrong?"

"News," he said, "from Mecklenburg."

"Pray tell me quickly."

It was Bute who took the letter from the King's trembling hand and read that the Grand Duchess of Mecklenburg-Strelitz had died and that in the circumstances the wedding would have to be postponed.

The Princess Augusta sat down heavily. It was what she feared—some impediment, something that would stand in the way of getting George married promptly.

Was she imagining it or did she see a look of relief in the King's eyes? Was he saying to himself: It could happen that the marriage does not take place after all. And there is Sarah . . .

Bute took charge of the situation as he had on so many occasions, promptly, tactfully and resourcefully, thought the Princess fondly.

"This is sad news," he said, "but I do not see why the death of our little Queen's mother need delay the wedding. Poor little lady, she will be so desolate and in need of comfort

. . . the comfort her husband can give her. I think Your Majesty should write immediately and insist that the plans are not held back in any way whatsoever.''

"It is very sad . . . for Charlotte,'' said George.

"I knew,'' said Bute warmly, "that you would want to comfort her. Let us write of your feelings without delay. And we will say that on no account should the Princess Charlotte . . . our little queen . . . delay her journey to her kingdom and her king.''

George allowed Lord Bute to lead him to his mother's writing table while the Princess watched her forceful lover. What an ally! How she adored him! More today, than in those weeks which had followed their first meeting in the tent when the new excitement had come into her life. More than ever, she thought fondly, after all these years.

Lady Sarah Lennox came down to breakfast at Holland House looking fresh and lovely, as though she had not a care in the world.

Her sister Lady Caroline Fox regarded her with some impatience while her brother-in-law looked up from his plate sardonically as she fell into her chair.

Lady Caroline found it difficult to forgive her for losing as she said the greatest chance that would ever come her way, for Lady Caroline was sure that had her foolish young sister played her cards as any wise girl would have done, she would now be betrothed to the King and not known throughout the Court as the girl he had jilted.

What was so irritating was Sarah's indifference. In fact Sarah's indifference was at the whole root of the trouble. If Sarah had shown some enthusiasm for the King's courtship in the first place, Caroline was sure George would have been so determined to marry her that nothing would have stopped him.

Sarah was holding something in her lap and her brother-in-law asked what it was she was regarding so tenderly. Lady Caroline gave a little shriek as Sarah held up the hedgehog.

"Not at the breakfast table!'' she cried.

But Sarah began to laugh and set the creature on the table.

"Is he not a little darling?'' demanded Sarah.

"I refuse to have him on the breakfast table,'' declared Lady Caroline.

But Sarah was looking appealingly at her brother-in-law.

Henry Fox thought her a little idiot, but she amused him and was so pretty so he said: "Don't be hard on poor Sarah, Caroline. She has suffered three bereavements so recently—the death of her little squirrel, that of Beau her horse . . ." Sarah's eyes filled with tears at the recollection. "Not to mention," went on Mr. Fox as though he were addressing the House of Commons, "the King of England."

"Oh, dear Mr. Fox," sighed Sarah plaintively, "do not bring up that stale matter again. I am so sick of the King and his wedding."

"Sarah, for God's sake try to be sensible," pleaded Caroline. "I know it is difficult for you . . ."

"Very," sighed Sarah mischievously. "Don't you love the way he rolls into a ball. Look at those spikes."

Caroline sighed and looked at her husband who shrugged his shoulders and turned his attention to his food.

"People are going to be sorry for you, Sarah," went on Caroline.

"Why?"

"Oh, don't be absurd. You are the most publicly jilted woman in England."

"I shall be very cool to him when we meet and show I don't care in the least."

"Try to be sensible. This is the King."

Sarah was silent, eating stolidly.

"The wedding will be delayed, I doubt not," Mr. Fox was saying, "on account of the death of the bride's mother."

"Perhaps," put in Lady Caroline hopefully, "it will not take place at all."

"Little fear or hope of that. I have no doubt that the Duke of Strelitz is not going to miss such an opportunity."

"He has more sense than some foolish people."

Sarah groaned. "How we do return to the same point in this house," she said.

"It is not every house which has a member of the family so foolish as to throw away a crown."

"George is a fool," cried Sarah. "If he had not been he wouldn't have let them persuade him and he would have asked me himself . . . not through Susan. If you ask me I'm well rid of him."

"Well rid of a crown, the power to do your family good, to bear a king?" said Caroline.

Sarah looked at her sister helplessly. "There are other

things we might talk of. What of our sister Emily's confinement? Is that not more important than my being jilted?''

''Nothing that has ever happened to this family is more important than your being jilted by the King.''

Sarah picked up her hedgehog and flounced out of the room.

''I'm sick of all this talk, Sukey,'' she said to the hedgehog, and she laughed for she had named him after her friend Susan Fox-Strangeways to whom she had given the nicknames of Sukey and Pussy. ''But Sukey was more suitable for you, Sukey,'' she said. ''You could hardly be Pussy could you? I have an idea *that* might have offended your dignity.''

Reaching her room she did what she enjoyed doing when she wished to soothe herself: Wrote to Susan.

''Dearest Susan . . .''

She paused and thought what fun it would be if Susan were here. Everything seemed a joke then, although Susan was far more serious than she was. If George had had any sense he would have fallen in love with Susan rather than her. She was sure Susan would have known how to deal with the matter. There! she was as bad as her sister and brother-in-law; the thing was constantly in her mind. It occurred to her that Susan might not yet have heard the news of the King's proposed marriage. Could it be that it had not yet reached Somerset?

She wrote rapidly:

To begin to astonish you as much as I was, I must tell you that the —— is going to be married to a Princess of Mecklenburg . . . Does not your choler rise at this . . . But you will think, I daresay, that I have been doing some terrible thing to deserve it, for you won't be easily brought to change your opinion of any person; but I assure you I have not. I have been in his company very often since I last wrote to you, but though nothing was said he always took pains to show me some preference by talking twice and they were mighty kind speeches and looks. Even last Thursday the day after the news came out, the hypocrite had the face to come up and speak to me with all the good humour in the world and seemed to want to speak to me but was afraid . . .

Sarah laid down her pen and thought: I am angry with him after all. He *has* behaved badly, and when I next see him I shall show him what I think of him.

She wrote rapidly and went on to say:

In short his behaviour is that of a man who has neither sense, good nature nor honesty. I shall have to see him on Thursday night, and I shall take care to show that I am not mortified to anybody, but if it is true that one can vex anyone with a reserved cold manner, he shall have it, I promise him.

"Now as to what I think about it myself, excepting this little revenge, I have almost forgiven him. Luckily for me I did not love him and only liked him, nor did the title weigh anything with me; so little at least, that my disappointment did not affect my spirits above one hour or two I believe. I did not cry, I assure you, which I believe you will, as I know you were more set upon it than I was. The thing I am most angry at is looking so like a fool . . . but I don't much care. If he were to change his mind again (which can't be though) and not give me a *very* good reason for his conduct I would not have him, for if he is so weak as to be governed by everybody I should have a bad time of it . . .

She paused, smiling. How easy it was to understand one's true feelings when one set them on paper to friends with whom one could be entirely candid as with dear Sukey. She was piqued. She did care a little. But not much . . . not so much as she had cared about the death of her squirrel or her darling Beau.

She took up her pen and wrote.

I charge you not to mention this to anyone but your parents and desire them not to speak of it, for it will be said we invent stories and he will hate us anyway, for one generally hates people that one is in the wrong with and that knows one has acted wrongly . . .

It was true, she thought. But George was perhaps too weak to hate anyone. He was at heart kind, she was sure, so perhaps it would not have been so bad to marry him.

She sighed and hastily finished off her letter.

His bride's mother had died. The wedding would be postponed. Was it possible . . . ?

When all was said and done there was some satisfaction in being a queen.

There was consternation at Holland House.

Lady Caroline was furious; she paced up and down the drawing room unable to control her anger.

"I never heard the like. How dare he! It's an added insult."

Mr. Fox tried to calm her. "It had to be. Sarah's position demands that she should be invited. In fact it would have been a bigger slight not to invite her than to do so."

"She must refuse," insisted Lady Caroline.

Lady Kildare, recently delivered of a child, said that she was unsure what should be done about the matter, but her husband said: "Sarah should go. What is going to be *said* if she refuses."

"It is the most humiliating business I ever heard," declared Lady Caroline.

"Let's see what Sarah herself thinks," suggested Mr. Fox.

"Sarah!" spat out Caroline. "Sarah has no opinions about anything but horses and hedgehogs . . . and perhaps squirrels. Sarah is a fool—as we have learned in the bitterest manner possible."

"Poor Sarah!" murmured Mr. Fox. "At least she should be allowed to give an opinion."

Mr. Fox summoned a servant and asked that the Lady Sarah come to the drawing room.

As soon as Sarah entered it was clear to the gathered family that she knew what matter was under discussion.

"I've decided to go," she announced.

"What!" cried Caroline.

Sarah shrugged her shoulders. "If I refuse he will think I am sulking."

"Which you have every reason to do."

"He might even think that I *care*. I am going to show him that I do not. I shall look at him . . . *insolently* . . . while he is marrying that woman and I shall make him feel so uncomfortable that he'll wish he had never seen me . . . or her. But I shall go. I have decided."

"I don't think you have given the matter serious thought," said Caroline.

"I have made up my mind," retorted Sarah. "And after all, the invitation is sent to me. I am invited to be the bridesmaid, remember, and it is for me to decide. All I'm telling you is that I have decided."

"It's madness," cried Caroline.

"I'm not so sure," put in Lord Kildare.

They were all waiting for Mr. Fox to express an opinion; after all he was the most important member of the family.

He lifted his shoulders. "To go or to stay away . . . either is not very comfortable. Which ever is done will raise comment.''

"At least Sarah should show she has some *pride*," insisted Caroline.

"But I don't think I have, sister . . . not much in any case. Everyone knows George is still dangling on his mother's apron strings, they know that she and Lord Bute arranged for him to marry this Charlotte person and he wasn't man enough to refuse. Poor Charlotte! I pity her.''

"I should have thought you would be envying her," snapped Caroline. "You would if you had any sense.''

"But you always said I had none of that useful commodity," smiled Sarah. "And . . . I have decided. I am going to be a bridesmaid at the King's wedding.''

Mr. Fox smiled at her, half amused, half exasperated. He deplored his sister-in-law's failure to achieve the royal marriage as much as anyone, but he couldn't help being fond of her.

We shall have further trouble with Sarah, he prophesied to himself.

Sarah flounced out of the room back to Sukey the hedge-hog and immediately sat down to write to Susan.

Dear Pussy,
I have only time to tell you that I have been asked to be bridesmaid and I have accepted it. I'm sorry to say it's against my sister Caroline's opinion a little. I beg you to tell me what your opinion is. I think it is not to be looked upon as a favour, but as a thing due to my rank. Why refuse it and make great talk, be abused by those who don't know and perhaps by those that do, for they are always in the right, you know . . . Those that think about it will say perhaps that I want spirit and pride, which is true enough, for I don't dislike it in the least, and I don't like to affect what I don't feel though ever so right . . .

Sarah put down her pen and laughed. Yes, there was no doubt writing to Susan helped her to understand her own feelings.

And even when Susan replied that she thought Sarah was wrong to be one of the King's bridesmaids Sarah clung to her opinions.

She was determined to go.

When George heard that Sarah had accepted the invitation

he did not know whether to be relieved or alarmed. While he was being married to this strange young woman, Sarah would be standing close by! He was sure he would not be able to think of anything but Sarah. If Sarah only knew how much he had wanted to marry her! But perhaps she did. Had he not made it plain? Scarcely perhaps, since he had so quickly been persuaded. But there were secrets people did not know. There had been Hannah. He thought of her, his beautiful Quaker, and how he had loved her and believed he always would, until he met Sarah. If he could have married Hannah, made her first Princess of Wales and then Queen of England perhaps he would never have noticed how beautiful Sarah was.

He tried not to think of Hannah, but he could not forget her. It was natural that he should think of her with his wedding day so close. How different this would be from that other wedding day when he and Hannah had stood before Dr. Wilmot and exchanged their marriage vows.

He shivered. How could he have been such a fool! But it had been no true marriage because Hannah had been married before to Isaac Axford, the Quaker grocer, one of her own sect. It was true that the marriage had taken place in Dr. Keith's Marriage Mill which was now declared illegal . . . but it was a true marriage all the same; and that made it impossible for the ceremony through which he had gone with Hannah to be anything but invalid. Besides, Hannah was dead. Or was she?

If he could be sure . . .

But he was supposed to be pining for the loss of Sarah, not thinking of Hannah. No, no, he was not supposed to be doing either. He was supposed to be thinking of welcoming his bride the Princess Charlotte.

George forced himself to think of Charlotte. He would be a good husband to her; they would have children, and when he was a father he would cease to be bothered by romantic follies.

But he could not dismiss Sarah from his mind; and while he made almost feverish preparations to receive his bride, images of Sarah continued to torment him.

In the nursery Caroline Matilda, the youngest of the family, was chattering about the wedding.

She was ten years old and had always felt herself to be apart from the family because she had been born four months after her father's death. So she had never known him. Neither had her brother Frederick William really, although it was true he had been born a year before she had, when their father was alive, but he could remember nothing of him, so he was as much in the dark as Caroline Matilda. Henry was sixteen and swaggered about the nursery, impatient because he was neither a boy nor a man, but very much despising his younger sister and brother. Then there was William who was eighteen, very much the man with no time to spare for ignorant little sisters. Elizabeth, the saintly one, had died what seemed like a long time ago to Caroline Matilda, but was in fact only some three years back; then there was Edward, Duke of York, who was twenty-two; and Augusta, haughty, eldest of them all, who was twenty-four years old; but she was not the most important member of the family. How could she be when there was George and although one year younger than Augusta, he was the King.

The thought that George was King of England made Caroline Matilda want to giggle, for George was less like a king than any of her brothers. He was always kind and even treated the youngest of them all as though she were worthy of some consideration. Now he was always giving audiences and receiving ministers, and even his family had to remember to show due respect to him, although he never asked for it.

Before he had become king he had had time to talk to Caroline Matilda about their father. She was constantly asking questions about Papa. It seemed to her so odd to have a father who had died before she was born.

She did not share George's delight in Lord Bute, for he scarcely noticed her. All his attention was for George. And Mamma of course did not notice her much either—only to lay down a lot of rules as to how the nursery was to be run.

She liked to listen to her brothers, Henry and Frederick, talking together—or rather Henry talked and Frederick listened. It wasn't only the gap in their ages which made Henry supreme. Henry was only sixteen but healthy, whereas Frederick always had colds and was often out of breath. Poor Frederick; he listened patiently, only too grateful that his brother talked to him.

Caroline Matilda knew better than to attempt to join in. Henry would soon have put her in her place if she had. He wasn't like dear George—dear King George, she thought with a little chuckle—and the reason was that everyone knew

George was king so he didn't always have to be *reminding* people how important he was.

Henry was saying: "It'll be different now George is king. They can't keep us cooped up forever."

Frederick timidly asked what would happen when they were no longer cooped up.

"We shall go to balls and banquets. We shan't just be the children in the nursery. You see. Of course you and Caro will be children for years yet . . ."

"Frederick will be as old as you are in five years' time," Caroline couldn't help putting in.

Henry looked at her coldly. "As for you, you are only a baby still."

"I'm ten years old which is only six years younger than you."

"And you're a girl."

"They marry before boys," Caroline reminded him cheekily while Frederick looked at her with amazement at her temerity. "After all," she went on, "the Princess Charlotte is only seventeen and that's a year older than you are now."

"That is not the point of the argument. The trouble with you, Caro, is that you don't think."

"I'm thinking all the time."

"What about?" challenged Henry.

"What I'm going to do when I grow up."

"What's that?"

"Run wild," she told them.

Henry laughed. She had voiced his own sentiments. So even little Caroline Matilda was longing for freedom; it all came of what he called being cooped up.

"It is Mamma who keeps us as we are," said Henry. "She's afraid we'll be contaminated by wicked people if we aren't kept shut away like this."

"George will be a good king," Caroline said, "so then there won't be any wickedness, and when there's no danger we won't have to be shut away."

"Poor George!" said Henry knowledgeably. "He's not looking forward to his wedding."

"Oh, but he loves the Princess Charlotte."

"How do you know?"

"Well, he must because she is going to be his wife."

"You don't know anything," Henry told her, "and you would therefore be wise to keep your mouth shut. Our brother wanted Sarah Lennox not this Charlotte, and I repeat he is not going to be pleased with this wedding.''

"But . . .'' began Caroline and was warned by a quick look from Frederick.

The door opened suddenly and Augusta their eldest sister looked in. They were immediately silent. One always was when Augusta arrived. It was well known that she delighted in carrying tales to their mother—whether to try to divert some of that affection which was lavished on George towards herself or because she liked telling tales and making trouble, no one was quite sure. But in any case her arrival was the signal to guard their tongues.

"What are you children chattering about?'' she wanted to know.

Henry flushed at the term, which amused Augusta; she always knew what would hurt people most and contrived to do it.

"I'll swear it's the wedding,'' she went on. "And Henry is telling you all about it. You should remember though that Henry knows very little. And sit up straight, Frederick. All humped up like that! No wonder you're always tired. And you supposed to be working at your embroidery, Caroline?''

Caroline said: "I had only just laid it down for a moment.''

"Then pick it up and make up for that moment of idleness. I shall be forced to tell Mamma how I found you all wasting time and telling each other stories about the wedding.''

"Oh, but we weren't!'' cried Caroline.

And Augusta looked at her in that way which implied she was lying because she, Augusta, had stood outside the door for fully five minutes before coming in.

Even when you were not guilty, thought Caroline, Augusta made you feel you were.

Augusta laughed unpleasantly and said: "Well, if you want to know that silly little Sarah Lennox is furious because she will not be Queen of England. I spoke to her yesterday at the drawing room. I showed I understood how she must be feeling. 'Poor Lady Sarah,' I said; and she tossed her silly head and pretended not to care. And something else I'll tell you. She is to be one of the bridesmaids. That will be fun, I promise you.''

Caroline Matilda contemplated what excitement existed in the outside world; and even while she listened avidly to what Augusta had to tell about the King's desire to marry Lady

Sarah—which had been rightly thwarted it seemed, according to her sister's account, as much by her, Augusta, as anyone— she was thinking of the story of Augusta's birth when their father and mother, then Prince and Princess of Wales, had fled from Hampton Court that their first child might be born at St. James's; and how the King and Queen—Caroline Matilda's grandfather and grandmother—had been so angry; and there had been no sheets at St. James's and nothing ready, so that the baby Augusta had to be wrapped in a tablecloth. What drama surrounded their lives. All except mine, thought Caroline Matilda. I have to stay in the nursery, "cooped up," while all the excitement goes on in the world outside.

And how her grandparents had quarrelled with her parents! They were always quarrelling, Henry told them. They were a quarrelling family.

Well, she would have some fun one day. She would be free to run wild.

In the meantime she listened to Augusta's account of the snubbing of silly Sarah Lennox who had believed mistakenly that she could be Queen of England.

And while the wedding was being discussed in the schoolroom, the Princess and Lord Bute were also talking of it.

There was to be no delay. In spite of the death of the Grand Duchess, the plans would go on as previously arranged.

"She will be here soon," said the Princess Dowager of Wales. "I confess I shall not feel safe until she is."

"Never fear," soothed Lord Bute. "All will be well."

He fervently hoped so. He was about to climb to the top of the pinnacle towards which he had patiently striven ever since he had seen the way to favour through George who was now the King.

Prime Minister, he thought. I shall rule this land. There is no end to the power which will be mine. Pitt will have to do as he's told . . . or go. And Pitt would never be able to let go; he was too ambitious.

I'll use Pitt, thought Bute. He's too good a man to lose. But he'll have to realize who is his master.

He smiled fondly at the Princess. They were in agreement. The sooner George was safely married the better. And the Princess Charlotte was ideal. Plain, so that she would not enslave George; daughter of a very minor dukedom, so that she should be forever grateful; and not speaking a word of

English so that she could not wheedle with her tongue at any rate.

All would be well—and once the wedding was over they would feel so safe.

George too was thinking of the wedding.

Sarah, Hannah, Charlotte. He saw them all in turn. The two first so vividly—the shadowy charm of Hannah, the vital beauty of Sarah; and he turned away from those two and saw a Princess whom he endowed with their grace and beauty.

Charlotte. He kept saying her name over and over again. And he longed for her coming because it would end the uncertainty, and he was sure that once he saw her, once he had taken his vows neither Sarah nor Hannah would torment him. They would be banished from his thoughts for ever, for no faithful husband gave a thought to other women.

"And I will be faithful," he assured himself. "I am impatient for her arrival and for the moment when she shall be joined to me . . . forever, I hope. And I pray God that He will make her fruitful."

And all through the hot August days the whole Court talked of the wedding.

Royal Wedding

The Court of Mecklenburg might be in mourning but there was to be no delay in the marriage ceremony. This was the order of the Duke.

He sent for Charlotte—bewildered Charlotte—who had so recently lost her mother, but was to gain a husband. Poor Christina had nothing to gain, thought Charlotte, but at least she remains at a Court familiar to her.

The Duke regarded his sister with the increased affection which he had felt for her since the King of England desired her for his bride.

"My dear sister," he said, embracing her somewhat curtly, as a duty, thought Charlotte, and as an acknowledgement of her new importance, "I understand your grief for your mother. It is a grief I share. I have been thinking of the postponement of your marriage and I can see no good that can come from it."

"A wedding so soon after a funeral . . ." began Charlotte.

But her brother silenced her. He had not summoned her that he might hear her views, but in order that she might hear his.

"It is the best way to forget your grief," he told her. "I have asked that there shall be no delay."

"But . . ."

"I am thinking of you, sister. This is what our mother would have wished. She knows you mourn in your heart. Your husband will comfort you."

"And Christina . . . ?"

Her brother raised his eyebrows. Christina had been foolish; she had fallen in love with an English duke. That would not have been an impossible union but for the clause in

Charlotte's marriage contract; as it was the affair had ceased to exist as far as the Duke was concerned, and Charlotte was extremely indiscreet to have mentioned it. But Charlotte could be indiscreet. There was that letter she had written to Frederick of Prussia. What tremendous impertinence! But by great good luck it had worked to her advantage, and he was delighted that she had written the letter. But in his secret thoughts he considered it most indiscreet.

What a mercy that Charlotte would soon be leaving for England.

Now he silenced her with a look.

He said: "The proxy marriage will take place almost immediately; and after that there will be little delay in your departure. The coronation is to be the 22nd of September; and you must have been married to him before that. So you see there is very little time."

"So soon . . ." gasped Charlotte.

Her brother smiled at her. "Your bridegroom is, where his wedding is concerned, a very impatient man."

The Duke came into Charlotte's bedroom. She was wrapped in a robe more splendid than any she had had before; beneath it she was shivering, though not with cold.

"Are you prepared?" asked her brother sternly.

"Yes," she answered.

He took her hand. "All is ready in the salon," he told her.

Flunkeys threw open the doors that they might pass through to that salon which was lighted by a thousand candles. The cost must have been great, thought Charlotte. But the petty Dukedom of Mecklenburg-Strelitz was allying itself with the throne of England, so it was not the time to count the cost of a few candles.

And this is all on account of me! thought Charlotte, struck more than ever before by the awesomeness of the occasion and all that it meant. She saw the ceremonial velvet sofa on which she was to lie and beside it Mr. Drummond, the representative of the King of England, who was to stand proxy for him in this preliminary ceremony.

The sight of the sofa filled her with dread because it brought with it a fresh realization of her responsibilities. This was not only leaving home, breaking up Christina's romance, it was living intimately with a stranger, bearing his children, with the eyes of the world on her because she would be the mother of the next King of England.

The sofa represented a state bed, their royal bed which she would have to share with a strange young man and therein perform rites of which she was ignorant.

She was trembling; her legs had become stubborn and were refusing to carry her towards that symbolic couch. It was not too late even now. Suppose she refused to continue with this. Suppose she cried out that they must let Christina marry her Englishman for she had decided not to marry hers. Christina longed for marriage; she was breaking her heart because it was being denied her; whereas she, Charlotte, was realizing in this solemn moment that she did not wish to marry. She did not want to leave her home; she wanted to stay here . . . remain a child for a little longer, doing her lessons—Latin, history, geography—making maps with Madame de Grabow, mending sewing. Why should she not protest that this was too sudden? There was something she suspected about this hurried wedding. Why so much haste? Was her bridegroom being hurried as she was? Was he in England crying out against the marriage as she was here? Why should she, who had once written a letter to Frederick the Great, hesitate now.

But it was because of that letter . . . This web was of her own making. But at least it showed that one had the power to direct one's own life.

"It is not too late." It was a message tapping out in her brain.

Her brother took her hand and pressed it impatiently.

"Come, come. We are waiting for you."

"No . . ." she whispered.

"Don't be a baby," hissed her brother angrily. "You are going to be Queen of England."

Don't be a baby. She was seventeen years old . . . old enough to leave her home, to marry, to bear children. It was the fate of all Princesses. All through history they had found themselves in positions like this. They were not expected to have any free will. They obeyed orders. They married for the good of their countries, where their fathers or brothers decided they should. And they had decided that she should be a queen as readily and as ruthlessly as they had decided Christina should lose her hopes of happiness.

She lay on the sofa and the coverlet was placed over her.

Beneath the coverlet she must expose her right leg; it was all part of the proxy ceremony.

Mr. Drummond, the Englishman, removed his boot and thrust his leg, bare to the knee, under the covers. When his flesh touched hers she tried to stop her teeth from chattering.

Now the symbol had been expressed, Mr. Drummond removed his leg and replaced his boot, while beneath the coverlet she arranged her robe to cover her own bare leg and rose from the couch.

The ceremony was over.

Her brother, all tenderness and affection, embraced her.

She was a very important person now. He called her Your Majesty.

"Preparations for the journey must not be delayed." The Duke was giving his orders throughout the schloss. "We must think of Her Majesty's coronation. There is very little time."

There were only two days left to her in Mecklenburg and these were to be spent in ceremonies. No longer did she eat her meals in the schoolroom under the scrutiny of Madame de Grabow. Now she dined in public. It was her very first experience of such ceremony.

She must sit at a separate table at the banquet which followed the proxy ceremony and beside her sat Christina, pale and sombre, looking as though she would never smile again, while since her mother could not be there her place was taken by the girls' great-aunt, the Princess Schwartzenburg. All the time the Princess talked of the great honour which had come to Charlotte and how proud they were, and how she must do her duty and be a docile wife and bear her husband many children. Christina said little; she ate scarcely anything. Poor sad Christina!

Charlotte began to feel that she would not be sorry to leave home . . . in the circumstances.

In the great salon her brother was seated with the English envoy Lord Harcourt, Mr. Drummond, and members of the English embassy; there were one hundred and fifty guests in all, and through the windows Charlotte could see the gardens lighted by forty thousand lamps.

All in honour of my marriage, she thought. I have become very important here.

But soon she would be on her way to her new country.

*   *   *

When she reached her bedroom she found her new dressers, Madame Haggerdorn and Mademoiselle von Schwellenburg
waiting for her. Everything was going to be so much more
ceremonious from now on.

Though these two ladies had been chosen to accompany her
to England, there had been some controversy about their
coming, for it seemed that the King would have wished her to
come without attendants and on her arrival choose English
ones—or have them chosen for her. But she had pleaded that
she be allowed at least two of her own countrywomen. "For I
do not speak the language," she had explained. She spoke
French tolerably well, her brother told her, and German
would be understood; so she need have no fears; but the
English envoy had agreed that two female attendants, provided
they were well chosen, might accompany her. She was also
allowed to bring Albert, her hairdresser.

As the new dressers—and it was clear that Madame Haggerdorn was in awe of Mademoiselle von Schwellenburg right
from the start—helped her to prepare for bed, Charlotte thought
nostalgically of Ida and the lack of ceremony of the old days.

Mademoiselle von Schwellenburg, putting herself in charge,
made it clear that she intended to extract the utmost ceremony
from the occasion. She signed for Madame Haggerdorn to hand
the nightgown and she herself slipped it over Charlotte's head.

"I trust there is nothing Your Majesty needs."

"No thank you," answered Charlotte.

"Then we beg Your Majesty's leave to retire."

Yes, thought Charlotte, retire and leave me alone.

So they left her and she lay in her bed unable to think;
scenes from this eventful day darting in and out of her mind.
She saw herself entering the brightly lighted salon; she heard
again her brother's impatient voice; she was lying on the
couch; she could feel the cold touch of the Englishman's flesh
against her own.

And through it all she saw the brooding unhappy eyes of
Christina.

I believe, she thought, frightened as I am of what the future
may hold, I shall not be sorry to go.

There was one more day of ceremony and then she left
Strelitz. For ever, she thought, and she knew in her heart that
it would be so.

Farewell, brother, she thought, you who are so glad to see me go. Farewell Christina, my poor broken-hearted sister.

Her brother embraced her with a show of that new affection. Affection for a crown rather than a sister, she thought cynically.

"You are going to a new country, sister. You are going to be a queen, but never forget you are a German; never forget your homeland."

She knew what that meant. If ever she had an opportunity to bring good to Mecklenburg-Strelitz she must never neglect to do so.

"You are the most illustrious member of the family now," he told her with a smile.

And goodbye Christina. Forgive me for what I have done to you . . . for if I had not written that letter it would have been your marriage we should have been celebrating. Of course there would not have been those thousands of candles; there would not have been the ceremonies; but you would have gone to your bridegroom so willingly and with such joy, whereas I go to mine . . .

But she had promised herself that she would not think of what awaited her in that remote land.

Mademoiselle von Schwellenburg's importance was growing hourly. The Queen must have this . . . must do that. She seemed to proclaim constantly: I am serving the Queen. No one in the Queen's retinue is as important as her dresser Schwellenburg; and both poor Haggerdorn and Albert seemed to agree with her.

Everyone was talking anxiously of the weather—none more so than the Duke, who lived in terror that something would happen to delay his sister's departure for England.

The day was overcast and inclined to be stormy when the cavalcade, consisting of thirty coaches, set out, and as they rode through the countryside the people from the villages came out to see them pass and gape in wonder, for it was a new experience to see a wedding procession and far more welcome than the soldiers to whom they were accustomed.

Charlotte took her last look at the schloss, trying to forget what she was leaving behind and to choke back the lump in her throat. She must smile all the while and speak gaily when anyone addressed her. Those were her brother's orders. She must not offend the English by letting them think that her great good fortune in marrying their king did not make up for all the bereavements she had suffered.

She would feel better, she told herself, when she reached Stade, for there she would meet the English party who had crossed the seas for the purpose of escorting her to her new country; once she was on the boat she would really feel that she had left the past behind.

As the party rode into Stade the wind was blowing fiercely but the bells were ringing and the cannons were firing in her honour.

Charlotte looked up at the lowering sky and said to Schwellenburg, "We shall never embark in weather like this."

"It would be most unpleasant, Your Majesty, and unsafe."

"So we have a little longer in Germany."

Charlotte sighed, uncertain whether to be pleased or sorry. At one moment she longed to get on, to come face to face with her bridegroom; but the next she was hoping to be able to postpone the encounter.

They had come to rest at a small schloss where they would spend the night; and as Lord Harcourt came to help her from her carriage he told her that the party from England had arrived and were waiting to greet her.

As she stepped inside the schloss she saw them waiting for her and how magnificent they seemed in their brocades and velvets, as they came forward to kneel and pay homage to their queen! Their queen! She could scarcely believe that that odd and rather ridiculous ceremony made her so.

"And Your Majesty, your new ladies in waiting, the Marchioness of Lorne and the Duchess of Ancaster."

She stared at them. She had never seen such women before. They were like goddesses. It was their rich garments. No, it was not. That smooth skin which they both possessed; those magnificent eyes; the abundant hair coiled about shapely heads; the grace; the charm. She had always known that she was plain; now she believed that she was ugly.

"At Your Majesty's service."

She heard herself say credulously in French, because so far most of these English seemed to prefer it to German, "Are all English women as beautiful as you?"

The ladies laughed and said: "Your Majesty is gracious."

It did not answer the question and as others were presented to her she scarcely noticed them for she was thinking of what the King would do when he saw her. If he were accustomed to women who looked like these two—and she had to face the fact that she had never seen any so lovely and there were two of them—what would he think of his new bride?

She was frightened now.

"Your Majesty is tired." It was kind Lord Harcourt at her elbow.

She admitted that she was and he suggested that she announce her intention to retire to the apartments which had been prepared for her.

There she studied herself in the mirror. How ugly her mouth was . . . so wide and thin! She thought of the beautifully moulded lips of the English women—pink tinted; she kept hearing the laughter in their voices when she had asked if all their countrywomen were as beautiful. And they had not answered.

Schwellenburg came in and because Charlotte was caught looking in the mirror she said: "The English women are so beautiful. I fear the King will be disappointed when he sees me."

"He chose Your Majesty," was the answer.

"Without seeing me."

"Both those women seem very flighty to me."

"I suppose when one is as beautiful as they are one can be forgiven all else."

"Nonsense, begging your Majesty's pardon."

"Oh, Schwellenburg, I'm apprehensive."

"What, Your Majesty! And you a Queen!"

"Of very short duration. What if he should decide that I'm too ugly to marry and sends me back."

"He could hardly do that. Your Majesty forgets that he's married to you already by proxy."

Charlotte sighed. It was not the answer she wished; she wanted reassurance; she longed to be told that she was not so ugly as she feared. But Schwellenburg would not flatter; she answered with the logical truth. Charlotte was plain; it was likely that if the King were expecting a beauty he would be disappointed; but all the same the proxy ceremony *had* taken place and whatever he thought he would have to take her now.

"It's all so hurried," she complained. "Schwellenburg, does it not seem to you a trifle mysterious?"

But to Schwellenburg it did not seem in the least mysterious. The marriage had been made as many royal marriages were. If Charlotte could provide her husband with children in Schwellenburg's opinion no one could complain.

Lord Harcourt was asking for an audience.

She greeted him with pleasure, but he was looking grave.

"I have messages from His Majesty the King," he told her. "He commands that we proceed to Cuxhaven without delay and there embark for England."

"At once?" she asked.

"We shall have a night's stay here and leave in the morning. I was planning to wait until the weather changed."

"Perhaps it may by the morning."

"I shall hope that it does, Your Majesty, but whatever it is like my orders are that we should sail."

She nodded; she had no great fear of the sea.

A peal of bells was heard followed by the salute of guns.

"The people of Stade are determined to give Your Majesty a good welcome," said Harcourt.

She frowned a little. "Am I worthy of all these honours?" she asked.

Lord Harcourt bowed and murmured: "Your Majesty is the Queen of England."

At Cuxhaven, when the royal party arrived, the wind was howling and the rain was pelting down. Lord Harcourt was anxious; so, Charlotte noticed, were the beautiful women who now rode beside her and were threatening to put Schwellenburg's nose out of joint.

They were a little mischievous, Charlotte felt, despising Schwellenburg and Haggerdorn for two frumps; Charlotte would be the first to admit that they were dowdy and no beauties; but at least she felt more at home with them in spite of Schwellenburg's domineering ways.

There was no help for it, they must go aboard. The ship was rocking uncomfortably and everyone except Charlotte was unhappily aware of this. Charlotte had never been to sea; therefore she had no notion what seasickness was. She had come to a decision; if the King did not like her then he must needs make the best of her. She had not asked for this marriage—although her brother had been more than eager for it. She would do her duty and if the King was not prepared to do his, she would try to shrug her shoulders and not care. After all, these two Englishwomen might be beautiful, but they were not Princesses, so what she lacked in beauty she made up for in rank . . . even though in that she was not of such a high standard.

Lady Lorne came to stand beside her at the rail as she stood watching, that she might see the last of her native land.

"Your Majesty seems unaffected by the rocking of the ship."

"Should I be affected by it?"

"Most of us are."

"And you?"

"Not yet. But with Your Majesty's permission if it becomes more uncomfortable I shall retire to my cabin."

"Pray do so. But you did not answer my question about the women of England. Are they all as beautiful as you and the Duchess of Ancaster?"

"I trust Your Majesty will not consider me unduly conceited when I tell you that we are both known as two of the outstanding beauties of the Court."

Charlotte's relief was obvious.

"I had imagined a Court of goddesses," she said.

"Your Majesty is too gracious."

"I don't mean to be . . . only truthful. You are without doubt very handsome, both of you. Tell me about your life at Court."

The Marchioness replied that she had first come to Court as Elizabeth Gunning some ten years before from Ireland—she and her sister and her mother.

"We came to seek our fortunes."

"And you found them?"

The Marchioness was silent for a few moments. "I suppose some would say we had. A year after we arrived I was married to the Duke of Hamilton."

"And you were happy?"

She smiled sadly. "It was a runaway marriage of a sort, Your Majesty. We were married in a Mayfair chapel at half-past twelve at night; and as the Duke had not thought to provide a wedding ring we used a curtain ring."

"It sounds . . . romantic," said Charlotte wistfully. "He must have been very much in love with you."

"That was true, Your Majesty. Then I was presented to the King and that was a great occasion."

"That would be . . . my husband's grandfather."

"Yes, Madam. He was most kind to me . . . but he was not considered as kind generally as his present Majesty."

"So you find the King . . . kind?"

"The King would never, I believe, be unkind to any. He is very different from his grandfather, who was inclined to be irascible, constantly flying into rages. Forgive me, Your Majesty, my tongue runs away with me."

"I have asked you to be frank. And so the King is different from his grandfather, then?"

"Very different. The King is tall and handsome and there is a charm about him . . . a gentleness . . ."

Charlotte was beginning to feel better. It was pleasant to chat with a woman like this and so get an idea of what was waiting for her.

"I hear from Lord Harcourt that he is impatient for the wedding."

"It is true. He has fixed the date of the coronation and I have heard that he wants his queen to share it with him."

Charlotte nodded, beginning to feel almost happy. She was curious about this beautiful woman and wanted to know why she was the Marchioness of Lorne when she had married the Duke of Hamilton.

"The Duke died six years after our marriage."

"And you have married again?"

"Yes. Your Majesty, to the Marquis of Lorne."

"So you became a marchioness instead of a duchess."

"My husband, Your Majesty, is the heir of the Duke of Argyll.'

Charlotte smiled. "So it is only a temporary loss of rank. Have you any children?"

"Yes, by my first husband I have a daughter and two sons; I have a little boy by my second marriage."

"You are a very fortunate woman. Was your sister as lucky?"

"My sister died a year ago of consumption. They said it was due to the white lead she used for her complexion."

"Oh . . . how terrible."

"I myself was very ill less than a year ago and I thought I was dying of the same disease; but my husband took me abroad and I have completely recovered."

Charlotte nodded. "White lead!" she murmured.

"Yes, Your Majesty, it produces a perfect whiteness which I have heard is most appealing."

Charlotte laughed more merrily than she had since the wedding ceremony. "Perhaps it is as well not to have such beauty that has to be preserved by such lethal means."

The Marchioness smiled and whispered that if Her Majesty would grant her permission she would retire to her cabin, for she was beginning to feel a little queasy.

Charlotte stood at the rail after the Marchioness had gone. She liked the feel of the wind on her face. She did not feel in the least ill.

She believed that she had really begun to look forward to the new life.

The ship was battling against the elements and all Charlotte's attendants lay groaning in their cabins or on their bunks praying for the journey to be over . . . or death.

But Charlotte was not in the least affected. A harpsichord had been placed on board for her entertainment and she spent a great deal of time playing this, though her ladies did not hear her, since every one of them, even the redoubtable Schwellenburg, was prostrated.

Lord Harcourt told her that they were days from the coast of England and that he had just learned that the storms had driven them almost on to that of Norway.

"It is a pity for my ladies that we did not wait for more propitious weather," commented Charlotte.

"Your Majesty, the King's orders were that we embark without delay."

"Why, Lord Harcourt, is he so very eager for our arrival?"

Lord Harcourt, smiling, bowed. "That, I am sure, His Majesty will make clear to you on your arrival."

The suggestion was that the King was so eager for *her* arrival. But how could he be so eager for someone he had never seen? Why had it been decided that he must marry without delay?

There was some mystery, Charlotte was sure.

Well, perhaps she would soon discover.

"Your Majesty has no one in attendance," said Lord Harcourt.

"Poor ladies, they are prostrate, all of them. The sea does not take to them as kindly as it does to me."

"Your Majesty is fortunate . . . in more ways than one."

Am I? wondered Charlotte. What will life be like with my new husband in England.

"I shall play the harpsichord to them," she announced. "Perhaps it will comfort them. If I leave the door of my salon open they will be able to hear it as they lie on their bunks."

Charlotte played and found pleasure in playing; but the poor ladies were unaware of anything but their own misery.

The wind dropped suddenly and the storm was over; sun dappled the grey waters turning them to green and opalesque.

One by one the ladies rose from their bunks. The change in them was miraculous. Schwellenburg became her old domineering self, Haggerdorn her faithful second; and the two English ladies put on their poised elegance as though it were a gown and were soon as beautiful as ever.

As these two dressed themselves and the horror of the last days faded and as the Duchess of Ancaster said she felt like a human being again, they discussed together the advisability of warning the Queen of the King's attachment to Sarah Lennox.

The Duchess of Ancaster thought it unwise; the Marchioness of Lorne was not so sure.

"She is so plain . . . That mouth of hers makes her look like a crocodile."

"Poor creature. George is going to be so disappointed. I'll swear they've told him she's a beauty."

"Queens are always credited with more beauty than they actually possess. George should know that and discount half of what he has heard."

"George is so unworldly. It would never occur to him to doubt."

"And what of the little Lennox?"

"What of her?"

"You know the King bitterly regrets not marrying her."

"Oh, that is over and George is such a *good* young man. They say he won't give Sarah a thought once he is married to Charlotte."

"Do you believe that?" asked the Duchess scornfully.

"No," answered the Marchioness. "But I believe that it is better for Charlotte to discover this for herself. Though we could at least try to make her a little more attractive."

"A difficult task," retorted the Duchess.

"Still . . . a little improvement might be possible. I shall try."

"Grim Schwellenburg will be most displeased."

"Let her. She doesn't know the competition Charlotte will have to face in Sarah Lennox."

"Sarah's a pretty little thing, but she's not exactly a beauty."

"She has something more than beauty. Charm. And she's young."

"So is Charlotte."

"More's the pity. She would have a better chance of winning George from Sarah if she were a little older, a little more experienced. I think her appearance could be improved a little . . . though that mouth would spoil anything. But I think we ought to try."

Albert was dressing Charlotte's hair.

The two English women looked on rather sadly and the Duchess of Ancaster suggested that Her Majesty might like to try an English style.

Charlotte answered promptly, "No, I should not."

"A little toupee . . . beautifully curled . . . would make a great deal of difference to Your Majesty's appearance," added the Marchioness.

Charlotte studied the hair of the two ladies and remarked coolly that she believed the style in which Albert dressed her hair was as becoming as theirs.

The ladies were silent. Perhaps she was right in thinking no hairstyle could add beauty to such a plain face.

"If the King wishes me to wear a periwig I will do so," added Charlotte. "But until he asks it I shall remain as I am."

"The King likes to see ladies dressed in a feminine English style."

"As you are dressed?" asked Charlotte.

"That is so, Your Majesty."

Charlotte studied them, her head on one side. "I do not think it is the style of dress that is becoming. I understand you are two of the most beautiful women of the King's Court, but it is not your dress which makes you so. No, I shall dress as I have always dressed, and shall not try to ape you, my ladies."

The two women exchanged glances. They had done what they could. The King was going to find his bride vastly different from lovely Sarah Lennox.

"The King," Charlotte was saying, "may dress as he likes and I shall dress as I please."

"Your Majesty will doubtless make your decisions when you have seen Court fashions."

"Doubtless, but I have no intention of changing my ways unless the King expressly wishes it."

She was gaining confidence. It was wonderful what the sea trip had done for her. To have seen these elegant women in the throes of seasickness while she herself sat playing the harpsichord for their comfort had done a great deal for her. The girl who had dared to write to Frederick the Great was not going to be persuaded into wearing fashions which she was not at all sure would suit her. Moreover, if she were dressed as they were the comparison would be even more unkind; and if she could not be a beauty, at least she would stand out by the strangeness of her costume.

"Tell me what you know of the King," she said, to show them that the subject of dress was not to be mentioned again.

The King had changed since his accession, they told her. He had always been serious, but now he was more so. He was often closeted for hours in the company of Lord Bute and his mother who acted as his chief adviser—much to the disgust of Mr. Pitt and Mr. Fox.

What were his amusements?

He danced a little. He was not exactly a good dancer, but he was a very skilful one; he played cards a little, but not for high stakes. He was going to reform the Court, everyone said; because in the days of his grandfather this had been at times scandalous.

"His Majesty rises early and therefore likes to retire early."

"Oh," cried Charlotte, "I do not relish going to bed with the chickens. And I have no intention of doing so."

The ladies were further surprised. It seemed that Charlotte was growing more and more confident as they came closer to the shores of England.

Lord Anson who was in command of the expedition told Lord Harcourt that he had decided to put in at Harwich instead of going to Greenwich as had been planned. The storms had driven them so far off course that it would be more convenient to go to Harwich. Moreover, he feared they might run into a French man-o'-war if they travelled farther south and Lord Harcourt could guess what that would mean.

Lord Harcourt expressed his misgivings that there would be

no welcome awaiting the Queen at Harwich as there most certainly would be at Greenwich where she was expected.

"Better an unwelcomed bride than a prisoner of the French," was Anson's sage reply, and Lord Harcourt agreed with him.

Thus Charlotte first stepped ashore at Harwich. It was three o'clock in the afternoon on the 7th of September and a fortnight since they had sailed away from Cuxhaven.

Everyone—except Charlotte—was relieved to set foot on dry land and as soon as it was realized that the Queen was in Harwich the Mayor summoned his aldermen to give her a welcome.

This had to be brief, for Lord Harcourt explained to the Mayor that they must leave Harwich without delay as they were expected in London immediately. So two hours later they had reached Colchester where at the house of a certain Mr. Enew they stopped to drink tea, which Lord Harcourt reminded the Queen she would find refreshing. She did, and she was particularly delighted to receive a box of eringo root which was one of the products of the town. Tasting this she found it to be a delicious sweetmeat and Lord Harcourt explained to her that the sweets were made from the roots of the eringo which was a kind of sea holly, and it was the custom of the inhabitants of Colchester to give boxes of this sweetmeat to members of the royal family who honoured their town by visiting it.

They left Colchester for Witham, where they were to spend the night at the mansion of Lord Abercorn; but alas Lord Abercorn was away in London being unaware that he was to receive such an honoured guest. However, those members of his family who were at home proceeded to show their loyalty to the Crown by arranging as impressive an occasion as they could manage at such short notice; and members of the nobility from the surrounding country—having heard of Charlotte's arrival—came hurrying to be presented to her.

She was beginning to feel that the English were really pleased to see her. Perhaps this was why next morning as she was prepared to continue the journey and knew that that day she would come face to face with her husband, she allowed Elizabeth to persuade her to adopt an English mode of dress. In fact she was rather pleased with the effect, for the English fashion was more becoming than the German, and when she did not look at the dazzling beauty of her two English ladies-in-waiting she felt she looked tolerably well. Her fly cap had laced lappets which were very fine; and the stomacher with which she had been presented was decorated with diamonds, her gown was a white brocade with gold embroidery. It was quite magnificent and more elegant than anything she had ever possessed.

When they set out and she saw how many people had come to see her she was glad she had worn a dress more in keeping with what these people had been accustomed to think of as high royal fashion. She sat in her coach smiling at them as she passed along.

At Romford the King's servants met her; they surrounded her coach and prepared to bring her into the capital; and along the road the cavalcade was joined by more soldiers, all in dazzling uniforms, all come to escort her on her way.

And so she came to London.

She was bewildered and fascinated—so much so that temporarily she forgot the ordeal before her. As her coach rattled over the cobbles past the magnificent buildings—such as she had never before imagined existed—the magic of the great city enveloped her. She saw the people jostling for a look at her; from the windows of the houses they called to her; she could not understand what they said, but she knew it for a welcome and she bowed and smiled and her delight in what she saw was obvious, so London took her to its heart. She was plain—they saw; but they liked her no less for that. She was a young bride for their young King; her coming would mean a wedding—a day of holiday and revelry—then a coronation.

"Long live the Queen!" shouted the people of London.

She saw the gaily coloured signs hanging from the shops; apprentices with their masters and their masters' wives; ladies in their chairs, elegantly scented, powdered and patched. There were men in brocaded coats, their quizzing glasses held up to the procession, delicate lace ruffles falling from their wrists; and there were beggars, ragged and dirty, and women with children in their arms and dragging at their skirts; there were the street traders who yelled their wares, to mingle with the shouts of loyal greeting. The ballad sellers, the pie men, the milk girls with their panniers on their shoulders, the pin woman, the apple woman, the gingerbread-seller . . . they were all there to play their part and add to the noise and squalor, the colour and excitement of the London streets.

Charlotte stared in amazement as the coach rumbled on.

The Marchioness was amused by the effect the London scene was having on Charlotte. She looked at the watch which hung at her side and declared: "Your Majesty will scarcely have time to dress for your wedding, which is to take place tonight."

"Tonight! But surely I shall have a day or so to . . . er . . . grow accustomed to the King?"

"It has been arranged, Madam, that it shall take place tonight."

The significance of this suddenly struck Charlotte. She was almost at St. James's. There she would come face to face with the man they had chosen to be her husband; she was to be hurried through a ceremony and then left with him alone.

I cannot do it, she thought. It is too much to ask.

The Marchioness was looking at her oddly.

"Your Majesty is not well," she began, then cried out in alarm for Charlotte had fallen sideways, her face ashen.

"Quick," cried the Marchioness to the Duchess, "the Queen is about to faint. We shall be there in a minute. She can't be laid at her bridegroom's feet . . . in a faint!"

The Duchess took a bottle of lavender water from her pocket and opening it threw the contents into Charlotte's face. As the sweet scent filled the carriage, Charlotte opened her eyes.

"She is recovered," whispered the Marchioness. "Oh, thank God! Your Majesty, we have arrived."

The coach had stopped before a garden gate and a young man was coming towards it.

"The Duke of York," whispered the Marchioness to Charlotte.

Using all her will power Charlotte threw off the faintness which had almost overwhelmed her in the coach and looked about her; it seemed as though a crowd of people were pressing in on her. Oh, God, help me, she thought. I am going to faint again.

A tall young man had stepped towards her. She knew at once who he was, for the miniature with which she had been presented was a fair likeness—flattering, of course, but there were the prominent blue eyes, the heavy jaw, the mouth which was trying hard to smile but which in repose could be sullen.

This was her husband . . . the man whose children she was

to bear . . . whose bed she would share this very night if it were true that they were to be married without delay.

Her knees felt weak and unable to support her. She was about to sink on to them when he took both her hands and kissed them.

He could not meet her eyes and she noticed this and she guessed that he was disappointed in her. She knew he must be. Doubtless they had told him she was—if not beautiful—tolerably attractive. And she felt so ill, so faint.

But he spoke to her kindly and his voice was tender. At least he was determined to hide his disappointment and she was grateful for that.

"My mother is waiting to greet you," the King told her. "Allow me to conduct you to her."

He took her hand and the rest of the company fell in behind them as they went into the Palace.

Beside Augusta, Dowager Princess of Wales, stood a tall man, middle aged, but still outstandingly handsome.

Charlotte guessed this was Lord Bute whose name she had heard mentioned many times as a great power in the land on account of his influence with the King and his mother.

The King presented her to his mother first and Charlotte was aware of a pair of shrewd eyes studying her; she was not sure of the meaning behind their expression but she fancied it was one of approval.

"My sister, the Princess Augusta," he said, "who wishes to welcome you into England and the family."

The Princess Augusta, a year older than the King, looked anything but pleased, thought Charlotte; she made a formal speech in French to which Charlotte responded; and after that Caroline Matilda was presented—a girl not much more than ten years old, Charlotte realized; and she too made her speech of welcome.

Then it was the turn of Lord Bute—"my dear friend," the King called him—and Charlotte's hand was most courteously kissed and Lord Bute told her, with emotion in his voice, how delighted he was to have her with them.

The Dowager Princess had risen and said that there was little time to spare, for the wedding was to take place at nine o'clock.

"Your wedding garments are all ready in the wardrobe room," she was told. "But it may well be that some alterations will be necessary.'' The Princess Dowager looked as though they could hardly have expected George's Queen to be quite so thin and little.

"So we will lose no time,'' said the Dowager Princess, and Charlotte was walking with her into another apartment. The King had remained behind with Lord Bute and a panic seized Charlotte. She had felt safer with her husband than with these women—the cold woman who was her mother-in-law; the supercilious girl who was her sister-in-law and the young Caroline Matilda who, she felt, was secretly amused. Why? Because she was thin and small and ugly, and the child felt this to be some sort of joke?

"Oh!'' cried Caroline Matilda as they entered the apartment in which the clothes were laid out. "Did you ever see such magnificent garments!''

Charlotte said in French: "I do not speak English.''

"Then,'' replied Caroline Matilda, "you will have to learn quickly, will you not?''

The Duchess and the Marchioness appeared suddenly and the Princess Dowager commanded them to assist the Queen to dress in the garments without delay.

Then she signed to her daughters to retire with her.

As soon as they had left, the sewing women came in, pins hanging on strips of paper from their belts, their small eyes which seemed to have sunk deep into their heads through so much close work, beady and alert, as the magnificent gown was slipped over Charlotte's head.

"Your Majesty is trembling,'' said the Marchioness.

"It is well for you to smile,'' retorted Charlotte. "You have been married twice. I never have before. So I find it no joke.''

Indeed not, she thought as the little sewing women seized her and lifted the gown up on the shoulders and in at the seams. It is like a bad dream that goes on and on, she thought. A nightmare.

At last the dress had been made to fit her. It was truly magnificent, being of white and silver; and her purple velvet mantle was fastened at one shoulder by a cluster of beautifully matching pearls. The King's present to Charlotte was a diamond tiara, and this with her stomacher of diamonds—also a gift from the King—was valued at £60,000; and when she put these on they scintillated so brilliantly that she was sure their glitter would take people's eyes from her face. Never had she seen such diamonds and she wondered fleetingly what Ida Von Bülow would say if she could see her now.

She wished that she could know what the King's thoughts had been when he had first seen her.

In his own apartments being dressed for the wedding George was attempting to deceive himself. He had been startled by his bride's appearance for, romantically, when he had thought of her he had pictured her so different; he had made a composite picture of Sarah Lennox and Hannah Lightfoot and deceived himself into thinking Charlotte would bear some resemblance to those women whom he had loved so devotedly at one time of his life. And to see her—pale, thin, small, with that wide mouth, he had been temporarily shocked. His inherent kindness had forced him to smile, to treat her with special tenderness and the most important thing in those first moments of meeting had not been his disappointment but his great desire to hide it.

He had kissed her warmly, had spoken to her tenderly and trusted she had not been aware of his distaste.

He determined to be a good husband to her. He must never think of another woman. Fate had been good to him where Hannah was concerned. When he thought of the difficulties that could have arisen out of that youthful indiscretion—and yet at the time what a passionate necessity it had been—he could tell himself that he had been obliged to pay for that folly by giving up Sarah. In any case the affair with Sarah was at an end. Charlotte was now his wife and it was his duty as her husband to be faithful to her and as a King to set an example of morality to his people.

So he would stop comparing Charlotte with Sarah. He would never give Sarah another thought. Hannah and Sarah belonged to the past. Charlotte was now and the future.

Lord Bute came into the apartment in the unceremonious way he now and then adopted to stress the intimacy between them.

"Your Majesty is smiling," he said. "I trust you are pleased with your bride."

"I already have an affection for her," lied the King, at the same time trying to believe it.

"I think she will make a good wife and, I pray, a fruitful one."

The King bowed his head in agreement. His spirits were

raised a little. It would make up for a good deal if he had children; and Charlotte's children would live under his roof; he could be a true father to them.

He was sad again, thinking of Hannah's children and his . . . living their lives in a Surrey household, not knowing who their true father was.

What mystery! What intrigue! It was a good thing that he was suitably married now. Over the indiscretions of the past he would build a solid family life.

Lord Bute was smiling at him quizzically. He believed his dear friend read his thoughts accurately.

In the Chapel Royal the Archbishop of Canterbury was waiting to perform the ceremony. It was nine o'clock and in her glittering wedding garments Charlotte felt more composed, although the mantle of velvet and ermine was so heavy it was all the time threatening to fall off her thin shoulders.

Charlotte was joined by her bridesmaids; there were ten of them, all daughters of dukes or earls and charming looking creatures they were, she thought—some, she noticed with chagrin, comparing with her two ladies-in-waiting for beauty, particularly the girl at the head of them who was quite lovely in her bridesmaid's gown of white and silver and the diamond coronet on her head.

She whispered to the Duke of Cumberland—the King's uncle whose name she knew as the victor of Culloden and who was giving her away—that the bridesmaids were charming and who was the leader of them.

Cumberland bent his head and gave her a very tender look which was a little grotesque on his poor face, so distorted by the palsy, although he was not an old man. He said: "Your Majesty, she is Lady Sarah Lennox, sister of the Duke of Richmond and sister-in-law to Mr. Fox, one of the King's chief ministers."

"She is charming," murmured Charlotte.

And she was aware of a slight ripple of amusement which she did not understand.

Her brothers-in-law the Duke of York and Prince William were close at hand, and Dr. Secker the Archbishop was ready to begin the ceremony.

"Dearly beloved, we are gathered together here in the sight of God, and in the face of this congregation . . ."

Charlotte glanced sideways at her young bridegroom. He seemed resolute, almost grimly determined.

I can be happy with him, I believe, she was thinking. There was a kindliness in his face which was comforting and led her to believe he would be tender towards her. Nowhere had she heard an unkind word spoken of him. He was a young man determined to be a good king and a good husband and if she were equally determined to be a good wife and queen what could go wrong?

"Look, O Lord, mercifully upon them from heaven and bless them as Thou did send Thy blessing upon Abraham and Sarah . . ."

The King started suddenly. He was looking at the chief bridesmaid, staring at her with longing and almost pleadingly as though he were asking her forgiveness. Charlotte was conscious of the look. She saw the beautiful young girl turn her head away and stare stonily in another direction.

There was something of which she had yet to learn, thought Charlotte; but she could guess. What had happened did not need words to explain it.

Lady Sarah Lennox! Abraham and *Sarah*! They would have met on many occasions. As the sister and daughter of a duke—and one of the leading dukes—that girl would have had many opportunities of meeting the King. And she was beautiful. She was all that Charlotte was not. Charlotte kept reminding herself that she had one asset though which made her more desirable: she was a princess.

The ceremony was over and the procession from the chapel had begun.

Charlotte was aware of the heaviness of her cloak and the hands which held her train were those of Sarah Lennox. The name kept repeating itself in her head. So it was Sarah Lennox he had wanted—that girl who was even lovelier than the Marchioness and the Duchess who had come to Stade to meet her, because she was young and fresh—a girl, whereas they were women.

It seemed that those small hands tugged viciously at the cloak—but that was not so. It was too heavy for her to support. She could feel it being pulled halfway down her back and saw several amused glances. She learned afterwards that Horace Walpole, that inveterate gossip and recorder of events, had noted that "the spectators knew as much of the Queen's upper half as the King himself.'' And in fact she thought they would drag the clothes completely from her back before they reached the banqueting hall.

At last they arrived there to find that there had been a delay in preparing the banquet; and as it had been reported that Charlotte had played the harpsichord to her seasick ladies, it was now suggested that she should play for the company until dinner was served. Having played and sung all her life Charlotte had no shyness on this score and played and sang so enchantingly that everyone applauded enthusiastically and declared that music had charms to soothe empty stomachs as well as savage breasts.

In time supper was served. The King sitting beside his bride was very attentive to her, as though, it was observed, he would make up for that lapse in the chapel when he had been so overcome at the mention of the name Sarah and had been unable to prevent himself gazing at the chief bridesmaid. Charlotte, fresh from her triumph on the harpsichord, felt excited and the King's attention was flattering. The more she knew him the more she liked him, and that she told herself, was a very promising start.

Supper over, the King took her hand and told her that they must mingle with the guests who would wish to be presented to her; this they did and the King seemed in no hurry to break up the party. Nor was Charlotte for as soon as it was over they would retire to their bedchamber and there be entirely alone.

It was as though everyone was aware of this and understood the feelings of the young married pair.

At last the Duke of Cumberland approached the King and said: ''When is Your Majesty going to break up the Company? I am exhausted and must needs leave without your permission if you won't give it.''

George immediately gave the required permission.

It was almost three o'clock in the morning and hopeful eyes were turned towards the royal couple. Now was the time for the nuptial celebration—the putting to bed of the bride and groom, the witnessing of the young couple in bed together, the sly comments, the whispered suggestions.

George had been dreading this and buoying himself up with the reminder that he was the King and could do as he wished, he announced his intention of abolishing the old custom which he found in extremely bad taste.

There would be no ceremony whatsoever. The King himself would conduct his bride to their bedchamber.

There was disappointment, for this ceremony was always enjoyed by all except the principal actors; however, the King's show of resolution was admired and no one could gainsay his orders. So, taking Charlotte by the hand he led her away to the nuptial bedchamber.

The King was apologetic.

"We met only for the first time today," he said, "and you will be feeling that I am almost a stranger."

"Indeed not," she answered. "I have heard little mentioned that did not concern you since the day the news arrived that you had spoken for me."

"Then . . . I am glad."

"I trust I am not as a stranger to you."

"No . . . as you heard of me, so I heard of you."

They faced each other nervously.

The King said: "I daresay you will agree with me that finding ourselves in this position we must do our duty."

"It is what I shall always wish to do . . . my duty."

And so while the Court speculated on what was happening in the royal bedchamber, George and Charlotte were solemnly doing their duty.

The Comic Coronation

It was the day after the wedding. Charlotte sat at her mirror while her attendants prepared her for the levee. They were watching her curiously and she knew why. They would very much like to know what she thought of married life. Charlotte was by no means discontented with it. The King could scarcely be called a passionate lover but he was kind. That was what pleased her so much. She had been dreading their first encounter and it had passed without undue discomfort; and she was now initiated into married life and knew what was expected of her and that if she could bear children she would be a successful Queen.

On waking she had immediately thought of the chief bridesmaid, for she was sure that the King had been thinking of her too, and no doubt wishing her in Charlotte's place. But she knew enough of the ways of Court to be aware of the fact that many a Queen had arrived in her new land to find her husband's mistress in possession of his affections. She did not believe Sarah Lennox was George's mistress; and she felt extraordinarily optimistic since her new intimacy with the King; she believed that now he was a husband he would soon stop hankering after that girl.

Her women were whispering together. There was one whom she had not noticed before; flamboyant and beautiful, though no longer young.

The woman was saying: "And my Lord Hardwicke met His Majesty coming from the bedchamber and His Majesty seemed in good spirits. He said it was a very fine day; to which my lord replied with accompanying leer: 'Yes, Sire, and it was a very fine night.' At which His Majesty was not amused."

The titter of laughter which followed this gave Charlotte an indication of the sort of joke these women were making, although they spoke in English. She had however caught the words His Majesty for those were two with which she had already become familiar.

I must learn English quickly, she thought. They must not be allowed to chatter so in my presence and I not know what they say.

She asked the Marchioness who the lady was.

"It is Elizabeth Chudleigh, Madam, whom the Princess Dowager has appointed to serve you."

"Pray present her to me."

Elizabeth Chudleigh swept a deep curtsey. Her eyes seemed to be filled with mischief—but how could Charlotte complain of that.

Elizabeth Chudleigh was thinking: My God, what have they given the poor boy now! I'll warrant he's thinking of pretty Sarah or perhaps his beautiful Hannah. What a tale I could tell little Crocodile-Mouth if I wished. Elizabeth was sure of herself. She had played her part in the Hannah Lightfoot affair, for the King—Prince of Wales then of course—had confided in her and asked her help. Was it not Elizabeth who had found the rooms in the Haymarket where George had had those clandestine meetings with his Quakeress? What a part she had played in the elopement! And what great good it had brought her for that sly old matron, the Princess Dowager, would have dismissed her from Court long ere this had Elizabeth not been in a position to work a little courteous blackmail. And Lord Bute was afraid of her too!

Well, Elizabeth was now deep in her own affairs; wondering how she was going to get the Duke of Kingston to marry her. He was her doting lover and she the mistress without whom he could not live—but she had married Hervey and she would have to extricate herself from that entanglement somehow. In the meantime she was biding her time and waiting on the newly arrived Queen.

Poor child! thought Elizabeth. Should one warn her of the King's infatuation for the Lennox girl? Should one tell her that if she were clever she could beat her mother-in-law at her own game. No. Keep out, thought Elizabeth. The great project was how to become the Duchess of Kingston. Let the Queen look after herself.

"You have been serving the Princess Dowager, I presume," said Charlotte in French.

"Yes, Your Majesty. I think she chose me because the King himself has always honoured me by his interest in my welfare."

"I am pleased to hear it."

"You are gracious, Madam. I shall hope to serve you faithfully, for that is what His Majesty would wish."

She is clever and wise, thought Charlotte. She is a woman of great experience. Did they say *Miss* Chudleigh. Odd that she had not married and become a Countess or Duchess. She would have to find out more about this intriguing woman.

She was ready for the levee and left for the drawing room. There she found her bridesmaids assembled and was quickly aware of Sarah Lennox, looking fresh and lovely and as beautiful in her gown of velvet as she had in her white and silver bridesmaid's clothes with the circlet of diamonds on her head.

As her position warranted she took her place near the throne, by which Charlotte was standing, as one by one the peers and peeresses came to do homage to her.

She felt suddenly alone because she could not speak English and once again she was determined to learn as quickly as she could.

The Marchioness was announcing the names of the people as they approached the Queen; they then knelt and kissed her hand and swore allegiance.

"Lord Westmorland," said the Marchioness; and that nobleman came forward peering from side to side for he was, the Marchioness whispered to her, almost blind.

Charlotte smiled at him kindly but he did not see her, and, to the outward consternation and secret amusement of all, he knelt and took the hand of Sarah Lennox who was standing close to the Queen.

"No . . . no . . ." hissed the Marchioness, while Sarah sprang back as though she had been bitten.

The Queen held out her hand and Lord Westmorland kissed it. Charlotte did not see the old man; she was aware only of the hush which had fallen on the assembly.

Charlotte had her first clash with her mother-in-law a few days later.

She was preparing to take Communion and her ladies had

put out all her new jewels, since this was an occasion when they believed she would wear them.

The Princess Augusta, the elder of George's sisters, had come to her apartment to see her and so was present when Charlotte announced that she did not believe it was seemly to take Communion in a tiara and stomacher of diamonds.

"Why not?" Augusta asked in her peremptory way. Charlotte resented the Princess's attitude towards her, but as they were both speaking in French—a language foreign to them both—she could never be sure whether she had interpreted correctly.

"It does not seem to me to show proper respect."

Augusta laughed; she had a harsh unpleasant laugh. She was resentful that George who was younger than she was should have married before her; and she had always thought it unfair that she, the first born, should have been a girl. This attitude did not endear her to Charlotte, though she was secretly amused that George had got a little Crocodile (it was a term which was being applied to Charlotte on account of that ungainly mouth of hers which everyone admitted did call the obnoxious creatures to mind) when he had set his heart on flighty Sarah Lennox. Augusta had done all she could to foil *that* romance and she had often succeeded in discomforting Madame Sarah; all the same this did not endear her to Charlotte, who was not only younger than herself, but above her in position, being Queen of England. And come from some wretched little State which no one had heard of before the suggested marriage! thought Augusta.

"*We* feel it would show a lack of respect to appear without them."

"I do not believe the disciples wore jewels at the Last Supper."

Impudent little crocodile, thought Augusta. So she would argue!

"They had none. That's why."

"I do not think jewels in keeping with the occasion," said Charlotte with a touch of that authority which she had displayed to her attendants on her way to London. "And I shall continue in the way I have been brought up to believe is the right one."

Augusta flushed angrily and asked leave to depart. This was given with alacrity, and once out of the apartment Augusta made haste to her mother's apartment.

"Charlotte is a most *arrogant* creature," she declared. "She despises our customs and tells me she will keep to those in which she was brought up and which are so much better than ours."

The Princess Dowager was alert. They would have to keep their eyes on Charlotte. The whole reason for marrying her to George was that they—she and Lord Bute—might keep their control of him.

"What is this?" she demanded.

Her daughter told her version of what had happened, and the Princess Dowager decided that something should be done. She went to the Queen's apartment just as Charlotte, simply clad without her jewels, was about to leave for Communion.

"But you are not going to Communion like that!" cried the outraged Princess Dowager.

"I am," answered Charlotte. Oh, yes, thought her mother-in-law, she is arrogant.

"No, my dear. We would consider that a direct insult to God."

"I am sure He would not."

So she was flippant, blasphemous. A very firm hand was needed.

"My dear daughter, now you are here you will want to learn our customs. You will not want to *offend* people by behaving as you do in your brother's little dukedom."

Charlotte flushed. "I cannot see what difference . . ."

"You will learn, my dear."

The Queen replied: "I shall first of all learn the language."

The Princess Dowager stood like a redoubtable old general blocking her way. The Queen was not going to pass.

She saw Elizabeth Chudleigh and told her rapidly in English to bring Lord Bute to her without delay.

Elizabeth, smiling secretly, hurried off. Meanwhile Charlotte, flustered, uncertain, never having considered that she would have to face such a situation, was undecided how to act.

"Let us sit down," said the Princess. "Where is your tiara? Pray fetch it," she said to one of the maids. It was brought and she put it gently on Charlotte's head. "How becoming! Why it makes you pretty." The eyes which regarded Charlotte were as cold as a snake's. "I cannot think why you do not wish to wear the King's gift on every occasion."

"It is charming," said Charlotte. "I have never possessed such jewels; but I do not consider them suitable to be worn at Communion."

Lord Bute had arrived. He looked deeply concerned; he kissed the Queen's hand and that of the Princess Dowager. The latter's eyes softened at the sight of him; hard as she was where everyone else was concerned she was soft for this man. Even now that they had been lovers for years her affection was apparent whenever she looked at him; it was in the inflection of her voice when she spoke to him.

"Lord Bute, the Queen wishes you to set her right on this little matter of custom. Lord Bute, my dear, *thinks* as the King thinks. They have never had a disagreement. He will tell you what should be done and you may believe him. Her Majesty wishes to go to Communion without her jewels. I have told her that she should wear them . . . that it would be considered most unseemly if she did not. She would offend people here if they thought she was not paying due respect to God and religion. That is so, my lord, is it not."

"It is assuredly so," said Lord Bute.

"I do not find it so," persisted Charlotte stubbornly. She was almost in tears, and angry with herself that she should be so over such a silly matter.

"I have told Her Majesty that she will learn our ways," said the Princess. "She must not be despondent if she does not grasp them all at once."

"I am sure Her Majesty will know our customs as well as we do ourselves . . . in a very short time."

"In the meantime . . ."

"In the meantime," interrupted the Princess Dowager, "you wish us to advise you. Rest assured, my dear daughter, that we shall be most happy to do so and save you from the embarrassment which would otherwise result."

Charlotte continued to look stubborn. It did not improve her looks.

What a plain creature she is! thought Bute. I wonder George doesn't rebel. Serve her right if he makes Sarah Lennox his mistress. Not that that sly old Fox will allow that. A pox on these silly squabbles, but Augusta was right of course to take this stand. The girl must not have her head turned by hearing herself referred to constantly as the Queen of England.

"I will have a word with His Majesty," he told her benignly. "I am sure when you hear his ruling you will be convinced."

There was one thing Charlotte had been taught in her home and that was that she must obey her husband, and if the King said she must wear her jewels to Communion, then she must.

She was distressed—more because of the folly of the situation than anything else, and perhaps because in her heart she guessed that this was an indication. Her powerful mother-in-law and Lord Bute expected her to do as she was told. She looked at them defiantly. She would not go to Communion—bejewelled or otherwise—until she had heard what the King had to say.

Lord Bute found the King in his apartments. He went in unceremoniously. He wanted the King and everyone to realize the intimacy between them.

"A little difficulty between the Queen and your mother," he whispered. "I am certain that between us we shall quickly put it to rights."

"A difficulty!" echoed the King.

"Yes, my dear Majesty . . . a matter of jewels. The Queen feels she should not wear them and your mother feels she should."

"Should it not be a matter for the Queen to decide?"

"This is for Communion. Perhaps an occasion for ceremony."

"I . . . I should not have thought so."

Bute was cautious. Here was a situation which he and the Princess Dowager had feared. If the Queen was allowed to have her own way she would quickly be advising the King and one of the first results of this would be to turn him from his mother. A matter of wearing or not wearing jewels was immaterial to Bute; but what was of the utmost importance was that the little Queen should not give herself airs, and that she must be made to understand that the Princess Dowager—and her dear friend Lord Bute—were the two who had guided His Majesty before his marriage and they intended to go on doing so.

"Your mother is of the opinion that it shows disrespect to religion not to wear the jewels and I agree with her."

The King looked startled.

"And I have assured her that on consideration Your Majesty will share our view."

"But . . ."

"Oh, these ladies! The Queen is charming. Perhaps she is no beauty but she is charming . . . charming . . . and I am sure she has already fallen in love with Your Majesty. That I can well understand and should indeed be surprised if it were not so. But being in love she feels she can lead you. Oh, it is the way with women."

"I have no intention of being led."

"So I thought. Your Majesty has often remarked on the trouble which has come through kings being led by women and I can remember your saying on more than one occasion that you had no intention of allowing this to happen to you."

"That's so. I should never allow any woman to persuade me from what I thought was right."

"How fortunate this country is to have such a king. When I consider the last reigns . . . No matter. We have come safely through and I know you are going to command me to explain to her dear little Majesty that it is your wish that she wears the jewels. Not that . . . between ourselves . . . we see anything of great importance in this. But I know Your Majesty will agree with me that we must make it clear to the Queen that you are determined not to be ruled by her and that it is her duty to obey her husband." Before George could speak, Bute hurried on. "This is a blessing, because in this very small matter we can set Her Majesty's feet on the right path. We can make known to her—so discreetly—Your Majesty's policy, for which—knowing women—I am sure she will respect you . . . far more than if you were to give way and allow her to rule you."

It all seemed a great pother about a small matter, George thought; but it was true that he was determined not to be governed by women; and Lord Bute was right—as usual—when he pointed out that Charlotte should be made aware of this in the beginning.

Shortly afterwards the Princess Dowager had the satisfaction of seeing the Queen go to Communion in her diamonds.

It was some three weeks after the wedding—a glorious day and the 22nd of September, the day fixed for the coronation. All along the route from the Palace to the Abbey, scaffolding had been set up in the streets and high prices were demanded for seats in windows. London was eager to see the new King crowned; he was popular because he was young, had been born in England, looked and spoke like an Englishman and was the first English king they had had since James II; and because they had never cared for him and had sent him packing, they preferred to recall Good Charles's days when that romantic monarch had come back to England on his Restoration and made England merry. That was a hundred years ago—and here was another, George, their king, newly ascended the throne and newly married. Of course they must come out on a glorious September day to shout their loyalty.

And there was the Queen, too—a German, not speaking English, which made them grimace. They were tired of Germans who couldn't—or wouldn't—speak English. But she was young and if she behaved herself they would accept her, for the King had chosen her in spite of the fact that he had had his eyes on Lady Sarah Lennox whom they would have far preferred. A lovely English girl was better than an ugly German one any day. Still, it was a coronation and a reign always meant new hopes of better times.

Charlotte awoke with a raging toothache and neuralgia. She decided not to mention this to Mademoiselle von Schwellenburg who was, she had to admit, becoming quite intolerable, setting herself up as the head of the women, making her own rule that no one should approach the Queen except through her. Charlotte would have to warn Schwellenburg that the English ladies would not like this at all. She had heard Miss Chudleigh make some retort to Schwellenburg which the latter did not understand—nor did Charlotte—but she guessed it was a witty quip by the manner in which the others laughed.

Miss Chudleigh and the Marchioness of Lorne were outwardly very friendly, but Charlotte believed there was a certain animosity between them because the Duke of Hamilton, first husband of the Marchioness, had at one time been betrothed to Elizabeth Chudleigh. These two women were, Charlotte feared, somewhat light-minded.

But Charlotte was in too much pain to think of them now. She lay in her bed dreading the moment when she would have to rise and prepare for the ceremony.

It came all too soon. Schwellenburg was bustling about her, talking in rapid German; this was an important occasion; only she should be in close contact with the Queen.

Charlotte felt too weary to reprove her, but she guessed that before long she would have to do something about Schwellenburg. She stood quietly while she was dressed in the splendour of purple velvet and ermine; she hoped the coronet she would have to wear would not be too heavy; her poor head would not be able to support it, she was sure.

Her spirits rose a little as she drove through the streets to the Abbey with George beside her. Each day she felt more affection for him; she wanted to write and tell her family how content she was with her husband. He was so kind and had never hinted in any way that he was in love with another woman—or had been before her arrival. She would like to tell them of her contentment. Her brother would not care; and how could she tell Christina when it would only make her regret her ill fortune the more bitterly; and if she told Ida von Bülow it would be gossiped all over the Court in no time and come to Christina's ears that way. No, she must keep her contentment to herself.

George looked magnifcent in his coronation robes; his face was flushed and his eyes seemed more blue than usual; he radiated purpose and that was what the people sensed; it was one of the reasons why they cheered him so loudly. "God save the King," they cried; and Charlotte had learned enough to know what that meant. And some said: "God save the Queen." She bowed and smiled at them and trusted the splendour of her garments made up for the plainness of her face.

The solemn ceremony proceeded in the beginning without a hitch. There was Dr. Secker, the Archbishop of Canterbury, in his cope of white and gold, informing all those who had gathered to witness the ceremony that he presented to them "George, the undoubted King of the realm."

With him Charlotte walked to the altar where the large Bible lay open.

Charlotte had rehearsed this part of the ceremony and had learned off by heart the words she would have to say.

"Will you solemnly promise and swear to govern the people of this Kingdom and the Dominions thereto belonging according to the statutes in Parliament agreed on and the laws and customs of the same?"

The King replied, laying his hand on the Bible: "I solemnly promise so to do."

Then it was Charlotte's turn. She was relieved that she managed to speak the words required of her.

More questions followed and finally: "Will you, to the utmost of your power, maintain the laws of God, the true profession of the gospel and the Protestant Reformed Religion established by the law?''

Again Charlotte made her reply faultlessly; and retiring from the altar she seated herself while the King went to St. Edward's Chair for the anointing.

The coronet was heavy and her head ached uncomfortably; and she was glad when they went once more to the altar to take Communion. George said to Dr. Secker: ''Should I not take off my crown when offering homage to the King of all Kings?''

Dr. Secker replied that he was unaware of the correct mode of procedure, and turned to one of the Bishops to ask his opinion.

As the Bishop did not know either, the King said that he was sure it would be more becoming in him to remove his crown and he believed the Queen should take her coronet off.

This, whispered the Archbishop, would disarrange the Queen's hair and he was sure that it was not expected.

''Well,'' said George, ''for this time we will regard Her Majesty's coronet as part of her costume and not as her crown.''

He then took off his crown and explained in German to the Queen what had taken place. Charlotte was astonished, because it was only a short while before that she had been commanded to wear her jewels when taking Communion. She wondered whether the King remembered this; and if so why she had been forced to wear her jewels on that occasion and he to dispense with his on this.

Communion over, the King and Queen prepared to leave the Abbey and as they did so one of the biggest jewels fell from the King's crown. There was a shocked silence. A bad omen, it was whispered, if ever there was one!

After an undignified scrambling to recover the jewel it was soon found; but all eyes seemed to be on the gap where it should have been and this incident cast a certain gloom over the proceedings.

This was the first of a series of mishaps. When the company led by the King and Queen arrived at Westminster Hall where the banquet was to be held they found it in darkness. Lord Talbot, who was Lord Steward and, with the Earl Marshall, was in charge of the coronation, had thought it would be an excellent idea to have all the candles lighted simultaneously as soon as the King and the Queen were at the threshold, and had arranged it should take place by means of flax fuses.

There was a gasp of astonishment as the royal couple stumbled into the darkness; and then it seemed to Charlotte that the hall was on fire. The jabbing of her tooth was so painful that she had to smother an exclamation. The candles were suddenly alight but pieces of burning flax hung in the air for a few seconds before they floated down on the guests. So the desired admiration was replaced first by startled fear and then relief when it was discovered that no one was injured.

The candles made a brilliant show and the smell of spiced meats and delicacies filled the hall. No one could eat of course until the King and Queen were served, and Charlotte saw that on the dais on which their table had been set, although it was glittering with glass and cutlery, chairs were lacking.

Lord Talbot and Lord Effingham, who was acting as Deputy Earl Marshall, were rushing round in a panic demanding chairs for their Majesties; but in spite of all the great efforts to provide a banquet such as those present would never forget, it was difficult to find two chairs suitable for the King and the Queen.

Lord Effingham, wig awry, eventually hurried on to the dais, a chair in his arms, followed by Lord Talbot with another. These were set at the table and a sigh of relief went up throughout the hall for everyone was very hungry and the ceremonious serving of the King and Queen had to take place before they could eat.

"It would seem, my lord," said George mildly, "that the arrangements for our coronation can scarcely be called efficiently made."

Effingham muttered: "It is so I fear, Sire. It seems some matters have been neglected." He added more brightly: "But I have taken care that the next coronation will be regulated in the exactest manner possible."

George burst out laughing, and told Charlotte what the Earl had said. Effingham was overcome with confusion—and far more embarrassed than he had been over the lack of chairs. But the more George considered his remark the more it amused him. He called Lord Bute and insisted that Effingham repeat what he had said. This Effingham did, mumbling and growing more and more scarlet.

Meanwhile the Lord Mayor of London and the Aldermen

of the City had discovered that no places had been laid for them, and the Mayor was declaring in a loud voice that he considered this a disgrace. He was the Lord Mayor of London and did my Lord Effingham and my Lord Talbot know that London was the capital city and bowed to no one . . . not even kings. The biggest omission that could have been made was to fail to provide places for the Mayor and Aldermen.

Lord Effingham, escaping from the amused King, was obliged to face the furious Lord Mayor.

"My Lord Mayor," whispered Effingham, "I pray you leave quietly with your Aldermen. Some recompense shall be made . . ."

"There's only one recompense," retorted the Mayor. "And that is table places."

"My Lord Mayor . . ."

"The city of London is giving a banquet to the King which is costing £10,000. Have you the effrontery, my lord, to tell me then that there is no place for the Mayor and Aldermen at the King's coronation banquet? The city will not have it, sir."

Talbot came to the aid of the harassed Effingham and whispered that the Lord Mayor and Aldermen should have the table which had been reserved for the Knights of the Bath.

Effingham was relieved and the Lord Mayor and Aldermen were satisfied. But then there were the Knights of the Bath to be faced and a similar scene was enacted with them. At length Effingham fitted them into other tables which caused such crowding that there was a great murmur of complaint to which derisive comments were added when it was discovered that there was not enough food to go round and that the incompetent organizers had miscalculated once more.

The most farcical incident of all was yet to come. It was the custom of the Lord Steward—in this instance the unfortunate Lord Talbot—to ride a horse into the hall and up to the dais and there pay his respects to the King and Queen. Talbot had intended to ride to the dais, make his gracious speech and then back the horse out of the hall keeping his face and that of the horse towards their Majesties. He had practised this in the empty hall; but this was a day of mishaps, and Talbot had forgotten that the horse had gone through his paces perfectly when the hall was empty but now it was full of chattering laughing grumbling people; it was lighted by thousands of flickering candles and was not the same comfortable spot by any means.

The horse and rider appeared in the hall. The horse seemed to take one look at the royal couple and turn his back on them; in vain did Talbot attempt to ride him to the dais; the horse would only turn and present his hindquarters.

There was wild laughter throughout the hall, while the discomfited Talbot endeavoured to guide his horse up to the dais. It was with the greatest difficulty that he did finally bring the prancing animal to the edge of the dais; but by then everyone—including the King and Queen—were too convulsed by laughter to hear his loyal speech.

It was a farce of a coronation. Yet it was a coronation all the same. And from that day those about the King noticed a new resolution in his manner. The first to be aware of this was Lord Bute, and although he was certain of his hold on the King's affections and therefore was certain of his own powers, from that time he did begin to be a trifle uneasy.

Conflict with the Princess Dowager

Now began the happiest weeks of Charlotte's life. George found her amicable, eager to learn; and the fact that she could speak only German and French, which cut her off from society considerably, made her turn to him for guidance and protection. Apart from her appearance she was all that he asked of a wife; and as he was a man who could only be at peace if he believed he was doing what was right, he began to enjoy his marriage. There were whole days when he did not give Sarah a thought; and even when he caught a glimpse of a Quaker's habit in the streets he would assure himself that together he and Charlotte would be such an example to all married people throughout the land that youthful indiscretions would count as nothing.

He had suppressed his own wishes; he had married Charlotte for the good of the country; and it was his duty to make that for her good and his own.

He was physically contented; he was not a sensual man, although he had a fondness for women and could always be deeply affected by feminine charms. It gave him pleasure to contemplate these and to know that a less respectable man in his position would have nourished that emotion they aroused. Not so, George. He was going to be a faithful husband and introduce a new respectability into the Court and country.

So he devoted himself to Charlotte, who congratulated herself that the most fortunate aspect of her marriage was her husband's determination to cherish her.

He quickly discovered her love of music and told her that they must have musical evenings during which she could display her skill at the harpsichord and hear some of the musicians of the Court. She would love the Opera he was sure, and within a few days of the coronation he had taken her to hear one. It was a state occasion; the people were still affectionate towards their King and Queen and when they entered the royal box they received a loyal ovation.

Later, he told her, when she had learned English he would take her to the play. She would enjoy the play, he was sure; but he saw no reason why she should not see the Beggar's Opera which had just been revived.

He told her the story of the highwayman and London low life to which she listened avidly, not understanding it completely, for London low life was something quite different from anything she had ever imagined.

"In my grandfather's day it was considered treasonable," he told her.

She could not understand how the antics of criminals and gaol birds could affect the Crown.

"Oh, some of the characters were meant to be caricatures of the King's ministers. But that is all different now. The allusions have no point. And we are not afraid of a little ridicule."

He spoke almost complacently; the cheers of the people were still ringing in his ears and he believed everything was going to be so different under his reign.

He drove with her a little way out into the country. She was enchanted with her new land which was so beautiful at this time of year when the leaves were russet and gold and the grass still green.

"It would be pleasant," said George, "if we had a house where we could live apart from the Court . . . well, not entirely so, but a place where we could be free from continual ceremony. I think I will buy you a house."

"A house for me!" cried Charlotte, enchanted.

"Which," George reminded her, "you will invite me to share with you."

They talked of houses.

"I never liked Hampton Court," he told her in a rush of confidence. "My grandfather once struck me there . . . and I always remember it."

"Struck you. He must have been a disagreeable old man."

"He was. I don't think he meant me to take it so seriously. He had a very quick temper and I suppose he thought me particularly stupid. In any case he struck me, and I have never liked the place since."

"Then I shall not like it either," declared Charlotte.

"But I never liked it even before that incident," went on the King. "It's too flat. I asked Capability Brown to do something about the gardens and he refused me. He said there was nothing to do there and he declined out of respect for himself and his profession."

"Capability!" she said. "It is an odd name."

"His name is Lancelot. But he is called Capability because, when shown a garden, if he wishes to work on it he remarks; 'This has great capabilities.' He is a despot about gardens . . . but a genius; and it is said that there is no gardener in the world to compare with him. He can transform a place."

"And he refused to touch Hampton?"

"He refused to touch Hampton," repeated George with satisfaction. "I want you to come to see Wanstead House which is on the market."

How she enjoyed these excursions with the King. He brought to them a cosy intimacy. They might have been a nobleman and his wife with no state duties, choosing their first home together.

Wanstead House was enchanting. "One of the finest houses in the country," said George. "If you had stayed here on your way to St. James's, you would have thought the Palace a mean place in comparison."

"It is a little farther in the country than we hoped," suggested Charlotte. "It is beautiful, I admit. I have never seen a house which delighted me more; but if we lived here we should not be able to visit it often."

George nodded. Charlotte was proving herself to be a practical young woman.

"There would be a journey through the city," he said. "Oh, yes, you are right. It is too far from St. James's. We should never be able to retreat without a fuss. I suggest that we go back and take a look at Sir John Sheffield's house. He wants £21,000 for it."

Charlotte was delighted when she saw Buckingham House. She declared that for position it was exactly right, being so near St. James's.

They both decided it would suit them and went through the vast house talking excitedly in German about what alterations they would have made.

The King took the matter of Buckingham House up with

his ministers and it was finally decided that if the King would give up Somerset House which would be used for public benefit, the country would settle Buckingham House on the Queen.

This seemed a reasonable and very pleasant arrangement, and Charlotte and George gave themselves up to the happy occupation of planning a house.

Very shortly reconstruction was in progress and the house became known as the Queen's House. Happiness had its effect on Charlotte's appearance.

One of the Court wits remarked: "The bloom of her ugliness is wearing off."

Mademoiselle von Schwellenburg grew more important every day—in her own opinion. It was inconceivable, she reasoned, that these English women who surrounded her mistress should have more standing than she had. She was German; she had known her mistress when she was merely the insignificant sister of the Duke of Mecklenburg-Strelitz; therefore she was a specially privileged person.

Albert? He was merely the hairdresser—a lower servant. Haggerdorn—a woman without spirit, meant to serve such as Mademoiselle von Schwellenburg.

She had inaugurated a new method of dressing the Queen. As it was beneath her dignity to take active part in the operation, she would direct it.

She attempted to make this clear to the English women by signs and grimaces which they pretended not to understand. Then she approached Charlotte and asked her to explain to the ladies that as Her Majesty's personal attendant she was in authority over them.

In her happy frame of mind Charlotte wanted to please everyone and told the English, in French, that in future Mademoiselle von Schwellenburg would direct them.

Elizabeth Chudleigh listened with outward decorum, but immediately talked over the matter with the others.

"You can see very well what is going to happen," she declared. "Everything in this place will become German. It is always the same with these Germans. They want to impose their dullness on everyone else. I shall be looking like a *hausfrau* very soon and so will the rest of you, and there will be no entertainment but music . . . music . . . music. And worse still, no one will be able to approach the Queen except through Schwellenburg."

"The Queen seems to want to give the loathsome creature a special place in her household, so what can we do about it?" asked the Duchess of Ancaster.

"Plenty," retorted Miss Chudleigh; and proceeded to act. Under her devious and expert direction the knowledge soon reached the ears of the Princess Dowager that Mademoiselle von Schwellenburg had a great influence with the Queen, that she gave her orders in the Queen's apartment and that the English maids of honour were in revolt.

Miss Chudleigh was summoned to the Princess's apartment and gave her opinion that Mademoiselle von Schwellenburg was an ambitious woman and she was certain that in her odious German, in which she chattered volubly, she was making all sorts of plans to run the Court in accordance with her German ideas.

One could trust Miss Chudleigh to scent trouble even if one could trust her in no other way; and the Princess Dowager graciously thanked her, implying she would be grateful for more news, that it would be well for Miss Chudleigh to work faithfully for her since her position at Court was a somewhat precarious one owing to her rather dubious relationship with the Duke of Kingston. To which implication Miss Chudleigh responded with equal grace and innuendo. She was in possession of some secrets concerning the King and a certain Quaker lady; and she did—having helped to arrange that affair—know a little more about it than most; and she was sure that in the hands of the scribblers and lampoonists it would make a story that would not amuse but shock the people of England; but she was keeping quiet because just as the Princess Dowager wished to please her so did she wish to retain the esteem of the Princess Dowager.

The Princess Dowager inclined her head in acknowledgement of a delicate situation. Elizabeth Chudleigh's place was safe at Court however disreputably she behaved; though Elizabeth Chudleigh would do well to remember that there were some limits beyond which a Princess would not go even to avoid involving her son in a hideous scandal.

The situation was clearly understood between them; and as in moments of uncertainty, as the Princess Dowager had always done, she sent for Lord Bute.

He came quickly. She looked at him anxiously, wondering

if he were changing. Was he a little less devoted? Did he spend more time with the King than with her? Naturally he must keep his eyes on the King for all their sakes—but was he slightly less attentive to her than in the past? And had the change come about since George's elevation to the throne?

As he bent and kissed her she felt it was unworthy of her to entertain such thoughts for a moment. She was not a promiscuous woman; she did not seek a host of lovers; the liaison between herself and Lord Bute was as a marriage, lacking nothing but the benefit of clergy. She could trust him and he could trust her. Their goal was the same and they would march together towards it.

"Disturbing news, dearest, from the Chudleigh woman."

"Trust her to scent trouble."

"She has her uses . . . if one can trust her."

"Ah, if one can trust her! What's the trouble now?"

"Schwellenburg; she is giving herself airs, making trouble with the other women and in fact setting herself up as a little queen. You know what that can mean. Very soon she will be selling honours; she will be making Charlotte the centre of a coterie of power. You know the signs."

"I know them full well. With the shining example of Sarah Churchill not far behind us we have good reason to be suspicious of these ambitious women near a queen. But with this one the answer should be simple."

"What do you have in mind?"

"Send her packing."

The Princess Dowager laughed. "Trust you to find the solution. Why didn't I think of it?"

"Because you thought to please me by letting me suggest it."

She gave him a tender look. "We had better go to see George about it, and suggest it would be better if Schwellenburg left."

"We'll ask him to come here."

"My dear! Sometimes I think you forget he is the King."

He turned to her and there was a fierceness in his look which, while it alarmed her slightly, delighted her.

"He is still our George. Nothing can alter that. We will ask him to come here."

Yes, she thought as he ordered a page to go to the King and request his presence in his mother's apartment, her dear

Lord Bute had become more sure of himself since the King's accession.

"I do not think," said George, "that Charlotte will care to relinquish that woman. She came from Germany with her. It is natural that she should want to keep her."

"It is a situation all Princesses have to face," his mother pointed out. "We come with our attendants and after a while must do without them. Moreover, Schwellenburg is making trouble with the other women."

"It is better to have a peaceful atmosphere in the Queen's apartments," said Bute softly. "It is better for the Queen."

"Yes, I suppose so," sighed George. "But I don't care to ask Charlotte to give up this woman."

"Your Majesty need not distress yourself on that score," said Bute promptly. "What are your subjects for but to do that work which is distasteful to Your Majesty?"

He smiled at the Princess Dowager as though to say: See how easily our battles are won?

Mademoiselle von Schwellenburg was incensed.

"But, Madam, this is monstrous. This cannot be. They will send me away. Who will care for you? I . . . only I . . . know how to do that! I came with you from Germany . . ."

Charlotte said: "This is nonsense. Who says you are to go?"

"It is orders. They come from the King. I am to go, to leave the Palace within a few days. My transport is provided. Back to Mecklenburg, they say. Oh, no, no, it is impossible."

Charlotte was aghast. Not so much at the prospect of losing Schwellenburg, whose overbearing ways were often hard to bear, but that her dismissal should have been decided on without reference to herself.

She went to the King and asked him what this meant; and what was her position here in England if she could not decide who should be her own servants.

George looked embarrassed. "It is the custom," he explained, "for foreign servants to go back to their homes after a certain period. They come, you see, to help you settle in. Well, now, I should say you had settled in, wouldn't you?"

"I do not understand this. I do not wish Schwellenburg to go . . . unless I myself dismiss her. Tell me this, pray. Was it your mother who asked you to order this?"

George admitted that this was so.

"Then will you ask her to come here so that I can hear the reasons from her lips."

"You make too much of this, Charlotte. You shall have other women to replace her . . . women who understand our ways."

"All the same I wish to speak to the Princess Dowager in your presence."

George looked uneasy. He hoped Charlotte was not going to turn into a virago, just as he had been congratulating himself that he had acquired a pleasant, docile wife.

But he wanted to please her; and secretly he could see her point. After all, as Queen she should be allowed to choose her servants surely.

The Princess Dowager came with Lord Bute at the King's summons, and when they saw Charlotte's distress they knew the reason for it.

"Her Majesty is concerned," the King explained, "that you should have asked for the dismissal of Mademoiselle von Schwellenburg."

"I know exactly how you feel, my dear," said the Princess Dowager fixing her cold eyes on the Queen. "Did I not suffer in exactly the same way when I first came to this country? Of course I quickly began to realize that those who had lived here longer than I knew best . . ."

"I cannot see what harm Mademoiselle von Schwellenburg is doing here."

The Princess looked pained. The Queen had no manners; she had actually interrupted her. No doubt the little upstart was suffering from conceit. Where had she come from? Some little Dukedom that no one had ever heard of! When it had been known that the English ambassadors were going there, that wit Horace Walpole had said, "Let us hope they will be able to find it!" But of course these were the sort of people who gave themselves airs. The Princess Augusta did not look too searchingly into her own origins, but at least *she* had been absolutely docile all through *her* married life. And if an ambitious woman should not have a few political ambitions when she was free to do so, when could she ever display her talents? If this little Madam was the Queen she herself was the King's mother; and but for the death of her husband she herself would have been queen. No, little Charlotte must be promptly put in her place—which was, queen or not, considerably lower than that of the King's mother.

"Then my dear, you must try to understand. That woman is overbearing. She is causing trouble among your attendants. It is a common enough situation—and she must go."

The young woman who had dared write a letter to Frederick the Great came to life at such an ultimatum. She herself was not so very fond of Schwellenburg that she would be heartbroken to lose her. Who could be as fond as that of Schwellenburg? But she would have to find someone to take her place. Haggerdorn was too meek; and there must be someone with whom she could speak her native tongue. No, she was not going to be robbed of Schwellenburg as easily as that—if only to show her mother-in-law that she would not be treated in such an undignified manner.

"I do not wish her to go. She is useful to me. Until I learn to speak English I must have someone who speaks German with me. You cannot imagine how difficult it would be."

"*I* cannot imagine!" cried the Princess Dowager. "My dear Charlotte, this happened to me, but I had the good sense to accept it as the natural course of events."

This conversation had taken place in German which George understood better than Lord Bute; but it was obvious to the latter that the tempers of both ladies were rapidly rising.

Then Charlotte went to the King and lifting her eyes appealingly to him said: "I ask this favour. Allow me to keep Mademoiselle von Schwellenburg."

George was in a dilemma. He did not wish to displease his mother; yet he did not see how he could refuse such a simple request from his bride. In fact he was on her side. He could not see why the tiresome Schwellenburg should not receive a warning that she must change her attitude—and then all would be well.

It was the solution. He smiled delightedly and his smile included Lord Bute who, he was sure, with masculine perspicacity, would be on his side. This was a quarrel between two women; and he felt as a husband he must support his wife, although it would be going against his mother.

He wavered for a moment and the Princess Dowager was about to speak when he said: "Mademoiselle von Schwellenburg shall stay and I know that the Queen will warn her."

"But . . ." began the Princess.

"I will warn her," said Charlotte quickly.

"Yes . . . yes . . ." went on the King. "You must tell her that if she does not behave er . . . becomingly . . . she will have to go."

"This will not do," began the Princess Dowager, but Lord Bute was flashing a warning at her.

The King spoke with dignity. "But Your Highness must understand that I have said it shall be so." He looked at the clock. "And now I think our attendants are waiting to assist at our dressing."

It was dismissal. Even the Princess Dowager had to accept it.

Lord Bute, in recognition of the King's order, gave his arm to the Princess Dowager and there was nothing they could do but retire.

"Can you believe it!" cried the Princess when they were alone in her apartments. "What can have happened to George?"

"My dearest, you are always telling him that he must be a king. At last he has taken the admonition to heart and become one."

"You mean he is going to begin setting himself up against us?"

"I saw that in his face today, which tells me that he wishes it known—to us—that in future if there is a difference of opinion between us, he will make the decision."

"That gives me great cause for alarm."

"It is a change, of course; and one of which we must be wary. We must, however, make sure that in future we all agree."

"But if he is going to imagine that he is the King and his word is law . . ."

"The last king believed all that, yet I have heard it said that it was really Queen Caroline who ruled."

"It was true."

"Yet George II thought he did. Why should George III be denied such a pleasant delusion?"

"You are so clever."

"We must be, my dearest, and we must not have any repetition of that Schwellenburg scene."

"But I have determined that the woman shall go."

"Your Highness must forget that determination. The woman is of no importance."

"But she is going to guide Charlotte . . ."

"My dear, we must see that Charlotte is not important either."

"The Queen!"

"Yes, the Queen. She has been brought over here to fill the royal nurseries. If she does that she will be well occupied. The King does not care for women's interference. He has said so often enough to me. We will foster that and in the meantime keep our eyes on Charlotte."

The Princess nodded. "You go on influencing the King, my love; and leave Charlotte to me."

The Princess Dowager had presented the Queen with several new women.

"Because, my dear Charlotte, you set such store on having Germans about you, I am sending you Miss Pascal. She came from Germany and has served me well. I give her to you."

Charlotte, flushed with victory over the retention of Schwellenburg, accepted gracefully. Then there was Miss Laverock and Miss Vernon.

"All excellent women," declared the Princess Dowager. And she believed that they and Miss Chudleigh would do very good service in the Queen's household—for the Princess Dowager, of course; for the chief duty of these women—while they went about the tasks allotted to them no doubt by the dominating Schwellenburg—was to spy for the Princess and report to her all that Queen Charlotte did and said.

Lord Bute—as always—was right. There should be no more disagreements with the King. And if the Princess and Lord Bute knew exactly what was happening in the Queen's private apartments they would be able to shape their policy so much more easily; and at the same time make sure that the upstart little Queen should be nothing but the mother of the new royal family.

The Great Commoner

The Dowager Princess Augusta had been right when the thought had occurred to her that Lord Bute was more interested in the King than in herself. She had always regarded him as a husband; and it seemed natural that he should be absorbed—almost completely absorbed—in the welfare of her son, for she was sure that the family spirit had so engulfed Lord Bute that he thought of George as his son. Everything he did for George was for George's good—and as he had pointed out to her, what was for George's good was for theirs; for their one aim was to see George reigning over his kingdom, happy and secure.

He had talked to her at length about the Monarchy, and they were in complete agreement.

As Lord Bute saw it, a king should be the supreme ruler. This had been the case in the past. Charles II had had great power. And what a statesman he had proved himself to be—conducting secret policies with the French behind his government's back and, Lord Bute was quick to point out, to the great advantage not only of himself but his country. But then Charles was a Stuart—as Lord Bute himself was, and although he could not claim direct connection, the name being the same, the link must be there.

Lord Bute would like to see George absolute Monarch.

"But there is the Constitution," the Princess had pointed out.

"Made for William the Dutchman. Naturally, the people wanted it then. The man was a foreigner; and they had just turned out James II, who lacked the intelligence of his brother. And after that there was Anne, who was a woman, and then they looked to the House of Hanover. Neither of the two

89

previous Georges cared about England, and the English sensed that. But now it is changed. Our George is an Englishman—born and bred in England. It is time this country returned to true kingship.''

"And the Government?''

"Ah, my love has put her finger on the trouble. While we have Mr. Pitt at the head of affairs this country will be ruled by its government and not by its king.''

"And what do you propose, my love?''

"To rid ourselves of Mr. Pitt.''

"The people's idol?''

"The people quickly forget their idols.''

"And you think Mr. Pitt will agree to retire?''

"Mr. Pitt, my dearest, must be brought to such a pass that he can do nothing else but retire.''

"It will need very careful handling.''

Lord Bute smiled at her. "Shall we call on His Majesty.''

The Princess nodded, and rising slipped her arm through that of her lover.

Both the Princess and Lord Bute were aware of the King's new determination when they found him at his desk studying state papers.

He greeted them warmly, embracing them both.

"Your Majesty will forgive this intrusion on your time,'' murmured Lord Bute.

"My dear friend, I am always happy to see you.''

"And your mother, I trust?'' asked the Princess.

"My dearest mother, you know it.''

"The Princess and I have been talking of the war,'' said Bute.

George frowned. He hated wars. Killing! he thought. Men who are strong one moment and killed—or even worse maimed—the next. A terrible price to pay for power. Yet, Mr. Pitt had assured him that it was necessary for the welfare of the people.

"We were saying,'' added his mother, "What a blessing it would be if there could be an end to all this bloodshed.''

"I am in absolute agreement with you.''

"I fear,'' said Bute sadly, "that Mr. Pitt has other ideas.''

"Mr. Pitt is of course a great statesman,'' said the King. "I hear that he is known throughout the country—and abroad—as the greatest Englishman.''

"Yes. The Great Commoner," laughed Bute. "I admit that at one time he did good work for the country, as Your Majesty and I have often agreed. Success goes to a man's head. It was the same with the Duke of Marlborough. Resounding victories throughout Europe. Blenheim, Oudenarde, Malplaquet. Wonderful! Wonderful! And all adding greatly to the glory of England—and the Duke. And Pitt? Victories in North America and India . . . an Empire no less. But the trouble with these heroes is that they do not know when to stop."

"You mean," said George, "that first they fight for the glory of England and then for their own."

"Your Majesty has a pretty turn of wit. Yes, that is what I mean."

"And you think that the war is no longer necessary?"

"I think Mr. Pitt should be ordered to bring his war to an end."

The Princess gasped. Was dear Lord Bute a little too blunt? Dare one attack the Great Commoner in such terms? What if it were passed on to the man himself? Would he turn and attempt to flick Lord Bute from his path as he might a fly? Oh, but Lord Bute was no lightweight to be flicked aside. Might it not be Pitt himself who would come off worst from such an encounter?

Still, it was against their policy to emerge too far out into the open.

George was astonished at such comment on the great Mr. Pitt, for he himself, the King no less, was overwhelmed in the presence of the Great Commoner who, although he always showed the utmost respect for the Crown—in fact he was apt to grovel before royalty—always conveyed the impression that he was the first minister and real leader of the country's policy, in other words the ruler, not King George.

"I think," went on Bute, "that Your Majesty should study the possibilities of an early peace. The French are eager for it, and I am sure Your Majesty will agree with me that it could be brought about without any loss of face."

"I should like to see an end to the war," the King agreed. "The thought of all the bloodshed appals me."

"I knew that Your Majesty, Her Highness and I would be of one mind," murmured Bute.

Then, with the Princess, he sat with the King at his table and they studied the state papers together.

The Princess noted that although the King listened to Bute, he no longer deferred to him in quite the old way; and when they left she said: "There *is* a change in George. It is becoming more and more apparent."

"It is inevitable," replied Bute complacently. "Each day he becomes more and more aware that he is King."

"He is not so ready to agree."

"We must be more sure of our arguments. He is still very inexperienced."

"And Pitt . . . ? Do you think we were perhaps a little too frank?"

Bute's smile grew even more complacent. "When George came to the throne Pitt was supreme. He had proved his policies. He was the people's idol and the late King believed that he could do no wrong. He was the most successful politician in Europe. Such success breeds envy, and there are many powerful men in the Government whose greatest desire is to see Pitt expelled from it."

"And you have talked with these men?"

"I have . . . sounded them, shall we say. Bedford, Hardwicke, Grenville and . . . Fox. They are all on the side of peace. In fact they are ready to range themselves against Pitt."

"Fox!"

"Yes, my love. Fox himself."

The Princess was satisfied. Of course her dear lord knew what he was doing.

With these men on his side he would have a good chance of ousting Pitt and with their help achieve that for which he had cautiously and assiduously worked even before George had come to the throne.

Lord Bute—with Fox as his lieutenant—would rule England.

As William Pitt's carriage took him through the London streets he was recognized and acclaimed. The Great Commoner was the people's idol. He had brought an Empire to England and prosperity overseas meant prosperity at home. There was a war, yes; and wars meant taxation and loss of lives; but there was work to be had and even a soldier at war was better than a soldier starving in the streets.

Pitt acknowledged the cheers with somewhat disdainful dignity. Although he was almost obsequious to the King, he could be almost contemptuous of the people in the streets;

they did not seem to resent this. He was the great Pitt and the more he showed his contempt for them the more they seemed to respect him. His hawklike eyes stared straight ahead and he sat very straight, so that he never failed to appear the tall and imposing figure he was. He was immaculate in full dress coat and tie wig as usual; and looked as scrupulously well dressed on any occasion as he did on this visit to the King.

He guessed the reason for the King's summons was connected with the French desire for peace negotiations; and he had made up his mind that he was not going to give way to the inexperienced young man who happened to be the King. He would have to explain to him patiently why, in his opinion, peace was undesirable at this stage; and being Pitt he had no doubt that he could do so effectively. He had enemies, of course the chief of whom was Lord Bute, who had, at one time, declared his support of Pitt's policies. But Bute was an ambitious man and his peculiar relations with the Princess Dowager—but perhaps one should not say peculiar at all, for they were, alas for the morality of the country, all too common—had doubtless given him the notion that he could lead the King whither he, Bute, desired him to go.

Bute must be taught a lesson in this respect.

The King received his minister with the respect which he had always accorded to him. Pitt bowed low; they exchanged a few courteous pleasantries and then the King broached the subject, to discuss which he had sent for his minister.

"I have been considering the French offer of a negotiated peace," said the King. "It would seem that the country is growing tired of war and some of my ministers are of the opinion that now is the time to let counsels take the place of arms."

"Your Majesty has considered that the nation has never known trade as it does now?"

"I know," said the King firmly, "that many of my ministers feel the burden of taxation on certain members of the community to be too great."

"Your Majesty will doubtless explain to them that all progress must be paid for."

"We have had great benefits and I am the first to admit this. We have done well and now perhaps is the time to call a halt."

"Your Majesty, can we be sure that the French are sincere?"

"We can attempt to find out."

"It is my belief that if we are to have peace with France, Sire, it is not for us to negotiate terms but to dictate them, and they should be in our favour."

"They would yield all North America and a large share of their Indian interests; and all they ask is possession of Minorca. This could be called terms decidedly in our favour."

Pitt was momentarily silent. The war was his war. He had conceived it; he had carried it through; and he saw it as the answer to England's problems. When he had taken charge, England had been a little island off the coast of Europe with a population of only seven million and there were twenty-seven million Frenchmen just across the Channel. British stock was low; it was linked with that of Hanover through its kings; Pitt had believed that if some drastic action were not promptly taken the country would sink to such insignificance that it could scarcely have been called a country. It might even have been a dependency of France. Then he had outlined his plans to the late King; he had been given power, and what had happened? He had turned the sphere of influence from Europe, where he knew no great gains could ever be firmly consolidated and had cast his eyes on wider horizons. He had dreamed of an Empire and had created one. In a few short years England had risen from an inconsiderable little kingdom to the greatest power in the world. The people in the streets knew this. They were singing *Rule Britannia* and *Hearts of Oak*; they walked with pride and dignity; and commerce was thriving in the City of London. The people of London had no doubt who had brought this about. It was Pitt who had wiped out nepotism, who had shown the King that armies could not be led by princes, simply because they were his sons. Pitt had carved out an Empire and the country was reaping the benefits of prosperity.

No one was more aware of this than Pitt.

He said slowly: "I had been considering the necessity of declaring war on Spain."

The King looked startled.

"I have just learned that France and Spain are preparing to make a secret treaty."

"For what reason?" demanded the King.

"Your Majesty will remember the strong family connection between the two houses. Two Bourbon kings—a kind of family compact. And the reason? because Spain wishes to attack Portugal, who has always been an ally of ours. I see Your Majesty feels as I do. A hasty peace could be a disaster to England . . . particularly when we are in such a masterly position. I could never persuade my government to make peace in such a way that I know some of Your Majesty's ministers are clamouring for.''

Pitt's manner suggested that the matter was closed; and the King was still too inexperienced, too in awe of this man to contradict him.

When Pitt called a cabinet meeting and put forward his proposals for war on Spain, he was met by a chorus of disapproval. Far from declaring war on Spain the cabinet wanted peace with France.

Pitt pointed out the disadvantages of negotiating peace. England was rapidly rising; she was the greatest power; there was no need to consider peace at this juncture. It was the French who earnestly needed it. To agree to sit down and arrange peace terms was to give up a game which they were winning. He would only agree to a peace which brought about the utter humiliation of France; and this they could do by remaining in the field a little longer. But to agree to work out a peace and give concessions on both sides—which such an arrangement would inevitably involve—was throwing away a hard-won advantage.

Lord Bute spoke against him; and everyone knew that Bute had the King behind him.

"I suggest that we immediately withdraw our ambassador from Madrid,'' insisted Pitt.

Fox rose to express an adverse opinion and for some minutes these two formidable adversaries faced each other; and to his shocked amazement Pitt discovered that Fox had many supporters. Led by Fox, George Grenville (one of Pitt's own brothers-in-law), Lord Hardwicke, the Duke of Bedford and Bute, his critics stood against him. To his dismay he found that only his two other brothers-in-law, Richard, Lord Temple and James Grenville stood with him; the cabinet had defeated the great Pitt. That had seemed inconceivable and in this he was aware of the hand of Bute.

Pitt could see no alternative but resignation.

In the streets it was whispered with awe: "Pitt has resigned."
The people of the capital were incensed. Pitt was their hero.
They remembered the days when trade had been poor, when
there had been no work for thousands. Pitt had made London
one of the great ports of the world. And Pitt had been
turned out!

It was not to be endured.

Who had turned him out? they wanted to know. It was the
Scotsman. They did not want Scotsmen in England. Let them
go back where they belonged, which was beyond the Border.
They wanted Englishmen who knew what was best for
England; they wanted Mr. Pitt, the Great Commoner. They
were proud of Mr. Pitt. He was no duke nor earl; he did not
seek honours for himself; he sought trade and prosperity for
England. And the Scotsman and his mistress had turned out
Pitt.

They were sure it was the Scotsman who was responsible
for this. There had been jokes about the Scotsman and the
Princess Dowager for years. These intensified; they grew a
little more lewd, a little more cruel.

Lord Bute, riding through the streets, was recognized and
md was thrown at his carriage.

"Go back where you belong. And take the lady with you.
We can do without you both."

Bute was shocked.

"We don't want Scotch coal burned in the King's chamber. We don't want Newcastle coal either. We want Pitt
coal."

It was a phrase which had come into being a few months
ago and appealed to the people. They wanted Pitt coal and
were going to have it.

Bute went to the King at the earliest opportunity and said
that they must find some means of bringing Pitt back into the
Government. The people wanted it. They were getting restive
and he felt it would be unwise to go so strongly against their
wishes.

"Whatever a new ministry did would be abused by the
people," he told the King. "They are determined to have Pitt
back and I think we should recall him."

The King was in complete agreement, for he too deplored
the resignation of Pitt.

"It was not what we intended," said Bute, "but the man is arrogant; he could not allow anything but his own desires. Therefore he thinks to discountenance us by resigning."

"Which," pointed out George, "he has done."

"There is only one thing left to us," added Bute. "If Your Majesty summoned Pitt we might come to a compromise. He could state his terms for rejoining the cabinet and I have no doubt that he is as eager to come back as we are to have him."

Pitt smiled complacently when the summons came. He knew full well that they couldn't do without him. As his carriage rode through the streets the people cheered him; they had quickly discovered that he was on his way to see the King and guessed the reason why.

"They can't do without Pitt," was the comment.

So it was with the utmost confidence that Pitt entered the King's presence. George was a young man, in great need of guidance; but one of his attractive qualities the minister decided, was his eagerness to do his duty. If he could be weaned from Bute's influence there would be little trouble from him.

Bute! He had been thinking of him. How was he going to break the influence of years? Bute had been George's constant companion since the King was a child. Even in the days when Frederick, Prince of Wales, was alive, Bute had been almost a member of the household, behaving like a favoured uncle and later a father figure. Something would have to be done about Bute.

He had made up his mind. Only if he could arrange for Bute to serve under him, could he put his reins on that ambitious man.

He gave the King that deep respect which he never failed to show in the presence of royalty and offered his terms. He would form a new cabinet; in it Lord Bute should have a place, on condition that he agreed to give unqualified support to Pitt.

When George discussed this with Lord Bute they realized what Pitt meant. The arrangement would completely break Bute's power. He would have to be Pitt's lieutenant; in fact it would sweep away everything Bute had been working for over many years.

It was an impossible condition, Bute told the King, and Pitt must be asked to propose some other alternative.

Pitt's reply was for a cabinet made up of his friends. He would be Secretary of State, with Lord Temple First Lord of the Treasury; and no one who did not support his policies should have a place in his cabinet.

Bute, with the Princess Dowager, came to the King's apartments to discuss these developments. Bute derisively laughed. "He'll be asking for the Crown next. Who ever heard of such a proposition! No one to have any power unless he agrees to submit to Mr. Pitt! The man's gout seems to have gone to his head and swollen it out of all proportion—though God knows it was big enough before."

"You'll never be king, George," pointed out his mother, "while Pitt rules England."

George was in complete agreement with his mother and Bute. Nor was he inclined to hide his anger from Pitt.

"You want to reduce me to these terms," he wrote, "by disavowing my own act. No, Mr. Pitt, before I submit to these conditions I will first put the crown on your head and submit my neck to the axe."

"But," George wanted to know when this reply had been despatched, "where do we go from here? Could you form a ministry?"

Lord Bute was sure that he could; but he was remembering with some apprehension that mud had been thrown at his coach and that there were shouts of adulation every time Pitt appeared in the streets of London.

"The people will be against us because Pitt is not with us," he complained. "They see that fellow as a sort of God."

He did not say what their opinion of him was, but he knew well enough. He was aware that George shuddered to hear the comments which were made in the streets about his mother and her lover, and Bute knew George well enough to fear that such constant reminders might affect his attitude towards them both since George was at heart a prude, and his great scheme was to bring morality back to England. They must be very careful.

"Our best plan," suggested Bute, "would be to offer Pitt some recompense . . . the greater the better. It would have to be something so tempting that he could not refuse it. Then when he accepted we should make the people see that it was a form of bribe. This should reduce his popularity considerably."

Both the Princess Dowager and the King saw the wisdom of this; and they set about planning what they would offer him.

"The obvious post that comes to mind is a governor-generalship of Canada," said Bute. "That would ensure his being three thousand miles away from England. What could be more desirable?"

"You think he would take it?"

"We could try. We could offer him £5,000 a year."

"He has never been a man to take much account of money."

"He has a special feeling for Canada. He regards it as his conquest. There is a possibility that he will accept; and once he has, we can set it about that Mr. Pitt has accepted Canada—in other words, deserted England for the sake of the new country."

It was, agreed George, an excellent idea, and forthwith a letter was drafted to Mr. Pitt. Knowing his interest in the dominion of Canada which had in fact been his conquest, the King had the greatest pleasure in offering Mr. Pitt the Governor-Generalship with an income of £5,000 a year.

Pitt's answer to this was prompt and to the point. Even if he were allowed to retain his seat in the House of Commons, he would still reject the project because he intended to stay in England where his heart was.

The next offer was of the Duchy of Lancaster—an exceedingly luscious plum; since all he would have to do was accept revenues from the Crown.

But Mr. Pitt was too wily to fall into this trap.

Then came the final offer. His wife should become a peeress—Baroness of Chatham; and he himself should have a pension of £3,000 a year for three lives, which meant that on his death his wife would have it, then his son, and if his wife died before he died, it would go to his grandson.

The previous offers had been rejected with scorn; but over this last Pitt hesitated.

When he had told his wife of the last offer he had seen a gleam of satisfaction in her eyes. So Hester would like to be Baroness Chatham! He was deeply in love with Hester and had been for some time before they married. She was one of the Grenvilles—a girl surrounded by brothers, and in the days before his marriage Pitt had often been a guest at Wootton

Hall where he had fascinated not only Hester but her brothers with his eloquence and that undeniable air of greatness; he had married Hester seven years ago and they had five children— three boys and two girls—the youngest, James, being only a few months old. Pitt was devoted to his family. They and his career were all that mattered to him; Hester mattered in particular.

She had betrayed to him by a look that she would enjoy possessing the title; and it was in his power to give it to her. He knew too that she liked the idea of the pension. £3,000 a year—and not only for him. They were not poor by any means. Hester had brought a large dowry; he had a little from his family; and the Duchess of Marlborough in her eccentric way had left him £10,000 for, she had written, his noble defence for the support of the laws of England. Yet with this new offer there came no conditions. He could accept it and relinquish nothing. A temporary absence from the centre of the stage might even be desirable, for he suffered excruciatingly from the gout.

The King and Bute were surprised and immensely gratified when he accepted this offer.

"No," cried Bute, "we shall tell the people in our own way what has happened."

The first move was to appoint Charles Wyndham, Earl of Egremont, to succeed Pitt as Secretary of State for the Southern Department and Bute saw that it should be made absolutely clear to the public that Pitt had accepted a pension and peerage in exchange for his office.

It was written in the Court Circular:

> The Right Honourable William Pitt having resigned the Seals into the King's hands, His Majesty was this day pleased to appoint the Earl of Egremont to be one of His Majesty's principal Secretaries of State. And in consideration of the great and important service of the said Mr. Pitt, His Majesty has been graciously pleased to direct that a warrant be prepared for granting to the Lady Hester Pitt, his wife, a Barony of Great Britain, by the name, style and title of Baroness Chatham to her heirs male; and also to confer on the said William Pitt, an annuity of three thousand pounds sterling, during his own life and that of Lady Hester Pitt and their son John Pitt, Esq.

The people were astonished—as Bute had intended they should be—when they heard this news. Nor did Bute intend that it should rest there. Like most politicians he had his dependants in the literary world whom he used to further his own cause.

Very soon a song was being sung in the streets of London—a sneer at the fallen idol.

> *Three thousand a year's no contemptible thing,*
> *To accept from the hand of a patriot King,*
> *(With thanks to the bargain for service and merit),*
> *Which he wife and son all three shall inherit.*
> *With limited honours to her and her heirs*
> *So farewell to old England. Adieu to all cares.*

Pitt had no intention of being misrepresented. As a politician who, even his enemies had to admit, had done a great deal for his country, he had not been overpaid with his peerage and £3,000 a year pension. But he would not have the people assuming that he had taken this in exchange for leaving his post.

He had a letter circulated which told the true story:

Finding to my great surprise," he wrote, "that the cause and manner of my resigning the Seals is grossly misrepresented in the City, as well as that the most gracious and spontaneous remarks of His Majesty's approbation of my services, which marks followed my resignation, having been infamously traduced as a bargain for my forsaking the public, I am under the necessity of declaring the truth of both these facts, in a manner which I am sure no gentleman will contradict. A difference of opinion with regard to measures to be taken against Spain, of the highest importance and honour of the Crown, and to the most essential National interests (and this founded on what Spain has already done, not on what that Court may further intend to do) was the cause of my resigning the Seals. Lord Temple and I submitted in writing and signed by us, our most humble sentiments to His Majesty; which being overruled by the united opinion of all the rest of the King's servants, I resigned the Seals on the 5th of this month, in order not to remain responsible for measures which I was no longer able to guide. Most gracious public marks of His Majesty's approbation followed my resignation. They are unmerited and unsolicited and I shall ever be proud to have received them from the best of Sovereigns.

When this was handed round the City and the obvious truth

of it realized, Pitt's popularity shot up again; and Lord Bute's attempts to discredit him had entirely failed.

All the public had to realize was that though he no longer had a place in the cabinet, he had no intention of forsaking his duty.

The Princess Dowager, unaware of public feeling, was delighted with the turn of events.

With Lord Bute she called on her son and embracing him cried: "Thank God. Now, George, you are in truth King of England."

A Visit to a Quaker House

The King and Queen were taking breakfast together. This was a very pleasant part of the day, Charlotte often thought. George was always so courteous and she really believed he was growing fonder of her, which surprised and delighted her, for she was fully aware of her lack of beauty; and there was no doubt that George with his golden hair, blue eyes and fresh complexion was a handsome man. In Court dress he looked truly magnificent; he even looked pleasant in the early morning.

He took only a dish of tea at breakfast.

"I must be on my guard," he told Charlotte, "against getting fat. It is a characteristic of the family."

"But a dish of tea! It seems so little. I really think I should persuade you to take a little more."

He smiled at her rather cautiously. He wanted her to know that although he was determined to be a good husband to her, he was not allowing any interference even in the matter of a dish of tea.

Tactfully he changed the subject. "You will be interested in this Lord Mayor's Show. I doubt you have ever seen anything like it."

"I am constantly seeing things which I have never seen before. It makes life very interesting."

He looked at her covertly. They had been married nearly two months. Was there any sign yet? He had certainly not failed in his conjugal duties. It might even be that already she was with child.

"We shall be the guests of the City, I believe," she was saying. "How I love the City. I find it absorbingly interesting."

"How are you getting on with your English?"

"Oh . . . tolerably well. I am taking my lesson every day."

"Try speaking it."

She did, haltingly, and he corrected her. She was laughing with him over her odd pronunciation. What a blessing, she said, that he could speak German so well.

"Even when I speak English proficiently we shall speak in German, shall we not, when we are alone together. We shall make it our *intimate* language."

He nodded. "Although you must work hard at your English."

"Oh, George, I will."

"I think my grandfather made a great mistake in not speaking it well. Now . . . the plans for the 9th."

She smiled cosily. How he liked making plans! He would go to such trouble to arrange the guests for the most informal ball even when he must have very important state matters on his mind. There was the affair of Mr. Pitt for one thing.

She ventured: "There is much talk of Mr. Pitt."

He frowned. "Oh, he is no longer in the cabinet."

"I did learn that there is a great deal of feeling in the City about his resignation."

"Who told you this?"

"Oh . . . I do not remember. It is often talked of. It seems a pity. He is a great man, they say; and it is sad that his talents should not be used in the service of the nation."

George was not having this. He must make her understand that he had no intention of talking politics with her. It was not a woman's place to interfere. He had seen too much of women's meddling. He was beginning to think that his mother interfered too much; but she was old and wise and he had always listened to her. But he was not going to have Charlotte becoming another Princess Dowager.

Queens and mistresses of kings had often sought to dominate them. It was not going to be said that George III was so dominated . . . except by his mother when he was young.

George was beginning to think that one day he might have to tell his mother that he would make up his own mind. So he did not want Charlotte beginning to interfere.

He said shortly: "That matter is settled. It is of no interest to you. I will show you the route the Lord Mayor's Show will take." He spread a map on the table and Charlotte was immediately absorbed. It was like the old days with Madame de Grabow. Now she followed George's finger as it traced the route.

"And where shall we be?" asked Charlotte.

George had turned a faint pink and she wondered why.

He stammered as he answered: "There . . . there is a house opposite Bow Church in Cheapside where it is possible to get a fine view of the Lord Mayor's Show. Its owners have invited us to see it from their house."

"How strange," murmured Charlotte.

"It is not at all strange," replied George almost too vehemently. "It is a very fine house and it is in fact . . . most suitable. There are balconies from which we can see everything in ease and comfort. And these people are Quakers. I . . . I think the Quakers are very fine people indeed. I . . . I have always felt that this was a religion . . . had I not been king of this realm . . . which I could have followed."

He was looking at her almost defiantly, and she said: "You must tell me more of this Quaker religion. You have known many Quakers, I suppose."

George grew a shade pale and, turning, went to the window and looked out.

He said in a muffled voice: "My position makes it necessary for me to meet many of my subjects."

The Queen was puzzled. What was the reason for this strange vehemence and embarrassment? Was it because he was asking her to see the procession from a house which he did not consider suitable for a queen? Or was it because he really felt strongly about becoming a Quaker? Of course that was impossible.

How restricted we are, thought Charlotte, and she saw poor Christina's face with the sad expression which had been there from the time her sister had heard that her marriage would not take place.

Poor Christina! There was no freedom for a princess . . . or a king for that matter.

"George," she said, "do you feel strongly about this Quaker matter?"

Her words did nothing to ease the tension. "Of course not," he said sharply; and then: "I have matters to which I must attend."

He left her at the breakfast table, wondering why his mood should suddenly have changed.

It was almost as though he were hiding some secret.

Charlotte was being dressed for the Lord Mayor's Show. It

was a state occasion so she would be most splendidly attired. Her women had dressed her hair in what they called coronation ringlets; these were crowned with a circle of diamonds. Her gown was silk and gold and silver brocade; her stomacher glittered with diamonds and she was not displeased with the reflection which looked back at her. Such clothes could take the plainness out of the most ordinary face; and Charlotte was always pleased to win the admiration of spectators.

The little page boy, dressed in scarlet and silver, was standing by waiting to carry her train, and Elizabeth Chudleigh was chattering away to the Marchioness of Lorne; they did not know that Charlotte was understanding a little more English every day.

"So it's to be the house of the Quaker," laughed Elizabeth Chudleigh.

"Well, he has been said to have a special fondness for them."

"This is the Barclays. Very rich bankers, the Barclays. Prosperous simplicity is the order of the day. I'm sure H.M. is glad that the house chosen was not in St. James's Market."

"Would Hannah's family have had him?"

The women tittered together. How strange! thought Charlotte. Had she translated that conversation correctly? She was not sure; but George himself had said something about Quakers.

What was this Quaker mystery? There was *something* she was sure. Perhaps she would find out today.

"They say the people are massing in the streets," went on Elizabeth. "Pitt's supporters are all out. I don't think they are going to send up happy cheers for the Favourite, do you?"

"When have they ever?"

"Never. But with Mr. Pitt riding in the procession they could get really offensive about Master Bute and Her R.H."

Pitt! Bute! The Princess! Charlotte could guess what these frivolous women were talking about.

She herself disliked the Princess Dowager and was sure her mother-in-law disliked her in return. It was rather disgraceful that she should be so talked about on account of Lord Bute.

What did the King think? Whatever he thought he kept it to himself. He was very fond of them both—more fond, Charlotte suspected, than of her.

She smiled to herself. That was going to change. George was not going to remain his mother's boy now that he was a husband.

She had a suspicion that he might soon be a father, but she was not sure yet. When he was, everything would be changed. The important people in his life would be his wife, his sons and daughters—not his dominating mother and her paramour.

Charlotte, glittering with diamonds, pink with the pleasure of contemplating the excitement of what was very possibly the case, left her apartments to take her place beside the King in the coach in which they would drive to the Quaker household from where they would see the show.

Pitt was reluctant to be a part of the procession, but Lady Hester was certain that he should.

"If you don't," she said, "the people will believe that you are ashamed to face them and in a day or so they will be saying that the lies Bute put about against you are true."

Pitt smiled. "They will have read my correction."

"Slander sticks," insisted Lady Hester, and Pitt had to agree that she was right.

"But the banquet is to honour the King. I do not wish to bring about an uncomfortable situation by appearing."

"You should be there. I am certain of it. You must convince the people of the City that you are still one of them. You resigned because the cabinet did not agree with you. You accepted the pension and my title as just rewards for your work . . . and Heaven knows you deserve them. You have the future to think of, William. You must go."

So Pitt gave way and he and his brother-in-law, Lord Temple, joined the procession in their coach.

The Princess Dowager was deeply concerned about her lover. He would have to ride through the city and the people of London blamed him for the dismissal of Pitt.

Bute assured her that he had taken precautions against any unpleasantness which might occur: "I have hired strong men to follow my coach and they will be on the spot when needed."

"So you expect trouble!" cried the Princess Dowager.

"Let us say that I always believe in being prepared for it."

The Princess shuddered. Since the resignation of Pitt, the temper of the public towards her and her lover had grown more hostile.

In the past the people had sung songs about them, had contented themselves with whispered scandal. They had merely been silent when they rode through the streets. Now they had changed. They shouted after her carriage and she knew they did after Lord Bute's, too. When she had last driven through certain streets placards had been waved before her coach so that she could not fail to see them. On them had been crudely drawn a jackboot and petticoat. Some of the people even carried the boot and petticoat. They shouted obscenities after her carriage.

The petticoat was meant to represent her and the jackboot was a play on her lover's name. He was John—therefore Jack—and Boot stood for Bute.

The country was governed by Jackboot and Petticoat, called these people, and they were by no means reticent about the relationship they believed to exist between these two; nor did they hesitate to discuss it in lewd and lurid terms.

The Princess shuddered.

"I wish you were not riding in the procession," she said, but Bute only smiled at her. Of course he must be there. It was an occasion when all men of standing must be present. She need have no fear. He had arranged for protection from the mob should it be needed.

Had he not always been able to take care of himself?

Charlotte sat in the state coach with the King. The journey from St. James's Palace to Cheapside was just over two miles, but although they had left the Palace at noon they were still on the way after three o'clock on account of the roads being so jammed with the people who had come to see the show; and because of the carriages, carts and sedans of the spectators the procession made slow progress. The people were able to come up to the coach and stare in at the King and Queen. George greeted them with warm, affectionate smiles; and Charlotte did her best to look pleasant.

"God save the King . . . and the Queen!" cried the people.

About the state coach were the Grenadier Guards, the Horse Guards and the Yeomen of the Guards, all in their brilliant uniforms, making a show to delight the people. But just ahead of them was the coach in which the Princess Dowager was riding with her daughters, the Princesses Augusta and Caroline Matilda, and Charlotte could hear the shouts of derision which were hurled at that particular vehicle.

"Where's the Scotch Stallion?" called a voice in the crowd. George heard it and his lips tightened. He did not like to hear his mother thus insulted; but it occurred to him that the relationship between Lord Bute and his mother was so close as to give rise to speculation. He refused to believe that they were anything but good friends; in his great desire to bring morality back to the Court he could not face any other conclusion. These were the two people to whom he was closest; he could not allow himself to believe they were living in a manner of which he would heartily disapprove. Therefore he preferred to believe the people were wrong, and it distressed him deeply.

Moreover, he was thinking of Hannah. How could he help it when he was to be guest of Quakers? Perhaps he should have refused the Barclays' offer of their home. But that would have aroused more comment than accepting it.

The shadow of Hannah Lightfoot hung over him. Sometimes he remembered the biblical admonition: The sins ye do by two and two ye pay for one by one.

He glanced sideways at Charlotte. She had no idea of his feelings. She must remain in ignorance. He was fond of her; he had forced himself to be fond of her because it was right and proper that he should be; he had forced himself to forget Sarah Lennox; but he could not shut Hannah Lightfoot out of his mind, and today he could not stop himself thinking of that ceremony of marriage through which he had gone when he and Hannah had stood before Dr. Wilmot. It was a mock marriage. Hannah was already married to Isaac Axford. But Axford had no longer considered himself married to her because they had not seen each other for years and in any case they had been married at Dr. Keith's Marriage Mill which had since been declared illegal.

At that time he and Hannah had believed their marriage to have been legal, and he could not get the thought of that marriage out of his head. It was going round and round, refusing to be dismissed; peeping out at him at odd moments like a mischievous sprite determined to ruin his peace of mind.

Sometimes his head ached with thinking of it.

Charlotte must not know. Charlotte would do as she was told. He was glad she could not speak English; that necessarily kept her apart. It was the wish of his mother and Lord Bute that she should not have any friends without their knowledge. They wanted to keep Charlotte in the background.

And so did he.

How slow was the journey! It was nearly four o'clock and they were only just turning into Cheapside.

Nearly four hours since they had left the Palace!

"I'm hungry," Charlotte was saying.

The first of the coaches in which George's uncle, the old Duke of Cumberland, was sitting must by now have reached the Barclays' home; and after that was George's Aunt Amelia and his brother the Duke of York, both with their separate coaches and servants. So many carriages and their retinues and after that there were George's brothers William Henry and Frederick before the Princess Dowager and her daughters.

Charlotte said: "What a lot of food the Lord Mayor will need to provide for us all."

"It will do them good," replied the King. "They were eager enough to sit down at our expense at the coronation."

One of the Barclays had spread a red carpet on the pavement before the house, so that the King and Queen need not step on the cobbles.

Charlotte, handed from the coach by the chamberlain, entered the house where one of the counting houses had been transformed into a parlour. On the stairs leading from this room the Barclay family were assembled to greet their Majesties. They looked very sombre in their grey Quaker costumes, for although palace servants had been sent to the house to show the family how to conduct themselves in the presence of royalty, Mr. Barclay had said that it would be against his principles to change his dress or manners. He respected the King but the only one he could bow down to was God.

Charlotte murmured in German that she could not reply in English to Mr. Barclay's loyal speech of welcome but the King was immediately behind her and he expressed their joint pleasure; he seemed very moved by the reception he received from these good people.

In the streets the crowd was calling for a glimpse of the King and the Queen and George said they should show themselves without delay, for the people had been waiting long enough.

Tumultuous cheers filled the street when their Majesties appeared on the balconies; and after some minutes they went back into the house to receive the members of the family.

The girls of the family looked charming in their austere garments and the King seemed deeply moved by the sight of them. There were seven daughters of the house and the King insisted on kissing them all as well as their mother. His emotion was noted by all who beheld him; and when one of the very young members of the household, a little girl of five, came forward, it was clear that the whole royal family was enchanted with her.

The child was grave but not shy, and she stood before the King regarding him solemnly.

"Tell me what you think of me," said George, who loved children.

"I am thinking that thou art the King," said the child.

"I hope I meet with your approval."

"I love the King," she said; then she lowered her eyes and added: "Though I am not allowed to love fine things."

"I am sure you are a good girl and do as you are told."

"My grandpapa forbids me to curtsey to thee."

There were tears in the King's eyes as he replied: "Then, my sweet child, I should not ask it of thee."

Everyone was moved and the Princess Dowager picked up the child and kissed her.

"What an enchanting little creature!" said the Duke of York, and looked as though he were about to bestow his kisses on the child.

But her mother had taken her hand and was leading her away, as she feared too much adulation might turn the little girl's head.

There was a shout of applause as she left.

Mrs. Barclay was whispering to some of the ladies that there was a buffet in one of the counting rooms which had been turned into a dining room; and if the company could be prevailed upon to follow her she would lead them to it, for she was sure they must be very hungry. The King said he would not eat but would talk with Mr. Barclay as there were many points about his doctrines that he would like to discuss with him; so the Queen with the rest of the company went into the counting-house dining room and partook of the refreshment.

Meanwhile the King was deep in discussion with Mr. Barclay and to the latter's astonishment showed some considerable understanding of Mr. Barclay's faith.

"I have always admired the Society of Friends," said the King, which delighted Mr. Barclay, for there was always a certain danger in belonging to a minority; one could never be sure when those who did not share one's views were going to make it an issue for complaint. So it was comforting to know that the King was in sympathy with them.

Mr. Barclay begged the honour of presenting the King with a copy of *Apology*, a book which set out clearly all the tenets of the Quaker faith.

The King thanked him and accepted the book.

"I assure you," he said, with emotion, "that I have always felt strong respect for your friendly society."

It was time to watch the Lord Mayor's procession from one of the balconies—the purpose for which the King and Queen had come to the house; and they were conducted out by Mr. and Mrs. Barclay to the pleasure of the people who were waiting in the streets to cheer them.

The Lord Mayor's procession was long and colourful and considerably enlivened by the Lady Mayoress. When she put her head out of the mayoral coach to pay homage to their Majesties her enormous headdress was caught in the window sash and she remained, her head stuck out uncomfortably as the coach rattled on. There were shouts of delight from the crowd and protests from the lady; and the whole procession had to be stopped while the footman extricated the lady and made it possible for her to put her head back in the carriage.

Everyone was laughing, except the Lady Mayoress; and Charlotte recalled the coronation and a similar series of accidents.

She was reminded how serious George had been on that occasion. It was indeed a solemn one. But he was even more serious today, which was strange.

It occurred to Charlotte then that there might be some strange connection between George and the Quakers. She must try to discover what it was, for as a good wife she must be interested in what concerned her husband.

Lord Bute sat well back in his coach. He had consoled the Princess, but he was not feeling very secure. He knew the mood of the people and that they blamed him for Pitt's retirement from the cabinet.

He heard the shouts. "Pitt. God bless him. We want Pitt."

It was coming. He sat back in his coach. He heard the hurrahs and the shouts of approval. It was some seconds before he realized that they had mistaken him for Pitt.

He kept well back. If only the coachman could whip up the

horses. This slow trundling along through a mob that could be murderous if it recognized the true occupant of the coach, was alarming.

The coach jerked forward and he with it. A face stared in at him; for a few seconds Bute stared back. Then the face became almost demoniacal in its delight.

"He's no Pitt. It's the Scotch Stallion himself."

The crowd was round his coach, preventing its moving backwards or forwards. Someone threw a stone through the window. Bute narrowly avoided it.

"Go back to your heathen land beyond the Border," cried a voice.

They were trying to cut the traces of the horse.

"We'll hang him on a tree where he belongs."

Oh, God, this is the end, thought Bute. On a day such as this the taverns would have been crowded while the people waited for the procession; they were inflamed by liquor and in such a mood they were capable of anything.

Where were the "bruisers" whom he had hired to follow him, for he had suspected something like this might happen. They were in fact battling their way through the mob to reach his coach. Suddenly he saw one on either side of the coach. The others would be doing their work.

"Get back," shouted one of them. "You're breaking the law."

"Whose law? Bute's law? We take no account of that. We want the Scotch Boy. He won't sleep in my lady's bed again. We're going to hang him high . . ."

The door of the coach was opened suddenly. Bute saw that another coach had drawn up close. In it was Lord Hardwicke. One of the bruisers held off the mob while Lord Bute leapt from his own coach to that of Lord Hardwicke.

Lord Hardwicke's driver shouted to the mob to stand aside unless they wished to be run over and because of the urgency of the moment he drove through them. They scattered from right and left; and they satisfied their fury by destroying Lord Bute's fine carriage while his lordship, beside his rescuer Lord Hardwicke, rode on to Guildhall.

He was safe, but it was a depressing indication of popular feeling.

Charlotte and George drove from the Barclays' house to Guildhall where various ceremonies had to be endured; and it was nine o'clock before they sat down to the banquet.

Although they were received warmly by the Mayor and his Aldermen and the City merchants, when Pitt and Lord Temple entered the Guildhall the rafters shook with the cheers; and the hosts made no secret of who were the honoured guests.

The King was out of favour. He had allowed Mr. Pitt to be dismissed and the City of London which stood for Trade stood for Mr. Pitt. It would not be forgotten in a hurry what Mr. Pitt had done for the prosperity of London in the years when he had been at the helm.

The City heartily disapproved of the King's treatment of their Great Commoner and the City of London was a law unto itself; it would not hesitate to express its disapproval of the King's action, for it considered that the prosperity of London was more important to England than all the kings and queens put together.

Still, George was not so unpopular as he might have been had he been older. He was young, a new king, and everyone knew that he did not rule. He was told what he must do and he did it. England was ruled by Jackboot and Petticoat and the City had shown what it thought of them.

The King and Queen sat at a table in the front of the hall which had been set especially for them. Over it was a canopy and they could not complain of their reception for the Lord Mayor himself served the King and the Lady Mayoress the Queen, even though, when the King proposed the health of the City of London, there were some murmurs about government policy not being conducive to its health; and this compared ill with the wild enthusiasm accorded to Pitt.

However, unlike the coronation banquet, this was expertly organized and there were four hundred and fourteen dishes with the accompanying wines—ample for the entire company of noblemen, ministers, aldermen and all city dignitaries.

The ball that followed was equally successful; but at midnight the King made clear his wish to depart.

The coaches were sent for, but it was discovered that the footmen and coachmen had been having a party on their own and that many of them were in such a state of drunkenness that they were unable to drive.

The Princess Dowager, extremely anxious as to what had happened to Lord Bute, for she had heard rumours of his ride through the City, was very angry. She longed to be in her apartments, her lover beside her, so that she could assure herself that all was well with him.

She paced up and down giving vent to her fury while George tried to soothe her by telling her that they must expect their servants to want a little entertainment when so much was being lavished on themselves.

The King's geniality was noted with approval; the Princess Dowager's impatience with dislike.

Tomorrow the shouts against Jackboot and Petticoat would be intensified; but the Princess Dowager was too worried and too exhausted to give that a thought.

At length coachmen were found to drive the coaches and the royal party was able to set off for St. James's. Even the coachman who drove them was not entirely sober and this was evident when the royal coach turned into the gateway of St. James's Palace, for he did not judge his distance sufficiently well, and the coach came into collision with one of the posts. The King and the Queen were thrown from their seats and the roof caved in; the glass windows were broken; but to their astonishment neither George nor Charlotte was hurt.

George descended from the coach and helped Charlotte out.

"Your Majesty . . ." stammered the coachman.

But George only waved him aside. "We will walk to our own apartments," he said.

What a strange day, thought Charlotte, in the royal bed while George lay beside her. She felt as though she were jolting in the coach; she could still hear the shouts of the people; could see the splendour of the Guildhall; but most clearly of all the Quaker household.

How friendly George had been to them! She had never seen him quite like that before.

She must ask him to explain to her this affinity he had for Quakers.

When she fell asleep it was to dream of people in austere grey robes looking like nuns in the brilliant assembly. But in the weeks that followed she forgot George's strangeness on that day, for an exciting probability had become a fact.

The Queen was pregnant.

The Birth of a Child

When George heard that Charlotte could expect a child during the following summer he was overcome by joy. But for the conflict prevailing among the members of his government this, he believed, could have been the happiest time of his life. He longed for a large family and Charlotte had shown, by becoming so quickly pregnant, that she was fertile.

He was growing more and more devoted to Charlotte who was a good and loving wife, and he scarcely ever thought of Sarah Lennox. But he could not help remembering those other occasions—similar in a way—when Hannah had told him that she was expecting a baby. This was different. No need for subterfuge here—only rejoicing.

If only Pitt had been content to accept the ruling of his cabinet how easy everything would have been. But with the weeks which followed the Lord Mayor's banquet the people grew more and more restive. It did not help when in January it was necessary to declare war on Spain and Pitt's policy was vindicated. People stood about in groups in the streets and demanded of each other: "Was this not the very issue on which Pitt resigned? And here they are declaring war after all. So Pitt was right . . . and they were wrong. And who rules now? Lord Bute. Newcastle may call himself First Lord of the Treasury, but it is Bute who controls affairs."

Bute! They hated him. It was unsafe for him to venture in the streets. "Jackboot!" they shouted after his carriage; and he could never be sure whether he was going to be attacked by the mob.

Bute had been working towards this position of power over many years, but now it was his he was beginning to wonder if it had been worth while. He loved power; but he was fond of

116

the King and truly wished to bring good to the country; and although he was aware of being overshadowed by the greatness of Pitt, he deeply regretted his departure. Perhaps this was not really what he had worked for after all. What he had desired was to be in control, yes, but with Pitt beside him—or a little behind him—to advise out of his great wisdom.

If Pitt had been prepared to take second place . . . But Pitt was a man of great pride and dignity. He would have everything his way or he would have nothing.

Bute still had the affection of the King and the Princess, and they both still regarded him with admiration as well as affection, which gave him great encouragement, and his speeches in Parliament were often so eloquent that many revised their opinion of him. Lacking the genius of men like Pitt and Fox, he was none the less something more than a man who had come to power because he had had the good fortune to attract the right mistress.

Newcastle was an encumbrance and he felt he would be well rid of him. George did not like the man either, so he did not have to prepare the King to dislike him. Bute felt that if he could rid the Government of Newcastle he could perhaps make some headway. The opportunity came over the subsidy which England had been paying to Frederick of Prussia so that he might prosecute the war in Europe. Bute was against continuing with this, whereas Newcastle was of the opposite opinion.

Newcastle threatened to resign and went to the King who had been prepared by Bute.

"I fear Your Majesty," said Newcastle, "that I disagree with Lord Bute over this matter of aid to Prussia. The time may have come when I should retire into private life."

"Then, my lord, I must fill your place as best I can," retorted the King.

Newcastle was taken aback; after all the years he had served the House of Hanover he had expected some protestation; but even he was quick enough to see that the King was welcoming his resignation and had no intention of persuading him to rescind it.

Thus Newcastle resigned and Lord Bute held that position for which he had long schemed and plotted. He had become First Lord of the Treasury and was elected a Knight of the Garter. The Princess Dowager wept tears of joy to see him in his regalia; the King embraced him and told him that this was one of the happiest days of his life. Only Bute was a little uneasy, realizing how weighty affairs of state can be.

However, he appointed Sir Francis Dashwood Chancellor of the Exchequer and George Grenville Secretary of State for the Northern Department—the post just evacuated by himself. Lord Henly remained Lord Chancellor; the Duke of Bedford was Lord Privy Seal, Lord Granville Lord President of the Council, and the Earl of Egremont Secretary of State for the Southern Department.

With such a strong cabinet he felt his confidence rising. He told the King and the Princess Dowager that his first aim would be to bring about a lasting and honourable peace.

The Queen was now heavily pregnant and her child was expected to be born in the following August.

Buckingham House was ready for habitation in June and she and the King decided that they would move in and enjoy it during the summer months. Furniture and pictures were brought from Hampton and St. James's to help furnish it, and when it was ready Charlotte was delighted, particularly when people called it the Queen's House.

There was a housewarming party to which the Court was invited and George, with his usual meticulous attention to detail, made the plans.

There would be a concert, of course; both King and Queen were determined on that, and as it was brilliant summer it would be an alfresco occasion. The King selected a certain Mr. Kuffe, who was a German, to take charge of the arrangements. Besides the concert there was to be a ball and the gardens would be illuminated.

Crowds waited outside to see the guests arrive and they were delighted by the sight of the King and his pregnant Queen on the balcony, for this pregnancy had won back the popularity which the King had lost at the time of Pitt's resignation. Now he was their young king again. He could be said to be handsome though his fair skin was now often marred by pimples; but his very blue eyes were not as prominent as his grandfather's and his jaw was only sullen in repose.

If he would rid himself of the odious Bute and take back their idol Pitt they would have nothing of which to complain.

But settling into Buckingham House was a joyous occasion and the crowds had come to cheer and applaud.

It was a delightful ball, Charlotte decided; and she wished that they could have more balls.

She confided this to George in the privacy of their apartments when the successful festivities had come to an end.

He shook his head. "It would not be good for you in your condition."

"But George, I shall not be in this condition after August," she reminded him.

"It may well be," he said, "that you soon will be again."

She considered this a little dolefully, for she had been feeling the heat rather too much and she had suffered certain discomforts. It would all be worth while once the child was born, but the idea of starting again almost immediately was a little subduing.

However, she did not protest. After all, she would not be content with one child only.

Charlotte was feeling wan and exhausted. The Princess Dowager called on her and expressed her concern.

"You should be in the country," she said. "There is nothing like country air when you are carrying."

"But I love this house."

"You should go to the country," insisted Augusta.

It was not only the Queen's health which made her feel this would be advisable. Charlotte was beginning to speak a little English and was taking too much interest in what was going on around her. She had expressed a view on Mr. Pitt and what was more distressing was that she had commented to one of her women—so Miss Pascal had reported—that she believed the King to be especially interested in the Quaker religion and she herself would like to know something of it so that she could discuss it with His Majesty if the subject should arise.

Quite clearly she was beginning to learn too much of what was going on around her. She and Lord Bute had brought Charlotte to England to bear the King's children, not to meddle and probe.

So the Queen should go to Richmond and live in retirement there.

Princess Augusta directed her cold smile on her daughter-in-law.

"Richmond! That is the answer. I shall know no peace until you are there. I shall instruct your ladies that they are not to bother you with too much chatter."

"I enjoy my conversation with them. It enables me to improve my English."

"All in good time. Don't forget you are carrying the heir to the throne."

"It may not be a boy."

"Of course it will be a boy," insisted Augusta, as though, thought Charlotte, it will be my fault if it is not—her own firstborn was a girl in any case. "And if this one is not a boy the next one will be."

Oh dear, thought Charlotte, how they do talk about the next before this one has appeared.

"I shall prepare a schedule for you, my dear. You will wish for a little exercise and when the King is with you at Richmond you will take that together. I doubt not the King will be with you whenever he can spare the time from state duties. You will have your reading, your English lessons, your sewing. But I do not think your ladies should tire you too much at this stage. I shall give instructions that they shall spend only half an hour a week in conversation with you."

"Oh, but . . ."

The Princess Dowager held up a playful finger which accorded strangely with her cold and calculating glance.

"It is all for your good, my dear," she said. "We cannot allow anything to go wrong now, can we?"

So Charlotte left Buckingham House and went to Richmond where the weeks of waiting passed slowly and monotonously.

George joined Charlotte at Richmond, and here began to live the life of the country gentleman. Richmond was near enough to St. James's to enable him to return for levees and important state occasions; but the thought of being a father and living a life of domestic happiness greatly appealed to him; and at Richmond he had time to be the devoted husband.

He enjoyed the rural life and nothing pleased him so much as to go among the local people and talk to them, waving ceremony aside and asking them questions about their work and lives. He was particularly interested in the farms and would talk at great length with the farmers and even their labourers on agricultural matters.

He became very popular in Richmond and he was delighted that the local people there touched their forelocks or curtsied, according to sex, and called a "Good morning, sir" instead of cheering for His Majesty.

And then there were the days with Charlotte. They both had a love of music and he would listen approvingly while she sang or played the harpsichord. Sitting with Charlotte, talking to her in German, he was happy; she sewed or embroidered and as he did not like to sit idly, he took up the craft of buttonmaking to which he applied a great deal of patience.

But he did not forget the state matters in spite of the simple life. Every morning he arose at five to light the fire in his bedroom which his servants had laid the night before. Then he would go back to bed until the room was warmed up. After washing and dressing he would study state papers until it was time to breakfast with Charlotte.

Each morning he surveyed her with pleasure. She appeared in good health and there was no doubt that the simple life and Richmond air agreed with her. She was a goodly size and some of the experienced were saying the way she carried the child implied that it was a boy.

At eight o'clock they took breakfast.

"Just a dish of tea for me, my dear Charlotte." His usual remark.

To which she replied: "Oh, but George, it is not enough."

But he would sternly resist her efforts to press food on him. He was not going to indulge his inherited love of rich food—and incur the obesity which went with it, he told her. It was all part of the discipline of his life. He put it from him as he had Hannah Lightfoot and Sarah Lennox; and he accepted his dish of tea as though it was exactly all he desired, in the same way as he accepted the plain woman sitting opposite him.

Such happy days they were in spite of all the conflict in the Government. Charlotte had no intention of concerning herself with that. Her thoughts were concentrated on the child.

On one of his visits to St. James's, George heard the news. It was Mr. Fox who told him—slyly, thought George, taking pleasure in the discomfiture which he must know such a revelation would cause.

"Your Majesty, my sister-in-law Sarah Lennox was married a few days ago."

George felt his face growing pink.

"Oh . . . is that so?"

"Yes, Sire. In view of Your Majesty's kind interest in her I thought you would wish to know."

"Er . . . yes . . ."

"A quiet wedding in the chapel at Holland House. Not perhaps a brilliant match, but . . ."

"Who was the bridegroom?" asked George quickly.

"Bunbury, Sire, Thomas Charles Bunbury. He is a fortunate man. He is not rich and of course heir to the baronetcy. But it is a match of her making and Your Majesty will agree with me that happiness does not depend on riches."

"H'm," grunted George, and turned away to speak to someone else. But he was not listening to what was said; he was thinking of Sarah, married to someone else; Sarah who might have been his wife.

The King returned to Richmond. How plain Charlotte was—plainer than ever now that her body was bulky! She was grotesque. He thought of Sarah, Sarah teaching him that dance, with the silly name, the Betty Blue, was it? Sarah laughing and teasing and making hay in the gardens of Holland House. He had given up Sarah for Charlotte—and now Sarah had another lover: Bunbury.

Silly name, thought George angrily. Who was Bunbury? A petty baronet . . . not even that until his father died . . . and no fortune either. But Sarah had never looked for title and fortune. If she had would she ever have refused the King? And she had refused him at one time . . . although later she would have accepted him and then he was persuaded to take Charlotte instead. He might have had Sarah . . . and he had Charlotte.

There was no longer contentment for him at Richmond. He could not bear to look at Charlotte. His mind and body were crying out for Sarah and wherever he looked he saw her . . . with Bunbury.

He could not stay within walls; he went out and walked. It started to rain and he went on walking. The rain soothed him; it soaked through his clothes; it was inside his boots, but he didn't care.

He found some savage pleasure in the discomfort.

He was cold and shivering when he returned; he felt feverish and was sneezing violently.

The King was suffering from acute influenza; he was delirious and to the doctors' consternation his chest was covered with a rash which they could not identify as being a symptom of a known disease.

Charlotte insisted on nursing him and she was in despair because when she brought the doctors to bleed him he cried out that he did not want them. They should not touch him. His behaviour was very strange, and he was not like the reasonable, amenable young man they had known before.

"Go away! Go away!" he cried. "Leave me alone . . . all of you."

There was great consternation throughout the Court, for it was believed the King might die. And then what? A Regency? What a state of affairs. A young king suddenly stricken down and the heir to the throne not yet born!

Charlotte now showed a strength of character which astonished those about her. This was the young woman who had written a letter to Frederick of Prussia. Nobody was going to turn her out of the sick room—not the King's mother, nor Lord Bute. She was his wife and she was in command.

She ordered the doctors to bleed the King; and by this time George was far too ill to protest. She was in the sick room night and day and there was nothing anyone could do to shift her.

Under her care and that of the doctors George began to get better; and the day came when he was sitting up in bed asking for a little food, no longer feverish and quite lucid in his mind.

"You will soon be well again," Charlotte told him.

"That must be so, for I have affairs to attend to."

"Ah. You will not get up until you are well enough, I promise you."

The King felt a surge of resentment. He was not going to be ruled by this bulky little creature. If she thought so, she must be quickly disillusioned.

"I shall get up tomorrow," he said.

Charlotte regarded him tenderly and shook her head.

How dared she, who was not beautiful Sarah, how dared she tell him what he must or must not do.

When he heard from the doctors that the Queen had been a wonderful nurse, and that no one could have been so devoted, he softened towards her. She was a good woman; it was not her fault that she was not beautiful; she could not be blamed because beautiful Sarah had married Bunbury.

"I hear you have been a good nurse," he told her. He must try to love her. She was carrying their child who might be the heir to the throne if he were a boy . . . and if it were a girl and there were no more children that child might be the Queen.

He must be good to Charlotte. He must forget Sarah Lennox and love his wife.

"Of course I was your nurse. As if I would allow anyone else to nurse you."

She had changed; she was less humble; she had been for a while in authority. If he allowed her she would be ready to advise him and guide him. That must not be. He could allow no woman to guide him—particularly one who failed to charm him.

"And you are going to stay there until you are quite well." Spoken with loving firmness.

He said quietly but firmly, "I shall get up tomorrow."

And he did. She protested, but he swept aside her protests.

He would not be dictated to. He was the King and he would make the decisions.

It was said that the King had risen far too soon from his sick bed; and sometimes George felt this to be true, but he was not going to allow Charlotte to decide what he should or should not do.

It was the beginning of August and the Queen's time was drawing near. One morning at breakfast George said to her: "The heir to the throne must be born in London."

"Oh, but it is much more peaceful here at Richmond," cried Charlotte.

"That may be so, but it is one of our traditions."

Charlotte was sad. The last weeks had been so enjoyable. She loved Richmond and she would always remember it as the place in which she had known the greatest happiness of her life.

She brightened when she thought of Buckingham House. That was not so bad. Too near St. James's, of course, but far more pleasant than that grim old palace which she had always thought looked like a prison.

"There is the new house . . ." she began.

But George shook his head. "It will not be ready. You must tell your women to prepare for the journey back to St. James's. And I think we should not delay it."

Charlotte protested, but George waved her objections aside.

George was growing very stubborn, and although he might be persuaded to change his mind about certain matters by Lord Bute and his mother, Charlotte had never had the power to persuade him.

He let her talk while he sipped his tea.

Then he said as though she had not mentioned her dislike of the place: "So, my dear, pray tell your women. We should leave this week, I think."

So there was nothing she could do but obey. It was not important, she told herself. Soon she would have her baby; and she would bring the child to Richmond.

She longed for the child. She wanted to write home and tell them what it was like when one was about to become a mother.

But that would be too cruel . . . for poor Christina.

So Charlotte meekly told her women to prepare and in a short time she was installed in that grim old palace of St. James's, there to await the desired event.

The morning of the 11th August dawned bright and warm; and it was very clear to all those surrounding the Queen that she was on the point of giving birth.

Schwellenburg, who had quickly forgotten her injunctions to behave with less arrogance, was in command and bullying poor Haggerdorn until she did not know which way to turn.

"Summon all the ladies," she commanded, "for the Queen's time is near."

Haggerdorn did as she was bid and a feeling of excitement ran all through the Palace. Crowds had begun to collect in the streets. This was the King's first child and if it were a boy he would be Prince of Wales; even if it were a girl there would be reason for rejoicing, for it was a very good sign that the Queen had so quickly shown that she could bear children; and there had been no alarms during her pregnancy either. Everything seemed well and normal. Married in September 1761; having her first child August 1762. Who could do better than that? Who could rival such promptitude?

Soon the Princess Dowager's carriage was seen driving to St. James's. On this day the people were kinder to her and gave her a cold silence. There were no reminders of the immoral life they liked to tell her she lived. Even Lord Bute's carriage was allowed to pass in silence.

No rancour at the time of a royal birth.

The ministers of the cabinet began to arrive: Egremont, Devonshire, George Grenville, Halifax and the rest. Then came the Archbishop of Canterbury and during the morning the excitement mounted.

The ladies of the bedchamber, all together in an anteroom, were not permitted to enter the bedchamber, much to the disgust of Mademoiselle von Schwellenburg. Even the ministers were not allowed in; the Archbishop of Canterbury alone enjoyed this privilege.

In another part of the Palace George waited. He was anxious; hating the thought of pain he was praying that Charlotte would be quickly delivered; he was thanking God for giving him a fertile wife; and he asked that the child should be a boy.

"Although," he hastened to add, "the sex of this one is not so very important. Let Charlotte come through well and the child be healthy and I shall ask nothing more of this occasion."

How long the waiting was! George remembered when Hannah's children were born. He had not suffered in the same way because he had not known the precise time of her travail.

He must stop himself thinking of Hannah. Hannah was dead. "Dead, dead," he repeated. And the mischievous voice which he heard now and then in his head whispered: "Is she, George? Are you sure of it?"

"Hannah is dead," he repeated. "The children are well cared for. Hannah is dead . . . *dead*."

"You are too vehement, George," said the voice. "And if she were not dead . . ."

"Hannah *is* dead," he whispered.

All through that day the tension was rising. George did not go to bed, and it was in the early hours of the morning that one of the women had come to tell him that the Queen's pains were becoming more frequent.

"It can be any time now, Sire."

Any time. He looked at his watch. Four o'clock. It could be in a matter of minutes; it could be hours.

And all this time he must wait. He must think of Charlotte. Charlotte was the important one now. He would not think of anyone but Charlotte.

He prayed that Lord Cantelupe would soon be with him, for it was that noble gentleman's duty as Vice Chamberlain to the Queen to bring him the message that the child was born. He would be well rewarded—five hundred pounds for a girl, one thousand pounds for a boy. All part of a Vice Chamberlain's perquisites.

Let it be soon.

*   *   *

Charlotte lay exhausted on her bed.

How long? she prayed. It had seemed to go on for so many hours.

"What is the time?" she whispered.

"It won't be long now," was the soothing answer.

Someone whispered to her that it was nearly seven o'clock.

Seven o'clock and it was three when the pains had begun to be violent.

She would not cry out; she felt she must prevent that at all costs. In the anteroom her ladies would be listening, waiting for the cry of the child.

She pictured them whispering together—Miss Chudleigh, the Marchioness, Miss Pascal, Miss Vernon and of course Schwellenburg and poor Haggerdorn.

Oh, no, they must not hear her cry out. At a royal birth there must be only rejoicing. No one must remember the pain.

Soon, she told herself, my child will be born.

And she steeled herself to bear the agony.

The cry of a child. And followed by a buzz of excitement that seemed to run right through the palace.

"The child is born. Girl or boy?"

Someone said it was a girl; and Lord Huntingdon who could not wait for Lord Cantelupe, whose prerogative it was to deliver the message, ran to the King's apartment to tell him he was the father of a fine daughter.

"And the Queen?" asked George with tears in his eyes.

"That I did not discover," Huntingdon told him.

George replied: "I am but little anxious as to the sex of the child as long as the Queen is safe."

He waited for no more but went with all haste to the lying-in chamber where Charlotte's *accoucheur* Mr. Hunter (for she had insisted that she be attended by this man instead of an ordinary midwife) greeted the King with the news that he was the father of a strong, large and pretty boy.

"Boy! But I was told a girl."

"Your Majesty may see for yourself. You cannot doubt the sex of the child."

And there he was, a screaming healthy boy—perfect in every way.

The King wept unashamedly and so did everyone else in

the bedchamber; then he went to the bed where Charlotte smiled up at him.

"We have a son," she said.

And he knelt, and taking her hand kissed it.

London was wild with joy. Married less than a year and already a healthy son. This was a good augury.

Now there would be a christening—balls, *fêtes*, thanksgiving services. After all wasn't the child the Prince of Wales? All over the City the bells were ringing and guns were firing the salute.

"It's a boy," people called to each other from their windows, in the streets, to the craft on the river. "A good strong healthy boy."

They were always on the look out for omens and it so happened that a captured ship, the *Hermione*, had been brought up the Thames that day; it contained gold which was being taken to the vaults of the Bank of England, and through the crowds of people—rejoicing in the birth of the heir to the throne—trundled the bullion-laden carts.

"Gold!" cried the people. "Captured gold to enrich the nation! On the day he is born, it is taken to the bank. If there was ever a sign this is it."

They said the baby had been born with a golden spoon in his mouth.

The baby was to be named George Augustus Frederick, and the ceremonial baptism was fixed to take place a fortnight after his birth. There were no qualms about this child; he screamed lustily, demanded his food with an arrogance which his doting mother called royal, and showed everyone that he had a firm footing on life.

When so many royal infants were delicate this was a blessing Charlotte never ceased to be grateful for. In fact she thought of nothing but her little prince.

The people clustered round St. James's demanding news of his progress; when he was carried on to the balcony they went wild with joy. The most popular person in the kingdom was the little Prince of Wales and next to him his parents for producing him.

Now, thought Charlotte, I know what it is to be completely happy. All the weary months of waiting were forgotten when she held this child in her arms. Her first thoughts on waking were for him. She could not wait for his nurses to bring him to her. She must go to him; she must look into that pink face and assure herself that all was well with him.

George shared her delight. This little boy was constantly in his thoughts. This pink bawling infant would one day be the King. George solemnly vowed that he would do all in his power to leave him a kingdom of which he could be truly proud.

The discontent which had been raging through the City since the dismissal of Pitt was overshadowed by the joy in the royal birth. When the Prince of Wales was taken into Hyde Park for an airing crowds followed him and his nurses, and they laughed with pleasure when he showed them what a fine pair of lungs he had or lay smiling complacently on his satin pillows.

"God bless him," they cried. "He's a lusty, jolly young dog and no mistake."

It was the custom on such an occasion for the Queen to invite any who cared to call at the Palace to partake of cake and caudle at her expense. The caudle was a warm concoction of wine and eggs which was supposed to be good for invalids and children; and as was to be expected crowds gathered in the waiting rooms to partake of the Queen's hospitality. The Yeomen of the Guard had to be summoned to keep order; and even so, people were caught stuffing their pockets with cake, and these had to be severely reprimanded and warned of dire punishment if the offence was repeated. During the cake and caudle week 500 pounds of cake and eight gallons of caudle were used up every day.

But the people enjoyed it and wished there was a royal birth every week.

And then came the day of baptism—a quiet ceremony in the Queen's drawing room. It was half past six in the evening and the Queen lay on her bed of state there.

She had lost a great deal of her plainness, for her eyes were alight with a serene pleasure. She was dressed in a white and silver gown as she had been at her wedding, and was wearing her stomacher of diamonds, the King's wedding gift. Against the background of the state bed—crimson velvet and gold braid, white satin and Brussels lace—she made a magnificent picture. The bloom of her ugliness had indeed worn off.

Little George, carried by his governess on his white satin pillow decorated with gold, screamed lustily in protest.

His grandmother, the Princess Dowager, took him from his governess which did not please him and his screams grew louder, but this only made everyone smile. "He's a self-willed little rogue," said the King fondly and prophetically. The sponsors came forward—the Duke of Cumberland and the nobleman who had come from Mecklenburg to stand proxy for the Duke of that land, Charlotte's brother.

The Archbishop of York baptized the child; the King wept with emotion; and the Queen looked on feeling that there was no happiness in the world greater than this she was now experiencing.

The ceremony over Charlotte took her child in her arms and held him for a few minutes. Then she gave him to the governess that he might be put in his cradle. There he lay protected by a "Chinese Fence" which had been erected round the cradle so that no one could touch him.

Those who had attended the ceremony crowded about the cradle admiringly.

Charlotte thought of little but her baby. He was her life. She had no intention of passing him over to his governess and nurses. George agreed with her. He was all for simple living. They had a beautiful baby. Why should they not enjoy him?

Charlotte had a wax model made of him which was exactly like the child.

"Now," she said, "I shall always remember him as a baby."

A glass case was made to fit over it and she had placed it on her dressing table so that she could gaze at it whenever the original was not with her.

For three months this child was constantly in her thoughts; and soon after that she discovered that she was once more pregnant.

Wilkes and Liberty

While Charlotte was occupied with one baby and awaiting the arrival of another, the King was finding himself more and more unpleasantly involved in state affairs.

He had always believed that when Lord Bute achieved his ambition, which was to hold the highest post in the Government, all his troubles would be at an end. He had looked on Bute as a kind of god, omniscient, omnipotent; but it was not turning out that way.

Pitt had resigned and they had needed Pitt. And it seemed that everyone in the country was against Bute.

The King had said: "Those who are against Lord Bute are against me." That had been his doctrine; and now it followed, therefore, that the attacks on Bute were in a way attacks on the King.

This worried George; he would dream of disasters; and always in these he, personally, was being persecuted. He began to look for slights in all those who came near him and to imagine that he heard them tittering behind his back.

When he was with Charlotte and the baby, when he saw her growing more and more obviously pregnant with the second, he could forget this. He could revel in the quiet country life of Richmond whither Charlotte had gone so that the baby could enjoy the air; and there he felt at peace; but as soon as he was obliged to return to St. James's, which in the present uncertain state of affairs was very often, the uneasiness, the feeling of persecution returned.

It was difficult to speak of it to anyone. In the old days he would have consulted Lord Bute. But Bute had troubles of his own and in his inability to master them had made George realize that his idol had feet of clay.

*   *   *

Lord Bute was indeed uneasy. His big bite of success had given him acute indigestion. He was beginning to wonder whether it was not more exciting to plan and to strive towards a goal than to reach it. He was haunted by an uneasy fear that he might not be enough of a politician to handle the intricate state craft.

His great plan had been to secure peace. He believed in peace. He had been for Pitt's war policy in the beginning; but the country had had enough of war. In secret he had been entering into negotiations with the Court of Versailles through the Sardinian ambassador and to act alone and secretly was a dangerous manoeuvre. Charles II had managed it expertly and amorally while bringing good to his country, but John Stuart, Earl of Bute, was no Charles Stuart, King of England. He lacked the power for one thing as well as that careless genius. He was a worried man. He was at odds with George Grenville whose support he had relied on; and he was beginning to wonder whom he could trust to stand beside him.

His thoughts suddenly hit on Henry Fox; and this seemed a brilliant idea.

Fox would have to be lured from the Opposition to their side, but Bute believed that Fox was ambitious enough to accept the offer.

He sought an audience with the King and told him that he could not trust Grenville to support the new peace treaty and that he needed a strong man as leader of the House of Commons and it must be someone who was clever enough to carry it through.

"I see you have someone in mind," said George.

"Fox," answered Bute.

The King's face grew pink. Fox! Sarah's brother-in-law! He had hated Fox ever since he had given up Sarah, for he was sure that the man was jeering at him for allowing himself to be persuaded by his mother.

"He is the only man wily enough to do it."

"He never would. It would mean deserting his party, being disloyal to Pitt."

"All Fox would care about was being loyal to himself."

"But you really believe . . ."

"I am convinced it is the only course left to us."

Left to *us*! thought the King. So Bute was including him in his failure. He was shocked to find that for the first time in his life he was critical of his dear friend.

"We cannot afford to be squeamish," said Bute.

The King recoiled. This was shocking. Nothing seemed as it had in the past. Everything was turning against him. He could have wept.

"So Your Majesty gives your consent to my approaching Fox."

The King nodded, turning away.

Mr. Fox returned to Holland House cynically amused after his interview with Lord Bute. He would, he had said, consider the noble lord's proposals, but they did not fill him with any great enthusiasm. Lord Bute was almost pathetic in his desire to include Mr. Fox in his confidence. So my Lord Bute was learning sense after all.

. And His Majesty? Mr. Fox had asked. How did he feel about having Mr. Fox as the leader of the House of Commons?

His Majesty was as eager as Lord Bute, so said the lord.

Well, thought Mr. Fox, they must be anxious. George had not been able to look him in the face after jilting Sarah. Perhaps now that Sarah had married Bunbury he felt that little matter was settled. Bunbury in place of a king! *Mr.* Bunbury— who would become Sir Charles one day. Not much of a match to set beside that with a king. But Sarah had chosen him and seemed happy—although how long that would last Mr. Fox was not sure and his feelings were sceptical.

However, the important matter of the moment was not Sarah but the future of Henry Fox.

He found his wife in the drawing room and told her that he had just come from St. James's.

Lady Caroline raised her eyebrows.

"Bute is asking me to take over the leadership of the House of Commons."

"No!"

"Yes, my dear, yes. They are most eager to have me. Even His Majesty raises no objections."

"They are in trouble," said Lady Caroline. "Best leave them to it."

"H'm."

"You can't be considering this proposal?"

Fox nodded slowly. "For a while . . . perhaps it would not be such a bad thing."

"You know you promised you were going to give up politics."

"I haven't forgotten."

"But you are considering taking up this offer?"

He slipped his arm through hers. "For a while," he said. "I promise to make a fortune from it and retire with a high sounding title in a blaze of glory."

She laughed at him; they understood each other. He was a cynic; he loved money even more than power; he was only vulnerable where Lady Caroline was concerned. Ever since their romantic elopement they had been lovers.

So Caroline understood. It would be the finale; and when it was over they would live as she had planned they should—away from the anxieties of state . . . enjoying life.

Mr. Fox was granted an audience in the King's chamber at St. James's. As he expected, Bute was with George.

Mr. Fox's expression was a little sardonic. He was not the handsomest of men with his bulky figure and dark face; it was when he talked—not with Mr. Pitt's brilliant oratory, but with those sudden flashes of spontaneous wit—that he could even triumph over Mr. Pitt.

George looked at him with mild distaste.

Never would trust that fellow, he thought; but it was no use; they would have to have him. Lord Bute had explained that they were lost without a strong man to lead the Commons and make sure that the signing of the Peace of Paris was brought to a successful conclusion.

"So Mr. Fox, sir," said George, "Lord Bute tells me that you are ready to take on the leadership of the House of Commons."

"Reluctantly, Sire, but since it is the wish of Your Majesty . . ."

Fox smiled ironically, as though, thought George, the sly creature—so rightly named—knew how he hated to be forced into this position and was reminding him of it.

"Lord Bute feels that your services could be invaluable."

"And since Your Majesty is in agreement with him I offer them with all my heart."

"His Majesty and I agree that it is necessary to get these essential matters passed through the Commons and the Lords. At the moment there is great opposition. This must be wiped out. We must have a majority vote in favour of the peace."

"It is not an impossible achievement."

"We have powerful enemies."

Mr. Fox smiled what George thought of as the foxy smile.

"We can secure their support in the time honoured way."

"And that?"

"Bribes, Your Majesty. Bribes."

"Bribes! But this is something I cannot countenance."

"Then the measures will be defeated, and I can be of no use to you. But if Your Majesty and you, my lord, ask me to bring these measures safely through I tell you I can do it. And I give you the blunt remedy. Bribes!"

The King had turned away; Bute was watching him uneasily. Fox shrugged his shoulders.

"Your Majesty and you, my lord, cannot consider bribes? Then I can only say that I can be of no use to you. You will understand that in coming to your side I shall be in opposition to my old friends."

"Unpopularity is the price we must all pay for parliamentary service," said Bute bitterly.

"Not all, my lord. Consider Mr. Pitt. He cannot move through the City without a crowd of worshippers following his coach. They are ready to kneel and kiss the hem of his garment."

George frowned. He did not like blasphemy.

"As for myself," went on Fox, "I am ready to face unpopularity if I can do His Majesty essential service."

Bute said quickly: "His Majesty and I are eager to see this peace treaty carried through, no matter at what cost."

He waited with great apprehension for the King to speak, but George said nothing.

The King was depressed and disillusioned. His head ached; he wanted to get rid of Mr. Fox. He was certain that that odious man was laughing at him, jeering at him for having lost Sarah; he would go away and whisper about him to that wife of his, Sarah's sister, who was a little like Sarah.

Bute was watching him anxiously, thinking: He has such strange moods nowadays. One can never be sure what he is thinking.

But Fox was preparing to take his leave and to throw himself into his new task as leader of the House of Commons who knew exactly how to administer those bribes which would get unpopular measures passed through Parliament.

* * *

Mr. Fox was true to his word. He set about his new duties with alacrity. Bribes were offered in cash and in the form of titles; and places in the Government were given in order to form one which would be solidly behind Fox and obey his commands to vote as performing dogs do at the crack of the whip.

The Dukes of Devonshire, Newcastle and Grafton were expelled from their offices to make way for complacent men; and by December Fox was ready to go into the attack. Crowds surrounded the Houses of Parliament knowing what issues were at stake. Pitt was still the hero of the piece; Bute the black-hearted villain.

In the Lords Bute had to defend Fox's policy; and in the Commons Fox had to face Pitt, who had arrived, swathed in bandages, wrapped in flannel, suffering hideously from his old complaint of gout.

Pitt harangued the Government for three hours; he pointed out that their enemies had not yet been beaten; that if peace were made now they would recover and get to their feet again. Peace was a danger to England. Pitt's eloquence was, as ever, spellbinding, but his gout got the better of him and before he had delivered the final summing up he was obliged to retire to his seat. Then Fox rose and with reasoning, cold against Pitt's heat, logical against emotionalism, he defended the Government's policy for peace. France and Spain had agreed to great concessions, and England was suffering from acute taxation.

Listening, Pitt seemed to sense defeat; in any case he was in agony. While Fox was speaking he got up and hobbled from the House, thus leaving his supporters without a leader.

The motion was carried for the Government—319 to 65.

A triumph for the Government, for Fox's policy and for peace.

It was hardly to be expected that Pitt's supporters would quietly accept this state of affairs. It was known how the Government majority had been achieved. Bribery! was whispered throughout the streets; and the mob marched carrying a jackboot and petticoat which they ceremoniously hung on a gibbet.

The feeling against Bute was rising. He was the arch enemy, the Scot who had dared to try to rule England, the lover of the Princess Dowager who with her ruled the King, and therefore ruled England.

Even the King came in for his share of criticism and his popularity waned alarmingly.

When he went to call on his mother, crowds following his carriage shouted: "Going to have your napkins changed, George?" And: "When are you going to be weaned?"

George did not like it. It wounded him deeply; when he came back to his apartments he would weep and his headaches would begin; he felt that everyone was against him.

When he could escape to Richmond, to the quiet life with Charlotte, he felt better. But he could not be a King and live the quiet life of a country gentleman.

Bute was feeling ill; he had lost his swagger. It was an uncomfortable feeling, every time he went out, wondering whether the mob were going to set on him and murder him.

Power such as this had been his goal; now it was his it was very different from the dream.

And then John Wilkes went into the attack.

John Wilkes was the son of a malt distiller of Clerkenwell, who had started a paper, in conjunction with a friend named Charles Churchill, in which he determined to attack the anomalies of the day. He had a seat in Parliament and was an ardent supporter of Pitt. As a man who must be in the thick of any controversy, the conflict between Pitt and the Government, under Fox's leadership, was irresistible to him.

Wilkes was an extremely ugly man; his features were irregular and his squint diabolical; to counterbalance this he had developed a very keen wit and courtly manners, and with these he endeavoured to bring down what he called the unworthy mighty from their seats. The first of these was of course Lord Bute.

As a young man he had been sent on the Grand Tour; on his return his parents had wished him to marry Mary Mead the daughter of a London grocer—a very rich one—and he had obliged. The marriage was a failure. Poor Mary could not keep pace with her husband's wit and brilliance. Wilkes came well out of the affair for he acquired not only a large slice of his wife's fortune but the custody of his daughter, Mary, who was the one person in his life for whom he cared.

His great energy had had to find an outlet and he joined societies of ill repute such as the Hell Fire Club and Sir

Francis Dashwood's club, the latter known as the Order of St. Francis. The motive of these clubs was profligacy, and obscenity, all to be conducted in the most witty manner. The members of the Order of St. Francis met in a ruined Cistercian Abbey at Medmenham and there indulged in practices with which they tried to shock each other, by mocking the Church, and they were said on one occasion to have given the sacrament to a monkey.

Membership of this society had brought Wilkes influential friends, among whom were Pitt's supporters, Sir Francis Dashwood and Lord Sandwich, and through them Wilkes became the High Sheriff of Buckinghamshire; and after an unsuccessful attempt to enter Parliament for Berwick-on-Tweed he was elected for Aylesbury.

He was not a great success in Parliament, lacking the necessary eloquence; but his wit and humour secured him many friends; he was a most entertaining companion; he even made fun of his ugliness. He had never, he said, like Narcissus, hung over a stream and admired his countenance; one would not find him stealing sly glances at a mirror, a habit he had noticed among those to whom Nature had been a little more kind when dealing out good features. He made a cult of his ugliness. He was extremely virile; he had a deep need of sexual satisfaction; and in a short time he had gone through his fortune and his wife's and was looking for a means of making money.

He discovered a talent for journalism; it was an exciting profession. To express one's views in print, to hear them quoted, to be a power in the land—that was exactly what Wilkes wanted.

If there was one man in the country whom Wilkes wished to send toppling from his pedestal, that man was Lord Bute. Bute was all that he was not—handsome, pompous and a lover to whom the Dowager Princess of Wales had been faithful for years; Wilkes was envious; he was cleverer than Bute, but Bute was a rich man and he a poor one. Bute had become head of the Government and he, brilliant Wilkes, was a failure in Parliament.

And now Bute was forcing his desires on the country and he had done it through bribes. Here was a subject for a journalist.

One of the papers, *The Monitor*, was criticizing the Government, but it was a scrappy little sheet, hardly worthy to be called a newspaper; and in retaliation Lord Bute had founded two papers, *The Briton* and *The Auditor*, and had set up the novelist Tobias Smollett as editor of the former. Under brilliant editorship *The Briton* was attracting some attention and was helping to put the case for Bute, who was becoming less unpopular as a result. This was something which Wilkes could not endure. He went to his crony Charles Churchill, a man who lived as disreputably as Wilkes himself, had separated from his wife as Wilkes had, and had made some reputation as a poet.

"We should found a rival paper to *The Briton*," he suggested. "In it we could keep the country informed on Mr. Bute."

"What could we tell them that they don't already know?"

That made Wilkes laugh. "We'll find plenty, never fear. Bribes! And what a gallant gentleman! I'll swear the people would like to know how very well he performs in the Princess's bed."

"Wilkes, you're a devil," cried Churchill.

"And doing you the honour of accepting you as the same, my friend. Now to business."

In a very short time they were ready to bring out their paper.

"What shall we call it?" Churchill wanted to know.

Wilkes was thoughtful; then a lewd smile spread across his ugly face. "Why not the *North* Briton? After all it is going to be dedicated to the destruction of a gentleman from across the Border. Yes, that is it. *The North Briton*."

And so *The North Briton* came into existence.

From its first number it was a success. There was nothing the people liked better than to see the great ridiculed, and when it was done with wit and humour it appealed more than ever.

Wilkes saw that it was presented, and people were buying it in their thousands. Fox was represented as Bute's faithful henchman. They had brought about their measures and how? Wilkes was hiding nothing. He had the information at his fingertips. He knew how the peace treaty had been brought safely through the Commons and Lords. Bribery! Bribery and Corruption was something which Wilkes and Churchill in *The North Briton* were going to expose to public view. Wilkes and Churchill were for Liberty. Freedom of action; freedom of speech. That was what they stood for; and they were no respectors of persons either. No one was going to be considered if he offended against the laws of decency laid down by Wilkes and Churchill. And Bribery was an offence which made them cry out Shame.

But the chief butt was the Scotsman. Very, very handsome, he was. He had a wife and numerous children. But he still had time and energy to serve the Princess Dowager. Did the people realize they had a boudoir genius in their midst?

Another method of attack was a more serious one. George III was likened to Edward III, the Dowager Princess of Wales to Queen Isabella. And Bute had to have a part in this drama so he was of course Roger Mortimer.

Together Wilkes and Churchill concocted a parody of Mountfort's *Fall of Mortimer* which they published with a dedication to that brilliant bedchamber performer, Lord Bute. The sales of *The North Briton* shot up; and Wilkes realized that this was the most amusing, the most exciting and the quickest way to change his financial position. It had been a stroke of genius to start the paper. All he had to remember was that they must stop at nothing; no one should be safe from their vitriolic pens. The simple fact was that the people loved scurrilous gossip; and the more shocking and the higher placed the people involved, the more the public liked it.

"They shall have what they want," sang out Wilkes; and proceeded to give it to them.

Henry Fox seeing the way trends were going, and by allying himself with Bute he was naturally catching some of the odium which was showered on that nobleman, saw no reason why he should continue in office.

Caroline was urging him to get out. He had promised, had he not, that as soon as he could do so, he would. He had told her that this last little fling was too important to be ignored. Well, he had done what was asked of him; he had shown them how to carry through the terms which Pitt had so violently rejected, so what further purpose could be served by remaining in office?

Walking in the grounds of Holland House, his arm through that of his wife, revelling in the signs of spring all around them, Henry Fox told her that she was right. He agreed with her.

Now that that odious man Wilkes had come out with his scandal sheet, no one was spared—certainly not those in high places. The Government was going to sway to the attack of ridicule.

If he were going to get out in that blaze of glory, then he should do so now, and the price of past services would be a title.

"What do you think of Lord Holland, my dear?" he asked, smiling complacently about the park.

"I think it would be ideal," Caroline told him; "but only if you leave the Government and come into retirement so that we can spend more time together which would give me great pleasure and enable you to escape from the mudslinging of that hideous Wilkes, the general scorn with which the Government is beginning to be regarded, and the growing unpopularity of my Lord Bute."

"Wise woman," commented Fox. "Tomorrow I go to see my lord and with him to the King. I doubt not soon that your husband will be a noble lord."

"The sooner the better since it means your escape from the Government."

Mr. Fox presented himself to Lord Bute.

Poor Bute! He was certainly losing his youthful looks. Being head of a government most definitely did not suit him. Fox laughed inwardly with grim satisfaction. These ambitious men who saw themselves as they were not! Let Bute go back to cosseting the Princess Dowager; he was very good at that. But countries needed more than cosseting.

"My lord, I have come to tell you that my health is failing, and as I have done that which I gave my word to do, I can see no point in remaining longer in the Government."

Bute was alarmed. While he had had Fox's support he had felt secure. Crafty as his name, this man was a brilliant politician, who could be called a worthy rival to Pitt. Bute had clung to high office fervently knowing that this man was supporting him; but now the sly fellow was withdrawing that support. He had had enough.

"This is ill news," began Bute.

"Nay, nay," cried Fox. "A man who is not in the best of health is a poor henchman. You, my lord, with that cleverness which has placed you in your present position, have no need of a poor sick fox. I have made up my mind to retire."

"This cannot be final."

"Alas, yes. My health demands it. I have promised my

wife that today I would come to you and tell you that I intend to offer my resignation. I can be of no further use to you. Therefore I shall go with the title you promised me, to show the people that I am considered worthy of my reward.''

"Title . . ." began Bute.

"Baron Holland of Foxley, Wiltshire," said Fox. "And I should hope to retain the post of paymaster."

Bute was astounded. How like Fox to ask for his title and a post which was almost a sinecure and brought in a considerable income.

"I think even my enemies would agree," said Fox smiling, "that the country owes me this."

The King was deeply disturbed. He had read Wilkes's sheet. Those terrible accusations against his mother and Lord Bute! Did everyone know of them except himself? What a simpleton he had been! All those years when they had been together he had thought they were just good friends. And they had been living together as husband and wife; and the whole world knew . . . except George, and was doubtless laughing at George for his simplicity.

The King buried his face in his hands. There were times when he felt that the whole world was against him. He could trust no one—not even his mother; not even Bute—those two on whom he had relied all his life.

Oh, yes, he could rely on Charlotte; because Charlotte was only a young girl who knew nothing of state affairs. She should never know. She should remain shut away from the Court which was wicked, anyway. Charlotte should retain her innocence; she should go on bearing his children. In August they would have another. Two already and not married two years! Yes, Charlotte was all he cared to think about these days. He was beginning to hate politics and mistrust politicians. But if he were going to be a good King he must understand these matters. The manner in which the peace had been passed through Parliament appalled him. Bribes! And that cynical Mr. Fox arranging it all!

What pleasure to escape to Richmond when he could; to walk with Charlotte in the gardens there; to sit beside the baby's cradle and marvel at the fact that he was such a lusty healthy little fellow.

And now Lord Bute was bringing Fox to him to tell him that the minister wished to offer his resignation, and as a reward for his services he would accept a Barony and become Baron Holland; he wished to retain the post of paymaster.

"So you are leaving the Government, Mr. Fox, sir," said the King disapprovingly.

"Your Majesty, my health has deteriorated and I am in no position to do honour to the high post which Your Majesty in your goodness bestowed on me."

George felt sick with annoyance and disappointment. Mr. Fox was lucky. When he wanted to extricate himself from a difficult situation he only had to resign; and get a title for doing it.

There was nothing to be done. They could only let him go.

On the 19th April the King opened Parliament and four days later number 45 of *The North Briton* appeared.

In this Wilkes commented on the Peace of Hubertsberg—which had followed the Peace of Paris—as "the most abandoned instance of ministerial effrontery ever attempted to be imposed on mankind."

George read the paper, for everyone was now reading *The North Briton*, anxiously scrutinizing it to make sure that they were not being ridiculed in it; and he found that Wilkes had dealt with him personally.

"The King's speech," wrote Wilkes, "has always been considered by the legislature and by the public at large as the speech of the Minister."

This was an attempt to imply that he had no intention of attacking the King but was blaming the chief minister, George Grenville.

"Every friend of this country," he went on, "must lament that a Prince of so many great and amiable qualities, whom England truly reveres, can be brought to give the sanction of his sacred name to the most odious measures and to the most unjustifiable public declarations from a throne ever renowned for truth, honour and unsullied virtue."

When George read this he was not in the least taken in by the implication of loyalty. This was a sneer at himself, suggesting that he was at best a puppet.

He was suffering from one of his headaches and he kept repeating the phrases of that article over and over again in his mind.

He wanted to get right away. He was weary of his office. If only he could be like Mr. Fox and get away to the pleasure of *his* wife's company. But he was the King; he could not resign.

George Grenville was asking for an audience. He came in clutching *The North Briton* and it was easy to see that he was as angry as the King.

"We cannot allow this to pass, Your Majesty."

"So I thought," agreed the King. "We are submitted to insult, but what can we do?"

"We can send a copy of *The North Briton* to the Law officers of the Crown. This, in my opinion, is a seditious libel."

"Let it be done," said George. "It is time we took some action against this man Wllkes."

Lord Halifax and the Earl of Egremont as Secretaries of State were only too ready to issue the warrant which Grenville demanded.

This gave permission for a strict and diligent search to be made in the offices of the seditious and treasonable paper *The North Briton* and for the authors of seditious libel to be arrested.

Halifax's secretary arrived at Wilkes's house one night and read the warrant to him, but Wilkes pointed out that his name was not mentioned on the warrant and therefore it was not legal. So forcefully did he argue that the secretary retired, but the next morning he had presented himself at the offices of *The North Briton*.

Wilkes was arguing with him when Charles Churchill came in and looking straight at Churchill, Wilkes said: "Good day, Mr. Thompson. How is Mrs. Thompson? Does she dine in the country?"

Churchill immediately guessed what was happening and that Wilkes was warning him, so he replied: "Mrs. Thompson is in good health, sir. I merely called to enquire after your health before joining her in the country."

And accepting Wilkes's kindest regards for Mrs. Thompson, Churchill disappeared and without delay went to the country to avoid arrest.

Wilkes's arguments were waved aside and he was taken away protesting that he would sue them all for a breach of the law.

London was in an uproar. Wilkes was arrested. This was a

threat against the freedom of the individual; freedom of speech was in jeopardy and Wilkes was the defender of Liberty.

Bute engaged Hogarth to draw a derisive cartoon of Wilkes, making him look even uglier than he was, so that it could be circulated throughout the City. Churchill, from a few miles out of the town, was able to retaliate with lampoons and songs about Bute and his followers. He made it clear to the people that Hogarth was in the pay of Bute, that he was an artist who worked for those who would pay him most, and his views were therefore worthless.

When, in May, Wilkes was brought up for trial he claimed privilege as a Member of Parliament and when he was released by Chief Justice Pratt, this was one of the biggest defeats the Government had suffered.

Arrogant and impudent Wilkes returned to his offices. Now he was going to fight them, and his first step was to issue writs against those who had caused his arrest.

The City waited in breathless amusement for what would happen next. The jeers at Lord Bute were more offensive than ever; the King was often received in a hostile silence. Wilkes was the defender of Liberty and the people's hero.

All through that trying summer George escaped to Richmond whenever possible, but by the beginning of August it was time for Charlotte to come back to St. James's to prepare for the birth of the child.

Charlotte had been taking her English lessons regularly and had progressed considerably. Her accent was decidedly German but she was no longer in the irritating position of being unable to understand what people around her were saying. Not that she was allowed to talk to many people. There were her women who attended to her needs but Schwellenburg had installed herself at their head and in spite of that warning they could not shift her from the position she had chosen for herself. There were so often those occasions when Charlotte could only express herself in German; then either Schwellenburg or Haggerdorn were needed.

Charlotte was aware of the manner in which she was restricted, but reminded herself that she had been pregnant most of the time she had been in England.

Occasionally she heard scraps of conversation. She knew that Elizabeth Chudleigh, that bold lady-in-waiting, was the mistress of the Duke of Kingston, which surprised her, for the

Duke had given her the impression that he was a scholarly man and being so much older than Elizabeth hardly the sort of lover one would have expected her to take. But perhaps it was his title which attracted her, although that was not much help to her as he did not marry her.

She wondered why Elizabeth was allowed to remain at Court, for her conduct was a little disreputable.

She mentioned this to George who said he agreed with her. His mother though had recommended her and might be offended if Elizabeth were dismissed without consulting her.

"When next we meet I shall mention the matter," said Charlotte.

And George, who was preoccupied, merely nodded. Poor George, he did seem to be weighed down by his cares now. But he was delighted with her pregnancy of course.

"Why," she laughed, "I have little time to see England. All the time I have been here I have either been going to have a baby or having one."

"Which is very laudable," added the King.

Yes, thought Charlotte, but there should be a little breathing space between babies.

When she next saw the Princess Dowager she did mention Elizabeth Chudleigh but the Princess Dowager looked confused and muttered that she thought the woman was a good servant.

"She is a little frivolous," suggested Charlotte.

"Most of these women are."

"Doubtless you do not know that she is the Duke of Kingston's mistress."

"There are always scandals." The Princess Dowager flushed a little. "I doubt not that few of us are spared."

It was very strange, thought Charlotte, because the Princess Dowager was usually so strict. When she, Charlotte, with George had attended balls after the birth of little George, the Princess had expressed her disapproval of such frivolity—even to celebrate the birth of a Prince of Wales. Now she was being very lenient to Miss Chudleigh. And when Charlotte recalled Miss Chudleigh's arrogant and altogether complacent manner it made one wonder whether she had not some hold over the Princess.

What a strange thought! Women get strange ideas during pregnancies, she told herself; but she remembered that later when she heard Elizabeth say something about the King's

fondness for Quakers and to say it with a little derisive laugh
which could mean almost anything.

Then Charlotte remembered the Lord Mayor's Show which
they had watched from the Barclay house in Cheapside. Yes,
the King *was* undoubtedly fond of Quakers.

St. James's! That grim dark prison of a palace. How
different from dear Richmond. What a pity she could not go
there to await the arrival of her second child. But no, the
child must be born in London; he might be king if anything
happened to little George—which God forbid. But Kings and
Queens had to be prepared for these contingencies.

All through the hot August days she waited. George was
frequently with her and often seemed worried; in fact he had
never been completely well since that illness he had had
before the birth of little George. Politics worried him. There
was always some trouble and now it was that ugly Mr.
Wilkes. Charlotte did not know what the trouble was all about,
only that it was trouble. She tried to learn something of it during
her brief sessions with her ladies who often disagreed together
about the rights and wrongs of the affair. And when she tried
to broach it with George he indulgently told her that she must
not bother her head with this unpleasantness; it would be bad
for the child. As for the Princess Dowager she said that the
King would doubtless tell her all he wished her to know.

Where was the determined girl who had written to King
Frederick? She seemed to have become lost in the mother.
When Charlotte had first come to England she had imagined herself ruling this country with her husband; she had
promised herself that she would try to understand state affairs
so that she could be of use to him.

But she was shut out from these affairs.

When my baby is born, she promised herself, it will be
different.

On the 16th August, one year and four days after the birth
of his brother George, Prince of Wales, Charlotte gave birth
to her second son.

He was a perfect child, strong and lusty. Now everyone
was saying that Charlotte was going to be a real breeder. Two
healthy boys in two years of marriage. What better sign than
that.

The King was delighted. His cares seemed to drop from

him. Nothing seemed to matter as he held the boy in his arms. Wilkes could rant and rave all he liked; his government could plague him; his disappointment in Bute was bitter, but he could endure that too when he thought of his growing family. Two boys and a wife who would bear him many more, he was sure. He was a lucky man.

The little boy was named Frederick Augustus and very soon he and his mother, with little brother George, were all enjoying the Richmond air.

A Wedding in the Family

It was hardly to be expected that Wilkes would not cause more trouble and that he was determined to do this became obvious during that autumn and winter.

The storm arose when he published an obscene poem called *An Essay on Woman* which was a burlesque on Pope's *Essay on Man*. There seemed to be little doubt that Wilkes himself had had a hand in the writing of this and as there were only twelve copies printed, he had apparently meant them only for circulation among those of his friends who delighted in pornography.

One of the copies came into the possession of Lord Sandwich. When Sandwich and Wilkes were both members of the Medmenham Circle they had been friends until Sandwich had one day called to the Devil to appear before him. Wilkes—knowing this was a habit of Sandwich's—had previously acquired an ape which he had dressed up to look like the Devil and just as Sandwich called out to the Devil to appear, Wilkes arranged that the ape should be let in. Sandwich was so alarmed that he turned and fled in abject terror—to the delight of Wilkes. Discovering the trick Wilkes had played on him Sandwich never forgave him, and when the *Essay on Woman* came into his hands he saw an opportunity of getting his revenge.

Only a few months earlier Sandwich had become one of the Secretaries of State and had changed his mode of life since the days when he had been one of the leading spirits of Medmenham. Now, expressing his horror that such a hideously obscene and blasphemous work should have been written and printed, he read parts of it to the House of Lords. Wilkes had written notes in the margin of the essay which he had signed with the Bishop of Warburton's name because Warburton had added notes in the margins of Pope's *Essay on Man:* and when Warburton heard that his name had been used on this foul document he rose in his wrath and castigated Wilkes whom he compared with the Devil. Then he apologized to the Devil for putting him in the same company as Wilkes. So fiercely did the Bishop rage that even those who had been inclined to support Wilkes turned against him. Wilkes had gone too far this time; and when Warburton suggested that proceedings should be taken against Wilkes, charging him with blasphemy, it was agreed that this should be done.

Meanwhile an attack was being made on Wilkes in the Commons, and during this the member for Camelford, Samuel Martin, referred to him as a coward and a scoundrel. Wilkes declared that he had no alternative but to challenge Martin to a duel.

Now the drama was at its height. Everyone waited for the outcome; and when Wilkes met Martin in Hyde Park and was wounded by him, popular excitement grew.

The rumour spread that Wilkes's enemies had deliberately commanded Martin to wound Wilkes; and the mobs were out. Always eager for excitement, they paraded the streets and when one of the city Sheriffs, on order from Parliament, proceeded to burn number 45 of *The North Briton* before the Royal Exchange, a crowd gathered to prevent him. *The North Briton* was captured and while one section of the crowd carried it through the streets in triumph, another remained by the fire to throw in jackboots and a petticoat or two to show who they thought were behind all the trouble.

Wilkes meanwhile, on pretext of being wounded in the duel with Martin, remained in his house and did not leave it although he was summoned to appear at the bar of the House of Commons to answer for his sins.

This Wilkes had no intention of doing, and when he saw that he could no longer avoid appearing before his judges he slipped over to the Continent where he fell in with a well-known courtesan named Corradini with whom he set up house. Friends of his, determined to support Wilkes and the cause of freedom, sent him money; and Wilkes settled down for a few months of pleasure, amused to think how he had outwitted them all on the other side of the Channel.

*   *   *

Wilkes's departure did not make matters easier. There was trouble over the tax which Dashwood as Chancellor of the Exchequer proposed should be levied on cider, and a clash in the Commons when George Grenville sought to defend the measure pointing out the necessity of imposing new taxes.

"Since there was such objection to the cider tax," said Grenville plaintively, "he wished gentlemen would tell him where to lay them."

Pitt rose and imitating Grenville's voice repeated the words of an old song: "Gentle shepherd, tell me where."

Grenville furiously demanded if it was to be permitted that gentlemen were to be treated with contempt. At which Pitt made a deep bow and hobbled out of the House. From then on the mob shouted after Grenville whenever he appeared; and he was known as the Gentle Shepherd.

This was typical of the day. The people seized on anything that caused ridicule and raised a smile. There was trouble and laughter side by side; and the mob was always ready to make a carnival of some poor politician's misfortune.

But their greatest target was Bute. No one could take the place of him. If his carriage appeared they would leave everything to follow it. Some were armed with cudgels; and the Princess Dowager lived in terror that something would happen to her lover. When he came to her she would embrace him warmly and tell him that she trembled to think of what could befall him.

"I cannot endure this," she said. "I am terrified."

Bute passed his hand over his brow. How he had changed! In the old days he had believed everything was possible; now he accepted defeat.

"Nothing is what I thought it would be. It is due to Pitt. If we had been able to keep Pitt all would have been well." He grimaced. "I am no Pitt, Augusta," he said.

"That man!" she said. "He deserted us."

Bute smiled and taking her hand kissed it. "So loyal. I don't deserve you, Augusta. Let us face the truth. I have failed."

"What nonsense! You don't know the meaning of failure."

"If you had been with me in the carriage this afternoon; if you had heard the shouts of the mob . . . seen their menacing faces . . ."

She shuddered. "Please don't talk of it."

"It exists, Augusta, my love. You see, I thought I could be

a great politician. The fact is, I can't. I haven't the genius for it . . . like Pitt and Fox. Men like that . . . they start up out of the crowd and they make the rest of us look like dwarfs in comparison.''

"My dear, you are overwrought. If I could do what I wished to that senseless mob . . .''

"They are not entirely senseless. They are aware of greatness. You have heard them cheer Pitt.''

"Don't talk of that man. But for him . . .''

"My dearest, he is a great politician. Let us face it. The country needs him at the head of affairs. While I am there I am bringing discredit to the King. Do you know that since I have been in office his popularity has waned considerably. And always they talk of us.''

"Oh, my dear, what do you propose to do about it?''

"Resign. Advise the King to call back Pitt and try to make some arrangement with him.''

Augusta put her face against his coat. It was not what they had planned. She and he had believed they would rule the country together; they would guide the King. But it had all gone wrong somewhere. It had started when Mr. Pitt refused to be guided and showed so clearly that if he were going to take a part in leading the country he would be in sole command.

To give up their plan was defeat. And yet if she wished to keep her lover safe, if she wished their relationship to continue in a dignified way, she must take him away from the glare of publicity.

What joy it would be not to have to fret as to what was happening to him every time he was in the streets! She wanted power; but she was a woman who most of all wanted a happy domestic life. She looked upon Bute as her husband—in fact more so than she had ever regarded Frederick.

His safety came first, and the ability to go on living together as husband and wife as they had for so many years.

"Yes,'' she said, "go to George and tell him that you can no longer continue.''

Bute embraced her warmly.

"To be with you . . . to have you care for me as you do . . . that is enough for any man,'' he said.

George showed no great surprise nor disappointment as he listened to Lord Bute.

"My health will not stand the strain,'' explained Bute.

"By remaining in office I can only do a disservice to Your Majesty."

George looked at his dearest friend with lack-lustre eyes. Who would ever have thought to hear him say that! Bute, always so full of vitality; the man to whom he had turned in his youthful dilemmas. And now he was confessing to age, ill-health and inability to hold his post.

"I believe you to be right," said the King.

Bute was hurt that George should take it so calmly. He had expected a show of deep regret, even pleading that he would continue in office. It was disconcerting. But George had changed lately. He too was disillusioned.

"If Pitt would take over the leadership," began Bute.

But the King shook his head. "He dictates to me. I will not be dictated to."

"Grenville is the man, then," went on Bute.

"Yes, I think it must be George Grenville."

Bute took his leave and reported to the Princess Dowager that the King had taken his decision to retire very calmly. He felt that George was slipping away from them and clearly believed that he could manage very well without them.

"You don't think," said the Princess Dowager, "that Charlotte is weaning him from us?"

"Charlotte! But she is never allowed to take part in anything."

"No, but he goes to Richmond and it is all very cosily domestic there. She is now speaking English tolerably well and can understand what is going on around her. She is not the meek creature some believe her to be. You remember that letter she wrote to Frederick of Prussia. Do you think a girl who could write such a letter would be content to remain in the background?"

"No, I do not. I think there is much in what you say."

"And he goes to her whenever possible. He seems to have an *affection* for her. These babies of hers . . . they make a bond between them. She is not yet pregnant again—or if she is I have not heard of it, but she had these two boys in a very short time, and the King is delighted with her. Oh, she's plain enough—but George was always amenable. Yes, I think Charlotte might well be influencing him."

"He has always said that he would never be influenced by women."

"Poor George," smiled Augusta. "He does not always understand himself."

The Princess Dowager called on the Queen at Richmond. Charlotte was looking well and told the Princess that she found life at Richmond to her taste, and it was very pleasant when the King could spare time from his duties to stay with his family.

The Princess studied her daughter-in-law carefully. No further signs of pregnancy. A pity! That would keep Charlotte occupied.

She was conducted to the nurseries where she was delighted with the children. Little George was bright-eyed and, his mother assured her, very intelligent. He was over a year old now and really taking notice. His nurses said that they had never known such a bright child.

The Princess Dowager sat nodding like an old mandarin. Mother's talk, she thought.

"And the baby?"

"Oh, little Fred is adorable."

"I wonder if he will be like his grandfather," smiled Augusta, softened by the charm of the children. "Oh, but he is just like his dear papa. Does George think so?"

"George thinks he takes a little after me," admitted Charlotte.

God help him! thought the Princess. No, he has his father's big eyes and chin. How could George see that crocodile mouth in such an enchanting little creature! Like Charlotte indeed! If George thought that he must be growing very fond and foolish.

That brought her to the matter uppermost in her mind and which had urged her to take the journey out to Richmond.

Was Charlotte beginning to influence George so that he no longer felt so affectionate towards his mother and Lord Bute? It was very likely.

"Dear George, the Government is so tiresome."

"Oh, yes. He was most upset over that horrible Mr. Wilkes."

He *is* talking to her, thought the Princess.

"These dreadful people who will not let us live in peace."

"And Mr. Grenville tries the King sorely," went on Charlotte. "George says that when Mr. Grenville has wearied him for two hours he looks at his watch to see if he cannot tire him for one hour more." Charlotte laughed, but was sober

almost immediately. "But the Government is most trying.
The King would be happier if Mr. Pitt would come back, but
of course Mr. Pitt never does anything except on his own
terms."

"So the King discusses these matters with you?"

Charlotte put her head on one side. It would not be truthful
to say that was so, but it was very tempting to do so. The
King answered her very briefly if she attempted to discuss
politics. She learned most of the news from her women. Yet
she hated to admit this to the Princess.

"These affairs are of the utmost importance," said Charlotte
evasively.

So this is the answer, thought the Princess. We are being
relegated to a back seat while he confides in this silly young
girl who knows nothing of state affairs in this country whatsoever. She is advising the King while he turns away from his
own mother and . . . her dearest friend and his.

Charlotte had too high an opinion of herself. She did not
know how *reluctant* George had been to marry her. She did
not know how he had hankered after Sarah Bunbury—Lennox
that was. She thought that when she had come over here
George had taken one look at her and fallen in love with her.
No wonder the silly little creature gave herself airs.

The Princess Dowager would not allow that.

"I am glad that you are happy with George, my dear," she
said quietly but in a deadly voice. "We were a little anxious
. . . just at first. I daresay you have heard about his obsession
with Sarah Lennox. There is bound to be tittle-tattle."

"Sarah Lennox . . ." echoed Charlotte, wrinkling her brow.

"Married Charles Bunbury about the time of the King's
illness. A pretty, empty-headed creature."

Charlotte remembered her at the wedding. The bridesmaid
who was the most beautiful girl she had ever seen. And
George had looked at her . . . longingly. She felt suddenly
sad.

"He wanted to marry her. It was quite impossible of
course. Then he saw sense and . . . he behaved as he knew a
king should. And how right it was. Here you are with two
beautiful babies. They couldn't be more beautiful, I am sure."

Charlotte sat still thinking of it. The wedding; the sacrifice
he had had to make. Yet he had never mentioned it; he had
never been unfaithful to her, she was sure. Poor George, to
have been robbed of his dreams as Christina had been of hers.

She often thought of Christina. Only Christina had no one; George had been presented with Charlotte; and he had married because it was his duty to marry; and they had two beautiful children. Sarah Lennox could not have produced more beautiful children. That was what the Princess was telling her.

She heard herself say: "It is sad for royal people that their wives and husbands should be chosen for them."

"It is all for the best. I had never seen my husband until I came to England, and it all turned out very happily. We had our children and then . . ."

And then, she thought, he died and I turned to the man I loved. Yes, she had been fortunate, but it was Charlotte and George she must think of.

"And now, my dear, you have your children."

Charlotte picked up the baby and held him tightly against her. All was well. George was a good husband; and she had the boys. Why should she care about Sarah Lennox?

"I am sure," went on the Princess, "that George has forgotten Sarah Lennox . . . just as he did the Quaker girl."

"The Quaker!"

"Oh, it is nothing. Past history one might say. But there was rather an unfortunate little matter."

"A Quaker girl," repeated Charlotte.

"Has he ever talked to you of her?"

"Never."

"Nor of Sarah Lennox?"

"No."

"Then he would not wish it to be known that I have mentioned these women."

"I shall not tell him."

"He would be distressed if you spoke of them. He always said that he would manage his own affairs."

Charlotte was silent.

"George was never one to like *interference*," went on the Princess Dowager. Was the message sinking in? Did she understand that George was capable of liking other women, that he was not the dull unadventurous husband she had no doubt been thinking him? Was she beginning to see that if she wished to keep George's affection she must not *interfere*?

The baby began to cry and Charlotte hastily picked him up. She had dismissed the nurse while she showed her children to the Princess Dowager and had the pleasure of knowing herself in command of them. It was not often so.

The baby was immediately soothed.

What had she to fear, she asked herself, when she had her little boys?

Sarah Lennox was safely married and out of the way; but she did wonder about the Quaker, for she had noticed on several occasions that George was deeply affected by them.

The Princess went back to her apartments well pleased with her interview. There she sent for her daughters, Augusta and Caroline Matilda. As they came into the apartment she thought how sulky Augusta looked nowadays; it was always so with princesses who were unmarried. Augusta was a year older than George and was naturally resentful that she had not been born a boy.

In fact, thought the Princess Dowager, perhaps Augusta would have made a better sovereign. They should find a husband for her before it is too late. Perhaps now that dear Lord Bute was free of his cares it would be more like it used to be and they could plan together.

Caroline Matilda, aged thirteen, showed signs of being the beauty of the family. She was very very fair, as the whole family were. The blue eyes, the fair skin, the shining hair—so pleasant in youth. But they must watch that she did not become too fat—a family failing.

Husbands, thought the Princess Dowager, for them both. She would certainly speak to Lord Bute.

She embraced the girls coolly—she had not much affection to show to any but Lord Bute and the King—and made a sign for them to sit down.

"I have visited the Queen at Richmond."

"Domestic bliss," sneered Augusta.

Poor girl, thought her mother. She is very envious. Yes, certainly a husband.

"She is happy enough with her two babies."

"What a fortunate thing that she happens to be fruitful. She has little else to offer."

"I don't think she's so bad," put in Caroline Matilda; and was silenced by looks from both mother and sister.

"She is getting a little arrogant, I fancy. I believe she imagines she advises the King."

"That explains why there is all this trouble with the Government," said Augusta, who enjoyed being spiteful.

"I am sure the King would never take her advice," said the Princess Dowager coolly.

"Then there is some other reason why the people are so dissatisfied."

How much did her daughter know? wondered the Princess Dowager. Did she know that the people paraded through the streets with jackboots and petticoats, that they made bonfires in which to burn them, erected gibbets on which to hang them?

"The people are never satisfied," said the Princess Dowager. "I want you two to be watchful of the Queen. She is not very old—not much older than Caroline Matilda here. She could be led astray."

The Princesses' eyes widened and their mother hurried on: "I mean that she could listen to gossip. She could become indiscreet and she might attempt to influence the King."

"George always said that he would never let a woman influence him. But what of Sarah Lennox?"

"I do not wish you to speak disrespectfully of the King because he happens to be your brother."

"But Your Highness will face the truth I am sure," said the Princess Augusta. "Everyone knows George was madly in love with Sarah Lennox."

"The woman is safely married now. Though I pity Bunbury. I do not wish you girls to talk of that unfortunate affair. But I do wish you to draw out Charlotte as much as possible. Discover whether the King really does confide in her . . ."

"In other words spy on her," said the Princess Augusta, "as you commanded us to do on the King when he was considering marrying Sarah Lennox."

"Nonsense," said her mother. "I merely wish you to *help* Charlotte."

The Princess Augusta was smiling sardonically. And in front of Caroline Matilda! There was no doubt about it, thought the Princess Dowager, her elder daughter was getting out of hand. She was becoming sardonic and cynical and very much aware that she was growing into an old maid.

She had not only Charlotte to worry about, but her own Augusta.

She dismissed her daughters; and decided that since Augusta was becoming so uncomfortable they certainly must find a husband for her.

The Princess Dowager did not wish the King to forget that although Lord Bute was no longer the head of the Government she still regarded him as the chief family adviser, and when she called on the King to speak to him about his sister's unmarried state she asked Lord Bute to meet her in the King's apartments.

They did not travel together; that would have been inviting the mob to hurl obscenities at them; it was bad enough now to go through the streets and see the jackboot and petticoat paraded or some of the posters which had been put up in prominent places.

The Princess liked to travel as quietly as possible and she knew that Lord Bute did too.

The King received them with affection, but not that deference he had shown in the past. She had no need now to tell him to be a king, as she constantly had been obliged to in the old days. George was very much aware of the burdens of state and wanted no one to remind him of them.

"It is of your sister Augusta that I have come to talk to you," said the Princess. "We have been discussing her future and we really feel it is time you did something for her."

"But what should be done?" asked George.

"She needs a husband. She grows more waspish every day. Don't forget she is a year older than you. We must do everything possible to find her a husband."

"It is not easy to find a Protestant Prince."

"That has always been the trouble. But we must marry her to someone. She needs marriage I am sure and she is becoming a little tiresome here at Court."

"Poor Augusta!" said George. "Certainly we must do what we can for her."

The Princess Dowager sighed. "She feels it deeply being the eldest and not born a boy. I shall never forget the night she was born and how we hurried from Hampton to St. James's because your father hoped she would be a boy and it was imperative that the heir to the throne be born there. There was nothing ready for us and the beds were unaired. Poor Augusta had to be wrapped in a tablecloth."

Both Lord Bute and the King had heard this story many times before, but they listened sympathetically.

"And when the Queen . . . your grandmother, George, came to see her she said she was a poor little mite to be born into a sad world. And so it seems. Poor Augusta! She has never been reconciled to being born a girl. So we must find a husband for her, George."

"We will do our best."

"And soon, George. There should not be a long delay. Augusta can no longer be called very young."

"We will consider the matter as urgent," said George. He looked to Bute and something of the old relationship was between them. "I found Grenville arrogant," he said. "And Pitt . . . well, Pitt is difficult too. I took your advice and summoned him. I felt it was necessary now that Egremont has died. But Pitt will return on his own terms. He wants to restore the Whigs. If Pitt would come as head of the Government all well and good. But now he will bring back the Whigs. I said to him: 'Mr. Pitt, my honour is concerned and I must support it.' So Grenville continues in office and plagues me and tires me and bores me."

"Ah, what times we live in," sighed Bute; but he had no consolation to offer.

It was very different, thought George, from the old days.

But he must devote himself to arranging a marriage for his elder sister. Poor Augusta! Naturally she wanted to marry and have children before it was too late. He understood that. He had his two at Richmond. How he wished he could escape to them and play with them and enjoy the life of a country squire.

But duty must come first. In a few days he was negotiating a marriage between his sister Augusta and Charles, Duke of Brunswick-Wolfenbüttel.

If George was displeased with George Grenville, so was Grenville with George.

For one thing Grenville knew that the King had approached Pitt and it was only because Pitt's terms were impossible that Grenville was invited to stay in office.

Having learned that Pitt had had an interview with the King, Grenville went on to discover that this had been brought about through the work of Bute; and that it was Bute in the first place who had suggested Pitt be approached.

Grenville in a rage went to see the King.

As soon as George received him he began one of his

lectures which the King found so tiresome, and as George yawned and watched the clock Grenville made no attempt to cut it short. At length the King, exasperated beyond endurance, said that he had other matters to which he must attend. Grenville replied that he would come to the point and tell His Majesty of his disquiet that Lord Bute, who had resigned from the Government at the people's desire, should still hold so much influence with His Majesty that he could suggest the recall of Mr. Pitt, and that that recall would have been brought about—but for Mr. Pitt's intransigence.

The King was trying to catch at the gist of this harangue when Grenville said: "Sire, I can only continue in office if I can be assured that Lord Bute does not enjoy secret conferences with Your Majesty."

"I will give you that assurance," replied the King. "But it is true that I invited Mr. Pitt to come and see me at Lord Bute's suggestion. It shall not happen again."

"I sincerely hope it will not," said the Minister grimly, knowing that if he resigned on account of Bute and the people knew—and he would make sure that they did—the King's unpopularity would increase and so would the lampoons and manifestations of the City's hatred against Bute.

"And Your Majesty, if I am to continue in office I must insist that Lord Bute leaves London."

"Leaves London!"

"Your Majesty it is a condition of my service. If Your Majesty feels that it is impossible to banish Lord Bute then I shall be compelled to deliver to you my seals of office."

George was angry, but he could see that he was at the Minister's mercy. Would any minister have dared to speak to his grandfather like that? There had been lampoons about George II and it was said that he was ruled by his wife and Sir Robert Walpole which doubtless had been true, but no one would have dared put such conditions to him as Grenville had just done to George III. Of course he was young, a novice at the art of ruling; and he was weary and tired and his head ached and he felt far from well. But he knew that he dared not lose Grenville at this time, so Bute would have to leave London.

George muttered: "I will ask Lord Bute to leave us for a while."

"And Your Majesty, it could not be permitted that one of

Lord Bute's friends take over his office of Keeper of the Privy Purse."

"Good God," cried George, humiliated into a display of anger, "Mr. Grenville, am I to be suspected after all I have done?"

Grenville murmured: "It is imperative to Your Majesty's Ministers and to the City of London that Lord Bute is not suspected of being Your Majesty's chief adviser."

The King turned away and when his minister had left, sent for Lord Bute to tell him that he must leave.

He was surprised at Bute's meek acceptance of dismissal, though he himself would have given a good deal to escape from his bickering ministers. But he was not particularly sorry either. When he thought of the old days when he had doted on this man, when he had been terrified of mounting the throne without him beside him, he was astonished that everything could have changed in a comparatively short time.

"It will only be a temporary absence," he murmured. "But I had no alternative but to agree to it."

Bute nodded.

"You will tell my mother?"

Bute answered that he would.

After he had gone the King sat thinking of them—Bute and his mother. In truth their relationship, of which the people in the streets had made him crudely familiar, shocked him. This was at the root of his changed feelings towards this man who had once been his dearest friend.

And yet, he thought, I went through a form of marriage with Hannah. And if that were a true marriage and if Hannah still lives then I am not married to Charlotte. We are living in sin as my mother is with Lord Bute.

No, it's not true, he told himself. I must shut that thought right out of my mind. For what with Mr. Pitt and Mr. Grenville, Mr. Wilkes and the rest I should go mad if I dwelt on that too.

He would not think of it. Bute would go away for a while and his mother must needs put up with his absence. After all, hadn't he been forced to give up Sarah completely? So why should his mother complain at giving up Bute for a few weeks?

They must forget their own troubles and set about arranging Augusta's marriage.

* * *

The Princess Augusta was very excited about her coming wedding. She had been presented with a picture of her future husband and was not displeased with it. Caroline Matilda was almost as excited.

"One wedding begets another," she said. "It will be my turn next. Oh, Augusta, just imagine! You'll go right away from us all to a strange land. I wonder what Brunswick's like. I suppose it's not far from Mecklenburg. How odd! You go there and Charlotte comes here."

"Nothing odd about it," said Augusta sharply. "It's just the nature of things."

"Oh, the nature of things!" cried Caroline Matilda, dancing round the apartment, her yellow hair streaming out behind her. "And the nature of things is that I'll be the next one. When do you think there'll be a wedding for me, Augusta?"

"Not for years. You're only a child."

"Thirteen. Charlotte was only seventeen. And as I told you, weddings come together. I'm longing to see Charles. I wonder if he's like his picture. Are you shivering with apprehension?"

"When you reach my age, child, you don't shiver with apprehension, you only sigh with relief."

Caroline Matilda giggled. "I hope he's a little more handsome than poor Charlotte."

"Hush! You are speaking of the Queen."

"Perhaps all Germans are *plain*."

"What about us? Are we not mostly German?"

"That was Grandfather. We're all English." Caroline Matilda surveyed her face thoughtfully in a mirror. "In fact," she went on complacently, "I think *I* am rather good looking."

Augusta laughed derisively and Caroline Matilda continued to giggle. Since Augusta knew she was to have a husband she had become much pleasanter to her young sister.

And in January Prince Charles Frederick of Brunswick arrived in England.

George took an immediate dislike to his prospective brother-in-law, and so did the Prince to him. Charles Frederick was twenty-nine and high spirited; on the way over he had been talking with the utmost indiscretion about English politics; he had stated that the King was inexperienced and had been led by the nose by Lord Bute, before that gentleman had been sent packing, while refusing the services of one of the greatest politicians alive, by whom he meant William Pitt. When this conversation was reported to the King and his ministers it did not endear them to the visitor.

As for the Princess Dowager, she declared that she had never liked his family. She had accepted him as her daughter's husband, she told Lord Bute, when he paid his secret visits to her—for it was not to be expected that they would give those up—but the old Duchess of Wolfenbüttel was the most disagreeable woman she had ever known, and everyone was aware that she had refused her daughter for George, although his grandfather had tried to foist the girl on to him.

If it was not for the fact that Augusta must have a husband she would never have agreed to the match. But Augusta really was a trying creature; her tongue was so sharp and she was interesting herself too deeply in politics. She was a supporter of Pitt's and with her brother, the Duke of York, was actually taking sides with the Opposition and those who were against the policy of the Court. Augusta was a real meddler. Well, let her meddle in Brunswick.

The Princess Dowager went to see her son to talk of the coming ceremonials.

"I don't see why we should go to any length to impress Brunswick," said Augusta.

"Nor I," agreed George.

"The fellow is an oaf. He would not know the difference between a Court ceremony or a country-house ball. So why go to the expense?"

"It would be a great expense. And don't forget we have already had to pay the fellow handsomely to take her."

"Eighty thousand pounds, an annuity of £5,000 a year on Ireland and £3,000 a year on Hanover. It's being an expensive matter getting rid of Augusta. Now for Heaven's sake, do not let us add to the expense."

"We won't; I am ordering that the servants should not have new livery."

George was looking better than he had for some months; he had always enjoyed working out details of household expenditure.

"And," he went on, "I have decided that he shall be lodged at Somerset House and that there will be no need to station guards there."

Augusta nodded, approving, but thinking at the same time: "In the old days he would have consulted one of us first."

"Doubtless he will be unaware," said the Princess Dowager, "that he is not being treated with the respect one would naturally give to a gentleman in his position. I believe manners are very crude in Brunswick."

This may have been so, but the Prince was immediately aware of the coldness of his reception and was furious. He was by no means meek and had no intention of hiding his displeasure. He had distinguished himself on the battlefield with the armies of Frederick the Great and since he had come to England to take an ageing princess off their hands he had expected better treatment.

The only one at the English Court who was pleased with him seemed to be his bride and she would have been pleased with any bridegroom. At least he was not deformed and she pretended not to notice his crudities. The ladies and gentlemen of the Court, taking their cue from the King, all showed their dislike of the bridegroom to such an extent that it would seem they were trying to influence the Princess Augusta against him.

But the Prince of Brunswick discovered a way of having his revenge. When he went out into the streets and the people crowded about his carriage to see him pass, he was extremely affable and showed his interest in them; he waved and smiled and very soon he had them cheering him. There was an occasion when he saw a soldier in the crowd who had served with him in the field; he acknowledged the man and they talked for a while with the crowd pressing close. That cemented his popularity. Here he was a visitor to England, a young bridegroom, and he was slighted and insulted. He was pushed into Somerset House without a guard and it was clear by the way he was unescorted that he was being humiliated.

The people were up in arms. This was a further cause for complaint against the King and his ministers. How dared they treat a visitor so! It was unpatriotic, unEnglish! Well, the people of London were going to teach their king manners.

So wherever he went it was: "Long live the Prince." The women threw kisses; the men cheered themselves hoarse; and the Prince was slyly delighted. There was only one thing which would have discountenanced the King and his ministers more, and he proceeded to do it. He made overtures to the leading members of the Opposition—for having studied English politics he was aware of the effect this would have—and was invited to dine with the Dukes of Cumberland and Newcastle; and not content with that he visited William Pitt at his Hayes residence.

"He's a scoundrel," spluttered the King; but he had to admit that the Prince had outwitted him and his ministers and that this was one more failure.

Four days after the Prince's arrival he and the Princess Augusta were married.

The Princess Augusta found she had married a masterful man. He was not much concerned with the niceties of life and her introduction to his somewhat coarse mode of living was a little startling. Temporarily she was robbed of that arrogance which had always prevented her from making friends and there was something pathetic about this once self-sufficient woman now faced with a new life in a land of which she knew nothing, with a husband almost a stranger to her; all she did understand was that it would be very different from life as she had lived it hitherto.

Caroline Matilda watched in awed silence. Marriage, she decided, was not the gay game she had once believed. Suppose when her turn came they gave her a husband like this prince. She shivered. She had pictured all husbands mild and gentle like her brother George.

The bridegroom kept up his feud with the Court and two days after the wedding when he and his bride, with the King and Queen, paid a visit to the Opera he had an opportunity of scoring over the King.

Charlotte, taking her cue from George, was very cool to the Prince, and Augusta was displeased with her. Who, Augusta asked herself, does she think she is, to put on such haughty airs! The sister of a little Duke of Mecklenburg and she dares to patronize Brunswick!

Charlotte was thinking how happy she was to have a husband like George. She shuddered, contemplating how different this man must be. George was so gentle, so tender, such a good father and husband. Poor Augusta! she pitied her.

Augusta was in no mood to be pitied by silly little Charlotte who was kept almost like a prisoner at Richmond and Buckingham House and was never allowed to voice an opinion. And who was she to be sorry for her, Augusta, when everyone knew George had had to be persuaded to marry her and had only done so out of a sense of duty?

As they entered the box, Augusta whispered: "The Opera House will be crowded tonight. Everyone will be here. I wonder if Sarah Bunbury will be? If she is, everyone will be looking at her . . . *everyone*. She is said to be the most beautiful woman at Court."

"I doubt they will look at her even so," said Charlotte. "Everyone will want to be looking at the bride and groom."

"Poor Sarah! She will have to be content to have George ogling her."

Charlotte flushed slightly but made no response. Did he, she wondered, still think of Sarah?

Charlotte had moved to the front of the box with the King and they stood together looking down on the audience. There was silence in the Opera House. It was most embarrassing. George sat down and Charlotte did the same and then the Princess Augusta and her husband came forward. Immediately the audience rose. A cry went up: "Long live the Prince and Princess."

There were loud hurrahs and "God bless the married pair." And Augusta and her husband stood there bowing and accepting the cheers.

Then to Charlotte's horror she noticed that the bridegroom had his back to the King.

This was an insult, an intentional insult.

She glanced at George who, she saw at once, was aware of what was happening. His blue eyes bulged a little more than usual but he gave no sign.

There was nothing he could do. The people were acclaiming the newly married pair so vociferously to make a contrast to the silence with which they had greeted their king and queen.

George had made up his mind.

He told Grenville: "They must leave immediately. I will not have them here."

"Sire, the visit was to last a few more weeks."

"I do not care for that, Mr. Grenville, sir. I say they shall leave the day after tomorrow and that is my final word on the subject."

George's mouth was set in stubborn lines. He was determined on this matter to have his way.

The Princess Dowager applauded his firmness. "I shall be glad to see the back of that man," she said, "and since

Augusta married him she appears to be more impossible than ever.''

So to the disgust of the Prince of Brunswick he was obliged to take his bride to her new home, for there was no longer to be hospitality for them in England.

The Princess Augusta protested that the weather was too inclement for them to set sail for a while, but the King was adamant; weather or not they should go at once. He would not be insulted in his own country.

The Princess stormed and wept for the prospect of leaving home became more alarming the nearer it grew. Her husband made no attempts to make her position easier. He had told her that she would have to accept his mistress Madame de Herzfeldt whom he had no intention of giving up.

"All that will be changed now," she told him; but he merely laughed at her.

"Listen," he said. "You bear a child and that's all you need worry about."

"I shall refuse to receive your mistress," she told him.

He roared with laughter. "It's not you she wants to receive. It's me. And we don't receive in Brunswick. You'll find it a bit different there, my girl, from your fancy English Court."

Oh, yes, undoubtedly the Princess was apprehensive and sought to delay departure as long as possible.

But George had never been fond of her as he had of Elizabeth the sister who had died, and as he was of young Caroline Matilda. Augusta had always been a troublemaker and he would be glad to see her go.

So the Princess could do nothing but set out with her husband on the day the King had appointed, and a very cold and blustery day it was, for at the best of times the end of January was not an ideal period to take a sea voyage; and so it proved, for when they were at sea a violent storm arose and as there was no news of their arrival from Holland, rumours that they were drowned began to circulate.

This was first whispered in the streets, then a great cry of anger rose up among the people. They had not wanted to go; they had been forced to set sail when the weather was so bad that they were certain to face great dangers.

This was due to the cruelty of the Princess Dowager and Lord Bute—and this time the King could not be exonerated.

It was the first time that the King had been so severely criticized and for a few days his popularity was at its lowest.

Then news arrived of the safe arrival of the Prince and Princess of Brunswick and the murmurings died down.

But the people's feelings for the King had suffered a severe decline. Previously they had blamed Jackboot and Petticoat; now he would stand alone. He was no longer their charming handsome King; his looks had undergone a change; the first flush of youth was over; and others would no longer be blamed for the disasters around the throne.

Meanwhile the poor Princess Augusta had arrived at her husband's Court to find that his palace was nothing more than a cold and gloomy wooden house with shabby furniture. And installed as its mistress was the flamboyant Madame de Herzfeldt whom the new husband greeted with exuberant spirits and with whom he retired to bed leaving his wife to settle into her new apartments alone.

The Princess began to feel that even a watery grave might have been preferable, and she could scarcely bear to think at all of her luxurious apartments in the English Court.

Why, why, why, she was to ask herself during the next years, did I ever think that marriage in any form was better than the single life? Oh, to be a virgin princess once more, to walk in the gardens of Kew or Richmond, to join a card party at St. James's or Buckingham House. Lucky Caroline Matilda who could still do this! Luckier Charlotte who had left a place similar to this to be the Queen of England!

But being Augusta, strong of will and in command of herself, she settled down to make the best of her uncongenial surroundings; and in due course she gave birth to a child.

It was a girl and she named her Caroline.

Marriage in a Masque

The year which followed the Princess Augusta's departure was a distressing one for the King. He felt his responsibilities weighing heavily upon him. He had lost Bute; it was not, he realized now, that Bute's advice had been so valuable, but that he himself had had such complete confidence in it. He now stood alone and he was not yet capable of doing it. He was well aware of his deficiencies and at the same time his sense of duty was so strong that he knew he must overcome them.

The wranglings in his Parliament, the estrangements from Bute and consequently his mother, although the Princess Dowager did her best to keep a firm hold on him, made it impossible for him to turn to anyone for help. He disliked his ministers; he realized the worth of Pitt but Pitt's autocratic demands made it impossible for George to ask him to form a Ministry. Had he turned to Charlotte they might have worked together, but Charlotte had no knowledge of state affairs; it was not that she lacked the intelligence, it was merely that she had been deliberately kept in the dark. Charlotte might have stood with him as Queen Caroline had with his grandfather, but George in his obstinacy had declared he would never allow a woman to interfere, thus Charlotte was kept apart; her only cares were for her children at Richmond.

George was not sleeping well; he was now and then troubled by strange rashes on his chest. He showed them to his doctors, but although purging, bleeding and ointments were applied these afflictions came and went irrespective of these treatments. Sometimes he felt dizzy and suffered from headaches. He began to feel a little uneasy, but he tried to keep these feelings to himself. He believed that if he could get a good government which could settle the country's trying affairs, if he could regain the affection of his people, if he

170

could grasp the handling of state matters with greater knowledge and the skill which only experience could give, he
would be a good ruler; and if he were, the doubts and fears
which tormented him and were responsible for sleepless nights,
which brought the rashes and the headaches, he was sure all
would be well. At least he had one great and burning ambition; to be a good king and do what was best for his people.

He would be up early in the morning, lighting his fire,
going back to bed for a few minutes while the room warmed
and then going through the state papers. Wilkes was fortunately safely in exile. Grenville—whom George thought of as
"Mr. Grenville" and refused to address as anything else—
was arrogant, believing himself indispensable, which perhaps
he was since Pitt could not replace him. But the King tried to
keep his mind off the intransigence of his ministers for when he
thought of them his head ached and the dizzy spells came on.

How delighted he was when he could leave the precincts of
St. James's and go to Richmond. What a pleasure to ride
through the country lanes, to chat with people who passed; to
be the king-squire with whom everyone was glad to have a
word. Pretty rosy-cheeked country girls bobbing their curt-
seys; toddlers hiding their faces in their mother's skirts. "Come,
come," he would say jovially, "do you not wish to say a
how-de-do to your king?" "Oh, Sir, he be shy, but you wait
till he's older and I tell him the King spoke to him and he hid
his face and wouldn't look!" Pat the child's head and tell him
to be good to his mother. Kiss the little girls—he loved the
little girls best of all in their little aprons and muslin frocks.
They were his most adorable subjects. He visited the farms,
discussing harvests with farmers, and once when he was
walking in the lanes he came upon a farm cart which had
stuck in a rut. The driver was trying to hoist it and George
joined him, putting his shoulder to the wheel. And what a
moment of pleasure when the driver recognized him and
stuttered and stammered his incredulous thanks. That was a
story which would be repeated throughout the country. It was
the kind of thing which he did naturally without thinking and
which won him the people's affection.

All would be well, he assured himself, if only he could
bring prosperity to England and prevent his ministers bickering together in the House of Commons. The figure of Pitt
swathed in bandages loomed over the King and the Government.
Although he was often in great pain from his gout, the

menace of Mr. Pitt was formidable. Yet if Mr. Pitt could be persuaded not to make such demands, to be a little less autocratic, how much easier life could have been; and how content the King would have been to work with such a brilliant minister. When he looked back he saw the great mistake he and Lord Bute had made when they had imagined that the latter could be as strong, as brilliant, as far-seeing and as great a politician as the Great Commoner.

Always he came back to the trials of state affairs. No wonder he wished to get away to Richmond.

George felt his responsibilities towards his family very deeply. His brothers were proving themselves to be somewhat wild, which was not surprising considering the restricted lives they had had. The Princess Dowager had been so afraid that they would be contaminated by the wickedness of the Court that she had kept them shut away until she could do so no longer. When they had been allowed to mingle with the world it was only natural that they, lacking their elder brother's purpose and position and his innate respectability, had turned to somewhat riotous living.

George could do nothing to restrain them, but he could find a husband for Caroline Matilda. His little sister—the youngest of the family—was fourteen years old. She should not be allowed to grow old and sour like poor Augusta. Fourteen was not really old enough for marriage, but opportunities must be seized when they came. He knew full well how difficult it was to provide Protestant matches for his family, and nothing but a Protestant match would do.

The opportunity came when the King learned that Frederick V of Denmark was seeking a bride for Prince Christian, heir to the throne of Denmark and the son of his first marriage.

A crown for Caroline Matilda! The Dowager Princess was excited.

"It is a very good offer, George," she said. "We could not hope for better. I think they should be betrothed without delay."

And what did Caroline Matilda say? George asked her, although whatever she said she would be obliged to accept the match.

Caroline Matilda in fact was delighted. She had forgotten Augusta's departure almost a year ago; and when she did later remember she told herself that all husbands were not like that horrid Prince of Brunswick. Christian of Denmark would be different. She saw him, tall, blond and handsome; and when his father died he would be king—not merely ruler of a little German principality, but king of a great country like Denmark.

Caroline Matilda was excited by the prospect.

On the 10th of January 1765 her betrothal was announced.

She immediately became a more important person, a princess who one day would be a queen. And there was nothing to worry about; it was only a betrothal; she was fourteen years old. They would wait at least until she was fifteen.

She went to see Charlotte and play with the babies. She was becoming very interested in married life. She herself hoped to have babies, many of them. But chiefly she saw herself in her royal robes, a crown on her flaxen hair.

The new year had come in happily for Charlotte for with it came the certainty that she was pregnant.

During the last year her English had improved greatly, and she spoke it now more or less fluently, but of course with a German accent. That was inevitable. But how much easier it made life! She was pleased that George was breaking away from his mother's influence, too; she was always hoping that he would share confidences with her; in fact during the last year when she had not been pregnant they had grown closer; it seemed that when Charlotte was not preoccupied by the prospect of bearing a child she could share a closer intimacy with her husband.

In a quiet and comfortable way she had a great affection for him and she was sure he had for her. The knowledge that he had greatly desired to marry Sarah Lennox and that he had given her up out of a sense of duty was not exactly comforting, particularly as she was obliged now and then to see Lady Sarah, who was an undoubted beauty, and although married to Sir Charles Bunbury, had many admirers. Sir Charles she had heard was more interested in racing than his wife, and Sarah was very fond of her cousin Lord William Gordon and was constantly seen in his company. Such Court gossip did not interest her although her women chattered about it constantly. The only matter that concerned her was that there was no mention of the King's having an attachment for Lady Sarah.

She did occasionally hear a whisper about a Quaker girl in whom George had once been interested, and oddly enough she could not shrug that aside as easily as she could the affair with Sarah Lennox. For one thing it was more secret, and that in itself suggested it was more to be feared. Everyone knew of the attachment for Sarah and many had remarked that the King scarcely looked at Sarah on the occasions when it was necessary for them to meet. They talked of the King's virtue and respectability. How many kings, who had all the opportunities in the world, had resisted temptations and remained faithful to their wives? It was difficult to recall one. Even sour old William of Orange had had his mistress. And it was not as though George was blessed with such a beautiful fascinating wife either.

Charlotte sighed. George was a good man and a good husband and she was lucky—and once again . . . pregnant. There would be a little gap between the birth of Fred and this child. It was what she had needed; the time between her darling firstborn and his little brother had been too short. Now young George, already a little autocrat of the nursery, but so beautiful, and so bright, would be three years old by the time the new baby appeared and little Fred would be two.

Oh, she was fortunate indeed. But she wished that the King's health would improve. He was young to have these vague ailments which seemed to upset him so. In a man of fifty or even forty they would have been understandable; but George was not yet thirty. It was the worries of state. Dear George, he was too conscientious.

But how pleased he was to hear that they might expect another child.

The King was extremely upset. He paced up and down his apartments. He did not wish to see anyone, but Charlotte went to him.

"George. You must tell me what is wrong."

George looked at her blankly as though he did not know who she was. She took his arm and looked into his face.

"Hannah . . ." he said. "Hannah . . ."

Her heart leaped and then seemed to stop for a second before it raced on. He was looking at her so oddly, as though he thought she were another person. And Hannah! That name which she had heard whispered before. Hannah Lightfoot, the Quaker.

"George . . . I beg of you, tell me what is on your mind."

His eyes seemed to come into focus. He looked more like himself. "Charlotte," he said. "Charlotte, my wife . . . the Queen."

"What has happened, George? You are ill."

"Oh, yes, yes . . ." he said.

"Pray sit down. I will call the doctors."

He shook his head but allowed her to lead him to a chair.

"Call no one," he said. Then as though speaking in a daze, "She is dead. Hannah is dead. This time it is true."

Charlotte knelt at his feet and taking his hand looked up pleadingly into his face.

"You must tell me," she urged and added: "If it will help you."

He seemed to consider this. His brow was wrinkled, his eyes wild.

Then he spoke a little incoherently: "Perhaps I should tell. Better. Charlotte, oh, Charlotte. It was wrong. It was wicked. I never should . . ."

She waited in breathless anxiety. What was the secret of Hannah Lightfoot? She must know.

"George," she said, "perhaps you should lie down."

"I feel dizzy," he said. "I can scarcely stand."

She took him to the bedchamber and he lay down while she sat beside the bed holding his hand.

"Charlotte, you are a good wife . . . a good queen."

"I want to be everything you wish me to be, George."

"All these years. What did Hannah *think* . . . ?"

And then he was telling the story, somewhat incoherently, it was true, but she saw him as a young boy of thirteen passing through St. James's Market and being aware of the beautiful Quaker sitting in the window of the linen draper's shop.

"The people had gathered to see us . . . my grandfather, my mother, myself . . . we were all going to the theatre; and the linen draper had taken the bales of linen from the window that his family might watch the procession pass by. Hannah told me that . . . afterwards."

"Yes, George."

"She was the most beautiful woman I had ever seen."

Charlotte winced, but the pressure of his hot fingers on her hand reminded her that however plain she was, he needed her; and he trusted her enough to confide in her.

"So we met. It was arranged for us and I loved her and she bore my children."

"Children, George? Where are they?"

"Being well cared for. I am assured of this, but I do not

see them now. They are growing too old. It would not be safe. But I know they are well cared for. That is taken good care of.''

There was silence while Charlotte thought of her little nursery and compared it with that of another presided over by a woman . . . the most beautiful he had ever seen, a woman who merely had to sit in a shop window to make him fall in love with her and risk all sorts of danger to be with her. Very different that must have been from marrying a plain princess who had been chosen for him.

But it was over. It was of the past and now he was king with a queen and two sons and another child on the way.

She told him this gently.

"Yes, it is over, but it haunts me, Charlotte. I think of her . . . What must she have thought of me . . . for allowing it . . . ? And in my heart I knew she wasn't dead.''

She listened to the incoherent fantastic story of how he had gone to the house . . . their house in Islington . . . and found that she was no longer there. She and the children had disappeared. The story they had told him was that she had died and been buried and the children were being taken care of.

"They showed me her grave, Charlotte. But it had another name over it. They cheated me. They told me she was dead . . . and I knew in my heart that she was not. It was a ridiculous story. They had buried her under another name to avoid scandal, they said. I should have asked questions, but I didn't, Charlotte . . . because I knew in my heart . . . And I understood what it would mean. I was the King and I had married the linen draper's niece.''

"Married!'' she cried aghast.

He nodded. "We went through a form of marriage. She was already married to Isaac Axford, but she said that was no true marriage and he thought so too for he had married again. It was never consummated. She ran away after the ceremony . . . ran away to me.''

"Married!'' repeated Charlotte.

"It satisfied her. She thought she was near death. It was after the child was born . . . the last one . . . and she feared the weight of sin. So I married her . . . and that made her happier. She was no longer afraid to die.''

He had closed his eyes; the telling had exhausted him mentally and physically.

He seemed to sleep and she sat by his bed, thinking: "Married! So they went through a form of marriage!'

Charlotte could not sleep for thinking of the strange confession her husband had made to her. When she had tried to broach the subject again he had looked at her coldly as though he did not know what she was talking about. A great fear came to her then. Was he pretending that he did not know or had he really been unaware of what he had said to her?

He was acting very strangely. There were times when he seemed bemused. He had changed in the last weeks. Could it be the result of the information he had received about Hannah Lightfoot's death? Who had told him? She imagined a letter arriving from Hannah herself, begging him to look after their children as she was dying. Was that not what any mother would do?

And George had actually gone through a ceremony of marriage with Hannah Lightfoot. So that wedding ceremony between herself and George in the Chapel Royal performed by the Archbishop of Canterbury was not the first George had undergone.

She thought she felt the child move within her and with that a faintness came to her, for with the movement of the child had come a thought. If George had been married before and that marriage of his had been legal, then he was not married to her, Charlotte; and little George and Fred were illegitimate and so was the child she carried in her womb.

She clutched the table. No, she thought. It is impossible. That could not be true . . . not of the Queen of England.

But the doubt persisted. It haunted her. It seemed to her that everywhere she went Hannah Lightfoot was mocking her. "I was his true wife. Some child hidden away somewhere in the country is the true King of England, not your little George whom they call the Prince of Wales."

It was unbearable. She could not endure it. She, Charlotte, Princess of Mecklenburg-Strelitz, brought to England to be the King's concubine, her children bastards. Oh, no! It was a nightmare. Yet he had told her of that marriage.

My God, she thought, I shall never be safe. My children will never be safe. In the years to come some young man could present himself to the Government, to the Archbishop, and say: "I am the true King of England."

There would be documents . . .

She must find out.

She tried to talk to George.

"You must tell me the truth. We cannot let this matter rest."

"Hannah is dead," he said. "I have evidence of that now. She was not before, but she is dead now."

"But you were married to her."

"It was not a true marriage."

"Why not? Why not?"

"She was married before."

"But she thought that was not a true marriage."

"It was at a Marriage Mill which was illegal."

"Then . . ."

"It was declared illegal, but the law had not been entered in the statute book at that time. It was a few months later. That was why she thought it was illegal."

"It frightens me."

"Don't think of it. Don't speak of it."

"But what if it were a true marriage? Then I am not your wife. What of our sons . . . What of them? What if they say that George, the Prince of Wales, is a bastard?"

"Stop," cried the King. "It is driving me mad."

And so it seemed. His doctors were anxious. The rash had broken out on his chest and he had a fever. They purged him and he was a little better.

Charlotte was hollow-eyed too.

The people of the Court said: "The Queen is anxious about the King. He certainly seems to have a strange illness."

Charlotte thought, we must do something. If we were not truly married before then we must be married now. But how? If they announced that they would be married again there would be immediate gossip and scandal. Those who had wondered about the Hannah Lightfoot story would begin to speak of it as a fact. Nothing could be more dangerous.

Charlotte could think clearly if the King was incapable of doing so.

The name of Hannah Lightfoot must never be mentioned at Court if she could help it. Those children must never know who their father was. A great wrong might have been done to Hannah and her children, and Charlotte and hers, but silence was the best way to right it.

She must speak to George. She must discover more; she

must find a way out of this difficulty if not for her own sake for that of those two boys in her nursery and the one who would be born later this year.

Alone in their bedroom she said to him, "I must talk of this. I fear it upsets you, but I have our children to think of."

George was mute, his features set in lines of abject melancholy.

"Who performed the ceremony when you married Hannah Lightfoot?"

"Dr. Wilmot," he said.

"Dr. Wilmot!" The name was not unfamiliar. He had been one of the court chaplains. She must discover more of this man.

While she pondered this an idea came to her. What if she arranged an entertainment . . . a court entertainment and there was a masque in which two people were married. It could seem like a mock ceremony, but they could say the necessary words. Everything that was essential could be performed. And the two chief players would be the King and Queen.

It was fantastic; but then so was the whole story.

A masque . . . when neither she nor the King cared for masques. Why not a quiet ceremony in the chapel at Kew? No. Quiet ceremonies had a way of being discovered. That would make it too serious. A masque was the idea with everyone looking on . . . and herself and the King and the priest . . . disguised in a domino.

The idea was forming shape. It is the only way, she thought.

Dr. Wilmot should be the priest. Whom else could she trust? He knew of the marriage so therefore there would be no one else in the secret.

And then she could be sure that she was married to the King, if only at this late date. And if George and Fred were bastards, the new child would not be.

"A *fête*. A court masque!" The words were whispered in astonishment. "The Queen is being gay at last. Who would have believed it . . . and another little one on the way!"

The Queen had announced that she and the King were devising a spectacle in which they were going to play a prominent part. The theme would be the glorification of marriage.

"That sounds a little more like them," grinned Elizabeth Chudleigh to the frivolous Marchioness. "I'll swear there'll be prayers and hymns of praise. And then we shall all have to declare ourselves ready to follow the good example of conjugal bliss set by their Majesties."

Still, a *fête* was a *fête* and everyone agreed that any *fête* was better than none at all.

The King had been keeping to his apartments lately and was seeing very little of people, even his ministers. They found him abstracted and his behaviour a little odd.

The Princess Dowager told Lord Bute when he came to her quietly in a closed carriage that she was anxious about George, who was behaving strangely. She was sure this absurd *fête* was Charlotte's idea and that they would have to be even more watchful of her.

"She is pregnant," Bute reminded the Princess, "and pregnant women get odd fancies."

The Princess grunted. "We'll be watchful," she said. "Madam Charlotte could get out of hand."

On the evening of the *fête* there was a banquet and dancing; and a troupe of dancers dressed as brides and their grooms performed before the company. The highlight of the evening was when the King and Queen standing on a dais apart from the rest of the company actually went through a form of marriage with one of the company disguised as a priest.

There was some surprise that this was considered in good taste since the words of the marriage ceremony were actually spoken.

"Poor George," was the comment, "he has no humour at all if he thinks this is the way to amuse his guests. As for Charlotte, she's as bad . . . or even worse. A dull pair."

The King and Queen sat apart from their guests both looking solemn.

Elizabeth Chudleigh commented: "Now if we had the old putting-the-pair-to-bed ceremony that would enliven things a little."

But of course there were no such frivolities at the Court of George and Charlotte.

The odd thing was that they should have thought to entertain the company by a mock marriage between the most stolidly married couple in the kingdom.

The company danced and feasted again and forgot the oddities of the King and Queen.

And Charlotte at least felt comforted by that evening's entertainment.

When a few days later Mr. George Grenville called on the King he found George sitting at his desk, his head in his hand, and he refused to look up when Grenville entered.

"Your Majesty . . ." began Grenville; but still the King sat there.

"Is anything wrong?"

George lowered his hands; his face was very red; and suddenly he burst into tears.

"Your Majesty is ill."

George did not deny it.

Grenville immediately sent for the King's doctors.

The doctors were in consultation with Grenville and a few of the King's top ministers.

"What ails him?" asked Grenville.

"His mind seems to be affected. He does not speak coherently; he is overcome by some sort of melancholy, some unnatural fear of disaster."

"Good God," cried Grenville. "You don't mean he's mad."

"He is decidedly disturbed," said Sir William Duncan, one of the chief doctors.

"This is disaster. The Prince of Wales is not yet three. It will mean a Regency."

"Come, sir. You go too fast. He has a violent chill, and there is a rash on his chest. This may be the delirium of passing fever."

Grenville looked relieved. "But this must be kept a secret until we are sure."

The doctors agreed with this; and Grenville said that either the Queen or the Princess Dowager should be informed, and perhaps they should choose the Princess Dowager as the Queen was pregnant.

The Princess was stunned.

"This is terrible," she cried. "George . . . deranged . . . and the Prince not yet three years old. Leave me. I will see you later. I must think about this."

And as soon as she was alone she sent an urgent message to Lord Bute.

He came at once, and she told him what the doctors had told her.

"He has been acting strangely lately. What does Charlotte say?"

"Charlotte does not know. The news was brought to me and I have given orders that she shall not be told."

"But she is the Queen."

The Princess shrugged her shoulders. "It is better that she does not know, until we have decided what should be done. I have said that because of her condition it is better for her to be told that the King is suffering from a chill and a fever and no one but his doctors must be with him for fear it is contagious."

Bute was struck by her calm. She did not waste time on sympathy for the King. She was immediately planning what effect his illness would have on the Crown, and who would be at hand to become the power in the land. The Princess Dowager was determined that she should be the one. Therefore the Queen was a menace, and the Queen should be kept in the dark.

"I shall give orders at once," she said, "that Charlotte shall not be told the nature of his illness; moreover, I shall ensure that Charlotte does not see him."

At Richmond with her children Charlotte received a message from her mother-in-law which told her that the King was suffering from a violent chill and fever. The doctors believed that the Queen should not visit him as it might be infectious and she had the child she was carrying to consider. She would be kept informed.

Charlotte thought: It is all this anxiety. The bickering ministers, the terrible lampoons about his mother and her lover. But in her heart she knew it was largely due to the Hannah Lightfoot affair.

But we are married now, she thought. And even if George and Frederick are bastards the children we have in the future will not be.

During the weeks that followed Charlotte was in a state of anxiety; at times she thought of ignoring the Princess's orders and going to see the King to tell him not to worry. They were married now for that which had taken place under the guise of a masque was a true ceremony. She had Dr. Wilmot's assurance on it. He must forget the past; he must never go to see his son by Hannah Lightfoot; he must forget that indiscretion of his youth and all would be well.

She went to her nursery to see the children. Young George, a very handsome child, was already aware of his importance. He knew he was Prince of Wales and his nurses were indulgent to him and he had already been informed that he would one day be king.

He was so bright, so precocious, so interested in everything —a perfect boy.

"Where is Papa?" he asked. "Why does he not come to see *me*."

"He will, my darling. As soon as he is able."

The little boy thought it strange that his father should be so dilatory in giving himself the pleasure of seeing the little Prince of Wales whom everyone adored.

Somewhere, thought Charlotte, there is another boy, who may be calling himself the Prince of Wales. But no, he would not dare! Hannah would have seen to that. She had been a sensible woman and she must have loved George to give him up as she did.

She tried to soothe herself, but as the weeks passed she began to feel apprehensive about the nature of George's illness since she was not allowed to see him.

The King's health improved and Charlotte was with him again. She was shocked by the change in him. His youth had gone for ever. He had a nervous way of speaking, repeating sentences and asking impatiently, "What? What?" before one had time to answer.

Charlotte talked to him of the children and that comforted him to some extent. She said not a word of the masque and the ceremony through which they had gone. She determined that never again if she could help it would she mention Hannah Lightfoot's name. Hannah was dead; Charlotte and George had been remarried—however oddly—and even though Charlotte refused to admit that that second strange ceremony had been necessary she was very relieved that it had taken place.

George suffered depressions. He believed that everyone was against him.

He wrote to Lord Bute:

Everyday I meet with some insult. I have been in a fever

. . . My very sleep is not free from thinking of the men I daily see . . . Excuse the incoherency of my letters. But a mind ulcerated by the treatment it meets with from all around it is the true cause of it.

When Bute received this letter he was disturbed. In the first place the fact that George had written to him seemed to imply that he had forgotten the break in their friendship and believed himself to be back in the old days of confidence.

He talked to the Princess about it and they were very disturbed.

But during a moment of intense clarity the King decided that he might at some time become unfit to govern and that it was necessary to bring into force a Regency Bill. He consulted Blackstone the authority on law who told him that a new Act would not be necessary as the present Act dealt with all possibilities. In the event of his dying or becoming unable to govern the Princess Dowager would automatically become Regent.

George said: "My mother is no longer young." And he thought: She and Lord Bute would rule together and neither of them is capable of it. "No," he went on, "I wish to introduce a new Regency Bill and I will name my Regent and it shall be a secret until I allow it to be known."

Blackstone said that this was a matter for him to discuss with his ministers and the King hastily called them together to tell them of his decision.

After much discussion the Bill was passed which would empower the King, in case of his death or incapacity, to name the Regent, limiting the choice to the Queen or members of his own family.

To Charlotte life had become alarming. She was not sure what was going to happen next. The illness of the King, and his strange behaviour which continued intermittently worried her.

And she knew that in the streets there were whispers about the King's strange malady.

But as the weeks passed he grew better; and in August in Buckingham House she gave birth to her third son. He was christened William; and as she held him against her and rejoiced in his coming she told herself that no one on earth could say *he* was not the legitimate son of the King and Queen of England.

The Royal Nursery

In the nursery at Kew, George reigned supreme. At four years old he was precocious, clever, bright, aware of his importance. He heard the servants whispering about the Prince of Wales and he knew it was himself.

"One day," he boasted to his brother Frederick, "George the Prince will be the King."

Poor Frederick tried to imagine how a boy of four could be king and wear a crown. Wouldn't it keep slipping off his head?

"Silly child," retorted George, "I'll have a big head then."

"God help us," said Lady Charlotte Finch, their governess. "It's big enough now."

Young George was seen surreptitiously touching his head to see if it really was big enough to carry the crown. The servants, watching, laughed together. "Master George can't wait," they said. "Not yet five and imagining himself the King already."

But of course they all loved George and did not mind his imperious ways one little bit. He was so handsome with his golden hair, almost red, and his clever way of talking, for George had never talked like a baby. His big blue eyes looked serenely on the world, knowing that it was made for his benefit.

"There is not much of his father in him," they said.

George enjoyed those rare days when he rode into London with his parents and the people cheered. There were always special cheers for George. He would bow and wave very solemnly because it was a duty of royalty graciously to accept the people's acclamation; and the more what his nurses called "old fashioned" he was, the more the people liked it. He enjoyed watching the guards from the windows of St. James's.

"One, two, one two," he would call to them; and they would salute or march to his orders. Everybody loved George.

185

"Why," he asked imperiously of Lady Charlotte, "can't we live at St. James's. There are no soldiers here."

"Kew is best for children," replied Lady Charlotte.

"I am not children. I am the Prince of Wales."

Then she would kiss him and say he was not going to let them forget that, was he?

"Could you forget?" he asked incredulously.

"Not with you around, my precious." Then he would feel very important until she said: "Now eat up your dinner and no more playing about with that nice fish."

"I like my meat days best," he confided.

"I don't doubt it," replied Lady Charlotte.

"I like meat days too," put in Frederick, who always liked what George liked.

"Well, this is the menu your Papa and Mamma have arranged for you, so we must keep to that, mustn't we? —otherwise we should be disobeying the King."

"When I'm king I'll eat meat every day."

"So shall I," echoed Frederick.

"Silly. You'll never be king."

Frederick looked as though he was going to cry. Poor little Fred, although only a year in time separated them, George seemed to be more than that year older.

"Never mind," said Lady Charlotte, "eat up this nice fish instead."

Frederick allowed it to be spooned into his mouth while George looked on contemptuously.

Heavens above, thought Lady Charlotte. If this is how he is at four what'll he be like at ten . . . at fifteen or eighteen when he comes of age? The King and Queen were undoubtedly right to insist that the children lived simply at Kew.

George was pushing his fish about his plate, breaking it into little bits which he told Fred were soldiers.

"It's fish not soldiers," said Lady Charlotte, "and to be eaten, not played with. Now eat it up or I shall have to go and see your Papa and Mamma and tell them that you are a naughty boy who won't eat his fish."

George looked at Lady Charlotte's nursery gown with contempt. "Pray," he said, "are you well dressed enough?"

Lady Charlotte raised shocked eyes to the ceiling.

"I should have thought," went on George, "that your gown would not be good even to visit the King in. When I am King . . ."

"Fish is to be eaten," said Lady Charlotte. "So I pray you treat it as it was meant to be treated."

The Prince was so struck with this observation that he shovelled two mouthfuls of fish into his mouth while he considered it. Then he remarked: "I like meat best."

Lady Charlotte was silent, thinking that the King was a little dogmatic about the children's food, for he was so anxious that they should not get fat.

He would come into the nursery and say: "Too much weight is not good for them, eh what? Too much fat not good for them. What?"

He had talked in this odd way since his illness, repeating his sentences and putting them in the form of questions which were not meant to be answered.

Perhaps he was right, but Lady Charlotte would not have pared all the fat from the children's meat. Breakfast was a dish containing two thirds milk and one of tea, not very well sweetened, and toast without butter. Dinner—which was taken at three in the afternoon and supper at half past eight—consisted of soup, usually clear and never fatty, lean meat (on meat days) with clear gravy and greens. They were encouraged to eat as much of the greens as they could, and when they had fish they were not allowed butter with it. They would have fruit tart from which the pastry had been removed so that it could scarcely be called fruit tart at all. On Thursdays and Sundays they might eat an ice and choose the flavour.

It was a simple diet and if anyone questioned the wisdom of it, the King would say: "They look healthy on it, eh? What? Are you suggesting the Princes are not healthy, eh? What?"

And everyone had to agree that the little boys with their pink faces and bright blue eyes did indeed look healthy.

"Now come," said Lady Charlotte, "after dinner we are going to visit the King and Queen."

Young George was looking at her gown and she said with a laugh: "Have no fear. I shall change my gown."

That seemed to content the boy and he turned his attention to the plate of fruit pie—minus piecrust—which had been placed before him.

Charlotte sat in the window at the Lodge waiting for the King's return.

"He should be here soon," she said to Schwellenburg in English, for she had insisted that they always speak English, because it was the only way of making any progress in that difficult language. "He will not wish to be late for the children."

"Vill not be," muttered Schwellenburg who showed her contempt for the language by what seemed like deliberate maltreatment.

"I think the King is looking better," went on Charlotte, gazing anxiously at Schwellenburg, but that lady merely grunted.

The Queen picked up her embroidery. The illness was over, and the King was well again; only it had been distressing while it lasted. It was frightening when people one knew suddenly seemed to lose their personalities, when they gazed at you without recognition. She shivered. For a time she had thought he had lost his reason. Did he think so too? He had wanted the Regency Bill passed through afterwards, so the thought may have come into his mind.

But he is well now, she thought; even though Schwellenburg would not admit it. All was well. Three boys in the nursery and there would be more children, she was sure. How she longed for a little girl!

Next time, she promised herself; and she forgot the King's illness. Soon it would be time for their governess to bring the two elder boys to their parents. The King would return and they would have a pleasant little family party, with young George surprising and delighting them by his precocious ways and his healthy looks.

If she could forget the King's illness and the slyness of the Princess Dowager in trying to keep her in the dark, she could be happy.

The King was with the Queen when the Princes arrived with Lady Charlotte Finch.

"Ha," said the King. "So here is my family, eh? What?"

Prince George looked at his father with solemn eyes.

"Why do you not wear your crown, Papa?"

"It is not to be worn when my children come to see me."

"But *I* would like to see it. *I* would like to wear it."

The Queen laughed and looked at the King, who smiled. Such a precocious little fellow. They couldn't help being proud of him.

"Frederick wishes to say something," said the Queen. "What is it, my pet?"

"It . . . it . . ." began Frederick and was overcome with confusion.

Young George looked contemptuously at his brother, but Charlotte said quickly: "Frederick means that it is too big for your little head, George. Why it would slip over your face and you wouldn't be able to see a thing."

"I wouldn't mind," said George. "I'd *feel*." He stretched out his hands as though playing blind man's buff and ran laughing round the room.

Lady Charlotte whispered to George, uneasily, and he turned and grinned at her, reminding her by a look that she had no power over him in the presence of his parents.

"Lady Charlotte is warning you, George," said the King. "You must obey her. She is your governess, eh? What?"

"What? What?" cried young George and began to laugh and caper round the room still faster.

"Lady Charlotte, I pray you bring the Prince to me," said the Queen.

Lady Charlotte caught the boy's hand and he looked at her mischievously and whispered: "What? What?"

"The Prince," said the Queen conversationally to the King, "is a little too full of high spirits."

Frederick wanted to say something and was tugging at his mother's skirt.

"What is it, my pet?"

"Am I?"

"What's that?" asked the King.

"What? What?" cried young George almost choking with laughter.

"Tell your Papa what you mean, my dear," said the Queen.

"Shall I have spirits too?" Frederick wanted to know.

"Yes, my dear, but not so many as George which will show that you behave better than he does."

Young George was astonished and Frederick elated. The Queen said: "Now come here, George, and tell me how you are getting on with your lessons."

George, a little subdued, wondering about his high spirits, listened to Lady Charlotte telling his mother how bright he was when he applied himself. The King listened gravely and the little boys were aware of the solemnity of the occasion.

George must work harder. He must *listen* to what he was told. He must obey his governess, his nurses, his mother and father, for he was after all only a little boy.

"But Prince of Wales," he told them slyly.

"Your Papa is the King and he always listens to everybody, that is why he is a good king. Are you going to be a good Prince of Wales?"

"I'd rather be a good king," said the irresponsible Prince.

"You must first be a good prince," the Queen told him; and listening, the King felt an emotion rising within him; she was a good mother and good wife; and there was something about her which made him wonder. Could she be pregnant again? Praise be to God, he hoped so. Being pregnant kept her contented. In between pregnancies she was inclined to meddle and that was something he would not have, loath as he was to disturb the harmony of their life. No, he liked Charlotte to remain at Kew or Richmond, away from the Court except for those ceremonies which it was imperative that she attend; then she kept her nose out of affairs and did not meddle. He couldn't tolerate a meddling woman. Women's mission in life was to bear children and Charlotte could do that very adequately indeed. Five years married and three boys to show and, if he were right, another child on the way. No one could complain about that. Although, thought George grimly, "those ministers of mine would if they had a chance." He had the most intransigent set of ministers that ever plagued any King. But George was beginning to think that he was capable of running the country's affairs. He gave a great deal of thought to them and once he had come to a decision he stuck to it. He had lost that doubt of his ability; and once he made up his mind he was certain that he was right.

When the children had left he said to Charlotte: "I had a notion that perhaps you're in a very happy condition once more."

"I am not certain," she told him. "But I think . . ."

He patted her shoulders.

"Well done," he said. "What?"

Mr. Pitt Falls Upstairs

Mr. Pitt lay in his bed, his limbs swathed in bandages, cursing his gout, but for which he would be leading the country now; no man had stopped him doing this; his implacable enemy was this accursed gout.

He longed to be back at the head of affairs but unfortunately it was rarely that he was well enough to go to the House of Commons. He was still a power though; as long as he lived the King and his government would continue to be aware of him.

It had always been so; he remembered a long ago occasion when Newcastle had come to see him in this very room; it had been winter and Newcastle who was always worried about his health had found the room too cold for him. "All very well for you in bed," he had said. "I'll catch my death in the ice house." And he had got fully clad into Hester's bed and pulled the coverlets about his ears and had stayed there while they talked business. But Newcastle was now out and the Marquis of Rockingham's ministry was in. And I have no faith in it, thought Mr. Pitt.

To be incapacitated, to know that your genius was being thwarted by your wretched body—could there be anything more frustrating?

Pitt knew himself to be the man who could establish the greatness of England and he was forced to lie in his bed for days at a stretch or to go to Bath to take the waters, to live the life of an invalid when he longed to be a Prime Minister. For nothing short of the head of affairs would be of any use to Pitt.

In his bed he railed against government measures; but what use was that when the pain of his gout was too great to allow him to go to the House of Commons. He wanted to be there arguing against the Stamp Act which George Grenville, his

191

own brother-in-law, had brought in when he was Chancellor of the Exchequer. Pitt was against the Stamp Act which was going to raise difficulties with the American Colonies. He had warned the house of this but he was too sick a man to go in and fight for what he believed. Protests had come thick and fast from America and there was considerable dissatisfaction there with the home country.

Pitt understood this. He wanted to get that Stamp Act repealed. If it were not he could see trouble. Why should England make laws for America? Why should the Colonists be expected to pay taxes to the English Government? It was an absurd imposition, said Pitt; and one which he would do all in his power to abolish.

He had talked to Hester about it. His wife was a brilliant woman who being devoted to him made his enthusiasm hers. He was constantly at loggerheads with her brothers now that they had become politicians; but in the early days when he had been a guest at their house they had all been overawed by his grasp of affairs, by his powers of divination which Hester said were supernatural because he could prophesy what would happen if such and such a thing were done. He had laughed at her and told her that it was long-sightedness—one of the most desirable gifts in a politician's life. It was in fact a complete concentration on the matter at hand. He had these gifts; and that was why she thought he was some sort of soothsayer.

To be with Hester, to talk with Hester, that was the greatest pleasure in life . . . No, he would be honest. The greatest moments were when he stood up in the House and swayed it the way he wished it to go. But Hester was the balm in his life. She was there not only to dress his painful limbs but to restore his pride and ambition, at moments like this when he believed that he, the greatest politician of his day, was being deprived of his birthright by his enemy, the Gout.

Hester came in to tell him that the Earl of Northington had arrived and was asking if he might see Pitt.

"Northington!" Pitt scrambled up in bed. "He comes from the King."

"So he tells me."

"He brings some message . . . some secret message, doubtless. George is weary of the Rockingham ministry, believe me. Hester, he wants me. He always has wanted me. By God, if he had not been under the influence of that fool Bute . . ."

"But Bute need no longer concern you."

"No, the only thing that really concerns me, Hester, is this accursed gout. You'd better bring Northington up at once."

"I thought I'd prepare you."

He nodded. "But until I know what the King wants of me it's hard to be ready with my reply. But bring him in, Hester. Bring him in."

"You won't commit yourself to anything rash."

"Rash! What's rash?"

"You know you are unfit just now to go back there. You must rest your feet. You know that."

"Yes, Hester, I know," he nodded grimly. "But let's see Northington and hear what it is he has come to say."

Accompanied by Hester, Robert Henley, first Earl of Northington, came into the bedroom. Of middle height, with florid complexion, he was quite a handsome man, but the signs of hard drinking were apparent. His language was punctuated with blasphemous expressions except when he was in the company of the King who strangely enough had an affection for him, and two years or so before had created him Viscount Henley and Earl of Northington.

Now he looked with sympathy at Pitt and gimaced.

"My God," he said. "I know just how you feel, William. Just looking at you brings back the memory." He looked down at his legs and shook his head at them. "It was the drink in my case they say. Not yours, though, William. Yours was an act of God. But if I'd known that these legs of mine were going to carry a Chancellor I'd have taken better care of them when I was young."

"Sympathy from a fellow sufferer," murmured Pitt, glancing at the letter which Northington was carrying and which he had not yet handed to him. "Very welcome. But you are not afflicted at the moment."

"That old devil gout has given me a little respite, William. I hope to God it'll be the same with you. When you read this letter you'll feel better I'll warrant."

"From . . ."

"You've guessed, William. From George himself. He's got no faith in Rockingham's crew and by God, nor have I."

Pitt held out his hand for the letter.

Richmond, Monday.
7th July, 1766.

Mr. Pitt, Your very dutiful and handsome conduct the last summer makes me desirous of having your thoughts on how an able and dignified ministry may be formed. I desire therefore you will come for this salutory purpose to Town.

I cannot conclude without expressing how entirely my ideas concerning the basis on which a new Administration should be erected, are consonant to the opinion you gave on that subject in Parliament a few days before you set out for Somersetshire.

I am conveying this through the channel of the Earl of Northington as there is no man in my service on whom I so thoroughly rely, and who I know agrees with me so perfectly in the contents of this letter.

George R.

Pitt looked at Northington significantly. Hester, watching, saw the look and knew what it meant. William looked five years younger; the lines of pain seemed to have been miraculously removed from his face.

"You can guess what this means," said William.

Hester cried: "The King is asking you to form a government."

Her husband handed her the letter. "That's what it means, would you not agree?"

"George knows he can't do without you, William," put in Northington.

"And you know you are not well enough," said Hester.

"My dear, I know only one thing. This is an opportunity I can't resist."

"But . . ."

"Listen. He has come eating out of my hand. A government on *my* terms. This is what I wanted. And now George is asking for it."

"George is growing up!" said Northington.

But Hester continued to look worried.

"Never fear," said her husband, "that is the best pick-me-up I could have had."

"So you will write to the King?" said Hester.

"Without delay."

Pitt was up; hobbling, it was true, but his improvement was miraculous.

This was the life. This was what he wanted. Now particularly he explained to Hester. Did she remember how he had given England her Empire? Had he not stopped that ridiculous frittering away of men and money in Europe and turned his attention to the world beyond the seas? Well, now they were going to lose the American colonies if he were not there to prevent it. "Your brother's—my dear Hester—I regret to say it—but your brother's iniquitous Stamp Duty will be the beginning of it all. I didn't bring America into our Empire to lose it. But we have fools for rulers, Hester, and that's the truth of it."

He sat down at his desk and wrote to the King; his style was fulsome; at this moment he admired the King.

Sir,

Penetrated with the deep sense of Your Majesty's boundless goodness to me, and with a heart overflowing with duty and zeal for the honour and happiness of the most gracious and benign Sovereign, I shall hasten to London as fast as I possibly can; happy could I change infirmity into the wings of expedition, the sooner to be permitted the high honour to lay at Your Majesty's feet the poor but sincere offering of the small services of Your Majesty's most dutiful subject and most devoted servant.

William Pitt.

George read William Pitt's letter with great pleasure. Pitt was the greatest politician in the country, but he never forgot the respect due to the King.

There were times when George faced a terrible possibility and because of this he wished to form a strong government in case it should be necessary to impose a Regency.

His perusal of state papers, his complete dedication to his role in life, his awareness that he had an ever-increasing knowledge of state affairs and that so many of his ministers had failed the country, gave him an impression that he knew as much as they did, that he was as capable of government. The shyness which had been due to his modesty in his youth disappeared; he had become stubborn and once he had made up his mind to a view he forced himself to believe it and cling to it at all costs. He was certain now that with Mr. Pitt, and Mr. Pitt's chosen henchmen, he and they could govern the country in the best possible manner.

So he was delighted to receive Mr. Pitt's letter.

Mr. Pitt would soon be with him and in discussing the new ministry he would forget that vague nagging fear which so far he had been unable to dismiss entirely. It had given him such a sense of insecurity to know that when that illness had beset him he had for some weeks failed to be himself. He could remember little of them but they had existed. He, George the King, had been a poor creature who could not control his own mind. A terrifying thought. But he had arranged for the Regency and the best way of ensuring that it did not happen again was to prepare in case it did.

Hannah was dead; and he need never think of her again. Charlotte was his wife and she was a good woman. She was expecting another child in September and during her pregnancies she hardly ever thought of anything else but the coming child.

Charlotte was a good wife—all that he wanted in a wife and he had nothing to complain of there. She accepted the fact that she must live quietly and not meddle.

"I'll not have women meddling," said the King aloud; and then he thought of his mother who had meddled for as long as he could remember.

"It shall stop," said George aloud.

But there was Lord Bute whom he had had to give up for a while but who had crept back after a time; and that was all due to the Princess Dowager whose lover he was. It was—as such relationships go—a respectable liaison; but George would never approve of it. And another thing that rankled was that for so long he had believed it to be a platonic friendship, and everyone had been aware of the true nature of that liaison, except George.

Bute had been kind to him in the past, but for what reason? In the hope of power when George came to the throne.

In that moment George made up his mind. He would never take Lord Bute's advice again. George's mouth was set in the familiar stubborn lines when he sat down and wrote to Lord Bute to tell him of his decision.

When he received the King's communication Lord Bute was astonished that George could write to him in such a way. When he thought of all the friendship of the past, the protestations of appreciation, the renewed affirmations that he would never happily ascend the throne unless Bute was beside him, it was unthinkable.

Bute was ambitious, George had written, and he wanted to form a party with himself at the head of it. Moreover his advice in the past had been singularly unsuccessful.

Oh, no. It could not be true! But it was; and when Bute tried to see the King he was told an audience was not at the time possible.

George had changed; the amenable eager young boy had disappeared completely; and in his place was a king—a simpleton, for he would always be that, but a man who was unaware of his own inadequacies.

"I protest," wrote Bute to the King. "I could scarcely believe my eyes when I read your letter. It is possible that you cannot see the difference between men setting up to be leaders of a party for seditious or ambitious purposes and me. I shall never be in politics in any way, and I should not ask any man to follow me since I have lost your royal favour. But I must insist that I am everlastingly devoted to Your Majesty. And I end by entreating my dear Prince to forgive me for troubling him with so tedious a letter. But I trust and pray Your Majesty will believe that I am more devoted to you than any man in this country ever was before."

Having sealed the letter and sent a messenger off with it, Lord Bute sat down heavily in his chair and leaned his elbows on his table. His mind went back to days long ago, when that other Prince of Wales, George's father, had been alive, and one rainy day at the races he had been brought into the royal tent to play whist while they waited for the rain to stop. That had been the beginning; then he had been *persona grata* with the family; even the Prince of Wales had been fond of him; and when he had died it was true Bute had seen possibilities of ingratiating himself with the simple young boy who was destined to be king when his ageing grandfather died. Then of course the boy's mother, the Dowager Princess of Wales, had fallen in love with him.

What a happy situation for a Scottish peer, debarred in so many ways from promotion simply because he was Scottish and not English, to find such favour in high places! And it had continued for so many years; there was a cosy domesticity about his relationship with the Princess, who was as devoted—perhaps even more so—to him as he was to her; and George had treated him as a father. And now . . . it had all changed.

He must report at once to the Princess for she might throw some light on the matter. As he rode through the streets he sat well back in his carriage. The people were slightly less hostile now, but they still talked of the jackboot and petticoat and could become offensive. If they made a riot, as they were constantly threatening to do, and it reached the King's ears, he would be more against him than ever. He might even forbid him to see the Princess Dowager. Oh, no, she would never allow that; and she still had some influence with the King.

The Princess received him as warmly as ever.

"Why are you disturbed?" she said. "Please tell me what is wrong. Come and sit here, beside me, my dear. I do not like to see you look so worried."

The Princess's servants had all discreetly disappeared as they had been doing for years on the arrival of her lover; and they could be sure of privacy.

"A most disturbing letter from the King. He does not wish to see me any more."

"Oh, no."

"It is true. Here it is."

The Princess read it and made clucking noises. "George is a fool!" she said. "He was always and always will be. He has no idea how to be a king."

"He is developing those ideas," retorted Bute. "He now believes he knows how to be a certain kind of king and, by God, he is going to be that kind of king. He has grown very stubborn. He makes up his mind and once it has been made up nothing on earth will shift him. And . . . he has turned against me."

"Something happened to George during that illness of his," mused the Princess. "He has grown very odd. That abrupt way of speaking . . . It's almost irascible. He was never like that before. He was rather slow and even stuttered now and then. The illness has changed his personality, I fear. But perhaps he will change again and become more like his old self."

Bute shook his head. "I do not think he will. He seems to have taken a great dislike to me and when I think of the affection he once had for me . . ."

"My dear, he is ungrateful; but we have each other."

"I was afraid that he might attempt to stop my visiting you."

"That is something *I* would never allow."

Bute smiled and turning to her embraced her warmly.

But he was thinking, a great deal of the excitement had

gone out of the relationship. Now they were almost like a staid old married couple.

When he left the Princess Dowager Lord Bute called on Miss Vansittart, a young lady of good family who had been extremely pretty and still was, although she was no longer young. But she was still much younger than Lord Bute who was over fifty.

She received him with pleasure and without surprise for in fact he had been calling on her for some time, finding her company a change after that of the Princess Dowager.

Miss Vansittart was humble and admired him wholeheartedly. She made no demands and that was very pleasant.

First they had talked and then it seemed so natural that they should become lovers in a quiet rather desultory way, which suited her nature and Lord Bute's declining years.

He told her that the King had turned against him and she was incredulous that the King could be so lacking in gratitude.

She soothed him and he told her that the Princess Dowager was as devoted to him as ever and that theirs was too strong a relationship for the King to stop it, although he might try.

"But I trust the Princess. She would never wish to part from me."

Miss Vansittart plainly adored him and he told her that he would speak to the Princess, and when there was a vacancy in her household it should go to Miss Vansittart.

Miss Vansittart shivered with delight at the prospect of serving the woman who for so many years had been a wife in all but name, to the wonderful Lord Bute; and he soothed the hurt the King had done him by basking in her admiration and explaining to her all the perquisites which fell into the laps of those who served in royal households. She would learn, for he would teach her, how to come by these rewards.

When he left her he felt better, but when he returned to his house his wife, that most accommodating of women, demanded to know if he had been visiting Miss Vansittart.

He admitted this was so, for since she had never complained of his relationship with the Princess Dowager why should she with Miss Vansittart?

But it seemed this was different. "This will have to stop," she told him. "This woman is no Princess Dowager. This is quite a different matter."

"I believe you are jealous," replied his lordship.

"Of course I'm jealous."

"Of this poor young woman?"

"Exactly. What has this poor young woman to offer but herself? With the Princess Dowager it was different."

"What a sordid view," he commented with distaste.

But his wife laughed at him and said that she was not prepared to have to listen to gossip about her husband and Miss Vansittart.

Lord Bute felt melancholy. Life had ceased to smile on him.

Four days after William Pitt had received the King's letter he was asking for an audience with His Majesty.

"Bring him in, bring him in," cried George. "Don't you know I wouldn't wish Mr. Pitt to be kept waiting, eh, eh?"

So Mr. Pitt came hobbling in and the King looked at him with emotion. The greatest mistake he had ever made, thought George, was to allow Bute to persuade him to banish Mr. Pitt.

But Mr. Pitt bore no grudges. The King asked after his family and gave news of his own.

"Young George is growing more bumptious every day. Frederick is imitating his brother; and I doubt not young William will be the same. As you know, the Queen is expecting another in September, ha! Well, well, we shall soon have a quiverful, eh, what?"

Mr. Pitt, elegant in spite of his afflictions, gracious and ceremonious, made a little speech about the blessings of family life and added that the royal family set an example to all the families in the land.

This pleased George whose eyes filled with tears at the thought of his and his wife's virtues and how well they filled their roles to the glory of England.

Then the conversation turned on the reason for Mr. Pitt's being in London and the King made it very clear that he placed himself in Mr. Pitt's hands.

He was disappointed in the Rockingham ministry; in fact ever since Mr. Pitt had ceased to lead the Government he had been disappointed.

Pitt's eyes gleamed with triumph when he heard this. He had come prepared to compromise; now he saw that there would be no need. It would be as he, Pitt, wished it to be.

He told the King that he would have great pleasure in

forming a government which he would submit to His Majesty for his approval.

George warmly shook his hand and said: "It is a great relief. You understand, eh? A great relief."

"I do understand, Sir. I trust Your Majesty will have no reason to regret your decision. Your Majesty knows full well that I shall use all my powers to make this ministry a success."

The King said: "Yes, yes, yes. I have never doubted that, eh? What? What?"

Mr. Pitt bowed himself from the presence. The King had changed and he could not help feeling a little uneasy. The quick way of talking with the inevitable "What? What?" was already being noticed. And the change had come with his recent indisposition . . . that mysterious illness which no one quite understood, and about which there were so many rumours.

A Regency? thought Pitt. He grimaced inwardly. Sufficient unto the day is the evil thereof. He would deal with such a contingency when and if it arose. In the meantime he had *carte blanche* to form a ministry.

Pitt presented his choice of a ministry to the King and it was accepted. The First Lord of the Treasury was the Duke of Grafton—a rather reckless choice perhaps, not because the Duke lacked ability and could not be trusted to support him, but because of the life he led. Descended from Charles II, Grafton had inherited many of that king's characteristics— chief of which was his love of women. His existing liaison was one of the scandals of the Court. This was with Nancy Parsons, a notorious courtesan, the daughter of a Bond Street tailor who had first lived with a West Indian merchant named Horton with whom she had gone to Jamaica; Jamaica did not suit her however and she soon returned to London where she took many lovers; chief of whom was the Duke of Grafton. The Duke's open dalliance with her—he was constantly seen with her at the races and in public places—his devotion to horse racing, his neglect of his wife, the mother of his three children, meant that his affairs were widely known and discussed. It was said by Horace Walpole, the wit and raconteur, that Grafton "postponed the world for a whore and a horserace" and he went on to voice some pointed criticism against "The Duke of Grafton's Mrs. Horton, the Duke of Dorset's Mrs. Horton, everybody's Mrs. Horton." And such was the man whom Pitt had chosen to be First Lord of the Treasury.

The Lord President was the Earl of Northington; the Chancellor of the Exchequer Mr. Charles Townsend; and the position of Lord Privy Seal Pitt reserved for himself.

When the news was out there was rejoicing through the City. Bonfires were lit in the streets. The Mayor decided that a banquet in honour of Mr. Pitt, the Great Commoner, be held at the Guildhall. There was a great deal of talk about the prosperity which Mr. Pitt had brought to the City when he had first become Prime Minister. Mr. Pitt had brought an Empire to England and the City knew that Empires meant trade and prosperity.

In the streets they shouted for Mr. Pitt. They waited for his carriage; if they saw it they gathered round it, cheering.

A great wave of optimism swept through London.

"Everything will be all right now," it was said. "Mr. Pitt is back."

Sewing, reading, walking a little in her apartments at Kew, going to see the children in their nursery, receiving visits from them, the trying months of pregnancy were passing slowly for Charlotte.

Though, she thought, I should be used to it by now. And there was one blessing: the more children she had the easier it became to give birth to them.

She saw little of her husband. He was occupied with the new Ministry and Mr. Pitt.

When he did come to see her she asked him questions, for there was so much excitement about that matter that the news had come to Kew. She wanted to know what had brought Mr. Pitt back and what his terms had been, because she knew that he had retired from the front bench because of some disagreement with the King and the majority of his ministers.

When George came to see her they walked together in the gardens. He wanted to know the minutest details. He always did. Why had roses been planted there? He would send for the gardeners and ask. They always had their answers ready and were prepared for him.

But when she asked him about government affairs he grew pink and he said: "Oh, state affairs . . . state affairs."

"Everyone seems so excited about this new turn."

"Shouldn't talk so much. Wait and see, eh?"

"Mr. Pitt must have many new plans."

"Don't doubt it, don't doubt it. Now are you taking regular

exercise? Necessary. Very necessary, eh? Feeling well are you? Feel the heat, eh, what? Usual in the circumstances, eh?''

''I'm as well as I always am at these times, but I should like to know . . .''

''Take care. Don't worry your head about matters outside your knowledge. Not good for the child. Not good for you, eh? I think a path would be good here. What do you think, eh?''

And so it went on.

At times Charlotte felt like a prisoner—a pampered prisoner who was to have all her comforts, most material things that she asked for, but never her freedom.

I am like a queen bee in a hive. I am looked after that I may go on bearing my young.

A few days after he had formed his ministry William Pitt made one of the greatest mistakes of his career. He accepted a peerage and became Viscount Pitt of Burton-Pynsent in the County of Somersetshire and Earl of Chatham in the County of Kent.

What possessed him to take such a step his friends could not be sure. He was suffering acutely from the gout; the first excitement of being in harness again was wearing off; he knew that the old enemy Gout was not going to allow him to carry out his plans; he felt old and tired; and as most of his colleagues possessed high sounding titles, it seemed only right and proper that he, who had done so much more in the service of his country, should have one too.

In any case he accepted the titles and by doing so lost the one which had counted for so much in the eyes of the people. He might now be the Earl of Chatham but he was no longer the Great Commoner.

''Illuminations for my Lord Chatham!'' cried the people of London. ''A banquet at the Guildhall! Not likely. They were to honour Mr. Pitt, not Lord Chatham. He's as self-seeking as the rest. He's not there to serve the country and us. He's there to get a fine handle to his name and what goes with it.''

There was no enthusiasm now in the streets. No one called Hurrah for Pitt. The people were sullenly silent.

Everyone was commenting on the change.

Lord Chesterfield wrote to his son: ''He has had a fall upstairs and has done himself so much hurt that he will never be able to stand on his legs again.''

But it was the shrewd Horace Walpole who summed up the position and pointed out that in accepting the title the new Earl had done more harm to the country than to himself. "While he held the love of the people," said Horace, "nothing was so formidable in Europe as his name. The talons of the lion were drawn when he was no longer awful in his own forest."

A sick man, driven almost to distraction by the pain of his gout, Pitt sought to defy public opinion which had previously wholeheartedly supported him and tried to govern with his ministry which had been made up from both parties; but because he had set Whigs and Tories, friends and enemies to work together and because he himself had ruined his own public image by his title, and chiefly because he was an extremely sick man, he was doomed to failure.

Edmund Burke was later to describe the Ministry as "a tessellated pavement without cement; here a bit of black stone and there a bit of white; patriots and courtiers, kind friends and republicans; Whigs and Tories; treacherous friends and open enemies . . . a very curious show, but utterly unsafe to touch and unsure to stand on."

That year there was a bad harvest and Chatham was obliged to lay an embargo on the importation of corn.

It was a very uneasy session and as the summer passed into autumn, the gout began to plague him more than ever.

In September Charlotte moved to Buckingham House to prepare for her confinement. It was necessary for the royal child to be born in London, but now that Buckingham House had become such a popular royal residence, Charlotte need not go to that grim old palace of St. James's.

Although she was not allowed to meddle, of course, she knew what was happening. She had heard that Mr. Pitt had become Lord Chatham and that the people were not very pleased with him because of this.

How she wished George would consult her. What a pleasure it would be if they could talk politics together. After all she was not exactly stupid. She was only ignorant because she was not allowed to learn.

She believed that the Princess Dowager was at the bottom of the plot to keep her away from affairs. That woman was downright jealous; and she was pleased to hear that her lover Lord Bute was out of favour with the King, and that George seemed at last to have escaped from his mother's apron strings.

What a blessing it was to be able to understand English. Now she could glean all sorts of interesting conversation from her women. Miss Chudleigh was really a most indiscreet woman. So much the better, thought Charlotte.

But on reflection she agreed that life in England was very different from what she had imagined. She had thought she was coming to England to rule with her husband; and here she was doing scarcely anything but being pregnant and bearing children.

Well, she had her three boys, and when she thought of them she could not help being delighted with them. It was after all so much more gratifying to be a mother than a great politician, though some women had managed to be both.

The leaves on the trees were beginning to turn russet. She could not be bothered to ask what all the shouting in the streets was about. The shortage of corn? The defection of Lord Chatham? It all seemed rather unimportant when a new life was about to begin.

I want a girl this time, she told Miss Chudleigh, and Miss Chudleigh replied that she was sure it would be a girl. It was the way Her Majesty was carrying and after three boys a girl often followed.

And on the 26th September Charlotte's child was born. A little girl. So she had her wish.

She was called Charlotte Augusta Matilda; and the Queen, delighted, happy now to be nothing but a mother, said that the child was her little Michaelmas Goose.

Domesticity at Kew

George had made up his mind to be a king and those about him had to learn to accept this fact. The Princess Dowager had reluctantly released her hold on him, although she still refused to believe that she had lost her influence over him entirely.

She had thought it would be enough that Charlotte should be prevented from usurping her place; this had been easy to achieve for Charlotte's ability to furnish the royal nurseries was really phenomenal. It seemed that no sooner had she been delivered of one child than another was on the way. After Charlotte Augusta Matilda, Edward had followed; and almost immediately she was pregnant again. Nor did she seem to suffer from this continual childbearing; in fact she seemed to thrive on it.

"She was intended for it," said the Princess Dowager to Lord Bute when he called on her. "And I will grant her this; she does it with remarkable speed and efficiency."

It was pleasant to reflect, was Lord Bute's comment, that the Queen could please the Princess Dowager in some respects.

"Oh, yes," said the Princess. "She is adequate. And as long as she does not attempt to meddle in politics I have no complaint to make."

She smiled benignly. She still doted on this man. He was as a husband to her and she was a woman who needed a husband. She was not promiscuous; she was not sensuous; but she needed the companionship, the at-oneness which was only to be found in a devoted husband; and Lord Bute had provided that, more so than her real husband the Prince of Wales had ever done; although she had had nothing to complain of in Frederick.

She had taken Miss Vansittart into her household recently, and the young woman had made herself very useful in the rather delicate matter of selling honours. She was a most discreet young woman; and the Princess Dowager needed the little money these sales brought in and could not of course be concerned in the sordid business of selling.

Since Miss Vansittart was a friend of Lord Bute's she knew she could absolutely rely on her. And if Lord Bute did visit her regularly, they never betrayed in her presence that there was anything between them but the most platonic friendship.

She loved Lord Bute with a wifely devotion; they had been together now for many years and she regarded their union as a true marriage.

Recently, however, she had been feeling a painful restriction in her throat which had alarmed her. She had said nothing of it, for she wanted no doctors telling her some unpleasant truth. The trouble would occur and then subside; but she was constantly aware of it; and she had uneasy suspicions, having heard of such symptoms before.

If she were going to die—oh not yet, but perhaps in a year or so—she would like to know that Lord Bute would have someone to comfort him; and nice, discreet, quiet Miss Vansittart would be the very one.

So far from discouraging that friendship, she kept Miss Vansittart beside her. Her love for this man, who had dominated her thoughts for so many years, was too deep, too abiding to be selfish.

In the meantime no one—not even Lord Bute—must guess of this thing which was there in her throat and which she fancied became a little more painful every time she was made aware of it.

George was impressing his personality on the Court which many declared was dull, dreary, unimaginative and completely devoid of the trappings of royalty. There was nothing royal about George—nor about Charlotte. George might have been a farmer, for he had a great interest in agriculture; Charlotte might have been any squire's lady sitting there in her country house breeding.

There was another characteristic which was beginning to be noticed and which was considered unkingly: the King was constantly concerning himself over trifling sums of money; he wanted to know the cost of things and would often shake his

head and say this and that was too costly. They must econo-
mize. Although there had been many complaints of extravagance
in kings in the past, George's carefulness was even more
deplored. As for Charlotte, she was, said her ladies-in-waiting,
becoming downright mean.

In fact Charlotte was constantly being asked to help her
family in Mecklenburg. She had become the great Queen of
England and it was imagined that she lived a life very different from that which she had known in humble Mecklenburg.
This was true; and Charlotte was pleased that her family
should be aware of this. She asked the King's advice and he
most beneficently came to her family's assistance. Her eldest
brother was given a pension; another brother was made Governor of Celle and another given a rewarding post in the
Hanoverian Army. Charlotte was not considered mean by her
family; but in her own apartments—where she followed the
King's habit of scrutinizing accounts—she was certainly considered parsimonious, a trait even more unpopular in royal
people than in commoners.

George had decided to bring a more religious way of life
back to his people. "I wish every child in my Dominions to
be able to read his Bible," he declared; and very soon he was
expressing a desire that the Sabbath Day be kept holy; that
there should be no entertainments on Sunday and that throughout the country there should be Sabbath Day Observance.

This desire in him was intensified when he thought of
scandals which surrounded his family. His brother Edward,
with whom he had been so close during his youth, had died a
year or so ago, but not before he had shocked George by his
wild life; his two brothers William of Gloucester and Henry,
who had become Duke of Cumberland since the death of the
Victor of Culloden, were continuously causing scandal through
their relationships with women; his mother's liaison with
Lord Bute was still talked of on the streets; lewd songs were
sung about Bute's prowess in bed and the Princess Dowager's
dependence on him. Jackboot and Petticoat remained a well-
known insult.

"It was necessary," said the King to Charlotte on those
rare occasions when he talked to her of anything apart from
the weather and children, "that our lives are exemplary. We
must show them, eh? You see that, Charlotte. What? You see
we must be beyond reproach, eh?"

Charlotte did see; and she pointed out that with her constant childbearing it was hardly likely that she could be anything else.

George replied that he had his duties as she had. But although he was determined to live a completely virtuous life he could not help his heart beating a little faster every time he saw a pretty woman.

He was disturbed when he heard that Sarah Lennox had given birth to a daughter who, it was said, was not her husband's, but that Sarah's cousin Lord William Gordon was the father.

"Shocking! Shocking!" said the King and thought wistfully of Sarah, adding to himself: "Lucky escape. I was well rid of that one."

But that did not prevent his thinking of her. However virtuous a man was, and intended to continue to be, he could not help erotic images coming into his mind, much as he tried to suppress them.

Then there was Elizabeth, Lady Pembroke, whom he had always admired. A beautiful woman, this Elizabeth, and not very happily married either. The Earl had eloped with a Miss Kitty Hunter some years before; George had been very sympathetic and had done his best to comfort Elizabeth, often holding her hand while he told her that if her husband failed to appreciate her, he, George, thought her one of the loveliest women he had ever seen. Elizabeth was grateful to him and if George had been slightly less virtuous he might have been her lover. But the Earl had returned and the marriage had been patched up. Yet he often dreamed of Elizabeth Pembroke.

There was Bridget, Lord Northington's eldest daughter—a charming girl. He had been rather fond of her too.

Charlotte was, he admitted in his franker moments, so very plain and unexciting. But he must remember that it was the duty of the King to set an example to his people; so he diverted these desires for beautiful women into stricter controls for his own household. He himself saw that the Sunday Observance was kept, and that gambling stakes were not too high.

It was soon being said that he was a petty tyrant in his household—obsessed by the need to live virtuously and force others to do the same.

He was beset by political anxieties. He had suffered great disappointment over Chatham whom he had thought would take the helm as he had in his grandfather's day and guide them to prosperity. But Chatham was not the same man that William Pitt had been. His title was like a cloak which suffocated his brilliance. He had lost the confidence of the people, and his infirmity had taken possession of him.

He kept to his house in Bond Street and lay in a darkened room cursing the gout which had laid him low; overcome by melancholia. He knew that in his present condition even if he could hobble to the House his mind would not be sufficiently alert to grapple with the problems of state.

George, up to this time, had a pathetic belief in Chatham. If Chatham would be the man he had once been, the country's affairs would be straightened out and all would go smoothly. But Lady Chatham was constantly writing to the King telling him that if only her husband's health matched his devotion to His Majesty and his zeal to serve him, Lord Chatham would be waiting on the King at this time.

Meanwhile there was trouble with the American Colonies who so bitterly resented interference from St. James's and were declaring that they could not and would not submit to taxation imposed by the British Government.

England needed a Pitt at this time and Pitt had turned into Lord Chatham and lay writhing on his bed.

All during the summer Chatham saw no one. Whenever any of his colleagues in the Government called, Lady Chatham assured them that her husband was too ill to be seen. There were rumours as to his reasons for hiding himself away. Had he quarrelled with the King? Had he gone mad? Grafton sought to control the party and failed. Chatham's policy of removing taxation from the American Colonies and establishing harmonious relations was overthrown and Townsend the Chancellor of the Exchequer imposed those taxes.

In his dark room Chatham lay a physical and mental wreck while his wife sought to keep this fact a secret from the world.

In his lucid moments Chatham wished above all things to resign and wrote to the King telling him so, but George would not let him go.

"Your name has been sufficient to enable my administration to proceed," he wrote. He was determined that ill as he was Chatham should remain ostensibly head of the Government.

But this could not continue; and some two years after he had taken office Chatham insisted on retiring and delivered up the Seal.

The King was so worried on receipt of this that he paced up and down his apartment for hours. The name of Pitt had been a magic one to him and he clung to the belief that while that man was head of the Government all would be well.

He was extremely anxious to settle this niggling business of the Colonists and he was sure that Pitt could have done it and that he was the only man who could.

But Chatham's resignation must perforce he accepted and Frederick second Earl of North became Leader of the House.

North was an old friend of George's. He had played with him in the nursery when North's father had been appointed his governor. George remembered Frederick North's playing in Addison's *Cato* when they had been very young and amateur theatricals had amused them so much. George had been Portius and his sister Augusta, Marcia. It all came back so clearly; and it was pleasant to talk over those days with Frederick who had grown into a witty man. He was very good tempered too, as well as being very like George to look at; in fact when they had been young they could have been brothers. The Prince of Wales, when they were boys, had said that the likeness was suspicious and joked with North's father that one of their wives must have played them false. The likeness was still undoubtedly remarkable; and not only that—North could be as obstinate as George himself, another trait they had in common.

He had the same prominent eyes which in his case were extremely short-sighted; he had a wide mouth and thick lips and with his plump cheeks and his eyes which rolled about "to no purpose" commented Walpole, he looked (Walpole again) like a blind trumpeter.

But George did not agree with these unkind observations. He saw Frederick North as his childhood friend, so like him in many ways that the friendship could comfortably continue.

If he could not have Chatham, North would do very well.

George was preparing to receive Christian VII of Denmark and Norway, husband of Caroline Matilda.

The Princess Dowager was delighted that her son-in-law was coming to England, but deplored the fact that he was not bringing Caroline Matilda with him.

She was with Lord Bute discussing this when news was brought to her that the King was descending from his coach to call on her.

"Oh, my dearest," she cried, "he had better not find you here."

They embraced and parted and she watched her lover disappear through the door which led to the secret staircase by which he would reach the street.

"So different," she sighed, "from the old days, when we were all together, the three of us. I can't think what has happened to George lately. Being king has gone to his head and he's surrounded by the wrong people and we shall have trouble." She touched her throat and the thought came to her then that she might not be here to see it.

George came in and greeted her as affectionately as ever. However much he tried to escape from her influence she was still his mother and he was too sentimental to forget that.

"My dearest son. How good it is to see you!"

"You are looking a little tired, Mother."

"Nonsense. It's the light. I am very much looking forward to Christian's visit."

"That is what I came to talk to you about. How strange that he should not be bringing Caroline Matilda with him. After all, it is Caroline Matilda we are really eager to see."

The Princess smiled. George was such a family man. She was pleased about that at least.

"I have heard strange rumours from Frederiksberg."

George nodded. "You think Caroline Matilda is unhappy?"

"Perhaps we shall be able to talk to Christian."

"Do you think he will listen?"

"He should listen to his mother-in-law if he has any courtesy."

"I wonder whether he has."

The Princess Dowager sighed. Neither of her daughters had done very well. Poor Augusta merely Duchess of Brunswick and living in that hateful town in a poor sort of wooden house while her husband's mistress flaunted her position under her nose. A fine comedown for proud Augusta! What had become of her sharp tongue? Was it any use to her in coping with this most indelicate situation which her boor of a husband insisted she accept? Well she had her daughter now, little Caroline Amelia Elizabeth, and the child must be a comfort to her, although naturally she would have preferred to have a son. But what that child would grow up like in such a court was beyond the Princess Dowager's divination.

As for Caroline Matilda, her position was as bad, for quite

clearly Christian did not have much affection for her—otherwise would he be travelling without her?

"He seems to be a weak-willed young man from what I hear," said the Princess Dowager. "I do wish he was bringing your sister so that I could hear from her own lips what is happening over there."

"I fear you would not be comforted. What?"

"Oh, you mean Christian's step-brother. There's no doubt that his mother will be wishing to see him inherit."

George nodded grimly. He felt so responsible for his sister's welfare and he had often wished that they had not hurried Caroline Matilda into marriage. Fifteen was so young; and he liked to have as many members of his family around him as possible. Continually shocked as he was at the wild life his brothers indulged in, he would particularly have enjoyed having a young sister, whom he could advise and on whom he could dote.

But poor little Caroline Matilda had been sent far from home to a young bridegroom—a weak, dissolute young man, more interested in some of his male attendants than in his young bride, and in the strange land she was confronted by this unfortunate scene. And there was a stepmother-in-law with a son whom naturally she would wish to inherit.

"Poor little Caroline Matilda," mused George. "I wonder if I shall be able to *talk* to Christian."

George was obtuse, thought his mother. Did he really believe that this little pervert would listen to him just because he was King of England!

"I have heard that Christian has taken Count von Holck as his favourite now."

George flushed and looked shocked. "It's all so unpleasant. What? But Caroline Matilda has her son, little Frederick, so . . ."

"So," said the Princess Dowager grimly, "our dissolute Christian is at least capable of begetting a child."

"I really find this so distasteful, I find it most distasteful," said George. "I shall do my best to make this known to Christian."

But when Christian arrived George saw how impossible it was to make any impression on the young man. He sent for Lord Weymouth and asked him to consult the Danish ambassador as to what would best please the young King and to ask for ideas on how to entertain him.

When Weymouth returned to George he said he had had a very direct answer.

"The way to entertain the King of Denmark is to amuse him," was the answer. "And the wilder and more perverted the entertainment the more he will be amused."

"This is most unpleasant, eh, what?" said the King; and Weymouth agreed that it was.

It was impossible for George to feel any affection for his brother-in-law. The very sight of the young man disgusted him. If he had seen him before the marriage he would never have agreed to it, but Caroline Matilda had been married by proxy.

There was no doubt of his character. He was not only perverted, he was depraved; and it seemed to be having its effect on his wits.

He was surrounded by courtiers whose main duty it was to praise and glorify him; and the visit depressed George, particularly when he learned that Christian spent his time in the brothels of London in which all kinds of unnatural spectacles had been arranged for his entertainment.

George decided that he would no longer attempt to entertain his brother-in-law, so he went down to Kew to be with Charlotte and the children for a while.

"I cannot help reminding myself how fortunate we are, eh? When I think of what a life my poor sister is leading in Denmark . . . and Augusta is not much better off in Brunswick. We have been lucky, eh? What?"

Charlotte agreed that they had. She was pregnant again, and that year gave birth to her second daughter; she called her Augusta Sophia.

She now had six children after seven years of marriage. It was pleasant to see the nurseries so full; but she was beginning to feel that she would like a little respite, if only for a few years.

Meanwhile that inveterate troublemaker, John Wilkes, was getting a little bored with exile and was thinking nostalgically of home.

When he had arrived he had found it most diverting to be welcomed as he was by the literary world of Paris. In the Hôtel de Saxe he had held his little court and later when he took up residence in Rue St. Nicaise he had that exciting and much sought after courtesan Corradini to live with him and share his exile. This he had found very much to his taste, and after a short residence in Paris they had travelled together to Rome and Naples, and it was in the latter city that he met his fellow countryman James Boswell and they, finding they possessed similar tastes mostly for women and literature, greatly enjoyed each other's companionship.

Wilkes had then intended to write a *History of England* but when Corradini left him for another lover he lost interest in the project and returned to Paris to look at a lodging in the Rue des Saints Pères.

Homesickness became more acute; if he had been able to make money with his literary efforts it would have been different; and so would it have been if Corradini had not deserted him. These two factors together made him decide that he did not wish to live among the French. He was pining for the streets of London, for the coffee and chocolate houses, for the taverns and his literary friends; he wanted to be in the thick of the fight, to live dangerously, to send out his scandal sheets and await the consequences. And he wanted money. There was his beloved daughter Mary to educate. She was the only person in the world he cared about and he wanted to give her all that he believed her worthy of, which was a good deal.

Grimly he walked the streets of Paris and dreamed of London. His ugly face had ceased to be comical; it was only melancholy, and that made his squint look more alarming and not mischievous at all, only sinister.

"I must get back," he told himself. "I'll die of melancholy here."

He waited avidly for news from London. Pitt was back . . . Chatham now. Oh, fool of a man to think the title of Earl could give him a greater name than Pitt. And Grafton was with him. Now there was a man who might give him a helping hand. He didn't trust Chatham who had washed his hands of him when he was in trouble; Wilkes was not going to ask favours of that man. But Grafton was a different matter. Grafton might do something.

He returned to London and there wrote to Grafton, who immediately went to see Chatham. This happened before Chatham had shut himself away and was suffering from that mysterious illness which robbed him of his mental powers; and Chatham's advice to Grafton was not to become involved with Mr. Wilkes.

So, dispirited, Wilkes returned to Paris, but within a year

he was back again in London and rented a house at the corner of Princes Court in Westminster.

George was disturbed when he received a letter from John Wilkes. The King was at Buckingham House which he enjoyed very much when he could not get to Kew or Richmond. But when Wilkes's servant arrived with the letter the peace of Buckingham House was definitely disturbed.

"What does this man want, eh?" George demanded of himself. "Trouble, eh? What? Here he comes after making a nuisance of himself . . . Ought to have stayed in France. Better go back as soon as possible."

And he was petitioning for a pardon, was he? And after that he'd be wanting compensation!

Wilkes might want to be in London, but London did not want him—at least the King didn't and there must be a good many of his ministers who didn't either.

George burned the letter and tried to forget the troublesome fellow. As if Wilkes was the kind to allow himself to be forgotten!

He kept quiet until the next general election and then he suddenly appeared at the hustings, asking the people of London to elect him to represent them. He failed with London but he did succeed in getting in at Middlesex.

Now the trouble started. The new member for Middlesex was an outlaw; he had been sentenced to exile; he had returned to England without permission; but nobly he surrendered himself to the King's Bench and was committed to prison.

Crowds gathered in the streets to see him taken there. He was in his element, the centre of attraction once more—Wilkes, with his wicked-looking face, his sinister squint and his cries of freedom.

"Such men," said the King, "could destroy the peace of nations."

The City was in a turmoil. People paraded the streets shouting: "Free Wilkes. Wilkes for Liberty." They would have rescued him and freed him on his way to prison but he had no desire to be freed. He wished to go to prison for he realized that while he was there he would hold the sympathy of the people; he would be Wilkes, imprisoned for speaking his mind.

His prison was in St. George's Fields and for days crowds

accumulated there to talk of Wilkes and demand his release; the great topic of conversation through the city was John Wilkes.

It was neccessary to call out the troops to disperse the mob and when he heard this Wilkes chuckled with delight, for nothing could have pleased him better.

When after a month in prison he was sentenced to a year and ten months imprisonment a fine was imposed and he appealed against this in both the Commons and the Lords.

Wilkes! Wilkes! Wilkes! He dominated the scene. Everyone was discussing the rights and wrongs of his case. The great battle took place in print. There were articles written under the pseudonym of Junius in a periodical supported by the Whigs, while Dr. Samuel Johnson made somewhat dull apologies for the Government.

It was Wilkes who was emerging from the conflict as the victor and when he brought a case against Lord Halifax he won and received heavy damages. Thus when he had gone to prison he had been penniless, but he emerged comfortably off.

The King was deeply concerned by almost everything around him. Nothing was as he had believed it was going to be. He had wanted to be the good King surrounded by contented subjects; and during this weary year there had been not only trouble with his ministers and the Wilkes controversy, but every month the situation between England and the American Colonies was growing more and more tense.

Even at Kew George could not escape from Wilkes. It was not that he discussed the man with Charlotte. At Kew life went on as he had decided it should, completely shut away from the outside world. The Queen was—naturally—pregnant, and next spring would give birth to her seventh child, and as she was still in her early twenties it seemed hardly likely that she would stop at seven.

The Prince of Wales was now seven years old, bright and more precocious than ever; he was always listening to gossip and repeating it to his parents to show them that he was well in the swim of affairs. He bullied—and at best patronized— his younger brothers and was indeed the little King of the nursery. He never failed to remind anyone who dared to reprimand him that after all he was the Prince of Wales; but his handsome looks, his bright intelligence, and his often engaging manners won him great affection and he was naturally adored by the nurses and maids of honour.

Even the Queen could not help spoiling him a little. He was her firstborn, a sign to the rest of the world that although she might be a plain and insignificant little woman, at least she could produce a charming son.

The people did not like her. She was aware of that. She would never forget driving through Richmond with the King beside her when a woman ran up to the carriage and began to curse her. It was horrible to be made aware of such hatred and to wonder what one had done to be the cause of it.

"Go back where you belong, you crocodile."

They hated her because she was a foreigner, because she was ugly. She was small and thin and her mouth made her look like a crocodile, it was true. She admitted to the resemblance when she herself looked in the glass.

The woman had taken off her shoe and thrown it at her. It had narrowly missed her face and hit the upholstery of the carriage.

"Go back. Go back where you belong, you German woman!"

A scene. The carriage stopping. The Guards arresting the poor creature who, they said, was mad. She could have been severely punished but both the King and Queen decided against that.

But the unreasoning hatred of a mob was a frightening thing, something of which she supposed all kings and queens were made aware at some time.

But in her rooms at Kew she felt a pleasant security; it was as though she were wrapped round in a cocoon which protected her from the world. When she had first come to England she had imagined herself ruling England with the King; now she knew she would never be allowed to do that. Therefore she would rule her own household at Kew . . . dear *little* Kew . . . where with her children she could live shut away from the unpleasantness of the world. Not for her to dabble in politics as the Princess Dowager had done—but only after her husband's death. She would content herself with ruling her own household.

And rule she did, taking an interest in the smallest details. Following the King's lead she must study the household accounts; she wanted to know how every penny was spent.

She became fascinated by economies—which did not endear her to the members of her household.

Albert, her hairdresser whom she had brought with her from Mecklenburg, was one who was in revolt.

He came to her one day and said: "Madam, I wish to return to Mecklenburg."

She was astonished. Leave England, this great and expanding country, for a little Dukedom! Albert must have taken leave of his senses.

"No, Madam," was the answer, "I could find a more lucrative post in the household of the Duke, I am sure. My skill is such that I should be welcomed there; and if Your Majesty would allow me to retire from your service on a pension . . ."

"A pension!" The Queen was horrified. More money given away. She could not bear to contemplate it.

Albert pointed out sadly that the expectations with which he had come to England had not materialized.

"That is often the case with many of us," she told him, and that was the end of the matter. Albert was not going to be allowed to leave.

The ladies-in-waiting said she was becoming like a miserly old country woman measuring out the preserves from the stillroom; and aware of their hostility she became more and more autocratic, although bowing to the King's will in all things.

She had made a rule that all her ladies should buy English goods.

"I myself," she told Lady Charlotte Finch, "shall wear an English nightdress." She smiled. "The King is pleased when I do. And, Lady Charlotte, I expect you to do the same."

Lady Charlotte, who liked to choose her own clothes, was a little deflated, but owing to her position in the nurseries could do nothing but obey.

"And the children's clothes should be English too."

"Then Your Majesty would wish me to order new English clothes for them."

"Good heavens, no. What a wicked waste! Only when the time comes, Lady Charlotte."

Lady Charlotte smiled. Like other ladies of the Court she liked to tease the Queen, without her knowing it, of course.

Charlotte asked for the lists of the children's clothes to be brought to her then. Each boy had six full dress suits a year besides several ordinary suits for ordinary day wear; once a fortnight they had new shoes, and new hats as they were required.

"The Prince of Wales seems to wear a great many hats."

"He enjoys playing ball with them, Your Majesty."

"Oh, the wicked waste! He must be stopped."

But even Charlotte was pleased at her son's high spirits.

"And William's shoes! Edward's too! Surely they cannot need so many pairs? A pair for spring and autumn should be adequate."

"They have a passion for kicking stones, Your Majesty. And if they can find anything to kick they will kick it."

"Then they must be forbidden to do so, the naughty little things. Where do they learn such habits?"

"From the Prince of Wales, Your Majesty."

It always came back to the Prince of Wales.

"He is a rogue," said his mother affectionately; but she doted on him to such an extent that she could even forget to be shocked by the extravagance he caused.

Such pleasant days at dear little Kew, waiting for her children to be born, bearing them, having the pleasure of seeing another little face in the nursery.

And of course the King came often to escape from state affairs, for a little respite such as he loved. There were times when Charlotte would have liked to reason with him, to ask him why he could not discuss affairs with her. How interesting it would have been if he had. It was not that she was meek by nature, far from it; but she could not forget those terrifying weeks of his illness when he had wandered in his mind and had been—yes, she had to admit it—somewhat deranged, when the Princess Dowager and Lord Bute had sought to keep her away from him—a foretaste of what her life would be like if ever she lost him.

Sometimes when George's eyes seemed to become more prominent than ever, when his speech became more rapid and was punctuated even more liberally than usual by those interminable "Whats," a terrible fear came to her that George might again suffer the same sort of illness which he had experienced that spring.

No, Kew meant refuge to him as it did to her. There he played the country gentleman; there he made his buttons and inspected the farms and talked about turning some of the park into arable land, supervised the children's education, diet, their wardrobes, their household. That was when he was happiest dealing with the little things of life which to him were of the utmost importance.

"Plenty of exercise," he would say, "and plenty of fresh air, eh? And not overloading with food. What? Vegetables. Good for you. And never wine. Make sure the children get lean meat."

He himself followed these rules which he laid down for the children, for he was certain they were necessary for all.

While the Wilkes trouble was at its height and there were riots in St. George's Square outside the jail, the King came to Kew for a little respite.

Charlotte who had listened to her women talking of Wilkes— as indeed everyone was—who had heard the servants whisper the man's name often when they were unaware that she could hear, mentioned him to the King which brought forth unusual indignation in His Majesty.

"Why, Charlotte," he said, "I thought you knew that I come here to escape from these tiresome matters. Didn't you? Didn't you, eh? What peace am I to get if I am to have nothing but Wilkes in St. James's and nothing but Wilkes at Kew, what? What?"

Charlotte said that that man's name seemed to be on all lips so she supposed it was natural it should be on hers, too.

"Not at Kew. I come to Kew to get away from all that. Not much use coming here to find Wilkes waiting for me, eh?"

To soothe him Charlotte asked if he would care to go into the children's house to see them dine. They would be just sitting down to dinner and delighted doubtless to see their father.

This suggestion restored the King's good humour and together he and the Queen left the main house at Kew and walked the little distance to the small one occupied by the children.

Charlotte was right; the children were just sitting down to their meal, Lady Charlotte Finch presiding.

Charlotte noted that it was a fish day and that there was nothing on the table which the King had laid down should not be eaten by his family.

The children greeted their parents with pleasure and cries of delight from little Edward which were echoed by little Charlotte who had only just become old enough to join the group at the table. The youngest, Augusta Sophia, was naturally not present.

The Prince of Wales made an announcement—which he made every fish day without fail—that he liked meat and when he was king he would eat it every day.

"Then," said the King, "you will be a very fat king."

"Fatter than you?" asked George.

"A great deal fatter . . . so fat that you won't be able to move about except in a carriage. You wouldn't like that would you? Eh? Eh?"

"Yes, I would," said the Prince of Wales.

"But I tell you you would not."

"I would," said the Prince of Wales almost sullenly. "I hate fish. I want meat."

The Queen looked at Lady Charlotte Finch who remarked that the Prince of Wales seemed to forget he was in the presence of the King and Queen.

"I didn't forget. How could I forget when they are here."

"The Prince of Wales forgets his manners, it seems. What?" said the King, looking so fiercely at Lady Charlotte that she flushed.

"I don't forget them," the Prince pointed out. "I don't always use them."

The Queen tried not to smile, but the boy knew by the twitching of her lips that he was being as amusing as ever and he went on imperiously: "And if I don't want to use them, I won't."

"Perhaps," said the King, still looking at Lady Charlotte, "the Prince of Wales should be requested to leave the room until he can find the manners he has mislaid. Eh? What?"

Little Edward began to look under the table as though he thought manners were something which they should be wearing or carrying in their pockets. Frederick who always followed his eldest brother said: "I won't eat fish either."

"Then," said the King, "you may leave the table and your brother may go with you. You understand me, eh?"

"Quite," said the Prince of Wales haughtily. "Come, Fred."

The two boys went with great dignity to the door and the Prince said as they disappeared: "I never could abide fish."

"The young puppies," said the King when the door shut on them and William told his parents about his new puppy and the Queen answered brightly trying to pretend that her two eldest sons had not been dismissed in disgrace.

"I will speak to them later," said the Queen comfortably. "Young George has such high spirits and Fred will follow him in everything."

The King grunted; he was already working out in his mind fresh arrangements involving more discipline in the nursery.

They sat with the younger children until they finished their dinner, and when they had been to their nursery they sat on together and the King talked in a rather excited manner about young George.

"But I have heard that he learns quickly and is very bright indeed at his lessons."

"He must learn humility," replied the King. "That must be taught him. You agree, eh? You'd admit he was showing some arrogance. You wouldn't approve of that, eh? What?"

"He has very high spirits and that is no bad thing. I think that on the whole we should be rather proud of him."

The King nodded, and said he would work out new rules for the children's household; and he would see that the Prince of Wales was taught a little more humility. He wondered how they were getting on with their music. They must love music. He had found more pleasure in music than any other entertainment. He believed that Handel was one of the best of musicians and he wanted the boys—and the girls in time—to be familiar with his works. Whether they had inherited his love of music or not they were to be made to like it . . . just as they would be made to like lean meat and fish when it was not their day for meat.

The door of the room was cautiously opened; the Queen turned sharply, but the King had not heard.

Charlotte saw Frederick's face, rather red, his blue eyes alight with purpose and behind him the taller figure of the Prince of Wales.

Suddenly Frederick shouted: "Wilkes and Number Forty Five forever."

The King leaped to his feet. There was a sound of scampering feet and rushing to the door George saw his elder sons disappear up the staircase.

Charlotte came and stood beside him.

Then George began to smile; Charlotte smiled too. Then they were both laughing.

"So you see," said the Queen demurely, "Your Majesty cannot get away from Wilkes even at Kew."

The children should be made aware of their public duty, said the King; and no one could deny that he was a devoted father. To give them an interest and to take their minds from their own petty importance he ordered that a model farm be made at Kew and there they could have their own animals and feel as the King said "a responsibility towards them." The King believed that what was entrancing to him must be to his children; and it was he who took more pleasure in the model farm than his sons did. When he was at Kew he would go to see how the milking was getting on and take a turn with the butter making.

"Come, George," he would say. "Come, Fred. You are not princes at this moment. You are farmers. Understand, eh? What's that? You'd rather be a prince, George. I've no doubt. I've no doubt. But you will have to learn to appreciate the joys of working the land, boy."

For the most part the boys did enjoy playing with their father. They were fond of the animals; but none of them showed the skill the King had in dealing with them.

The King had decided that on every Thursday Kew should be thrown open to the public so that they could wander about the grounds and the farm, and see the children at play. They would watch the games of cricket and rounders at which the elder Princes excelled; and the Prince of Wales always enjoyed an audience.

The act of throwing Kew open to the people proved to be a good one, for the King's popularity began to rise again and whatever else was said of him all agreed that he was a good father; and when he met any of his subjects wandering over his lawns he always behaved with the utmost courtesy and never expected them to treat him as a King.

He was a bit dull, they said; and there was nothing exciting about his Court; but he was a good husband and father and that was rare in Kings.

But this mingling with the public could be carried too far and when George decided that he wished the children to hold a Court of their own there was some criticism of this. Young Frederick who was at this time seven had when only a few months old been given the title of Bishop of Osnabrück, which amused the lampoonists so much that the child was always represented in Bishop's regalia when he appeared in cartoons—as he did constantly since he had received this title.

At the reception the five eldest children stood on a dais where they received the company in the utmost solemnity. The Prince of Wales, wearing the Order of the Garter, looked particularly jaunty and young Frederick, the youthful Bishop, wore the Order of the Bath.

The ceremony was subjected to the utmost ridicule which delighted those noblemen who, with their wives, had been obliged to bow before such young children.

The cartoonists were busy; examples of their work was handed round; and the Prince of Wales was drawn flying a kite while a Whig dignitary bowed low before him.

It was a mistake, George realized; and he was very susceptible to the feelings he aroused in his subjects. But even though this ceremony brought the jeers of the writers and artists, everyone went on admitting that the King was a good father and considering the state of the country and that he was therefore overwhelmed by anxieties brought about by the hostilities between his ministers and their ineptitude in solving the nation's affairs, he still had time to supervise his children's education.

George was a family man.

Scandal at Home

A family, though, could prove a heavy liability.

George had long known that his brothers were creating scandal by the lives they led. Deploring this, George reminded himself that this fault in them could to some extent be blamed on their upbringing. So eager had their mother been to shield them from contamination by the wicked world that she had kept them shut away until they were too old to go on leading the sheltered lives she had arranged for them. And the result! As soon as they were free they began living like libertines, desperately, feverishly trying to make up for lost time.

There had been Edward, the companion of his childhood, who had been his favourite brother. When they were boys they had shared confidences and it was to Edward that George had told the story of his love for Hannah Lightfoot, and it was Edward who had said that he would always stand beside his brother in everything he did. But when Edward broke free of maternal restraint he had given vent to such lechery that George could no longer feel the same affection for him; and Edward had chided his brother for his prudery. It had broken some of the links which bound them together, but the affection had still been there. George was affectionate by nature and the love for a brother could not be so easily destroyed. Edward Duke of York had gone to sea and, when ashore at Monaco, he had attended a ball, caught a chill and died.

That had been a shock to George, even though some of his affection had waned. He could not forget the friendship of their boyhood and he had been very sad for a long time over Edward's death.

Now he was to receive a fresh shock, this time through the

younger of the two brothers who remained to him, Henry the
Duke of Cumberland.

Young Cumberland came to George one day in an abject
mood so unusual with him that George guessed something
was very wrong. He soon discovered how wrong.

Cumberland said: "I have been a fool, George." And the
fact that he called him by his Christian name was an indication to the King that he was appealing to him as a brother.

George replied: "Doesn't surprise me. I've heard tales of
your doings from time to time. What have you been up to
now, eh, what?"

"It's Lord Grosvenor, George."

"Well, well, well, what of him, eh? what? Get on."

"He's suing me for damages."

"Suing a member of the royal family! He can't do that."

"Well, George, he is threatening to do it."

"On what grounds, eh?"

Cumberland hesitated and looked sheepish. "Well, you
see, I was very fond at one time of Lady Grosvenor."

"You idiot! You young fool! And now what?"

"He has brought a case against me for the seduction of
Lady Grosvenor."

"But this is not true," cried the King, knowing full well
that it was.

Cumberland nodded miserably.

"It must be stopped."

"It's too late. The case is about to be heard. I put off
telling you because I knew how shocked you'd be. You're
such a prude, George. You never understand these things."

"Oh, go away," said the King. "What is the use of my
trying to set an example when my own family undermine
everything I do?"

Cumberland wheedled: "There's nothing odd about it,
George. Most people sleep with someone else's wife at some
time."

The King flushed scarlet.

"Get out!" he said.

And Cumberland went, dejected but only a little. The king
had to know that this case was pending and he had felt it
would be better if he were the one first to break the news.

The whole of London was highly amused by the proceedings. The Duke of Cumberland had become very enamoured

of Henrietta, Lady Grosvenor, and had sought to seduce her. She had allowed herself to be seduced; and now her husband —in fact one of the biggest rakes in London—had decided to make capital of the affair. After all he should expect big damages from a royal duke.

And so he had brought the case and Lady Grosvenor had kept Cumberland's letters which was exceedingly practical of her and so helpful to her husband's case. The letters were read in Court; ill spelt and ungrammatical they were a boon to the lampoonists. All London knew what happened when a dissolute royal duke, who was clearly no scholar, pursued an equally dissolute noblewoman who was nothing loath.

The Princess Dowager was depressed about the affair; or perhaps it was something else which depressed her. She could no longer deceive herself. There was something very wrong with her throat. She felt listless at times and only wanted to shut herself in her apartments and be alone. Her great desire was that no one should know that there was anything wrong with her.

There were times when she was in great pain; then she would soothe herself with a little opium which would lull her to sleep, and after a rest she would feel better. Her great determination to hide this thing from everyone about her acted as a kind of crutch, and although many people thought she was looking tired at times they put this down to her increasing years. She was just past fifty—not so very old really and yet by no means young. It was understandable, she argued with herself, that occasionally she should have one of her bad days.

Secretly she was aware that this Thing in her throat was a killer; she had known others who had suffered from it. It was she guessed a tumour which would gradually grow more malignant as it sucked the life from her. But not yet. Not even Lord Bute should know. And when it was over there would be Miss Vansittart to comfort him. She was glad of that woman's existence. She would not regret leaving him so much if she could leave him in safe hands.

She was more philosophical, more self explorative than she had been before.

She smiled sometimes at her reflection in a mirror and when her face looked back at her no longer forced into vitality, but showing the pain that was gnawing away inside her, she would whisper to herself: "I can see that I truly love that man."

And she wept a little for the past—those glorious days when they had first met in the tent, and how discreet and kind and attentive he had been, keeping his distance until that day when after Fred's death it seemed right and proper for them to become lovers.

"No man was ever loved more," she murmured; and she thought how strange it was that she who had been able to be such a mild and docile wife to Frederick, who had never greatly cared for her children—George she had watched over with such devotion mainly because he was to be the King—should have had such single-minded passionate devotion to offer to one man. There were some women perhaps who made better wives than mothers. She was one of them.

And now George had moved away from her. He no longer confided. She had always urged him to be a king—in fact that had been the theme she had continually pressed on him—and now, in his way, he had become a king. He devoted himself to state affairs; he made decisions; his ministers knew that they had to keep in his good graces. That was, after all, being a king.

And there was trouble. Chatham a sick man; and these other ministers? "Poof!" said Augusta and thought how much better Lord Bute would have filled the role of Prime Minister. He had given up—but that was because everyone was against him, she assured herself. She would not believe that he could not have been as competent—perhaps far more—than Chatham . . . if he had had a chance.

Trouble everywhere and now Henry, this silly son of hers, had to make matters worse by being involved in this most unsavoury case.

They were laughing at him in the streets. They were prying into his intimate life. He had betrayed the secrets of his bedchamber. It was disgusting.

And of course the people revelled in it; and as they laughed over Cumberland and Lady Grosvenor they would remember the Dowager Princess and Lord Bute. There would be more jackboots and petticoats to be seen in the streets, she knew.

But it was so petty, so humiliating, so revolting.

But the pain was beginning to nag again; and she knew

from experience that it could quickly become so overwhelming that it submerged all else.

She groped for her bed and lay down. The pain was claiming her; there was nothing but the pain. The past dissolved, taking ambition with it.

The Princess Dowager knew that the pain was driving her from the scene of action and that whatever happened in the future she would have no part in it.

Henry came to see the King again. He was very dejected because the Court had given judgement against him.

"Well?" said the King. "What is it?"

"Ten thousand pounds damages for Grosvenor."

"What!"

"And three thousand costs. Thirteen thousand in all."

"Well, you'll have to pay it. What?"

"George, I haven't the money."

"Haven't the money? Should have thought of that before you started this . . . this . . . frolic. Thirteen thousand pounds!" The King seemed to be struck speechless with the distress of it.

"It'll have to be paid," said Cumberland. "Otherwise there will be a mighty scandal."

"You should have thought of it before you started on this frolic. You should have considered it, you idiot. You young fool. Where are we going to find this money, eh, what? You tell me. Do you think I am going to find it for you, eh? Get out, and don't let me hear any more of this matter. You hear me, eh?"

There was nothing Cumberland could do but retire, but he returned shortly after with his brother William Duke of Gloucester. Gloucester was sympathetic with Cumberland. He could hardly be anything else. His own amatory adventures were inflammable enough to burst at any moment into a roaring scandal. He would go with his brother, he said, and together they would try to persuade the King that he must help pay Grosvenor's damages or the family would be in disrepute.

George saw the point of this. He was weary of the affair. It was no use arguing. He wanted to talk it over with someone, but he would not do so with Charlotte. He had no wish to sully his wife's ears with stories of this sort. It was quite disgusting.

No, he must decide this matter alone, and after much thought he came to the conclusion that the best way out of this indelicate situation was to pay the damages as quickly as possible. In fact, although he did not care to admit this, the loss of the money hurt him even more than the scandal. Wantonly to throw away thirteen thousand pounds for the pleasure of sleeping with one woman seemed to him not only criminal but criminal folly.

What about the folly of marrying Hannah Lightfoot? asked his conscience, always at his elbow these days.

At least I was respectable. I married her.

Ha, ha! said his conscience. What Cumberland has done is not half as shocking or perhaps as callous as what you did to Hannah Lightfoot. And what of Sarah Lennox? You publicly jilted that girl because you hadn't the courage to insist on marrying her in the face of opposition from Bute and your mother.

One must not blame young men and women too much, he conceded; and wondered how he could procure the thirteen thousand pounds which clearly must be found.

He decided to consult Lord North.

North came to see him at once and was not surprised that the King wished to consult him about Cumberland's misdemeanour.

Dear Fred North! thought the King; he had not changed very much. There he sat opposite the King, for George would have no formality between himself and such an old friend, particularly on an occasion like this, and he looked so like George that it was almost like gazing into a mirror.

North's bulging eyes rolled shortsightedly about the room.

"My two brothers have been to see me," said the King. "You know about this distressing law-suit and that they have found for Grosvenor. The money has to be paid in a week and I do not see how so large a sum as thirteen thousand pounds can be provided in so short a time. I pray you, my dear North, tell me what can be done about it."

North's eyes seemed to focus on the King, but he could not see him clearly. He shook his head and the flesh on his cheeks waggled in a manner which might have seemed comical to some, but the King did not notice it.

"The money must be found," he said at last.

"Or," added the King, "it will bring more dishonour on the family, eh?"

"That would be so, sir. I believe His Highness is no longer the lady's lover."

"I'm not surprised," stuttered the King. "This is enough to put anyone off. What? Bringing a case . . . dragging the family, the royal family, sir, through the law courts. And have the verdict go against a royal duke! Sometimes I think they enjoy plaguing us, eh? What do you think. What?"

North said that the Duke's reputation was not good. He already had a new mistress; he hadn't even waited for the case to be settled. "Mrs. Horton, widow of a Derbyshire Squire. A very fascinating woman, sir, so I've heard. Walpole says her eyelashes are a yard long and she has the most amorous eyes in the world."

"Then God help him."

"That scandalmonger Walpole says she could have turned the Duke's head if her lashes had only been three quarters of a yard long." North tittered. "Gossip," he went on. "So much gossip. Not good at all for the family, sir. We must settle this affair without delay for the sooner it's settled the sooner it's forgotten. And Your Majesty will doubtless feel inclined to speak to His Highness, to point out his duty to the State, sir, from which he must not be allowed to diverge so far again . . . not, I'm sure Your Majesty will agree with me, for eyelashes two yards long."

"It's true, North. Absolutely true. I'll speak to the young idiot. And the money, eh, what?"

"From the Civil List. There's no other way."

The King sighed with relief.

"Thirteen thousand pounds!" he murmured. "But as you say, North, there's no other way."

Family scandals were in the air and by an odd quirk of fate one followed quickly on another.

There was very disturbing news from Denmark.

When George read the letters he could scarcely believe them; he set out with all haste to his mother, for he felt that it was to her only that he could talk of this terrible disaster to the family.

When she heard that the King wished to see her, the Princess Dowager hastily arose from her bed. She did not call her women but herself painted her face to take away the strained look and sallow tinge of her skin which was growing more and more apparent every day. When she received the King she was relieved to see that her changing looks went unnoticed. Perhaps this was because he was himself in a state of extreme agitation.

"Mother," he cried, embracing her, "there is terrible news from Denmark."

The Princess Dowager felt her throat begin to throb, but she said calmly: "News, George? What is it?"

"They have arrested Caroline Matilda."

"Arrested the Queen! On what charges?"

"Treason and adultery."

"It's impossible!"

"No, mother. I have proof of it. It's in these letters. There is one from Caroline Matilda herself. She is a prisoner near Elsinore, and she fears for her life."

"They wouldn't dare."

"She is far away. And you know what Christian is."

"The villainous little pervert," cried Augusta, her voice harsh with fear. What was happening to her family? That horrible case only just over and here was Caroline Matilda accused of adultery . . . and treason.

"They say they have found evidence of a plot against the King between Caroline Matilda and a man named Struensee. They are saying foul things against Caroline Matilda and Struensee. They have both been arrested. They say it will be the traitor's death for Struensee and possibly Caroline Matilda. What should we do, eh, what?"

"It's barbarous," whispered the Princess Dowager.

"She is in their hands . . . a prisoner. My little sister! We should never have allowed her to go. Better far if she had stayed here . . . and never married at all. There is Augusta in Brunswick . . . I shudder to think what is happening there. But this . . . this is monstrous, eh?"

"We cannot allow her to remain a prisoner, George. It's an insult to our family."

"That's true. We'll have to stop it. How dare they! My sister's life is in danger so they tell me. They will take her out and execute her . . . barbarously! What can we do, eh? What can we do what, what, what . . . Sometimes I feel as though I'm going mad."

"George! For God's sake, don't say that."

For a second or so they looked at each other in horror and then the Princess Dowager said very quietly: "We must find a way to save Caroline Matilda. I think George that this is a matter which you will have to lay before your ministers."

George nodded. He had had to call in North and use the Civil List to extricate Henry from his scandal, but this was a matter between nations. This was a far more serious and dangerous affair.

Scandal Abroad

From the window of her prison on the Sound near Elsinore, Caroline Matilda could see the lights of Copenhagen. The city was *en fête* to celebrate her downfall, so she had been told. So much was she hated.

And not more than I hate them . . . all of them, she thought. But George will come and take me away. They will have to remember that I am the sister of the King of England and he is a good king; he loves his family; he would never desert his little sister.

Oh please, George, send quickly.

She closed her eyes to shut out the sight of those garish illuminations and thought of home. Kew and Richmond; Hampton and Kensington; Buckingham House of which Charlotte was so proud. Lucky Charlotte, who had been married to a stranger just as she had, but that stranger was George—the dearest and kindest of men.

Oh, George, send quickly. Take me away from here. Bring me home.

Everything had gone wrong since she left home; everything would be right once she was back. Her mother would scold her; she would blame her; but she would answer back. What of you, Mother, you and Lord Bute. Why shouldn't I have a lover too? I had to do something; and I hated the King and Struensee was so clever, so handsome, so skilful, everything that Christian was not.

When her mother had come to see her two years ago she knew that the Princess Dowager was prepared to remonstrate with her. But she had given her no opportunity. John Frederick Struensee had been constantly in her company then and they had taken a mischievous delight in never allowing the Princess Dowager to have a word alone with her daughter. Even when the Princess asked it, she, Caroline Matilda had given orders that they were to be constantly interrupted.

"For if," she had said to John Frederick, "she begins to scold me for my friendship with you, I shall not be able to prevent myself asking about hers with Bute. Far better for family relations if the subject of our extra-marital relationships are not allowed to be brought up."

That was in the carefree days; the Princess Dowager had gone home dissatisfied and Caroline Matilda and her lover had continued to enjoy life.

How had it all started? Oh, God, she thought, those awful days when I arrived and saw this thing they had given me for a husband. What can they expect of a girl of fifteen, taken from her home to a strange land, handed to a strange man who is little more than a lunatic, even parted from the few attendants she had brought with her and surrounded by others whose language she does not fully understand! How could I have dealt with the situation I found? Christian has been compared with the Emperor Caligula and I don't find the description wildly exaggerated. And waiting for me was Juliana Maria, my husband's stepmother, who had a son of her own, Frederick, and naturally she would feel some resentment towards me and she must hope that I would be barren so that her son would inherit the throne. And as if that were not enough there was Sophia Magdalena the Queen Dowager, widow of Christian's grandfather, quiet and dull, watching everything with those old brooding eyes of hers.

What a situation for a young inexperienced girl to find herself in!

And when Christian had taken Count von Holck to be his constant companion, day and night, appointing him Marshall of the Court so that he could be in constant attendance, she had felt outraged. How dared they marry her to such a man!

But they had managed to have a child. She had her little Frederick who was some consolation; but she was too young to be shut away and merely play the mother in a hostile Court.

Those two women Juliana Maria and Sophia Magdalena had put their heads together and clucked over the decadent behaviour of Christian and insisted on his taking a mistress. But it was von Holck who had all the influence with Christian and he tried to run not only Christian's household but hers. He had succeeded in having dismissed old Frau von Plessen who had been her Mistress of the Robes. She had not felt any great affection for Frau von Plessen who had been most severe in her criticism, but now she realized how important that criticism, and the advice which went with it, were; and that had Frau von Plessen stayed with her, she might not be where she was today.

How she had raged when Christian had gone on his travels and not taken her with him. The idea of him in England had tormented her; a wave of terrible homesickness came over her at that time and she hated her husband, hated her life and vowed that she would not be treated in this way.

On his travels Christian had taken with him a young physician named John Frederick Struensee and had found him to be a very good physician indeed, with the result that on his return, Struensee remained in the royal service. At first Caroline Matilda had disliked him as she disliked all those who were her husband's friends.

She herself suffered from ill health now and then; she had her family's tendency to put on weight and believed she had a touch of dropsy.

She kept to her apartments and Christian for some odd reason suddenly became interested in her. When he came to her apartments and found her lying on her bed, he asked what ailed her and she said that she thought it might be dropsy.

"I shall see one of the doctors," she added.

"I'll send Struensee," Christian told her.

"I don't want that man near me."

"He's the best doctor in Denmark."

"I don't think so and I will decide on my own doctor."

"You'll have Struensee," said Christian threateningly. This was typical of him. Why should he have cared what doctor she had? Did he care for her? Certainly not. He merely wanted to go against her wishes.

Christian strode out of her apartment and she sent for one of her women and told her to call a doctor of her choosing.

She would show Christian that she had no intention of bending to his will on every occasion. If he sent Struensee— but of course if he met von Holck on the way from her apartments he would probably forget all about her and her need for a doctor—that man would find another doctor attending her.

The door of the apartment opened and there was Struensee.

Angrily she demanded what he wanted.

He bowed and said he came on the King's command.

"I do not wish . . ." she began.

"The King wishes that I attend you, Madam."

Tears of mortification filled her eyes; everyone would be listening. She was like a slave, forced to obey the King's will.

"Come," said Struensee, "allow me to examine you. I swear I will use all my skill to make you well again."

There was a magnetism about the man. She had to admit it on that first occasion. He showed the utmost attention while she talked of her ailment and it was the first time since she had come to Denmark that anyone had made her feel so important.

When he rose to go he said: "With Your Majesty's permission I will come and see you later in the day. We will see what effect the ointments have had then."

She found she was waiting eagerly for his return.

They had not become lovers immediately. The deadly attraction was there for her, but she was not sure that he was aware of her feelings for him.

When she was better she told her women that Struensee was a wonderful doctor, a miraculous healer; he had not only cured her he had brought her out of her depression; he had dispelled her homesickness completely, for why should she want to be in a place where Struensee was not.

He visited her often; he told her that she would be wise to come to some understanding with her husband. Should she not accept him as he was. Let him have friends like the Count von Holck, but she should live on amicable terms with him.

She listened to him and since Christian did the same there was a slight improvement in the relationship between the King and the Queen. When a small pox scare came to Copenhagen Struensee inoculated the Crown Prince and the operation was an absolute success. Struensee was now installed in his own apartments at the Christiansberg Palace, and there he and Caroline Matilda had become lovers.

In those first days they had been reckless. Caroline Matilda was in love; and the whole world was changed. She no longer railed against the fate which had brought her to Denmark. She would not be anywhere else than Denmark. Let Christian have his friends. What did she care?

Her women's attitude towards her was becoming furtive; she caught them exchanging sly smiles. Once when Struensee was coming from her bedchamber in the early morning he had heard a door quietly shut.

He said: "We are being watched."

Then they were careful.

"Who knows," said Struensee, "what form Christian's revenge would take?"

"He doesn't want me."

"He might not want anyone else to have you."

So for a while they met less frequently, but this state of affairs Caroline Matilda declared to be unendurable and very soon they were meeting more frequently than ever, and since it was not possible to keep their relationship a secret, they did not attempt to. The whole Court was aware of the nature of the friendship between Struensee and the Queen.

But Struensee was more than a skilled doctor and a practised lover; he was an ambitious man. His great aim was political power.

He was already dabbling in politics; the King's feeling for him and the Queen's devotion, allied to his own ability to plot, gave him high hopes of success. He envisaged Denmark ruled by a Regent Queen with himself the power behind the throne; and to do this it would be necessary to have the King shut up as a lunatic. Christian was showing signs of mental instability, so it was not an impossible dream.

Struensee's power had grown rapidly; he had undermined the Government; and all the time he was working towards that goal which was to rule Denmark. The King was almost as much under his spell as Caroline Matilda was; this was evident when Count von Holck fell from favour. Who else but Struensee could have brought that about? The man fascinated the royal pair equally. He became Master of Requests and later a Cabinet Minister; and following on that his rise was so rapid that it was said that an order from him carried more weight than one from the King. He took the title of Count; he filled the cabinet with his own creatures; he had climbed where he wished to, but his political ambition would never be entirely satisfied until he was to all intents and purposes the ruler of Denmark.

He had not taken into consideration the people's reaction. Who was this adventurer? they had asked. What right had he to set himself up? A doctor who had pleased the King and because the King was a near imbecile and the Queen a wanton he would rule the land!

We should have seen the disaster, thought Caroline Matilda. The writing on the wall was very plain.

Had Christian seen it? One could never tell what penetrated his clouded mind. But he had been kinder to her since Struensee had become her lover. He showed no objection to their intimacy; in fact at times she had believed he encouraged it.

He had told her that they should have another child and this was true. So she had sacrificed herself, stayed away from her lover, been a wife to Christian until she became pregnant again.

It was after this that she noticed the change in Struensee. His caresses were mechanical. He was concerned with power not with a woman.

Naturally everyone was suspicious at the birth of little Louisa Augusta. "The King's?" asked the people openly. "Or Struensee's?"

During those first months after the child's birth she had not cared so deeply that Struensee was no longer her ardent lover. She had her baby, and the child, with little Frederick, absorbed her. She had begun to think that with her children she could be happiest and she was beginning to suspect that Struensee's deep feelings had been more for the Queen than the woman.

She should have been prepared. Riots in the streets. Lewd placards about the Queen and her lover. And in the Court plots to remove Struensee.

He was more long-sighted than she was, and saw the danger coming.

She remembered the occasion when he came to her and told her that he believed he should leave the country.

"Why?" she had demanded. "Would you desert me?"

That brought forth protestations of devotion. He would never leave her while she needed him, but . . .

"Then you will stay here," she told him coolly.

"There are wild rumours," he replied. "They are saying that you and I intend to put the King away, to set up a Regency and take control together."

"Well," she had replied, "are they wrong?"

He could not understand her. She was no longer his devoted mistress. She had remembered, since the birth of her child, that she was a queen. He was responsible for the change in their relationship, she told herself. Had he never shown during that period when he thought he could do without her that love for her had its roots in the power she could bring to him, she would not have changed.

It was hardly likely that Juliana Maria would stand by and do nothing. She had her own son Frederick to consider. Some time before she had gone to Fredensborg from where she watched events at Court with great concentration. She was surrounded by supporters; and there she had plotted.

In the Christiansberg Palace a masked ball was being held. Caroline Matilda and Struensee were dancing together when the conspirators entered. Conspirators! They would call themselves the patriots. Their schemes had matured in the apartments of Juliana Maria; and the people were with them.

Struensee was arrested. She saw him carried off under her eyes; but she had not believed that they would dare touch her.

She had cried: "I am the Queen. Take your hands from me."

But they took no heed of her orders and struggling she was carried away and no one in the great hall attempted to prevent this outrage.

Her first thoughts were for her children. She begged not to be parted from them. They had become more important to her than anything else. The guards considered and at length her little daughter was brought to her. Her son Frederick was not allowed to see her; he was the Crown Prince and belonged to the state. But at least she had Louisa.

And so they had brought her to the prison on the Sound and the days of captivity had begun.

What was happening in Copenhagen, in Frederiksberg, in London, she wondered; and her thoughts dwelt on London. George would hear what was happening to her and he would never allow these people to treat a sister of his in this way.

She had wanted to scream at them: "Do you realize that I am the sister of the King of England?" But she had remained silent. She would get messages to him; and he would never desert her. People might laugh at George, say he was simple, respectably bourgeois, but he was kind and he would never desert his sister.

What frightening days she endured in prison when she had heard news of Struensee's trial; when they tortured him and under torture he confessed to his intrigue with her—all the details, the private intimate details; and she knew that they did not wish to incriminate him only, but her. They wanted to take her out of this prison to her execution. They wanted to humiliate her, to kill her.

And they had brought to her her lover's confession. Is this true? they demanded. And she regarded them silently. It was true. She had loved this man; there had been a time when nothing in the world had been important to her but him; and now they had him under restraint; the penalty for his sins was horrible death.

She had cried: "The fault is mine. I take the blame." And that had pleased them; that was what they had wanted her to say.

So they had brought their case against her; she was to be divorced from the King; her lover was to die . . . barbarously. And herself? What of herself?

She had waited for news of her lover's death. There was no news; and one April day she was overcome by a terrible melancholy; and she said to herself: "This is the day."

Later she heard that she was right. She shuddered to think of the torturing of that once handsome body; she could not shut out of her mind the thought of his corpse.

And herself. What of herself? Her only hope lay with George.

George paced up and down his mother's apartment.

"What do you think they will do to her, eh, what? Are they planning to execute her as they did Struensee?"

"We cannot allow it," said the Princess Dowager.

"No, we will not allow it. Caroline Matilda." George's eyes grew soft. His little sister who was so bright and pretty. Something must be done to save her.

"I will speak to North," he said. "We must delay no longer. Who knows what these Danes will do next. We must prove to them the might of England, eh?"

"How I wish this marriage had never taken place."

"And I!" agreed George. "But what can we do? Can we leave our women unmarried . . . spinsters, eh? What? Not a good prospect for them. And so few Protestant Sovereigns in Europe."

"None could be worse than this Christian. A lunatic, George. Nothing more. My poor, poor daughter."

The Princess Dowager had become a little more sentimental since she felt so ill. Now she was thinking of Caroline Matilda, her youngest, the posthumous child of the Prince of Wales. She remembered so well those months when she had awaited the child's birth and dear Lord Bute had been waiting too. When Caroline Matilda had come into the world, the Princess Dowager had ceased to mourn for her husband; then she had turned happily to Lord Bute. This had happened all those years ago; and now this daughter of hers was in great trouble; and she felt too ill to listen, to care as she should have done.

"I will speak to North," George was saying. "We cannot allow these people to forget that their queen is our sister. She must be treated with the respect due to the Crown."

The Princess Dowager nodded, and George noticed her listlessness for the first time. She was different; in the spring light her face looked sallow and ravaged.

"You are ill," he said suddenly.

"No . . . no . . . no," she protested.

"This has upset you, I fear."

"Yes," she answered. Let it go at that. She was not going to admit to George how ill she was. She was going on fighting to the end.

The news from Denmark was bad. There were strong opinions there that the Queen deserved the same fate as Struensee, so why should she not suffer it?

The Danish ambassador faced the King and his ministers. He should not forget, they reminded him, that the Queen of Denmark was an English princess.

"My government would never tolerate the execution of an English princess," said the King.

The answer came from the Danish Court that they would settle their own affairs without help from England; and as a result a squadron was ordered to sail for Denmark.

Now the Danes were alarmed and just as diplomatic relations between the two countries were about to be broken off, they expressed a change of attitude. The Queen should be divorced; they would not take her life, but she should be exiled from Denmark.

The squadron was not sent to Denmark; but the position demanded some action; therefore two frigates and a sloop were ordered to Elsinore to make sure that the Queen was allowed to leave Denmark in safety.

George had discussed the affair at great length with his mother. Caroline Matilda had been guilty of adultery; they must remember that. They could not blame the Danish Government entirely for its treatment of her. She had admitted that Struensee had been her lover; he had paid the price; they must not demand a free pardon for Caroline Matilda merely

because she was an English princess. But they would remember that she was the King's sister; therefore the Navy
must make this gesture to the Danes that they might not forget
the exalted rank of the English princess.

The Danes had no wish for trouble with England. All they
wanted was to be rid of Caroline Matilda. It was enough that
she was divorced and exiled—although the British ambassador did succeed in getting her a pension of about £5,000 a
year.

So it was goodbye to Denmark. Caroline Matilda was
weeping bitterly. Not that she cared to leave this land in
which she had known such tempestuous years. She despised
her husband; she had been disappointed in her lover; and all
that was left to her was her children. And this was her
punishment; she was to be parted from them.

Frederick! Louisa! They were no longer hers. They belonged to the State of Denmark. And she was to be exiled—by
a freak of fortune—in the castle of Celle.

It was at Celle that her great-grandmother, Sophia Dorothea the tragic Queen of George I, had lived her happy
childhood; and poor Sophia Dorothea's life had run on similar
lines to that of Caroline Matilda, for married to the coarse and
inconsiderate George I, she had taken a lover, been discovered, her lover had been brutally murdered, her children taken
from her, and she exiled to spend the rest of her life in
solitude.

She remained in exile for more than twenty years, I believe, thought Caroline Matilda. I pray it will not be so long
for me.

And so ended Caroline Matilda's life in Denmark, as, her
children taken from her, her lover lost to her for ever, she
made her journey towards Celle.

The Princess Dowager
Takes Her Leave

The family troubles were not over. It was hardly likely that
Cumberland would learn his lesson; no sooner had the
Grosvenor scandal died down than he came to his brother in a
mood of something between contrition and truculence and
told him that he had something of importance to tell him.

"You will hear of it sooner or later," he told George,
"and I would rather you heard it first from my own lips."

George's spirits sank. He could see from his brother's
expression that it would be something which would not
please him.

"You'd better tell, eh?"

"I . . . I am married."

"Married," spluttered George. "But . . . but it's impossible. How . . . how can that be?"

"Your Majesty should know. You take your oath before
the priest and . . ."

Cumberland was looking sly, reminding George of that
ceremony he had undergone with Hannah Lightfoot.

George said: "You had better tell me the worst."

"She's beautiful. I would have made her my mistress but
she would have none of that. Marriage or nothing . . . so it
was marriage."

"Who is she?" asked George.

"Mrs. Horton. You've heard of her. There's been plenty of
scandal about us. Widow of a Derbyshire Squire. Lord Irnham's
daughter."

"But this is . . . impossible. You cannot marry a woman
like that!"

"I have, brother. That's what I'm telling you. It *is* possible . . . because it has been done."

"You . . . *idiot*."

"I thought you would say that."

George remembered hearing the gossip. The lady with the eyelashes a yard long. And his brother was a fool. One would have thought that having been caught over Grosvenor's wife he would have been more careful. But no. North had provided the thirteen thousand damages for that affair . . . and as soon as it was settled, this young idiot had gone off and committed another piece of folly. Would he never learn?

George was really angry. He thought how he had sacrificed lovely Sarah Lennox for plain Charlotte because he thought it was his duty—and here was his brother living with no restraint whatsoever, becoming involved in one scandal and then plunging straight into the next.

He said: "I . . . I will not receive her . . . nor you. You understand. Eh? What?"

Cumberland lifted his shoulders and accepted his dismissal.

Old George wouldn't keep it up, he knew. He was too good-hearted and he hated quarrels. He'd give way in time just as he had over the Grosvenor case.

The Princess Dowager asked the King to come and see her. She did not feel equal to making the journey to him, but she did not wish him to know it.

She was very worried about her family. Her sons were wild; there was no doubt about that. Her daughter Augusta was very dissatisfied with her life in Brunswick and what Augusta's daughter would grow up like she dared not think. It must be a very strange household with her father paying more attention to his mistress than to her mother; and how would proud Augusta react to that? And then Caroline Matilda— whose case was the worst of all and did not bear thinking of.

And now this news about Henry Frederick. Oh, what a fool. Women would be his downfall; and now he had been caught by this siren with the long eyelashes. How like him to be caught by *eyelashes*! He was without sense and without dignity.

She heard that he was extremely coarse; his only cultural interest being in music. But the whole family shared that interest. And now . . . this disastrous marriage.

When the King came to her she seated herself with her back to the light that he might not see the ravages pain had made on her face.

George was too indignant about this new turn in the family's affairs to notice.

He said: "You wished to speak about Henry Frederick I don't doubt, Mother, eh?"

"It's a sorry business."

"I won't receive them."

"That can't undo the mischief; and perhaps it is not wise . . ."

George's mouth was set along the stubborn lines with which she had now become familiar.

"I shall not receive them," he said; and she knew that that was an end of the matter.

She tried again though. "Family quarrels never did any good. In the last two reigns they were disastrous to the family and made it a laughing stock to the people. We do not wish that."

"True," agreed the King, "but I won't receive them."

He would change, of course. He was not vindictive. She knew what it would be. The couple would not be received for a while and then all would be forgiven. But it was no use telling George that in his present mood.

She changed the subject. "George, there should be some provision against this sort of thing."

"What provision could we take?"

"You could make a law that royal persons would not be allowed to marry without the Sovereign's consent."

"Ha! They would marry without it. Can you imagine Henry Frederick's coming to me to ask my permission? Eh? What? No. He would marry first and tell me afterwards. That is the respect I get from my brothers."

"What I mean is George that you could pass some Marriage Act. Then if any one of the family married without your consent the marriage would be invalid."

"The Parliament would never pass such a law."

"I think you should consider it, George."

But his mouth was set.

"The Parliament would not have it," he said.

And she felt the pain beginning to nag and when that happened she had no power to do anything, but will it to leave her.

*   *   *

The change in the Princess Dowager was now so apparent that she could no longer hide it.

"I fear," said George, "that this scandal of the Grosvenors and Caroline Matilda's tragedy has upset you far more than anything ever has before, eh?"

"I fear it has," replied the Princess Dowager, ready to admit anything but that her illness had a physical cause.

Lord Bute came to see her; he was distressed at the change in her, and implored her to see the doctors.

"My dear," she answered. "Of what use? I have nothing of which to complain. I am well enough really. It is just these family troubles."

"My dearest," replied Bute, "you should see the physicians. There might be something they could do."

"No," she answered. "I shall be all right very soon. It is just these family scandals. I have allowed them to affect me too deeply."

It was useless to try to persuade her. She had made up her mind.

When she was alone, she looked at herself in the mirror and tried to see this nagging burning thing which was in her throat.

She thought of her husband's mother—her indomitable mother-in-law Queen Caroline—who had been afflicted with an internal rupture which she thought indelicate and had suffered in silence even as she, Augusta, was suffering now, while she declared to the world that there was nothing wrong with her and refused to see the doctors.

She hated illness, just as Queen Caroline had done, and she would not recognize its existence.

But there came the day when it could no longer be hidden. She lay on her bed unable to protest and they brought the doctors to her. They quickly discovered the Thing in her throat and they gave their grave verdict to the King.

"A cancer in the throat, Your Majesty."

"And there is hope . . . eh? What?"

"No, Your Majesty. There is nothing that can be done. Her Highness cannot have many more weeks left to her."

George was heartbroken. His family feeling had always been strong; and from his childhood she had been there to guide him. Even now he would hear her strong voice breaking in on his dreams: "George, be a king."

"Everything that I am I owe to her," he told Charlotte, and Charlotte, good wife that she was, wept with him.

Lord Bute and the King were close again in a shared grief. Bute had been wrong; he had been immoral, but he had loved the Princess. He had been as a husband to her and her happiness had been centred in him. At such a time one could not allow one's respectability to intrude on one's deeper feelings.

"I cannot believe that she will leave us," cried the King. "How can anything be the same without her?"

When she received visitors, the Princess still went through a pretence that there was nothing seriously wrong with her.

The phrase: "When I am well . . ." was constantly on her lips. But they knew—and so did she—that she never would be well.

She brooded about those two men whom she would leave behind her and who she believed would suffer through her absence. Bute—he would grieve for her; but Miss Vansittart would comfort him; and he had his family and Lady Bute was a good sensible woman. He would not be left entirely alone.

And George? George was a fully-grown king now and he no longer confided in his mother. George had his advisers and how often they advised him to folly! But she should not grieve too much at leaving George for he did not take counsel with her now.

Charlotte? She felt guilty about Charlotte. Charlotte might have been a help to her husband. She was not a stupid woman. But she never would now. She herself and dear Lord Bute had decided what position Charlotte should occupy about the King when she first arrived in England and they—and her constant childbearing—had made it impossible for her to influence him in the smallest way. So now he stood alone—among his ministers. George, who was growing more and more aware of state affairs; George who saw himself as the King who would rule his country; who was developing a growing obstinacy; who believed that he knew best.

Trouble, trouble, thought the Princess Augusta. The family growing up and causing scandal. There were whisperings about her sons and she did not know how true the stories were —nor would she now. But she did foresee trouble with the family who seemed to have a genius for getting into it although they had a genius for nothing else. Trouble, she thought. But I shall not be here. It was all round the throne. It was brewing in America. Was George strong enough to hold it off? Was North strong enough to guide him? She did not know. All she knew was that she would not be there to see.

Her women dressed her to receive the King and the Queen. Perhaps, she thought, the last time. Another presentiment that the end was near. The pain in her throat was almost unendurable.

"Let me not betray it to them," she prayed.

Her women came in to tell her that the King and Queen had already arrived. She was astonished. It was so unlike George to be either too early or late. He was almost as precise about time as his grandfather had been.

George came in, took her hand and kissed it fervently. ·

"You are early, George, my dearest son."

"I mistook the time," lied George. He thought: She is dying and she will not admit it. Oh, my brave mother who has lived for me.

The Princess Dowager embraced Charlotte more warmly than usual.

Poor Charlotte, who had been shut out deliberately. It was a mistake, thought the Princess. Did I think that I was immortal, that I would go on forever, so that he had no need of someone to take my place?

She sat bolt upright on her chair trying to concentrate on what they were saying.

And George sat beside her, a pain in his heart because he knew he was going to lose her and that this could well be the last time they sat together like this.

He could have wept, but he knew that would distress her; and he wanted to tell her that he loved her, that she was his dearest mother and he would never forget her care for him.

But he dared not say these things for she would not wish it; and how much more painful it was to sit there beside her pretending that all was well.

When her son and daughter-in-law had left her the Princess Dowager collapsed on to her bed.

I cannot lie to them much longer, she thought.

She was right. She could not hold off the doctors now. She was too ill for pretence.

She was aware of the King at her bedside; she saw his eyes wide with grief, his lips twitch with emotion.

"Farewell, my good son George," whispered the Princess Dowager.

"Oh, dearest and best of mothers . . ." answered George. He turned in despair to the doctors. "Is there nothing . . . nothing that can be done, eh? Nothing . . . nothing. Eh? What?"

The doctors shook their heads.

There was nothing.

Gloucester's Secret Marriage

George could not now find solace even at Kew. He missed his mother deeply and he thought of her constantly. He felt that all his brothers and sisters were alien to him; and he was a sentimental man; he had wanted to believe they were such a happy family. He could not bear to think of Caroline Matilda, virtually a prisoner in exile, her punishment for entering into an adulterous intrigue which she made no attempt to deny. Indeed how could she, with the evidence against her? And this was his little sister. The news from Brunswick was sordid and unpleasant, although he believed his sister Augusta made the best of it and at least did not add to his humiliation by undignified conduct. But he had never loved Augusta; that year of seniority had always been between them. When they were young she had bullied him; and when they were older had shown her resentment because although she was the first born he was the boy. And now Cumberland's disgraceful marriage. And as for William, Duke of Gloucester, the only other brother left to him, there were whispers about *his* life to which George assiduously closed his eyes.

Charlotte was a comfort. She never caused him the slightest scandal. There she was calmly in the background, sewing, praying, living the quiet domestic life and being—he had to admit it—excessively dull. Not that she should ever know that he thought that. Not that he would betray by a look that he thought often of Sarah Lennox and wanted to hear all about the scandal she was creating, bearing another man's child and running off and leaving her husband. She had now left her lover and was, he heard, living quietly at Goodwood House under the protection of her brother, the Duke of Richmond. Sometimes he imagined that Richmond blamed him for what had happened to Sarah. There were often times when he thought Richmond went out of his way to plague him. But he felt that about many people. Yet occasionally there were times, though he felt well and his mind was lively, when he was a little afraid of that persecution mania which had been with him so strongly at the time of that fearful illness, on which even now he did not like to dwell.

But he still thought of Sarah . . . longingly . . . and of women like Elizabeth Pembroke. Ah, there was a beauty! Unsuccessfully married both of them; and he supposed his marriage with Charlotte would be called a success.

It has to be, he told himself desperately. I have to set an example.

But in his fancy he thought of other women. It was as far as he would ever progress in infidelity.

He must set that example, more especially because there was such licence in his Court.

There was Elizabeth Chudleigh, that old friend of his who had helped him to pursue his relationship with Hannah Lightfoot. How grateful he had been then! But would he have been wiser not to have taken that advice? Oh, it was easy to be wise after the event. But at that time Elizabeth Chudleigh had wished to please him and that was why she had acted as she had.

Elizabeth had been creating a certain amount of scandal. She had travelled widely in Europe, had become a close friend of King Frederick in Berlin; and when her husband Augustus Harvey asked her for a divorce because he wished to marry she hurried home. It had been a curious case. Elizabeth was eager to marry the Duke of Kingston whose mistress she had been for so many years, and when it was not possible to arrange the divorce, declared that she had never really been married, and now she had gone through a form of marriage with the Duke of Kingston.

It was all very complicated, thought the King; and he did not wish to hear of it. He did not wish to see Elizabeth because she reminded him of Hannah Lightfoot. So he was pleased to push her to the back of his mind, but her strange behaviour did underline the licentiousness of his Court which he was trying to combat.

All these women he admired were adventuresses, it seemed; and the admirable one was Charlotte—Charlotte with her little body, the plain face, the wide mouth which the lampoonists likened to a crocodile's. Charlotte, his wife. So plain, so good, so dull.

So he must commit his infidelities in dreams and in reality remain Charlotte's good husband. He gave evidence of this. Elizabeth had been born as also had been Ernest Augustus bringing the total up to eight. Five boys and three girls; and they had not yet been married ten years!

No one could doubt that they were doing their duty. But he was deeply disturbed about his brothers and he kept remembering his mother's injunctions to get a law passed which would prevent royal personages marrying without their Sovereign's consent.

He thought of those five boys and three girls and sincerely hoped that they would not bring him as much trouble as their aunts and uncles had.

And thinking of this he decided that his mother was right and that something should be done.

The King was preparing a message which would be delivered to his Parliament:

> His Majesty, being desirous, from paternal affection to his own family and anxious concern for the future welfare of his people, and the honour and dignity of his Crown, that the right of approving all marriages in the royal family (which ever has belonged to the Kings of this Realm as a matter of public concern) may be made effectual, recommends to both houses of Parliament to take into their serious consideration whether it may not be wise or expedient to supply the defects of the law now in being, and by some new provision more effectually to guard the descendants of his late Majesty King George II (other than the issue of Princesses who may have married or may hereafter marry into foreign families) from marrying without the approbation of His Majesty, his heirs and successors.

When this message was delivered to the two Houses it was received with hostility.

Chatham, on one of his rare appearances in the House of Lords, hobbled in, swathed in bandages, to thunder against the Act.

"New fangled and impudent," he cried. Others said: "This should be called 'An Act to encourage Fornication and Adultery in the Descendants of George III'."

Lord North came to see the King and shook his head over the Bill.

"It is most unpopular, Your Majesty."

"I am sure it is right," declared George obstinately. "This must go through."

The opposition continued. It was called a wicked act; but the King was determined.

He wrote to Lord North:

I do expect every nerve to be strained to carry the Bill through both Houses with a becoming firmness, for it is not a question which immediately relates to the administration but personally to myself, and therefore I have a right to expect a hearty support from everyone in my service and shall remember defaulters.

The last phrase was ominous. Although this was a constitutional Monarchy the King carried great weight, having the power to appoint ministers. There were some though who opposed him. One of these was Charles James Fox, a young man who was already beginning to make himself known in the House. Son of Lord Holland, nephew of Sarah Lennox, he was a man of overpowering personality.

He stood firmly against the Marriage Act and resigned because of it.

A plague on young Fox! thought the King. His own mother, daughter of the Duke of Richmond, had run away from home to marry Henry Fox. A mesalliance, thought the King. One could see the way that young man's mind worked.

But he was angry with Mr. Fox. He would remember him.

The Bill had a stormy passage and could not be passed through exactly as the King wished. It was amended. The consent of the Sovereign should only be necessary until the parties were twenty-six years of age, after which a marriage might take place unless Parliament objected. A year's notice of the proposed alliance must be given.

Modified as the Bill was there were still storms of protest; but eventually it was passed with a meagre majority.

No sooner had the Marriage Bill been passed than George received a communication from his brother William Henry Duke of Gloucester.

William Henry had a confession to make. Six years before he had married and because he believed that the King would not approve of his marriage he had kept it secret. Now, of course, that the Marriage Bill had been passed, he must come out into the open.

And the woman he had married was Lady Waldegrave, the widow of their tutor whom George had so intensely disliked. That was not all. Lady Waldegrave was, in the King's opinion, most unsuited to be the wife of a royal duke. She was the illegitimate daughter of Sir Edward Walpole and her mother was said to have been a milliner!

George was wounded—not only by this most unsuitable marriage but by the fact that for six years his brother had kept it secret from him.

"The fool! The idiot!" he shouted. "They have no sense . . . these brothers of mine. They think of nothing . . . nothing but the gratification of their senses. They don't look ahead. They forget they are royal and they allow themselves to be caught by adventuresses."

Charlotte, hearing the news, because it spread rapidly through the Court tried to comfort her husband.

"At least we set a good example," she reminded him.

He looked at her . . . plain little Charlotte, the mother of his numerous progeny. He had had to accept her; while his brothers chose these fascinating sirens whose unsuitability meant they must be doubly desirable, because even his reckless brothers would not be trapped into marriage unless they were.

The more he thought of them, the more his lips tightened, and the more angry he became.

"They shall not be received at Court," he said.

Then he was sad thinking of the old days.

"Gloucester was my favourite brother after Edward died. We were often together and when he was young he was so serious."

Charlotte nodded. "But that was only because he could not be anything else."

"He was a good religious boy . . . and so was Edward . . . when we were all together in the schoolroom."

"But they lost their seriousness with their freedom."

"A madness seemed to possess them," began George, and was silent suddenly. That word which his mother had always hated to hear on his lips! No, no . . . he thought . . . a wildness. He went on: "A reckless desire to find pleasure . . . everywhere. It seems as though they thought they had so much to make up for. I can't understand my brothers. Why do they have to behave in this way?''

Charlotte could not say. Her expression was prim. She was becoming very like her husband.

"I shall not receive them," said George. "I shall not accept this marriage. It may have been entered into before the Marriage Act but I shall not accept it all the same. Why should I, eh, what?''

But a further letter came from Gloucester. His wife was expecting a child. He hoped this would influence the King to accept them.

When George read this he threw it on to his table. His brothers were going to be forced to realize their responsibility. He had had to make sacrifices; so should they.

His family had displeased him and he was disappointed in them all. He remembered how he had adored Lord Bute and how he had been the last one to understand the relationship between that nobleman and his mother.

No, he was not going to be duped any more. They would have to understand that he was the King and he made the decisions. And why should his brothers enjoy the pleasures of matrimony with these fascinating women while he the King had constantly to think of his duty?

He wrote to his brother that after the birth of the child he would have the marriage as well as the birth "enquired into.''

This enraged Gloucester who replied that he must have an immediate enquiry, and if the King would not agree with this he would take the case personally to the House of Lords.

What could George do? He was hemmed in by the rules and regulations of Constitutional Monarchy. His power was limited; laws could be passed without his will. It was possible for the Lords to declare the marriage valid without his consent.

There was nothing to be done.

He gave way. He accepted Gloucester's marriage; but that did not mean Gloucester would be welcome at Court. He would not receive his brother; and Queen Charlotte declared that she had no intention of receiving the milliner's daughter.

Gloucester laughed at them, and with his wife set about indulging his favourite hobby: travel.

So the Gloucesters travelled all over the Continent and the Cumberlands enjoyed life at home; and neither of them cared that they were not received at Court. The Court was dull in any case. What else could it be, presided over by George and Charlotte?

George spent more and more time with his family. His children enchanted him. The model farm, the games of cricket, the wandering through the country lanes—that was the life for him.

But he knew in his heart that he would not hold out against his brothers. He could not forget how close they had all been in the schoolroom.

In due course he would receive them; he would be kind to their wives; because whatever they had done they were his brothers and he was a very sentimental man.

Loss of Sister,
Colony and Statesman

Harassed by family trouble, George was no less troubled by affairs of state.

The situation between his government and the American Colonists was growing more and more tense. The East India Company was in difficulties and the Government was forced not only to subsidize it but to give it a monopoly to export tea to America.

Previously their Bohea tea had been brought to England where a duty of one shilling in the pound was levied on it. Although tea which entered the American Colonies was taxed, the tax was much lower than that in England, being only threepence instead of a shilling, which meant that the Colonists were getting their tea at half the price of the English.

This was not the issue at stake, which was that the Americans refused to be taxed or governed by the Mother Country. It violated their rights, they insisted, and there were members of the British Government who agreed with them, notably Chatham.

Disaster was threatening, but neither the King nor Lord North could see this; they lacked the vision to put themselves in the place of the Colonists and were being dragged farther and farther into a disaster which was all the more to be deplored because it was unnecessary.

That the Colonists were in a fighting mood was apparent when a party of young men, disguised as Mohawk Indians boarded a vessel belonging to the East India Company and which was carrying a consignment of Bohea tea to the value of £18,000 and tipped it into Boston harbour.

It was a sign for disorder to break out throughout the American Colonies.

George and Lord North discussed the matter together and decided that a firm hand was needed. There must be no conciliatory measures. Those of the past, they agreed, were responsible for what was happening now.

There was a storm of protest in the Government. Charles James Fox was using his considerable talents to oppose Lord North.

Chatham, wrapped in flannel, arrived to make a protest in which he cried: "Let the Mother Country act like an affectionate parent towards a beloved child, pass an amnesty on their youthful errors, and clasp them once more in her arms."

North raged against the feeble conduct of the Opposition and a great problem faced the Government: to give the Colony independence in the hope that it would remain loyal to the Crown, or to force it to remain subservient to the Mother Country by force of arms.

North and the King chose the second alternative, and it was decided to send Lieutenant General Thomas Gage to subdue the Colonists. He told the King that the Colonists would be lions if they were lambs, but that if they themselves were resolute the Colonists would be very meek.

This misconception was not proved until too late, and George was soon writing to North:

The die is now cast and the Colonies must either submit or triumph. I do not wish to come to severer measures, but we must not retreat.

The die was indeed cast; and George was about to commit that error of judgement which was to haunt him for the rest of his life.

Then there was a further tragedy.

In her exile at Celle Caroline Matilda had settled down to a not uncomfortable existence. It was a relief to be free of the Danish Court and not to have to see Christian, that husband who disgusted her and had become almost a lunatic by now. All she regretted was the loss of her children and for them she did pine. News was, however, brought to her of them from time to time and she tried to make the best of life.

Remembering the old days when they had all practised

amateur theatricals she arranged for a theatre to be constructed in the castle; and this was done. There she gathered together a little band of actors and they performed plays in which Caroline Matilda took a prominent part. She would tell them of her childhood when her family had all enjoyed amateur theatricals and how Lord Bute, who had been almost like a father to them—for she had never known her own, having been born after his death—had been so clever at stage-managing and acting, in fact everything concerned with the theatre.

She read a great deal and was visited often by people who came from England. They brought her news from home which she welcomed.

Her resignation ended when she received a visit one day from a young Englishman, a Mr. Wraxall, who was gay, handsome and in search of adventure.

It was pleasant to have such a charming and amusing young man at her Court and when he told Caroline Matilda that he believed there were many people in Denmark who would welcome her back, they put their heads together to try to work out a scheme to bring about her return.

Caroline Matilda was not certain that she wished to go; but she was only twenty-three and although she had put on a great deal of weight she was still attractive; she was so fair that her hair was almost white and her eyes, so like George's, were blue and sparkling.

She was attracted to Mr. Wraxall and his devotion gave her great pleasure, so she found herself drawn more and more into his schemes.

They would sit together in the French garden within the castle grounds, and talk of the days when she would again mount the throne of Denmark.

"It will be wonderful," she told Mr. Wraxall, "to see my children again. Little Frederick must miss me and Louisa . . . she will not remember, but she will hear tales of me . . . perhaps unpleasant tales. They will turn her against me."

"They will not do that," Mr. Wraxall assured her, "because you are going to be there with them . . . before long."

It was so pleasant to bask in Mr. Wraxall's admiration and dream of the future that she wondered why she had ever been content to remain in exile.

They talked constantly of the glory that would be hers when she was back in her rightful place. She would start again; she would be the great Queen of the Danes; and when her little Frederick ruled she would be beside him. It was a very alluring picture . . . pleasant to imagine, exciting to talk of.

Sometimes when she was alone, though, she thought of the charms of Celle, of her delightful French garden, of her theatre, of the little world of which she was the centre. Apart from the fact that she was separated from her children she could have been perfectly happy here.

She thought of England where she had led an extremely sheltered life, shut away from fun, kept behind the scenes by a stern mother. Her mother was dead now, but she had heard that the English Court was dull. She had never greatly cared for Charlotte who had always seemed so insignificant. She loved George, of course, but he was scarcely the most exciting person in the world. That was England. And then Denmark. Exciting, yes, when she and Struensee had been lovers; but what had been the end of that! She shivered; she had come rather near to losing her life.

But she was young and she did not want to be like her great grandmother and spend twenty years in exile.

When she next saw Mr. Wraxall she pointed out to him that their plan could not possibly succeed unless they had money, and the only place where they could hope for that was from England.

"My brother," she said, "is the only one who could help us. If he gave his approval to this scheme I would be ready to act without delay."

Mr. Wraxall looked dismayed, but he had to agree that she was right. If the plan were to succeed, they would need money.

"And you think your brother would help us?"

She was thoughtful. Would George help? George was just a little mean, but was that over the small household matters? As for Charlotte, she had the reputation of being a miser, but Charlotte was not involved in this. She, poor insignificant creature, had no say in anything.

She did not really believe anything would come of the affair; it was something to dream about as one sat in the spring sunshine in the French garden.

Mr. Wraxall said he would go to London to see if he could arrange an interview with the King, which he was sure he would be able to do when the King knew he had come from his sister. Then he would ask George for his help and when they had it, they would go triumphantly ahead with their plan.

"Pray do that," said Caroline Matilda. "And I will await your return with the good news."

So Mr. Wraxall left for London and Caroline Matilda waited, without any great enthusiasm, for her brother's response.

The King's equerry stood before him.

"A gentleman, Your Majesty, who asks an audience. He says his name is Wraxall and that he comes from the Queen of Denmark."

George's emotions were in revolt. There had been so much trouble already, that he had come to expect nothing else from his relations.

Caroline Matilda with some request. He could guess what that request would be. She was tired of her exile; she wanted to return to Denmark or to come to England. She was tired of living in the shadows. But only there was she safe.

She was his little sister though, and he remembered her as a chubby baby and afterwards as the little girl with the bright eyes and eager smile who was always clamouring for a part in the family plays. He smiled fondly. But she was not the same. She had become the woman who had indulged in an adulterous intrigue and who had nearly involved her country in war. The scandal of her behaviour had swept through Europe.

"No, no," said George. "If people will not learn restraint, they must take the consequences."

He had had to restrain *his* impulses; he had had to give up Hannah, give up Sarah and marry Charlotte. Others had to make sacrifices.

His mouth was primly set.

"I do not know Mr. Wraxall," he said, "and I cannot see him."

But as usual his conscience would not let him rest. Caroline Matilda's face was constantly before him. He kept thinking of the day she had been born when he had first seen her and his mother had said: "You must take care of your little sister always, George, for remember, she has no father."

And he had vowed he would take care of her.

He asked one of his gentlemen-in-waiting to see Mr. Wraxall and find out what he wanted.

He listened to the plan. His help and money was needed to bring Caroline back to Denmark.

What a child she was! Did she not understand that she might be asking him to involve his country in war?

Had he not enough troubles? His two brothers had made unsatisfactory marriages; they were not received at Court because of this; and the eternal American question was in his mind day and night.

"Mr. Wraxall should be told that there is nothing England can do until the Queen of Denmark is securely back on the throne of Denmark. If she were, we would support her. You think you can make him understand, eh? What?"

And Mr. Wraxall being the most optimistic of gentlemen stayed on in London hoping that the King would change his mind.

Caroline Matilda waited listlessly in Celle for the return of Wraxall. She guessed that George would do nothing. George did not approve of the scheme; he knew it was doomed to failure right from the start.

One morning in May she arose early and sat at her window looking out over the gardens. The trees were in bud and some were already showing a glimpse of tiny leaves.

Oh, she thought, it is very beautiful here in Celle.

One of her women came to her with an expression half shocked, half excited.

"Madam," she said, "one of the pages is dead."

"Dead! Where is he?"

"He is in the pages' room."

Caroline Matilda went straight there and looked at the young boy who was lying on a couch. She shivered and turned away.

"How did it happen?"

"We do not know, Your Majesty," was the answer. "We can only believe it must have been something he ate."

"Have the doctors been called?"

"Yes, Your Majesty. They say it may well be something he has eaten."

"Poor child," she said, and lightly touched his forehead.

She could not get him out of her mind. Something he ate? Something tainted, by accident or by design?

How could one be sure? Poor child. What harm had he done anyone?

*   *   *

She lay in her bed; her women had come to help her dress.

"No news from England then?" she asked.

"None, Your Majesty."

"I doubt not we shall soon have Mr. Wraxall with us," she said.

They dressed her hair; they put on her gown; and she went walking in the French garden. One must take a little exercise. George had always said that the family had a tendency to fatness, and how right he was. She was beginning to feel the inconvenience of too much weight; it made one so breathless.

When she came in from the garden she felt a little unwell; so she retired to her apartments and lay down. Her throat felt hot and dry.

Her women came in and were alarmed at the sight of her; the rich colour which was characteristic of her family had left her cheeks; she looked oddly different.

"I am a little unwell," she said.

"Madame, should we call the doctors?"

She shook her head.

"It is like a red hot vice grasping my throat."

They did not say that the little page who had died recently had complained of the same symptoms.

When she allowed the doctors to come to her they saw at once that she was very ill.

George was a worried king. Events were not going as he and North had believed they should in North America. He regarded the Opposition's attitude as little short of treason. It was their continual haranguing of the Government and disagreement with its American policy which gave heart to the Colonists.

Chatham was making a nuisance of himself in the Lords.

"We shall be forced," he declared, "ultimately to retract. Let us retract while we can, not when we must."

Withdraw the troops from America? "Impossible!" said North. "Impossible!" echoed the King.

Chatham, Charles Fox and Edmund Burke were against the King and the Government. John Wilkes, who had become Lord Mayor of London, drew up a petition with the Livery of the City suggesting that the King dismiss his government because they were responsible for the existing bad relations between the Country and America. George, who had always hated Wilkes, retorted that when he wanted advice he would go to his government for it.

Meanwhile the conflict was going from bad to worse. Gage, as Commander in Chief, had attempted to seize the Colonists' arms at Concord and was defeated at Lexington, and shortly after there followed the disaster of Bunkers Hill.

And it was while George was tormented and distressed by this alarming event that news was brought to him from Celle.

When he read the letter he stared at it and tears filled his eyes.

His sister Caroline Matilda . . . dead!

It could not be. She was only twenty-four years old. It was true she had lived through a great deal but she was little more than a child.

He questioned the messenger.

"How, eh? Tell me. How did it happen . . . what?"

There was little to tell. The Queen had fallen sick of an affliction in her throat and in a few days she had died.

"But she was strong . . . she was healthy . . . and so young."

Oh, yes, she was young to die. How could it have happened? He heard the story of the page who had died, possibly through eating "something."

Had Caroline Matilda died for the same reason?

No one could say. No one could be sure. Poor ill-fated Caroline Matilda who had lived so quietly in the heart of her family and then for a few violent years as Queen of Denmark.

"It is all trouble," said George. "Sometimes I feel as though I am going mad."

Everyone at Court was talking about the trial of Elizabeth Chudleigh. George was horrifed at what had been unfolded. This was the woman whom he had regarded as his friend; and here she was exposed in the courts as the most scheming of adventuresses.

What a devious course she had travelled! Her life was one long tangle of lies. When she had been living at Court as spinster Elizabeth Chudleigh she had in fact been married to the Honourable Augustus John Hervey. There had even been a child of the union, who, perhaps fortunately, had died. Elizabeth had been unsure whether she would acknowledge her marriage to Hervey until his uncle, the Earl of Bristol, whose heir he was, had been on the point of dying. Then she

had considered it would not be such a bad thing to become
Countess of Bristol; but before the Earl had died she had
become the mistress of the Duke of Kingston and had decided
that she would rather be the Duchess of Kingston than the
Countess of Bristol. Because she did not wish to suffer the
scandal of a divorce she had pretended her marriage to Hervey
had not taken place and when there was an opportunity of
marrying the Duke of Kingston she had done so, forcing
Hervey to silence on their marriage.

During her spell as Duchess of Kingston Elizabeth had
flaunted her position; one of her many extravagances had
been to build a mansion in Knightsbridge which was known
as Kingston House.

The Duke, who was many years older than Elizabeth, did
not long survive the marriage; and he left his fortune to
Elizabeth on condition that she remained a widow since he
feared that her vast fortune might attract adventurers.

This caused some amusement among those who knew Elizabeth for the biggest adventuress of them all. Elizabeth, however, was not satisfied with the arrangement and the story of
her remarkable adventures would never have been known had
not her late husband's nephew, on information he had received from an ex-maid of Elizabeth's, brought a charge of
bigamy against Elizabeth which, if proved, would mean that
she had never been the Duke's true wife.

Elizabeth who had been travelling in Italy enjoying her
wealth was forced to come home to face the charges. She was
a woman who was in the thick of adventure even in Rome
where she had difficulty in obtaining the money she needed
from the English banker until she produced a pistol and
forced him to supply it. Nothing it seemed was too outrageous for Elizabeth to do.

And now the trial was entertaining the whole of London.
There was Elizabeth—the young adventuress, whose portrait
by Sir Joshua Reynolds had delighted London before her
arrival, which fact had decided her to leave Devonshire and
seek her fortune in the capital city. To London she had come,
found a place in the household of the Princess Dowager,
attracted the interest of the King—George II—secretly married Hervey, decided she had made a mistake, destroyed the
church register; and then when there had been a possibility of
Hervey's becoming Earl of Bristol, forged a new sheet in the
register to replace the old one she had destroyed. Then decid-

ing that Kingston had more to offer her she ignored her marriage with Hervey and married the Duke.

This was Elizabeth Chudleigh, the sparkling vivacious maid-of-honour who had befriended George when Prince of Wales, who had learned the secret of Hannah Lightfoot, who had used it to blackmail the Princess Dowager and Lord Bute and now faced a charge of bigamy.

No wonder everyone was talking about Elizabeth Chudleigh; it was far more interesting than all the dreary controversy about the American Colonies.

But the King could not escape from the American problem; he could not sleep for thinking of it. He grew more and more stubborn; he would not give way to these rebels; he was not going to be browbeaten. The fact that so many in his own kingdom believed his policy and that of North to be wrong made him stand more firmly behind his chief Minister.

"I am ever ready," he said, "to receive addresses and petitions, but *I* am the judge where."

That was the crux of the matter. He was going to be the judge. He was King George and he was going to rule. For years his mother had said to him: George, be a king. Well, now he was the King; and he was going to show it.

He no longer had the blind faith in Chatham that he once had had. There had been a time when he had believed that if Pitt would form a government all would be well; the people had believed it too; but Pitt had become Chatham and Chatham was a poor invalid, a man who suffered cruelly from the gout and who, it was said, had once lost his reason through his illness.

Lost his reason! The King shivered at the thought; and tried not to remember that period of his own life when his brain had become a little clouded. That was past. It should never happen again; but it haunted him like a grey ghost, always ready to leap out at him and torment him at unguarded moments.

Now when he spoke of Chatham he called him that "perfidious man," "that trumpet of sedition," for there were times when Chatham in the House of Lords thundered his disapproval of the Government with all the fire which had belonged to the Great Commoner.

Chatham was now urging the King at all costs to put an end to the strife in America, to stop this barbarous war against "our brethren." He wanted every oppressive Act passed since 1763 to be repealed.

Lord North, who like the King had become deeply affected by the struggle, wanted to retire, but George would not allow this. In this conflict with America, George declared, he had the majority of Englishmen behind him; he was stubborn; he had made up his mind that weakness was disaster. He shut his eyes to military losses; he had set himself on a course of action and he believed it would be folly to give it up. It would be construed as weakness and they could not afford to be weak.

He kept hearing his mother's voice ringing in his ears: "George, be a king."

It was alarming to learn that Americans were visiting the Court of France and the French were offering help in all forms, short of declaring war, and that there were many Frenchmen who were urging Louis XVI to go as far as that.

North was in a panic. He longed to escape from the storm which he had helped to raise. England needed a strong man now and there was one whom the French feared above all other Englishmen. William Pitt had brought humiliation and disaster to their country; he had snatched Canada, America and India from them; he had made England a force to be reckoned with. And Pitt was still in the field of action even though he masqueraded under the name of Chatham.

North sought to introduce two Bills which he believed would win the approval of both England and America. In the first the right of the English Parliament to tax Americans would be relinquished; in the second a commission would be set up to adjust all differences.

Charles Fox supported this Bill, but some members of the Opposition were against it. North had shown himself to be the enemy of America, they said, and the Americans would be too proud to accept such offers from him.

George himself clung to his desire to remain strong, but he did not oppose North's proposals; yet North again attempted to give up the seals and step into the background. He wrote to the King informing him of this desire.

Lord North, feels that both his mind and body grow every day more infirm and unable to struggle with the hardships of these arduous times.

But George would not let him go. His great desire was to keep North as head of his government, for he would never approach Chatham again.

Chatham, watching the way events were shaping was now seeing himself once more as the one man who could bring his country out of the morass of disaster into which she had fallen. It was Chatham who had brought America to England; how right that it should be Chatham who should heal the breach between the two countries.

He could not agree that America should be allowed to declare her Independence. He could not bear to let America go. He deplored the faulty statesmanship which had brought about this disastrous situation. But he was certain that it was not too late.

He hobbled into the House of Lords, his legs encased in flannel, supported by his son and his son-in-law.

"I rejoice," he cried, with a return of his old fire, "that the grave has not closed over me so that I can raise my voice against the dismemberment of this ancient and most noble monarchy. Pressed down as I am, I am little able to help my country at this perilous juncture, but while I have sense and memory I will never consent to deprive the royal offspring of the House of Brunswick, the heirs of the Princess Sophia, of their fairest inheritance . . ."

His voice faltered a little and then the old power rang out.

"I am not, I confess, well informed of the resources of this kingdom, but I trust it has still sufficient to maintain its just rights, though I know them not. But any state is better than despair. Let us make one effort and if we must fall, let us fall like men."

He sat down in his seat helped by the members of his family.

The Duke of Richmond replied that it was not practical to keep the American Colonies. They could not hold them and to continue to attempt to would weaken the country still further and make an attack by France possible. The country was not prepared for war.

Chatham rose and protested once more against the dismemberment of this ancient and most noble monarchy. The threat of French invasion made him laugh. He turned violently to the Duke of Richmond and then suddenly he swayed and would have fallen had his son not caught him in his arms.

The debate ended and Pitt was carried out to a nearby house in Downing Street.

There was no doubt that he was very ill.

A few days later he expressed a wish to go to his beloved house at Hayes and he was taken there.

In three weeks he was dead.

The body of the Great Commoner lay in state for two days and was buried in the north transept at Westminster Abbey.

"That," said the people, "is the end of Pitt, one of the greatest of English statesmen." But this was not quite the truth. The chief mourner was the dead man's second son, his firstborn being abroad. His son was William Pitt, named after his father; he was nineteen and he was determined to be as great a politician as the father he mourned.

So the great struggle had come to an end with ignominious defeat for the King and his country.

George knew this humiliating memory would haunt him for the rest of his life; and he was right: it did.

Often he was heard to murmur: "I shall never lay my head on my last pillow in peace as long as I remember my American Colonies."

In the meantime Charlotte had spent the greater part of her time being pregnant. Ernest had been born in June 1771; Augustus in January 1773; Adolphus in February 1774; Mary in April 1776; Sophia in November 1777; and Octavius in February 1779. So that by the year 1780 they had thirteen children.

And at the beginning of that year no one was very surprised to learn that Charlotte was pregnant again.

Fire Over London

The King's eldest sons were giving him great cause for alarm, particularly the Prince of Wales. In the past he had looked to his family for comfort and found it. That was when they were children. Alas, children grow up; and it seemed to be a tradition in the family that the Prince of Wales should be at enmity with the King.

"Why should he, of the whole family, have turned out so? eh?" he demanded of the Queen.

But she could not tell him. Poor Charlotte had had no opportunity to learn anything. In the nineteen years that she had been in England she had been kept as a prisoner—a queen bee in her cell, never allowed to know the secrets of politics, never asked an opinion. They had made of her a Queen Mother, nothing else; and they had kept her very busy at that.

She adored her eldest son; he had been the King of the nursery and well he had known it. With his rich colouring, his blue eyes and golden hair, he was beautiful; and if he was a little wild it was what everyone expected of such a little charmer.

Lady Charlotte Finch had declared him to be a handful, and worse still he carried his brother Frederick, who was a year younger than he was, along with him. But the young George had been full of curiosity; he had shown an aptitude for learning which delighted his father, who had never himself been good with his books. Young George, in the seclusion of the Bower Lodge at Kew, had shown good promise. There was nothing else to do but learn, so he learned. He had a good knowledge of the classics, spoke several languages, could draw and paint with a certain amount of talent and seemed avid for learning. High spirited, yes. Mischievous, certainly. Leading his brothers into trouble, it had to be admitted.

"He is such a *boy*," said his mother fondly and indeed wondered how such a plain creature as herself could have produced such a wonder.

Life at the Bower Lodge had been carefully laid out by the King. The children's domain was not to be contaminated by the Court. So influenced had George been by his mother that he had made the household of his children almost a replica of that which he had known as a boy. He did not pause to consider the conduct of his brothers which had brought such anxiety into his life; nor Caroline Matilda's unhappy experiences in Denmark. Even he himself had broken out over the Lightfoot affair and he could so easily have gone against his elders and married Sarah Lennox. He did not connect the wildness of his brothers with their sequestered childhood. And now here was young George threatening to be as difficult to control as George's brothers had been—if not more so.

It was not possible, naturally, to keep the Prince of Wales at Bower Lodge when he was eighteen, that time when princes were considered to be of age.

He would demand a household of his own and independence—and if he did not demand it, the people would for him.

They had always known that he was wilful; he had shown that in the schoolroom. He had swaggered before his brothers and sisters; he had bullied his tutors, slyly reminding them that they had better be careful and not forget that one day he would be king.

Boyishness, they had called it.

On his eighteenth birthday he had been given his own establishment in Buckingham House.

Now he showed how really troublesome he could be. He had taste for low company and liked to roam the streets with a band of friends—as bad as himself—incognito, going into taverns and coffee houses, talking about the politics of the day. He would extricate himself from any difficulty by blatant lying if the King saw fit to reproach him; and perhaps most alarming of all, he drank too much.

The King, abstemious and puritanical, was very shocked.

"You will grow fat if you drink or eat too much," he told his son. "It's a failing in the family."

The Prince pretended to be impressed and was laughing up his sleeve. Most grievous of all was that he had no respect for his father. He daren't announce this yet, but it was there between them and the King knew it. And what could he say to the Prince of Wales, his son, who was doubtless eager now to step into his shoes?

Moreover, the King was growing more and more unpopular. Lampoons were circulated about him. There were cartoons representing him in the most ridiculous situations. It was humiliating particularly as the Prince of Wales was so popular. He only had to appear in the streets to have a crowd cheering him.

"What a handsome fellow!" cried the people; and they told themselves it would be different when he was king. Gone would be the dull old Court presided over by old George who never did anything to amuse them in his private life except go to bed with old Charlotte and produce more and more children to be an expense on the State.

And here was young George, already indicating how different it was going to be when he came to the throne. It would be like the days of Charles II again. A merry England where there was a brilliant Court and a king who would be up to all sorts of gay adventures to amuse his people.

"It causes me great concern," said the King to Charlotte. "What do you think of it, eh, what?"

"He'll settle down," Charlotte assured her husband. "He is so young and after all he is only just experiencing freedom."

"Experiencing fiddlesticks!" retorted the King.

Charlotte was really more concerned about little Octavius who was not as strong as the others. The health of her children had never before been a great cause for anxiety; not only had she been able to breed but to breed strong children. But Octavius had been a little sickly from birth and though she might have thirteen the thought that she might lose one of them terrified her.

She had learned not to argue with her husband though, so she did not make any more attempt to defend George; fondly she went on believing that he would "settle down."

Charlotte was sewing when the King burst into her apartment. His blue eyes looked as though they would pop out of his head and the veins stood out at his temples.

Charlotte dismissed her women hastily. When the King looked like this she was always reminded of that terrible illness of his. Like him she was constantly dreading a return of it.

"I have some shocking news . . . most shocking . . . I

could scarce believe my ears. How long has this been going on? I do not know. It is a very degrading thing . . . yes, that is what I would call it . . . degrading. I will not have it. I will put a stop to it. This cannot be allowed to go on, eh. What? What? What?''

He was talking so rapidly that she was terrified. It was so like that other occasion.

"I pray you be seated and tell me what is distressing you."

"It's that son of ours . . . that George . . . that Prince of Wales. I don't know what he thinks he is doing. No sense of place . . . no sense of dignity, eh? What? What? There is trouble . . . trouble . . . everywhere and he has to add to it. What are we going to do about it, eh? eh?''

"I beg of Your Majesty to tell me what has happened."

"He's been to the play . . . been to Drury Lane and he's found a woman there . . . an actress . . . What does he think he's doing at his age, eh, what?''

George paused. He had been about fourteen when he had first seen Hannah Lightfoot; he had not been much older when he had arranged that she should desert her husband immediately after her marriage to him . . . to come away to that house at Islington to be with him. That was different. That was not flaunting his infatuation. That wasn't setting the whole town talking. That was secret . . . very secret. It was different, said George to himself, eh? eh? eh? What?

"Going to the play . . .'' echoed Charlotte.

"Yes, every night to see this, this . . . creature. And he has fallen in love with her. Calls her his dear Perdita. She's been playing in Winter's Tale or some such. Shakespeare. Cannot see why there is such a fuss for his plays.''

"But what of the Prince?''

"Making a fool of himself over this actress. Setting her up in an establishment. It's got to stop, I tell you. Can't go on. People talking. People will talk. He's the Prince of Wales . . . The woman's an actress . . . an adventuress . . . laughing at him. Older than he is . . . making a fine fool of him and everyone laughing at him behind his back. He has to be made to see, eh? What?''

"Perhaps if I spoke to him.''

George looked at his wife contemptuously. Charlotte speak to that young blade! What a hope that she could make an impression on him. When had Charlotte ever made an impression on anyone? All she could do was be a petty tyrant in her own household where she had the authority to dismiss a maid if she wanted to. A lot of good Charlotte's speaking to him would do!

"*I* shall speak to him," declared George.

The Prince could not ignore his father's summons. He swaggered in looking very handsome in his elaborate embroidered waistcoat and buckskin breeches.

Extravagant! thought the King. How much in debt is he? That'll be the next thing. Cards, tailors, and women. Why should my son be like this?

George smiled insolently at his father.

"Your Majesty requested a visit from me."

"Requested, eh? What? I know nothing of requests. I *commanded* you to come here. Do you understand, eh? what?"

The King was heated, the Prince incredibly cool. He did not care. There was nothing the King could do to him. He even had his friends in the House, ambitious politicians who were ready to form a Prince's party when the opportunity arose. It was Hanoverian history repeating itself. Princes of Wales always quarrelled with the Kings and if that King was their father all the fiercer was the quarrel. It was amusing in politics to have an Opposition led by the King-to-be while the King-that-was supported his government. The Prince enjoyed the situation immensely, particularly as that most amusing, witty and brilliant of statesmen, Charles James Fox, was making overtures to him. The fact was the King was an ignorant old bore, an old fool and apart from a love of music he had no feelings for culture whatsoever.

The Prince felt very superior to the King and was certainly not going to attempt to hide something which in any case he felt to be obvious.

The Prince bowed his head and waited with studied indifference for the storm to break.

"You're being talked about, young man."

"Your Majesty will know that I have always been talked about."

"I want no insolence," said the King. "You understand that, eh? What?"

The Prince raised his eyebrows.

"It's this woman . . . this actress . . . You know who I mean, eh?"

"I believe Your Majesty to be referring to Mrs. Mary Robinson."

"Ah, so you've no doubt of that. It's got to stop. You understand me? It's got to stop, eh? It's got to stop."

"Indeed."

"Pray, sir, none of your insolence. I do not think you grasp the extent of your duty to . . . er . . . to the State. You must lead a more sober life. You must be . . . er more . . ."

"Like Your Majesty?" said the Prince with the faintest sneer in his voice.

"You must remember that one day you *may* be King of this realm."

"I have yet to learn that there is any doubt of that."

"You be silent and listen to me. You will give up that actress. You will go to her and explain that your duties as Prince of Wales make it impossible for you to continue this er . . . this er . . ."

"Liaison," prompted the Prince.

"This disgusting association," cried the King. "You understand me, eh? what? You stand there smiling. Take that grin off your face. You will go to this woman and tell her. You will do it at once, eh? what? Answer me. I tell you to take that grin off your face."

"I thought Your Majesty's questions merely rhetorical and that in accordance with those habitually asked by Your Majesty required no answer."

"You insolent . . . puppy."

George advanced, his hand raised. He remembered suddenly an occasion when his grandfather had struck him. It was in Hampton Court and he had never liked the place since. But he had not been insolent like this young fellow. He had merely stammered.

He was increasingly remembering scenes from the past.

The Prince stolidly stood his ground, amused by his father's vehemence.

"I'll cut your allowance," cried the King.

"That is a matter for the Government."

Too clever, thought the King. And too much grace. He made his father feel clumsy. He was a social success whereas his father had been shy and gauche at his age. There was a world of difference between them. This George had all the airs and graces to make him popular. He was educated; he played the violincello with skill; he could chat in French and

Italian and had a better command of the English language than his father could ever have; and his clothes! The King thought them outrageous but he supposed those who liked fashion would admire them. Oh, this son of his, of whom he had once been so proud, had grown too far from him. George realized with a start that he no longer had any control over him.

"And," he said angrily, "you see too much of your uncle Cumberland. I daresay he thinks this is all very fine, eh, what? I daresay he thinks it's all very well to set actresses up in houses, eh? what?"

"We were discussing only one actress and one establishment, Your Majesty."

"I'll have no more of your insolence. You learn your ways from Cumberland and his wife, I'll swear. That woman, eh? Very experienced before your uncle was such a fool as to marry her. Eyelashes a yard long, I heard. Artful as Cleopatra and succeeded in making a fool of your uncle, eh? what?"

"My uncle seems very content to be made a fool of, Your Majesty."

"Don't answer me back."

"Ah, I understand. Another of those questions which require no answer. Your Majesty's pardon."

What could he say to such a one? He was too quick for him. He was the Prince of Wales; people were on his side. He himself was growing old, he supposed; although he was not really old in years. But he felt tired and incapable of handling this young man.

"You will see less of your uncle Cumberland and his wife. You will stop seeing this actress altogether, eh, what? I want no scandal. We cannot afford more scandals in the family. You understand me?"

"A question Your Majesty? Or a prophecy?"

Oh the insolence of the boy!

"You get out of my sight before I . . . before I . . ."

He needed no second order to do that. He bowed and pretending to stifle a yawn sauntered from the apartment.

Insolent puppy! What could he do with such a one?

George sat down, his brain was whirling. Everything went wrong. America! The Prince of Wales! Everything!

He covered his face with his hands and oddly enough he could see nothing but that woman of his brother's with the eyelashes a yard long and young George with his actress. He had made enquiries about the young woman; she was one of the most beautiful in London.

Gloucester had a beautiful wife. They were rogues all of them and he tried to be a virtuous man, a good King. As a result he had Charlotte. Charlotte and a large family who would flout him as the eldest was doing now.

Life was a tragedy and a disappointment.

It was as though Hannah and Sarah came to mock him.

It could have been different.

At first he tried to shut out of his mind the erotic images that crowded into it. Then he made no attempt to do so.

He sat thinking of what might have been.

Very shortly afterwards the shortcomings of the Prince of Wales were forgotten in a disaster which threatened to lay waste the whole of London and Westminster.

Ever since George's association with Hannah Lightfoot he had felt the need for tolerance in religious matters and although he favoured Quakers particularly he wanted to be remembered as the King under whom religious freedom had been encouraged.

England was fiercely Protestant and had been ever since the reign of Mary I, when the Smithfield fires had shocked the country. The history of England might have been different if James II had not become a Papist. Then he would have continued to reign and his son after him, and the House of Hanover would never have been known in England. George was King because his ancestors had been Protestants.

The laws against Catholics were unjust, he had always considered. Catholics could not hold land; Army officers could not be Catholics; the son of a Catholic who became a Protestant could claim his father's property; Catholic religious services were officially illegal, although for many years they had been held and no one had taken any action.

There had been no great religious fervour in England; the natural impulse was to go one's way and let others do the same. Occasionally minorities suffered a little and George had on several occasions shown his desire to protect them. He had begun by professing his friendship for the Quakers and when there had been certain comment about this had extended his benevolence to other sects.

Two years previously the Catholic Relief Bill was brought before Parliament, was passed through both Houses without much publicity, and George had very willingly given it his signature.

All would have been well but for Lord George Gordon, who at thirty years old was weak, unbalanced and had a grudge against life. He was a younger son of the Duke of Gordon; and his brother, William, had been the lover of Sarah Lennox which had brought him into some prominence because of Sarah's early relationship with the King.

He had had a commission in the Navy, but because he was not given a ship of his own he resigned. He was a strange man, fanatically religious while leading a life of debauchery. Six years previously he had entered Parliament where he sought to make a name for himself as he had in the Navy. He was very handsome and a good speaker, but he lacked something which was essential to success. He could grow hysterical; he was often the worse for drink and it was known that he often spent his nights in the brothels.

No one was very much aware of him. When he rose to speak in the House many members would slip out. He was there because of his family; and he was nothing on his own.

This rankled and looking about him for a way of calling attention to himself, he found it in the Catholic Relief Bill. He himself was a Protestant and had opposed the Bill, but his little protest was quite unimportant. Or was it? Well, they would see.

He hit on a way of making them take notice of him, and he became fanatically overjoyed at the result of his efforts.

First he had joined the Protestant Association of England which was delighted to welcome a Lord into its midst, and it was a very short step for Lord George between joining and becoming its President.

In Scotland the Society was very strong and there had been some dissension across the border when the Relief Bill was passed, the Protestant Association up there having encouraged its members to riot in one or two towns.

Now if Lord George could bring about the abolition of the Catholic Relief Act or, failing that, whip the Protestants of London to such a fury that they would behave as those in Scotland, he would be famous.

No one could laugh at him then; no one could think him insignificant. No one could say that if he were not a Gordon he would be nowhere.

Therefore he would start actions which would mean his name would be remembered in the history books of tomorrow while the Protestants of today claimed him as the hero who had saved them from the Catholic threat.

* * *

Having a mission, Lord George was indefatigable. His dark limp hair fell about his ears; his pale skin was damp with the sweat of exertion; the fanatic looked out from his wild eyes as he went to the newspaper offices to insert advertisements that the people might know he was working on their behalf. He had a petition for the Repeal of the Catholic Relief Act which had been signed by thousands; and anyone who wanted a copy of the petition and the signatures could get it at the various stated places.

Meanwhile in the Houses of Parliament he asked for the Repeal of the Act; he declared that he was speaking for thousands and that the Government would be ill advised to ignore him.

The Government ignored him.

Gordon then wrote a long pamphlet and asked for an audience with the King, and when George received him Gordon insisted on reading the pamphlet to him.

The King listened and then became tired of the excited fanatic who went on voicing arguments with which he could not agree. George yawned significantly, but Gordon went on. George looked at his watch, but if Gordon noticed his sovereign's impatience he gave no sign.

At last George could bear it no more. "Leave it," he said. "I will read the rest myself."

Gordon could do nothing but retire at that, but he was not content when he heard no more from the King. He demanded other interviews during which he harangued the King, told him that many Protestants went so far as to believe the King was a Papist, and demanded something be done.

The King, worried by the conduct of the Prince of Wales, his brothers, the health of Octavius, the ever present subject of America, dismissed him again.

But he was disturbed.

He sent for North.

"I begin to think this man Gordon is bent on stirring up trouble, eh? what?"

"Your Majesty, the man is a born agitator."

"He's saying they suspect me of being a Papist. What? Doesn't he know my family have always been stern Protestants. The man's a fool."

"A fool, sir, but a dangerous one. He is having meetings. His followers are everywhere. They're a formidable body."

"I don't think the Protestants are so fierce over their religion, eh?"

"Sir, I have had my servants at his meetings. It's not so much a matter of religion. He attracts the mob and the mob is glad of an opportunity to make trouble."

"Better find a way of stopping him."

North agreed that this was an excellent idea.

North, with his genius for taking the wrong action, attempted to bribe Lord George, promising him money and a post in Parliament if he would leave the Protestant Association.

Lord George's eyes gleamed. Money! He didn't want money. His family had money. A position in Parliament which he would not be allowed to hold? He had never been able to hold any position.

What Lord George wanted was fame; and now he saw that it would be his. North must be afraid of him if he attempted to bribe him. That showed how powerful he was.

Lord George was a man intoxicated with his own power. They had never listened to him in Parliament. Well, they should see that there were some who were only too ready to listen.

He left North and went home to plan his next action.

A few days later a notice appeared in the *Public Advertiser*.

All members of the Protestant Association were to assemble in St. George's Fields. There they would hold a rally and decide on some plan of action. Members should wear a blue cockade to distinguish them from the spectators.

It was a sweltering hot day. When Lord George arrived at St. George's Fields he was delighted to see what a crowd was already there. There were thousands of blue cockades and many without them, for the London crowd could never resist a spectacle and from all parts of the city they had come to see the fun.

Lord George was cheered wildly, and his eyes gleamed with satisfaction. This was what he needed. He addressed the assembly telling them that he was going to Parliament with his petition that the Catholic Relief Act might be repealed.

This statement was applauded; little bands of people from the Association marched round the fields singing hymns; and in due course they ranged themselves into an orderly procession to march to the Houses of Parliament.

On the way they were joined by many out for some sport. The crowd began to get nasty.

This will show them, thought Lord George. He was confident that after this session of Parliament the Act would be repealed and he would be the hero of the day—and the years to come. He would be Prime Minister for he would have the support of the people. He saw a glorious future before him.

The crowd surged about the entrance of the House. Some carried banners displaying the words "No Popery." As the Ministers began to arrive the mob jeered at them, threw refuse at them, and tore off their jackets and hats.

No one was hurt, however. Gordon was a little disappointed for, dishevelled as they were, the members showed no fear of the mob outside, and going into the House he presented his petition. This was seconded but completely defeated, for there were only nine votes in its favour.

Gordon was alarmed. It was in his power to incite the mob to violence but if he did so he would be guilty of treason; yet if he did not his petition would be dismissed and that was the end of the matter.

He left the House and spoke to the people.

"His Majesty is a good and gracious King," he said, "and when he hears that the people are surrounding the House he will command his Ministers to repeal the Bill."

He went back to the House and was asked if he intended to bring his friends in. If he did, one member warned him, drawing his sword, he would thrust it into Lord George's body for a start.

Lord George grew pale. He was excited by violence but only when it was directed against others; it was because he so feared it that he liked to think of others suffering it.

He turned and went out once more to speak to the mob.

He had the power to move them and they began to disperse.

George had gone to Kew to see the Queen. She was not as well as she usually was during pregnancies. Perhaps, he thought, it is the anxiety over Octavius.

Her confinement was due in September so she had three months to go.

"You are feeling the heat, eh?" he said.

"It has been so hot, but very pleasant here. But not so pleasant in London, I daresay. And I hear that there has been trouble."

"Trouble, eh, what? What trouble? Who said there was trouble?"

"This affair of the Catholics. I heard the women talking of it."

"Women talk too much. Shouldn't listen. Better go and see Octavius. Been better has he, eh?"

"I fancy he has been a little better," said Charlotte. Why won't he talk to me, she thought? Am I a fool that I am not supposed to understand? A brood mare? A queen bee? A cow for breeding? Is that the way he sees me?

She was beginning to dislike him. In the beginning she had thought him so good, for he had never been unkind. Or was it unkind to treat her as he had? His mother had started it but it had gone on since her death. She had not greatly cared because there were always the children, but now there was this trouble with George, and they were saying that Frederick was almost as bad. Frederick was teaching George to gamble and George was teaching Frederick to tipple. And neither of them ever came to see her. They despised her as they despised their father—perhaps even more.

Octavius was sleeping quietly and looked a little better.

"The Kew air is good for him," said the King. "Make sure he doesn't get too much rich food, eh? Plenty of vegetables. Not much meat, and fresh air. That's the best, eh, what?"

They were interrupted by a messenger from Lord North.

The King should return at once, for rioting had broken out all over London.

Charlotte said: "George, at such a time I should be with you."

"You, eh? What? Nonsense. Never heard such nonsense. What of the child, eh? Next thing we'll be hearing you'll have had a miscarriage, eh?"

It was always the same. She was always kept out of affairs. Get on with the breeding. Leave state matters to the King and his ministers.

She almost hated him as she watched him leave.

The child moved within her. Three months and then another birth and again and again.

No! She would rebel. She found no pleasure in her relations with the King. She never had. She smiled grimly, imagining his comment if he had heard her say that.

"Pleasure, eh? Why pleasure? It's for the procreation of children, eh? what?"

* * *

Fires were springing up all over London. There was an ominous red light in the sky by night. The mob had gone mad. These were not, said North, the members of the Protestant Association; this was the rabble, the scum, that element in every big city which is ready to come to the surface when emotions boil up. These were the thieves and the vagabonds, the jailbirds, the criminals. They burned, they looted and shouted "No Popery" without knowing what it meant.

The houses of well-known Catholics were the first targets. Members of Parliament were the next; and of course the prisons. Newgate was burned to the ground; Clerkenwell Prison was broken into and prisoners released to swell the throng. There was murder in the streets.

George remained in St. James's. The mob hovered, uncertain. The guard was doubled and the King never hesitated to show himself, but made a point of mingling with the soldiers and talking to them and bringing refreshments to them during the night watches.

But something would have to be done.

Lord North discussed this with the King.

"Action is needed without delay," said the King. "We dare not let this continue. It grows worse. What do you say, eh?"

"Action, yes, sir, but what action?"

"We have an army. We must use it."

North was aghast. "Fire on the people, sir?"

"Fire on them or let them destroy the capital."

Lord North was horrified.

He left the King to consult the cabinet.

George, who had always hated bloodshed of any sort, was thoughtful. That he should be the one to ask his soldiers to fire on his own subjects was abhorrent to him.

The mob, he thought. Poor deluded creatures. No sense. Led away. But I have my City to think of. They're bent on destruction. They have to be stopped.

He was not a man to shirk the unpleasant. What had to be done had to be done and if it meant killing a few of his subjects to save many more, he would be ready to give the order.

"Fire," was the order, "if peaceful methods are ineffective." All householders were to close their doors and keep within. The soldiers had a right to fire without awaiting orders.

The result of this order was to quell the riots. In a very short time the city was quiet. Three hundred rioters had been killed; some had died of drinking too much pilfered liquor, others had been burned to death, having in a drunken stupor fallen into the flames which they themselves had provoked. But the terror was over.

One hundred and ninety-two rioters were convicted, twenty-five of whom were executed. And Lord George Gordon was taken to the Tower on a charge of High Treason.

The King was overcome with melancholy. He had given orders to fire on his own subjects and many had lost their lives.

The Dean of St. Paul's remarked that the King by ordering the soldiers to fire on the mob had saved the cities of London and Westminster. This was true, but George was none the less grieved.

And all through that hot summer he was sad; but he did rejoice in September when another son was born.

They called him Alfred. Alas, he was delicate like Octavius.

"We shall have to take great care of this little one, eh?" said the King.

"Perhaps we have had too many," replied the Queen with unusual spirit; and the King regarded her oddly.

Dear Mrs. Delany

Charlotte sat at her table while her women curled and craped her hair. Nothing they do will make me beautiful, she thought. Schwellenburg stood superintending; Miss Pascal—who had become Mrs. Thielke—was the one who really did the work.

They had brought the newspapers to her, for she liked to read them while her hair was done, but she could not concentrate on them this morning. She was thinking of Alfred.

He had looked very wan last night and she was very anxious about him, but trying hard not to show her anxiety. She did not want the children to know.

"We now ready for de podwering," said Schwellenburg in her atrocious English which Charlotte was sure she could have improved had she tried.

"Yes, yes." She put down the paper and went into her closet.

While she was there the King came in. He looked distraught and she knew that he had had some news of their child. His hands were trembling with emotion.

"Charlotte," he said, "our poor darling child."

And she dismissed the women that they might be alone together.

"You have news?" she asked.

"The doctors say that he cannot live throughout this day."

She was biting her lips, trying to hold back the tears.

"My dearest Charlotte," said the King, "he is our baby and we love him dearly, eh? But . . . we have the others . . ."

She nodded and the King took her hand and kept it in his.

And after a while they rose and went to the room in which their child lay dying.

George shut himself in his study. There was nothing he could do but wait. He thought of little Alfred, so trusting, such a good baby. He had the innocence of a child who relies on his parents and has not yet learned how to plague them.

287

The Prince of Wales was growing tired of Mrs. Robinson and she was giving him trouble. Threatening this and that. She would have to be paid off heavily.

A lesson to him, eh? Serve him right. Teach him what such women are. It was never like that with Hannah. She had made no demands. Thank God he had not got himself into the sort of trouble which surrounded the Prince of Wales.

But his thoughts now were with little Alfred who had lived long enough to make them love him, so that his passing would be a bitter grief.

He sat down and wrote to his chaplain, the Bishop of Worcester, because he found some relief in writing:

> There is no probability and indeed, scarce a possibility, that my youngest child can survive the day. Knowing you are acquainted with the tender feelings of the Queen's heart, convinces me that you will be uneasy till apprised that she is calling the only solid assistant under affliction, religion, to her assistance.

It was true. Charlotte was a religious woman and faith would carry her through this trial and all others.

And he too must rely on religion. He needed help. Affairs of state were heavy on him. He would never forget those fearful days of the Gordon Riots. Gordon had been tried for treason last year and because of his very good advocate, had been acquitted. Thank God he had acted with promptitude over that affair, although he had been torn with doubts as to the advisability about calling out the soldiery to fire on the people. It was an example of how one must always do one's duty, however unpleasant.

The cares of his family weighed heavily upon him; he was never sure when he was going to hear of some fresh escapade of the Prince of Wales or his brothers. And now there was this illness of the youngest child which the doctors had told him would be fatal.

The doctors were right. Shortly after the King had written that letter to the Bishop of Worcester, little Alfred was dead.

The King paced up and down his apartments. His head was aching, his thoughts were whirling.

"God will never fill my cup of sorrow so full that I cannot bear it," he whispered. "That's true. It must be true."

But his mind was filled with doubts.

George's great happiness was with the younger members of

his family. He preferred, he said, to hear nothing of the Prince of Wales, for he was very disappointed in that young man who seemed to be of the opinion that the manner in which the heir to the throne should spend his time was at boxing booths, race tracks and gaming houses—and, in the company of the most immoral people. A new Court was being raised about the Prince. It was a Court which, it was universally said, was what a Court should be. Who wanted a staid family establishment consisting of babies and dull domesticity? Who wanted a plain little queen who was rarely seen and didn't behave like a queen, although those who served her had little to say against her except that she was parsimonious within her household and behaved like some impoverished lady of the manor rather than the Queen of England. Who wanted a king who never gave balls and banquets; never rode among his people sparkling with gems; who never provided them with a scandal; and the only excitement he had given them was when he was ill some years ago and rumour had it that he had been mentally deranged?

No, the Prince of Wales had the look of royalty, the manner of royalty. Florid, handsome, already beginning to show signs of corpulence—not unpleasant in the young— splendid, with the most perfect manners, with wit and a spirit of adventure! Already he had scandalized the Court over his affaire with Mrs. Robinson; and he could be seen driving a carriage with a pair of the finest horses up Richmond Hill on a sparkling morning to call on another lady love.

It will be different when the Prince of Wales is king, it was said.

There would be extravagances; there were already debts, it was whispered, massive debts. But the Prince was worth it. There was nothing dull about the Prince of Wales.

But the King was perpetually anxious and that made his thoughts whirl and his head ache. When anyone came to him on a matter of importance his first thought was: Does it concern the Prince of Wales?

No, the King's happiness was with the little ones and he could scarcely bear to tear himself away from the heart of his family. What joy to see them in their little drawing room, curtseying, playing their music or listening to it. George had insisted that they all be taught to love music.

His favourite was the little Prince Octavius, perhaps because he was not so strong as the others; and now that little Alfred was dead he was the baby.

The family was at Windsor, which was even farther from St. James's than Kew and George was glad to be there in the Queen's Lodge where there was such a happy family atmosphere.

Waiting on the Queen was Elizabeth Pembroke, whom he had known since she was seventeen. He too had been seventeen at that time and had greatly admired her. He had been very sorry when her husband had run away with Kitty Hunter; he had wanted to comfort dear Elizabeth. Pembroke had returned to her and Kitty Hunter had married and faded out of the picture. Poor Elizabeth! Not a very happy life, George used to think. But one of the most beautiful and charming women he had ever known. He liked her to be there, part of the domestic background. She was still lovely and he always thought Charlotte looked particularly plain beside Elizabeth.

In the Queen's drawing room the children were gathered and there was Elizabeth waiting on Charlotte and that woman Schwellenburg "with whom I could well do without," thought the King. But poor Charlotte, he supposed, must have some say in the management of her own household. So she kept her.

The Queen was saying: "I want Your Majesty to meet Mrs. Delany."

An old lady was making her curtsey; she had bright intelligent eyes and was clearly very aware of the honour done to her, first to be received in the Queen's drawing room and then to be presented to the King.

The King sat down and did Mrs. Delany the further honour of requesting her to sit with him. There was an air of goodness about the old lady which appealed to him.

She had been brought to the Queen's notice by the Duchess of Portland who was very fond of her, and the Queen had received her on more than one occasion. She had on this day asked the Queen to accept one of her flower pieces which she believed were quite original, and the Queen had graciously accepted it.

"Perhaps," said the Queen to one of her ladies, "His Majesty would like to see the specimen of Mrs. Delany's work which she has presented to me."

"Your Majesty is most gracious," said the old lady. "I fear I was over presumptuous in offering this lowly tribute of my humble duty and earnest gratitude."

Charlotte who had taken to the old lady said that she found the work delightful.

Here it was. Would the King give his opinion?

The King examined the specimen which consisted of pieces

of coloured paper of all shapes stuck on to a plain piece of paper making a mosaic of delightful shapes and colours.

George was always interested in other people's work and the simpler it was the more it delighted him. He wanted to know how the work was done and insisted that Mrs. Delany explain to him in detail.

There was nothing Mrs. Delany enjoyed more than talking of her work and Charlotte watched them benignly, listening to George's continual questions (Eh? What? What?) It was all soothing and natural, although she was always watching that he did not start to speak too rapidly. Always her mind went back to that other and most fearful occasion. But he had been well for so long now, so perhaps she need not worry any more.

If George were ill . . . there was the Prince. She thought of him longingly. Why did he not come to see her now? He would always be her favourite; she remembered every detail of his childhood and now . . . well perhaps it was fortunate that he did not come and see her, for the King might be there and the Prince did upset him so.

"These flower pieces are delightful," said the King. "I think they are very clever, what? Little bits of paper, eh?" He turned to Charlotte and explained in detail the process of the paper mosaic he had just learned from Mrs. Delany.

The old lady was flushed with pleasure. She clearly adored the King and he had taken her to his heart immediately. He was calling her already "my dear Mrs. Delany."

The children came in to pay their respects to their parents and Mrs. Delany was invited to stay.

George swooped on Octavius.

"And how is my son, eh? Glad to see his papa, eh, what? What?"

"Very glad, Papa," said the child.

"And now I must present you to Mrs. Delany who makes clever paper mosaics. Perhaps you might ask her to show you the one she has presented to the Queen, eh? And tell you how it is done, eh, what?"

Octavius was brought to Mrs. Delany and being delighted by the necklace she was wearing stretched out to touch it.

Mrs. Delany overcome with emotion, kissed the child's hand; and George to show what a fancy he had taken to this woman said: "Kiss his cheek, Mrs. Delany. Kiss his cheek."

And this she did with tears in her eyes.

"Now, Mrs. Delany, the children will perform for you.

For this is the concert hour. Now are we ready, eh? I hope you have included some Handel in the programme. There is no composer to my mind to compare with him, Mrs. Delany. I trust he is a favourite of yours, eh? what?''

Mrs. Delany was ready to make any favourites of the King and Queen hers.

And in the second drawing room the concert was held—a family affair. Little Prince Ernest, nine years old, carrying a chair almost as big as he was for Mrs. Delany to sit on.

The King sat back listening to his little daughters singing together. What a charming scene! There was dear Elizabeth Pembroke, pensive and beautiful, beside the Queen and dear Mrs. Delany so happy to be honoured, such a good and loyal subject.

What a pity, mused the King fleetingly, wondering what the Prince of Wales was doing at this moment, that one's children cannot always remain young.

But even the young can cause distress. Nine months after the death of Prince Alfred, little Octavius was taken seriously ill.

This was an even greater tragedy than the loss of Alfred, for Octavius was four years old and the most lovely and charming of the children. The King had adored him and had spent hours playing games with him in the nurseries.

"This is more than I can bear," he said to the Queen.

Poor Charlotte! She shared those sentiments.

She was pregnant again and was not feeling as well as she usually did; and the anxiety concerning Octavius was terrible.

When the little boy died the King could scarcely contain his grief; he shut himself into his room and would see no one. But when he emerged he was obviously resigned.

"Many would regret that they had ever had so sweet a child since they were forced to part with him. I do not feel that. I am thankful to God for having graciously allowed me to enjoy such a creature for four years."

He went to Charlotte and repeated these sentiments to her.

"You must agree with me, my dear."

And Charlotte did her best.

A few months later she gave birth to a daughter. They called her Amelia; she was a little frail but lovely, and she did much to make the King forget his grief for Alfred and Octavius.

More and more did the King seek the refuge of his family. Only in the heart of it with his young children around him could he be happy. North had resigned—a fact which had greatly upset the King; Charles James Fox was making a nuisance of himself and was allying himself more and more closely with the Prince of Wales; young William Pitt, Chatham's second son, was making himself heard in Parliament; and the King was favouring young Pitt because he was the enemy of Fox. When Pitt was appointed First Lord of the Treasury and Chancellor of the Exchequer there was derisive laughter through the Commons, for Pitt was not then twenty-five years old. Pitt was on his mettle. He was going to show these old fools what a young man could do. He had his father's tradition behind him and he carried with it all the confidence and courage of youth. George believed in this young man. He knew there would be no lip service to royalty, but George did not seek that. He wanted a man of principles at the head of affairs who would bring back honesty into government. George wanted a peaceful existence. He knew that he needed this. He had been aware of certain failings in his health—both physical and mental—and he was often worried. Let the lampoon writers say that the country was in a schoolboy's care, he trusted that schoolboy and because of this felt he could escape more and more often to the pleasant domesticity of his private life which was what he needed and indeed what he must have.

He dared not think towards what disasters the Prince of Wales might be heading. He now had a place in the House of Lords and had already given his vote in support of Fox. He was decorating Carlton House at great expense; he had discovered the virtues of Brighton where he had started to build a fantastic Pavilion, and worst of all there were rumours that he had offered marriage to a Catholic widow, Mrs. Maria Fitzherbert.

The King shut his ears; he did not want to know what the Prince of Wales was doing. He felt ill when he contemplated this son of his; it made him dizzy; it made him talk even to himself at a great rate. It alarmed him.

No he wanted to get down to the country. It was Windsor he frequented now. There he had farms to inspect; he would ride and walk about the country; he could come home and play with the children. His greatest happiness was in Baby Amelia, the most adorable of creatures. He loved that child. Not that he did not love all the children, but the adorable girl who held out her arms to him when he came near her was, he admitted secretly, his favourite.

The Duchess of Portland died suddenly and when the Queen

told him of this he immediately thought of his dear friend Mrs. Delany.

"For," he said, "I do not know how much she relied on the Duchess, but I do not believe dear Mrs. Delany is so comfortably placed as I could wish. What do you think, eh? What?"

The Queen said that she thought poor Mrs. Delany was not very comfortably placed.

"Then," replied the King, "we must do something about it, eh? What? Can't allow that dear lady to be in difficulties."

He had the answer. She should have a little house all her own and it should be at Windsor so that he could call on her any time he wished. And she should have an annuity of three hundred pounds a year so that she need have no anxiety.

Wasn't there a niece, a Miss Port, or someone? She should come and live with her. He would busy himself to see that everything was as it should be.

This was the sort of task he enjoyed. It did not worry him in the least; it only stimulated him.

He would see about stocking the house.

"Let her know," he said to the Queen, "that she is to bring nothing to Windsor but herself, her clothes and her niece. Now let me see what will she want, eh? What? Now the furniture. Leave it to me . . . leave it to me . . ."

He saw to everything. Plate, linen, china, glass, wine in the cellars and there was even sweetmeats and pickles in the stillroom.

It was a strange task for a king; but no one was surprised. A king who went round to the farms on his estate and helped make the butter was capable of anything.

When Mrs. Delany arrived at the little house which the King had prepared it was to find George himself on the threshold waiting for her.

"Now," he said, "this is your home!" And he was so excited he could not wait to show her round. He was clearly charmed with his work and he kept shouting excited questions at her. "You like this, eh? What? There is everything you want, eh?"

Mrs. Delany, with tears in her eyes, thanked His Majesty. What had she done to deserve such bounty from the best king in the world?

There were tears in George's eyes too. Events like this gave him the greatest happiness. It took his mind off the exploits of the Prince of Wales, which, however much he tried to forget them, insisted on obtruding into his thoughts.

Miss Burney at Court

In the literary circle which Mrs. Delany had frequented in London she had made the acquaintance of Miss Fanny Burney a young lady who was enjoying a great deal of fame because of a novel which she had written called *Evelina*. The identity of the writer had been kept secret and had intrigued some of the most well-known people in the literary world of London, among these was Samuel Johnson and Mrs. Thrale. Fanny was an amusing and clever girl, and now that she had a house in Windsor Mrs. Delany asked her to visit her there.

Fanny was delighted to come, for she was very fond of Mrs. Delany, but she did confess that she was a little alarmed for she knew on what terms her friend was with the royal family, and it was almost certain that she would at some time meet the Queen or perhaps the King.

Mrs. Delany laughed away her guest's fears as she showed her round the house. Those were the very pickles which the King had chosen for her.

Fanny was very impressed, and when she retired to her room lost no time in writing in her journal a detailed description of everything she had seen. She had started this journal when she was a child and nothing would prevent her keeping it up.

It was a pleasant stay. The royal family were at Kew so Fanny was able to relax and enjoy the days. These were enlivened not only by Mary Port, Mrs. Delany's niece, but also by Mrs. Delany's great niece, an enchanting little girl to whom Fanny at once took a fancy. The child's father was also a guest at the same time.

The little girl was delighted with Fanny who was able to give her an account of her own family life which had been extremely happy. She told the little girl about her sisters and the games they had played together when they were young; and the child wanted to play them too.

And Fanny said she would show her at the first opportunity and everyone must join in. One day, under Fanny's guidance, the company was playing a childish game in the little drawing room when suddenly the door opened and a tall man came in. He said nothing but shut the door quietly behind him and stood watching the group at play.

He was dressed in black. Fanny thought: Surely he's a ghost. Then she saw the glittering diamond star on his coat and at once she knew.

For a moment the others did not see him and he and Fanny looked at each other appraisingly.

Then Miss Port, turning her head, seemed suddenly struck by horror. "Aunt," she whispered. "The King!"

Mrs. Delany had seen. She went towards the visitor to greet him, then it seemed to Fanny that everyone else had disappeared except herself, the King and Mrs. Delany.

Fanny stood against the wall hoping that she would be unnoticed while Mrs. Delany with calm assurance, but conveying a deep sense of the honour and happiness this visit gave her, curtsied and spoke to the King as to her health and his.

George was looking beyond Mrs. Delany to her visitor. He had heard of Fanny Burney. Indeed who had not? The whole of London had speculated about her identity until it was known. She was the friend of the great Dr. Johnson. The Queen had read *Evelina* and had told the King it was most commendable and that she had heard it was the first novel to appear since Richardson's *Clarissa*—and a great deal more moral; and the Queen had been told as soon as she returned to Windsor Lodge that Miss Burney was a guest in Mrs. Delany's house.

The King said: "Is that Miss Burney, eh?"

"Yes, Your Majesty," answered Fanny, dropping a curtsey.

The King looked at her piercingly for some seconds.

"You are enjoying your stay here with my dear friend Mrs. Delany?"

"Yes, sir. Very much."

"That is good, eh, what?" He nodded to Fanny and turned to Mrs. Delany. "You will be asking me how the Princess Elizabeth is. I am worried about her health. Ever since I lost my sons . . ."

Mrs. Delany was nodding sympathetically.

"Well," went on the King, "I have to tell you, dear Mrs. Delany, that the Princess has been blooded twelve times this last fortnight. Seventy-five ounces of blood she has lost. It's a lot, eh? What? What do you think, eh? What?"

Mrs. Delany said she thought it was a great deal.

"They're blistering her, too. I am anxious, most anxious." He was aware of Fanny again. "Pray, does Miss Burney draw too?" he asked.

"I believe not, sir," replied Mrs. Delany. "At least she has not told me if she does."

The King laughed slyly. "Ah, that's nothing. She's apt not to tell. She never does tell, you know. Her father once talked to me about her book." He moved towards Fanny and studied her intently. "But what? What?" he went on. "How was it?"

He was speaking so quickly that Fanny, unaccustomed to his manners, did not understand the question.

"Sir?" she began.

"How came it about, eh? What?"

"I wrote it for my own amusement, sir."

"But publishing it . . . printing it . . . eh? What? How was that, eh? What?"

"Well, sir, that was because . . ."

For the life of her Fanny could not think of the answer to his question. But the King was not a man to give up. He was very interested in detail; and he wanted to know why Fanny had published her book if she had written merely for her own amusement, just as he had wanted to know how Mrs. Delany did her mosaics.

"I thought, sir, that . . . er . . . it would look well in print."

The King laughed; he walked over to Mrs. Delany. "That's fair," he said. "Very fair and honest."

He stood at some distance looking at Fanny; every now and then laughing and saying "Yes, very fair and honest."

The Queen arrived to see dear Mrs. Delany and to talk to her about the treatment the Princess Elizabeth was having.

She was delighted, too, to see the famous Miss Burney, and was gracious when Fanny was presented. Fanny was invited to sit beside her and the King came and joined them. He told the Queen that Miss Burney had had her book printed because she thought it would look well in print. And he laughed again.

They talked of literature for Fanny's benefit and behaved with such courtesy towards her that she was charmed. As she began to grow used to the King's unusual ways of speaking it was easier for her to understand and to know when the "ehs" and "whats" demanded an answer.

"Shakespeare," said the King. "Was there ever such stuff as a great part of Shakespeare? Only one must not say so. But what do you think, eh? What? Is it not sad stuff, eh? What?"

Poor Fanny. How could one writer deny the greatest of her kind. And yet how could she argue with the King. This unfortunately was one of the questions which demanded an answer.

"Oh yes, sir," she said, "though mixed with such excellencies that . . ."

The King burst into laughter. He found Fanny very amusing. "Of course it is not to be said. But it's true, eh? Only it's Shakespeare and nobody dare abuse *him*. Some of those characters of his. Poof. Stuff. Sad stuff. But one would be stoned for saying so."

Everyone seemed to be very happy and Fanny found the company of the royal pair not nearly so alarming as she had feared it might be.

The Queen was so gracious and determined to be kind; and the King clearly wanted to be pleasant.

When the royal pair had left Mrs. Delany said that it was obvious to her that they had taken a liking to Fanny. This was confirmed on further visits to the little drawing room.

Shortly afterwards Fanny was offered a post in the Queen's household as second keeper of the robes, with which she would receive a drawing room in the Queen's Lodge at Windsor with a bedroom opening from it, a footman of her own, together with an allowance of two hundred pounds a year.

Fanny was uneasy. It was no part of her ambition to become a royal servant. But having become acquainted with the King and Queen in such an intimate and friendly manner through Mrs. Delany, it was very difficult to refuse.

So she accepted and in a short time was installed in Charlotte's household.

Madame Schwellenburg quickly resented the newcomer who was clearly specially favoured by the Queen. Schwellenburg would grumble to herself about people who were sent in and who had no idea how to wait on a Queen. Fanny disliked the old woman and told herself that if she was sent away she did not greatly care, except that she was growing fond of the Queen and every day felt a great desire to serve her.

Charlotte sensed this and liked to have Fanny near her; she was considerate and made a point of not giving her any tasks that she might not be able to perform until she had watched others do them; and she made a point of dismissing Fanny when her hair was powdered in case Fanny's dress should be spoilt.

Fanny would stand waiting for her duties to be pointed out to her while the Queen read the papers. This was usually during the crimping and craping of her hair. Being aware of Fanny and her literary tastes the Queen would read out a paragraph or two for her benefit.

This Fanny found endearing; and although she had to admit that the Queen was not beautiful and did lack a certain grace and was inclined to be imperious in her own household and was mean almost to stinginess, she was kind and Fanny was soon adoring her.

She began to settle in happily apart from skirmishes with Schwellenburg who found fault with everything she did and, in fact, seemed to care for nothing but her position in the Queen's household and two horrible little frogs which she kept as pets. She was an inveterate card player and insisted on Fanny's playing with her, for she implied that one of the newcomer's duties was to amuse her. She despised novel-writing and told Fanny so in her unique English which always made Fanny laugh. "You lauf Miss Berners," she said. "Very well. I vill not to you talk. But I talk to selfs."

Fanny enjoyed visiting Mrs. Delany and telling her of life at Court.

It was the Princess Amelia's fourth birthday and Mrs. Delany had told Fanny that she was going to take advantage of the old custom of paying her respects and asked Fanny to accompany her.

As it was her birthday the little Princess was to parade on the castle terrace and there receive the homage of those who had called to give it. She looked very charming in a robe-coat which was covered with the finest muslin; she wore white gloves and carried a fan; on her golden head was a tightly fitting cap; she looked charmingly and incongruously grown up and was clearly delighted with herself. The King could not take his eyes from her. They were filled with tears as he watched the delightful creature parade between the spectators turning her head to smile and acknowledge the acclaim.

The Queen and the Princess were present, and when the little girl reached Mrs. Delany she stopped to smile at her and speak with her. "You haven't brought your niece," she said. "I wish you had."

Then she saw Fanny and looked up at her.

Fanny stooped to the child and said: "Your Royal Highness doesn't remember me."

The Princess laughed and put out her lips, indicating that she wished to kiss Fanny. Receiving the kiss Fanny blushed, wondering whether this was a seemly thing to do in public.

The Princess had seen her fan and took it. She examined it with interest. Then she gave it back to Fanny. "Oh," she said, "a brown fan!"

The King who had come up to see why his daughter was delaying told her to curtsey to Mrs. Delany, which the child did with the utmost charm.

George, watching her, told himself that this beloved child made up for everything. He could never be entirely unhappy while he had her.

The King's Affliction

Life changed abruptly at Windsor.

It was April when Mrs. Delany became ill. She was eighty-eight years old and the outcome could not be unexpected.

Her death threw the King into a mood of melancholy which was not improved by the news that the Prince of Wales was heavily in debt and that he was losing thousands of pounds at the gaming tables; there was a great deal of talk about his marriage to Maria Fitzherbert and Fox had denied in the House of Commons that the marriage had taken place.

Another factor which disturbed him was that some time before when he was at St. James's a woman had stepped out of the crowd and tried to stab him. She was proved to be a certain Margaret Nicholson who was mad; but George could not forget the incident; and soon after the death of Mrs. Delany he began to suffer from bilious attacks and the rash, which he had had once before on his chest, broke out again.

Charlotte noticed that his speech was becoming more and more rapid and was punctuated more liberally with ehs and whats, and now he did not wait for the answers. He was taking the most violent exercise, and when the Queen timidly suggested that perhaps he was driving himself too hard he cried out in some excitement: "Can't get fat. Abhor obesity. It's a family characteristic. It has to be avoided. Can't avoid it by overeating and taking no exercise, eh?"

In June, Sir George Baker, his physician, suggested the King go for a month to Cheltenham.

"Your Majesty could take the waters which would be beneficial to your state. And another point if you were absent from London, long audiences and other tedious ceremonies could be avoided."

The King was loath to go. A sense of duty kept him in London until July and then as it was clear that his health was not improving he agreed to go to Cheltenham if the Queen and the Princesses went with him.

He stayed for a month and then when it became clear that neither the waters nor the rest from state duties was improving his health he decided to return.

He shook his head sadly and said: "I have, all at once, become an old man."

He felt a little better to be back at Kew. He was always happier there than anywhere else. He liked to walk in the gardens and look at the children's house and call in on them and play a few games with his darling Amelia.

In spite of his ill-health he insisted on taking exercise and his servants were greatly shocked when one day out walking he was caught in a heavy shower of rain and did not return immediately but went on walking. When he came back and took off his boots, the water poured out of them.

"Fresh air! Rain! Never hurt anyone, eh?" was his comment.

A few days later he was caught in the wet again and as he was due to go to St. James's to attend a levee he did not bother to change his boots and stockings. When he came back to Kew it was obvious that he had caught a chill.

The Queen scolded him and told him she would herself prepare a cordial and when he had drunk it he should retire to bed immediately.

He wanted no cordial, he replied. He didn't believe in cordials. Vegetables, fruit, cold water. They were the best healers. He ate a pear and drank a glass of cold water.

It was one o'clock in the morning when he was seized with cramp in the stomach. So agonizing was the pain that he awakened the Queen.

She was terrified, for she thought he was dying, and leaping out of bed ran into the corridor in her night shift to the acute embarrassment of the pages. But they immediately realized the urgency and as the doctors were not at Kew they called in a nearby apothecary.

The King was having a fit, said the apothecary; and tried to administer a cordial.

The King had regained a little of his senses and refused the cordial, but the Queen begged the apothecary to administer it in some way in spite of the King's protests, and with the help of the pages the liquid was forced down George's throat.

In a short time the fit subsided and he lay quietly in his bed.

*   *   *

There was no doubt now that the King was seriously ill and the malady had taken an alarming turn, for the King talked incessantly and at great speed, and at times it was not very clear what he meant; his mind seemed to dart from one subject to another and before saying what he wished to about one he would be on to the next.

A few days after the fit in the night he went to church with the Queen and the Princesses and while the sermon was being delivered he suddenly rose in his seat and started to embrace the Queen and the Princesses.

"You know what it is to be nervous," he cried.

The Queen was terrified; in fact she was growing more and more alarmed every day. She did her best to calm him.

"Please, George we are in church . . . *church*, do you understand."

The helpless manner in which he looked about him made her want to weep; but he allowed her to take his hand and force him back into his seat.

Thank God, she thought, that the wall of the pew was high enough to prevent their being seen by the rest of the congregation.

They went quietly back to the Palace and she persuaded him to rest in his room.

This could not go on. The doctors must decide what ailed the King, but deep in the Queen's heart was a fear which had been with her ever since his derangement all those years ago.

"He recovered from that," she told herself. "He will recover from this."

A few days later the King went to a concert and when he returned he grasped the Queen's arm and said to her, "The music seemed to affect my head. I could scarcely hear it."

"It is because you are not well. When you are well you will enjoy music as much as you ever did."

He looked at her in a wild, almost unrecognizing manner. "Shall I, Charlotte?" he said. "Shall I?"

"But of course. The doctors are going to cure you."

"Of what?" he whispered.

She did not answer; she could not look at him; but he gripped her arm fiercely and cried: "Tell me of what, Charlotte. Tell me of what?"

She looked up at him bravely. "Of your illness," she answered.

Then he released her and turning his head away burst into tears.

"I wish to God I may die," he said, "for I am going mad."

What can I do? Charlotte asked herself. How could she keep this distressing illness from becoming public knowledge?

She thought of the Prince of Wales who for so long had despised his father. What would he be feeling now? He had disappointed them; the charming child of the nursery had become the gay young man about town. He was all that his parents were not; he was becoming known as the First Gentleman of Europe; and although she knew he was so wild—and perhaps wicked—she could not help loving him and . . . yes, admiring him.

What would he do now?

The King came bursting into her apartments. All his movements were violent and he seemed in a desperate hurry.

"Ah, Charlotte . . . here we are! Fresh air, Charlotte. It's good for you. Must have it, eh, what? Are you ready? Come on . . . a five mile walk. Good for you. Mustn't get fat. Too much fat in the family, eh, what?"

She remonstrated with him. Was he not taking too much exercise? Did the doctors not say he should go more slowly? What about a drive? That would be better. They could go farther afield.

He did not seem to be listening, but when she led him to the carriage he got in without a word. She sat down beside him and let him talk of the beauties of the countryside. And how he talked. He talked of farms, of button-making, of Mrs. Delany's paper mosaics, pleasant subjects like the Princess Amelia and unpleasant ones like the Prince of Wales.

Suddenly the King shouted to the driver to stop.

The carriage came to rest by an oak tree. The King alighted, bowed to the oak, approached it with great dignity and shook one of the lower branches. For some seconds he stood there talking as though to the tree; and watching, being aware of the driver and the footman looking on, Charlotte felt a great fear and depression sweep over her.

After a while the King bowed, shook the oak branch again and took his seat in the caariage.

"I think," he said, "that I have put our case clearly to the King of Prussia."

*   *   *

There were rumours throughout the Court and the City.

What is happening to the King? Is it true that his mind is deranged?

The Prince of Wales consulted with his friend what this would mean. A Regency? With the Prince in command. And it seemed very desirable to them all.

The Prince of Wales came to Kew to see for himself if the rumours were true.

He was astonished at the sight of his father who had changed considerably in the last few months. He had been right when he had said that suddenly he had become an old man.

He received the Prince with dignity and made no reference to their disagreements. The Queen was on the verge of hysteria; she feared the King would become violent. She could not much longer, she knew, keep his state from the attendants; and she lived in terror of what he would do next.

It was inevitable that the Prince of Wales who had given him so much cause for that anxiety which had without doubt hastened him to his present condition should bring affairs to a climax.

During dinner the King suddenly began shouting at his son, talking fast and incoherently, but it was obvious that he was abusing him as he rose from his place and went to where his son was sitting.

He began to shout at him and the Prince of Wales, rising in his chair, touched his arm gently and said: "Father, I beg of you lower your voice."

The King was seized with a sudden fury against his son. He took him by the throat and throwing him against the wall appeared to be about to strangle him.

"Who shall dare tell the King of England he shall not speak out, eh? What? Tell me that? Tell me that? Tell me that?"

The footmen rushed forward to rescue the Prince; the Princesses rose to their feet, all colour drained from their faces; the Queen sat clenching and unclenching her hands, her lips tightly pressed together as she forced herself not to scream out that she could endure no more.

Colonel Digby, Charlotte's Chamberlain, bowed to the King who was struggling to free himself from the footmen and suggested that he allow him to conduct him to bed.

"Don't dare touch me, sir," screamed the King. "I will not go. Who are you?"

"I am Colonel Digby, sir," was the calm reply. "Your Majesty has been very good to me often and now I am going to be good to you, for you must come to bed. It is necessary to your life."

The King was so struck by this speech that he grew silent. Tears filled his eyes as Colonel Digby, taking him by the arm, led him away.

The Prince of Wales was almost fainting and his eldest sisters hurried to bathe his forehead with Hungary water.

The Queen said to two of her women: "Pray conduct me to my apartments."

They obeyed and when she reached them she threw herself on to her bed and gave way to fits of laughter of a wild, hysterical kind.

Her women were terrified; and she sat up in bed and cried: "What will become of me? What will become of us all?"

Having reached his room the King seemed to grow calmer.

"Where is the Queen, eh?" he kept demanding. "What have you done with the Queen, eh? What? You are trying to separate me from the Queen."

"The Queen is indisposed, sir," Colonel Digby told him.

"Indisposed? The Queen ill? Then she will want me with her. I will go to the Queen. Do not stand in my way, sir. The Queen is ill; therefore I must be with her."

They could not restrain him from visiting the Queen and when she saw him, wild-eyed though quieter than he had been at the dinner table, Charlotte's fears rose. She had seen his attack on the Prince of Wales and she could not be sure what he would do next.

"You are ill," he said, "ill . . . ill, ill, ill. Eh? What? You must take care of the Queen." He glared at her women. "And now we must rest. Both of us. Charlotte, I beg of you do not talk to me so that I may fall asleep quickly. I need sleep. I need sleep. You understand, eh? What? I need sleep." He went on talking of his need to sleep and begging the Queen not to talk to him, which she had shown no sign of doing.

It was very distressing to all those who watched.

One of the women suggested that the Queen and he should have a separate room for the night so that he could be sure of uninterrupted rest.

"Part from the Queen!" he cried. "I could not be parted from the Queen."

It was arranged that the Queen should have a room leading from his so that she would not be far from him, and he went on begging the Queen not to talk to him, and he would not let her go to her room. It was past midnight when he left her and the Queen lay staring at the ceiling repeating to herself: "What next? What will become of us now?"

Into the Queen's bedroom walked a solitary figure. In his hand he carried a lighted candle.

He parted the bed curtains and Charlotte, who had been lightly dozing for the first time during that terrible night awoke to look up into the wild eyes of the King. The lighted candle quivered in his hand and she thought he had come to set fire to the bed hangings and kill her.

She started up in bed and he said soothingly: "So you are here, Charlotte. I thought they had tried to separate us."

"I am here," she told him, "and shall be with you as long as you need me."

He began to weep quietly; the tears splashing on to his nightgown.

"Good Charlotte," he said. "Ours was a good marriage. Good Charlotte."

He would not go; he went on talking without ceasing. Charlotte dared not move for fear his kindly mood turned to one of violence and it was half an hour before his attendants heard him and came to take him back to his bed.

There was a brooding silence throughout the castle. The ladies of the Queen's household lay sleepless in their beds. One fact was clear to them all, and it could no longer be denied: The King was mad.

In her room Fanny Burney could endure the suspense no longer.

At six o'clock she rose and, dressing hastily, went out into the draughty corridors.

The pages were all sleepless. Everyone was waiting tensely for what was going to happen now.

She went back to her room; she was cold, not only because it was always cold in the castle corridors where there was enough wind someone had said to sail a man-o'-war. She had not been there very long when she received a summons from the Queen, and she hastily went to the bedchamber where she found Charlotte sitting up in bed, pale and fearful.

"Ah, Miss Burney," said Charlotte. "How are you today?"

Fanny was so moved that she burst into tears. And to her amazement the Queen did the same.

For some minutes they both wept unrestrainedly.

Then the Queen said: "I thank you, Miss Burney. You have made me cry. It is a great relief to me. All this night long I have wanted to cry and been unable. I feel better now. I think I will get up."

While the Queen was at her toilet they could hear the King talking incessantly in the next room.

Another fearful day had begun.

There was no hope now of hiding the fact that the King was deranged.

The whole country was talking of it and what this would mean. There was to be a Regency. The King would be replaced by his son.

Pitt was trying to make the Regency a restricted one; Fox and Sheridan were trying to get full powers for the Prince of Wales; and meanwhile the King's doctors were wrangling together over the treatment he should receive. The King was removed from Windsor to Kew; he was not allowed to shave himself or have a knife at dinner. Once he tried to throw himself out of a window; then he would give himself up to praying and talking of religion. At times his struggling body was forced into a straitjacket. The fashionable Dr. Warren was called in; and it was said that he was a friend of the Prince of Wales and was there to serve his ends. The King disliked him and the Queen feared him. And she feared the King.

The King suddenly began to talk of women and seemed obsessed by them. He who had lived such a determinedly respectable life now seemed to be living an erotic one in his thoughts.

"You are the man who took Sarah Lennox away from me," he cried to a harmless footman. "Yes you were, eh, what?"

The man fled in fear of his life.

But the obsession with women marked a new phase. The King was now having periods of lucidity. He knew he had been ill, he knew the nature of his illness; he was sad because of it, but during those periods when he was aware he had suffered derangement his mind was sane again.

The lucidity would pass. He saw Elizabeth Pembroke and from the mind over which he had lost control came the imaginings of years. He believed he had divorced Charlotte; he believed he was married to Elizabeth. He addressed her as Queen Elizabeth and attempted to make love to her.

The barriers he himself had set up had crumbled. He was the man he would have been had he not suppressed that man.

He thought of women . . . women . . . women.

Then came the clarity; but Elizabeth was still there. He was married to Charlotte, of course—plain, unexciting Charlotte who had nevertheless borne him fifteen children. And he wanted Elizabeth.

He caught Elizabeth in a corridor. She must be his mistress, he told her. She must name anything she wanted and it should be hers.

Elizabeth talked to him gently, kindly, trying to turn his mind away from the subject.

The King's health was improving. The lucid periods were more frequent and of longer duration.

The King is going to recover, said his friends.

Three doctors had signed a bulletin announcing the entire cessation of His Majesty's illness.

The King was restored. His illness had made him popular once more. The people wanted to show him that they were pleased by his recovery. The City of London was ablaze with lights even as far out as Tooting; and between Greenwich and Kensington the lights blazed forth.

Everyone was singing God Save the King; and the ladies who served at White's Club had ''God Save the King'' worked in gold letters on their caps. There were services at St. Paul's, rejoicing everywhere.

The King was to go to Weymouth to recuperate and Weymouth was determined to vie with London in welcoming the King.

The town was lighted from end to end and at every few yards the bands blared forth ''God Save the King.''

Everyone wanted to tell George how pleased they were that he was well again. All the bathers on the seashore wore ''God Save the King'' on their caps and when George left his machine to step into the sea a band would strike up the national anthem.

It was all very gratifying, said the King's friends.

But the King looked to the future with sad eyes. There were times when his mind would be in a whirl, when he wanted to talk and never stop; there were thoughts of women in his mind . . . all the beautiful women he had missed and dreamed of.

He knew that there were occasions when he was wavering between lucidity and insanity, and in his heart he was aware that what had happened before would happen again. It was inevitable. He was trying to hold it off, but he was not strong enough.

And he looked at Charlotte and saw a little old woman—for this had aged her, even as it had him—a dowdy little old woman.

Poor Charlotte! he thought. What is she thinking now?

He would not ask her. He dared not ask her.

The people were singing:

> *"Our prayers are heard, and Providence restores*
> *A Patriot King to bless Britannia's shores."*

The people were easily moved. They loved one day and hated the next.

A patriot King who had lost America, who had given them the Prince of Wales, who had been mad for a while . . . and would be so again.

Ah! He had said it. It was the thought that stayed with him and which he knew would come true.

He would be known as the King who was mad.

Charlotte was thinking: What will become of us? This is not the end. It is the beginning.

BIBLIOGRAPHY

Walpole, Horace, *Memoirs and Portraits*

Walpole, Horace, *Memoirs of the Reign of George III*

Willson, Beckles, *George III: Monarch and Statesman*

Davies, J. D. Griffith, *George III: a record of a King's Reign*

Melville, Lewis, *Farmer George,* 2 vols.

Long, J.C., *George III*

Butterfield, Herbert, *George III and the Historians*

Colburn, Henry, *George III, His Court and Family*

Davies, A., *George III and the Constitution*

Thackeray, William Makepeace, *The Four Georges*

Boulton, William B., *In the Days of the Georges*

Edited by the Countess of Ilchester and Lord Stavordale, *The Life and Letters of Lady Sarah Lennox*

Fox, Henry, 1st Lord Holland, *A Short Political History of the Years 1760–1763*

Fitzgerald, Percy, *The Good Queen Charlotte*

Lindsay, John, *The Lovely Quaker*

Pendered, Mary, *The Fair Quaker*

Thoms, W. J., *Hannah Lightfoot*

Petrie, Sir Charles, *The Four Georges*

Massey, W., *History of the Reign of George III*

Redman, Alvin, *The House of Hanover*

Lloyd, Christopher, *Fanny Burney*

Masefield, Muriel, *The Story of Fanny Burney*

Wade, John, *The Diary and Letters of Madame d'Arblay*

Wade, John, *British History*

Edited by Sir Leslie Stephen and Sir Sidney Lee, *The Dictionary of National Biography*

Bayne-Powell, Rosamond, *18th Century London Life*

Aubrey, William Hickman Smith, *National and Domestic History of England*

About the Author

Jean Plaidy is an extremely popular author who is also known as Victoria Holt and Philippa Carr. She resides in England and has written over twenty novels for Fawcett, including both the Georgian Saga and the Plantagenet Saga series.